MESSENGERS
OF EVIL

MESSENGERS OF EVIL

BEING A FURTHER ACCOUNT OF
THE LURES AND DEVICES OF
FANTÔMAS

PIERRE SOUVESTRE
AND MARCEL ALLAIN

WILDSIDE PRESS

MESSENGERS OF EVIL

Published in 2009 by Wildside Press.
www.wildsidepress.com

I

THE DRAMA OF THE RUE NORVINS

On Monday, April 4th, 19 —, the evening paper *La Capitale* published the following article on its first page: —

A drama, over the motives of which there is a bewildering host of conjectures, was unfolded this morning on the heights of Montmartre. The Baroness de Vibray, well known in the Parisian world and among artists, whose generous patroness she was, has been found dead in the studio of the ceramic painter, Jacques Dollon. The young painter, rendered completely helpless by a soporific, lay stretched out beside her when the crime was discovered. We say 'crime' designedly, because, when the preliminary medical examination was completed, it was clear that the death of the Baroness de Vibray was due to the absorption of some poison.

The painter, Jacques Dollon, whom the enlightened attentions of Doctor Mayran had drawn from his condition of torpor, underwent a short examination from the superintendent of police, in the course of which he made remarks of so suspicious a nature that the examining magistrate put him under arrest then and there. At police headquarters they are absolutely dumb regarding this strange affair. Nevertheless, the personal investigation undertaken by us throws a little light on what is already called: *The Drama of the Rue Norvins.*

The Discovery of the Crime

This morning, about seven o'clock, Madame Béju, a housekeeper in the service of the painter, Jacques Dollon, who, with his sister, Mademoiselle Elizabeth Dollon, occupied lodge number six, in the Close of the rue Norvins, was on the ground-floor of the house, attending to her customary duties. She had been on the premises about half an hour, and, so far, had not noticed anything abnormal; however, astonished at not hearing any movements on the floor above, for the painter generally rose pretty early, Madame Béju decided to go upstairs and wake her master, who would be vexed at having let himself sleep so late. She had to pass through the studio to reach Monsieur Jacques Dollon's bedroom. No sooner had she raised the door curtain of the studio than she recoiled, horrorstruck!

Disorder reigned in the studio: a startling disorder!

Pieces of furniture displaced, some of them overturned, showed that something extraordinary had happened there. In the middle of the room, on the floor, lay the inanimate form of a person whom Madame Béju knew well, for she had seen her at the painter's house many a time — the Baroness de Vibray. Not far from her, buried in a large arm-chair, motionless, giving no sign of life, was Monsieur Jacques Dollon!

When the good woman saw the rigid attitude of these two persons, she realised that she was in the presence of a tragedy.

Stirred to the depths, she redescended the stairs, calling for help: shortly afterwards, the entire Close was in a state of ferment: house porters, neighbours, male and female, crowded round Madame Béju, endeavouring to understand her disconnected account of the terrifying spectacle she had come face to face with but a minute before.

Sudden death, suicide, crime — all were plausible suppositions. The more audacious of these gossip-mongers had ventured as far as the studio door; from that standpoint, a rapid glance round enabled them to get a clear idea of the truth of the housekeeper's statements: they returned to give a confirmation of them to the inquisitive and increasing crowd in the principal avenue of the Close.

'The police! The police must be informed!' cried the Close portress.

Whilst this woman, with considerable presence of mind, and aided by Madame Béju, exerted herself to keep out the people of the neighbourhood who had got wind of the tragedy, two men had set off to seek the police.

Lodge Number 6

On the summit of Montmartre is the rue Norvins. In shape it resembles a donkey's back, and at one particular spot it hugs the accentuated curve of the Butte. The Close of the rue Norvins is situated at number 47. It is separated from the street by a strong iron gate, the porter's lodge being at the side. The Close consists of a series of little dwellings, separated by wooden railings, up which climbing plants grow. Fine trees encircle these abodes with so thick a curtain of leafage that the inhabitants might think themselves buried in the depths of the country.

Lodge Number 6 is even more isolated than the others. It consists of a ground floor and a first floor, with an immense studio attached. Three years ago, Number 6 was leased to Monsieur Jacques Dollon, then a student at the Fine Arts School. It has been continuously occupied by the tenant and his sister, Miss Elizabeth Dollon, who has kept house for her brother. For the last fortnight the painter has been alone: his sister, who had gone to Switzerland to convalesce after a long illness, was expected back that same day, or the day following.

The reputation of the two young people is considered by their neighbours to be beyond criticism. The artist has led a regular and hard-working life: last year the Salon accorded him a medal of the second class.

His sister, an affable and unassuming girl, seemed always much attached to her brother. In that very Bohemian neighbourhood she is highly thought of as a girl of the most estimable character.

The Baroness de Vibray visited them frequently, and her motor-car used to attract attention in that high, remote suburb — the wilds of Montmartre. The old lady liked to dress in rather showy colours; she was considered eccentric, but was also known to be good and generous. She took a particular interest in the Dollons, whose family, so it was said, she had known in Provence. Jacques Dollon and his sister highly valued their intimacy with the Baroness de Vibray, who was known all over Paris as a patroness of artists and the arts.

First Verifications

Already slander and imagination between them had concocted the wildest stories, when Monsieur Agram, the eminent police super-intendent of the Clignancourt Quarter, appeared at the entrance to the Close. Accompanied by his secretary, he at once entered Number 6, charging the two policemen, who were assisting him, on no ac-count to allow anyone to enter, excepting the doctor, whom he had at once sent for.

He requested the portress to hold herself at his disposal in the garden, and made Madame Béju accompany him to the studio. Barely twenty minutes had elapsed since the housekeeper had been terror-struck by the dreadful spectacle which had met her eyes there. When she entered with the superintendent of police nothing had been altered. Madame de Vibray, horribly pale, her eyes closed, her lips violet-hued, lay stretched on the floor: her body had assumed the rigidity of a corpse. That of Jacques Dollon, huddled in an arm-chair, was in a state of immobility.

Monsieur Agram at once noticed long, intersecting streaks on the floor, such as might have been traced by heavy furniture dragged over the waxed boards of the flooring. A pungent medicinal odour caught the throats of the visitors: Madame Béju was about to open a window: the superintendent stopped her:

'Let things remain as they are for the present,' was his order. After casting an observant eye round the room he questioned the house-keeper:

'Is this state of disorder usual?'

'Never in this world, sir!' declared the good woman. 'Monsieur Dollon and his sister are very steady, very regular in their habits, espe-cially the young lady. It is true that she has been absent for nearly a month, but her brother has often been left alone, and he has always insisted on his studio being kept in good order.'

'Did Monsieur Dollon have many visitors?'

'Very seldom, monsieur. Sometimes his neighbours would come in; and then there was that poor lady lying there so deathly pale that it makes me ill to look at her. . . .'

Jacques Dollon lives

The conversation was interrupted by the arrival of the doctor employed in connection with relief for the poor. The superintendent of police pointed out to this Dr. Mayran the two inanimate figures. A glance of the doctor's trained eye sufficed to show him that Madame de Vibray had been dead for some time. Approaching Jacques Dollon, Dr. Mayran examined him attentively:

'Will you help me to lift him on to a bed or a table?' he asked. 'It seems to me that this one is not dead.'

'His bedroom is next to this!' cried Madame Béju. 'Oh, heavens above! If only the poor young man would recover!'

Silently the doctor, aided by the superintendent and a policeman, transported young Dollon into the next room.

'Air!' cried the doctor, 'give him air! Open all the windows! It seems to me a case of suspended animation! There is partial suffocation. This will probably yield to energetic treatment.'

Whilst good Madame Béju, whose legs were shaking under her, was carrying out the doctor's orders, the superintendent of police kept watch to see that nothing was touched. The doctor's attention was concentrated on Jacques Dollon. Monsieur Agram was searchng for some indication which might throw light on the drama. So far he had been unable to formulate any hypothesis. Should the moribund painter return to consciousness, the explanation he could give would certainly clear up the situation. At this point in the superintendent's cogitations, the doctor called out:

'He lives! He lives! Bring me a glass of water!'

Jacques Dollon was returning to consciousness! Slowly, painfully, his features contracting as at the remembrance of a horrible nightmare, the young man stretched his limbs, opened his eyes: he turned a dull gaze on those about him, a gaze which became one of stupefaction when he perceived these unknown faces gathered round his bed. His eyes fell on his housekeeper. He murmured:

'Mme . . . Bé-ju . . . je . . .,' and fell back into unconsciousness.

'Is he dead?' whispered Monsieur Agram.

The doctor smiled:

'Be reassured, monsieur: he lives; but he finds it terribly difficult to wake up. He has certainly swallowed some powerful narcotic and is still under its influence; but its effects will soon pass off now.'

The good doctor spoke the truth.

In a short time Jacques Dollon, making a violent effort, sat up. Casting scared and bewildered glances about him, he cried:

'Who are you? What do you want of me? . . . Ah, the ruffians! The bandits!'

'There is nothing to fear, monsieur. I am simply the doctor they have called in to attend to you! Be calm! . . . You must recover your senses, and tell us what has happened!'

Jacques Dollon pressed his hands to his forehead, as though in pain:

'How heavy my head is!' he muttered. 'What has happened to me? . . . Let me see! . . . Wait. . . . Ah . . . yes . . . that's it!'

At a sign from the doctor, the superintendent had stationed himself beside the bed, behind the young painter.

Keeping a finger on his patient's pulse, the doctor asked him, in a fatherly fashion, to tell him all about it.

'It is like this,' replied Jacques Dollon. . . . 'Yesterday evening I was sitting in my arm-chair reading. It was getting late. I had been working hard. . . . I was tired. . . . All of a sudden I was surrounded by masked men, clothed in long black garments: they flung themselves on me. Before I could make a movement I was gagged, bound with cords. . . . I felt something pointed driven into my leg — into my arm. . . . Then an overpowering drowsiness overcame me, the strangest visions passed before my eyes; I lost consciousness rapidly. . . . I wanted to move, to cry out . . . in vain . . . there was no strength in me . . . powerless . . . and that's all!'

'Is there nothing more?' asked the doctor.

After a minute's reflection Jacques answered:

'That is all.'

He now seemed fully awake. He moved: the movement was evidently painful: 'It hurts,' he said, instinctively putting his hand on his left thigh.

'Let us see what is wrong,' said the doctor, and was preparing to examine the place when a voice from the studio called:

'Monsieur!'

It was Monsieur Agram's secretary. The magistrate left his post by the bed and went into the studio.

'Monsieur,' said the secretary, 'I have just found this paper under the chair in which Monsieur Dollon was: will you acquaint yourself with its contents?'

The magistrate seized the paper: it was a letter, couched in the following terms:

Dear Madame,
    If you do not fear to climb the heights of Montmartre some evening, will you come to see the painted pottery I am

preparing for the Salon: you will be welcome, and will confer on us a great pleasure. I say 'us,' because I have excellent news of Elizabeth, who is returning shortly: perhaps she will be here to receive you with me.

I am your respectful and devoted
Jacques Dollon.

The magistrate was frowning as he handed back the letter to his secretary, saying: 'Keep it carefully.' Then he went into the bedroom, where the doctor was talking to the invalid. The doctor turned to Monsieur Agram:

'Monsieur Dollon has just asked me who you are: I did not think I ought to hide from him that you are a superintendent of police, monsieur.'

'Ah!' cried Jacques Dollon. 'Can you help me to discover what happened to me last night?'

'You have just told us yourself, monsieur,' replied the magistrate. . . . 'But have you nothing further to tell us? Can you not recollect whether or no you had a visitor before the arrival of the men who attacked you?'

'Why, no, monsieur, no one called.'

The doctor here intervened:

'The pain in the leg, Monsieur Dollon complained of, need not cause any anxiety. It is a very slight superficial wound. A slight swelling above the broken skin possibly indicates an intra-muscular puncture, which might have been made by someone unaccustomed to such operations, for it is a clumsy performance. It is a queer business! . . .'

Monsieur Agram, who had been steadily observing Jacques Dollon, persisted:

'Is there not a gap, monsieur, in your recollections of what occurred? . . . Were you quite alone yesterday evening? Were you not expecting anyone? . . . Are you certain that you did not have a visitor? Did not someone pay you a visit — someone you had asked to come and see you?'

Jacques Dollon opened his eyes — eyes of stupefaction — and stared at the superintendent:

'No, monsieur.'

'It is that ——' went on Monsieur Agram. Then stopping short, and drawing the doctor aside, he asked:

'Do you consider him in a fit state to bear a severe moral shock? . . . A confrontation?'

The doctor glanced at his patient:

'He appears to me to be quite himself again: you can act as you see fit, monsieur.'

Jacques Dollon, astonished at this confabulation, and vaguely uneasy, was, in fact, able to get up without help.

'Be good enough to go into your studio, monsieur,' said the magistrate.

Jacques Dollon complied without a word. No sooner did he cross the threshold than he recoiled, terror-struck.

He was shaking from head to foot; his lips were quivering; every feature expressed horrified shrinking from the spectacle confronting him.

'The — the — the Baroness de Vibray!' he barely articulated: 'how can it be possible?'

The superintendent of police did not lose a single movement made by the young painter, keeping a lynx-eyed watch on every expression that flitted across his countenance. He said:

'It certainly is the Baroness de Vibray, dead — assassinated, no doubt. How do you explain that?'

'But,' retorted Jacques Dollon, who appeared overwhelmed: 'I do not know! I do not understand!'

The magistrate replied:

'Yet, did you not invite her to your studio? Had you not asked her to come some evening soon? Had you not certain pieces of painted pottery to show her?'

'That is so,' confessed the painter: 'but I was not aware. . . . I did not know. . . .' He seemed about to faint. The doctor made him sit down in the chair where he had been found unconscious. Whilst he was recovering, Monsieur Agram continued his investigations. He opened a little cupboard, in which were several poisonous powders: this was shown by the writing on the flasks containing them. He spoke to the doctor, taking care that Jacques Dollon should not overhear him:

'Did you not say that this woman's death is due to poison?'

'It certainly looks like it. . . . A post-mortem will . . .'

The Arrest

Interrupting the doctor, Monsieur Agram went up to Jacques Dollon:

'In the exercise of your profession, monsieur, do you not make use of various poisons, of which you have a reserve supply here?'

'That is so,' confirmed Jacques Dollon, in a faint voice: 'But it is a very long time since I employed any of them.'

'Very good, monsieur.'

Monsieur Agram now made Madame Béju leave the room. He asked her to transmit an order to his policemen: they were to drive back the crowd. Soon a cab brought by a constable entered the Close, and drew up before the door of Number 6.

Jacques Dollon, supported by two people, descended and entered the cab.

Immediately a rumour spread that he had been arrested.

This rumour was correct.

Our Inquiry — Silence at Police Headquarters — Probable Motives of the Crime

Such are the details referring to this strange affair, which we have been able to procure from those who were present. But the motives which determined the arrest of Monsieur Dollon are obscure.

There are, however, two suspicious facts. The first is the puncture made in Monsieur Jacques Dollon's left leg: this puncture is aggravated by a scratch. According to the doctors, soporific, injected into the human body by the de Pravaz syringe, acts violently and efficaciously. It is beyond a doubt that Monsieur Jacques Dollon has been rendered unconscious in this manner.

To begin with, the painter's first version was considered the true one, namely, that he had been surprised by robbers, who rendered him unconscious; but, on reflection, this explanation would not hold water. Murderous house-thieves do not send people to sleep: they kill them. Add to this that nothing has been stolen from Monsieur Dollon: therefore, mere robbery was not the motive of the crime.

Besides, Monsieur Dollon maintained that he was alone; yet at that time Madame de Vibray was in his studio, and was there precisely because the artist himself had asked her to come. We know that the Baroness de Vibray, who was very wealthy, took a particular interest in this young man and his sister.

We should consider ourselves to blame, did we not now remind our readers that the names of those personages — Dollon, Vibray — implicated in the drama of the rue Norvins, have already figured in the chronicles of crimes, both recent and celebrated.

Thus the assassination of the Marquise de Langrune cannot have been forgotten, an assassination which has remained a mystery, which was perpetrated a few years ago, and brought into prominence the personalities of Monsieur Rambert and the charming Thérèse Auvernois. . . .

Madame de Vibray, who has just been so tragically done to death, was an intimate friend of the Marquise de Langrune. . . .

Monsieur Jacques Dollon is a son of Madame de Langrune's old steward. . . .

We do not, of course, pretend to connect, in any way whatever, the drama of the rue Norvins with the bygone drama which ended in the execution of Gurn, but we cannot pass over in silence the strange coincidence that, within the space of a few years, the same halo of mystery surrounds the same group of individuals. . . .

But let us return to our narrative:

Monsieur Jacques Dollon, interrogated by the superintendent of police, declared that he very rarely made use of the poisons locked up in the little cupboard of his studio. . . .

Notwithstanding this, it was discovered, during the course of the perquisition, that one of the phials containing poison had been recently opened, and that traces of the powder were still to be found on the floor. This powder is now being analysed, whilst the faculty are engaged in a post-mortem examination of the unfortunate victim's body; but, at the present moment, everything leads to the belief that there does not exist an immediate and certain link between this poison and the sudden death of the Baroness de Vibray.

It might easily be supposed, and this we believe is the view taken at Police Headquarters, that for a motive as yet unknown, a motive the judicial examination will certainly bring to light, the artist has poisoned his patroness; and, in order to put the authorities on the wrong scent (perhaps he hoped she would leave the studio before the death-agony commenced), he has devised this species of tableau, invented the story of the masked men.

In fact, the doctor who first attended him has declared that the puncture, clumsily made, might very well have been done by Jacques Dollon himself.

It is worth noting that not a soul saw the Baroness de Vibray enter Monsieur Dollon's house yesterday evening: as a rule, she comes in her motor-car, and all the neighbourhood can hear her arrival.

It seems evident that Jacques Dollon will abandon the line of defence he has adopted: it can hardly be described as rational.

There is little doubt but that we shall have sensational revelations regarding the crime of the rue Norvins.

Last Hour

Mademoiselle Elizabeth Dollon, to whom Police Headquarters has telegraphed that a serious accident has happened to her brother, has sent a reply telegram from Lausanne to the effect that she will return to-night.

The unfortunate girl is probably ignorant of all that has

1   See *Fantômas*.

occurred. Nevertheless, we believe that two detectives have left at once for the frontier, where they will meet her, and shadow her as far as Paris, in case she should get news on the way of what had occurred, and should either attempt to escape, or make an attempt on her life.

Decidedly, to-morrow promises to be a day full of vicissitudes.

This article, published on the first page of *La Capitale*, was signed:

JÉRÔME FANDOR.

II

THOMERY'S TWO LOVES

Two days before the sinister drama, details of which Jérôme Fandor had given in *La Capitale*, the smart little town house inhabited by the Baroness de Vibray, in the Avenue Henri-Martin, assumed a festive appearance.

This did not surprise her neighbours, for they knew the owner of this charming residence was very much a woman of the world, whose reception-rooms were constantly opened to the many distinguished Parisians forming her circle of acquaintances.

It was seven in the evening when the Baroness, dressed for dinner, passed from her own room into the small drawing-room adjoining. Crossing a carpet so thick and soft that it deadened the sound of footsteps, she pressed the button of an electric bell beside the fireplace. A major-domo, of the most correct appearance, presented himself.

"The Baroness rang for me?"

Madame de Vibray, who had instinctively sought the flattering approval of her mirror, half turned:

"I wish to know if anyone called this afternoon, Antoine?"

"For the Baroness?"

"Of course!" she replied, a note of impatience in her voice: "I want to know if anyone called to see *me* this afternoon?"

"No, madame."

"No one has telephoned from the Barbey-Nanteuil Bank?"

"No, madame."

Repressing a slight feeling of annoyance, Madame de Vibray changed the subject:

"You will have dinner served as soon as the guests arrive. They will not be later than half-past seven, I suppose."

Antoine bowed solemnly, vanished into the anteroom, and from thence gained the servants' hall.

Madame de Vibray quitted the small drawing-room. Traversing the great gallery with its glass roof, encircling the staircase, she entered the dining-room. Covers were laid for three.

Inspecting the table arrangements with the eye of a mistress of the house, she straightened the line of some plates, gave a touch of distinction to the flowers scattered over the table in a conventional disorder; then she went to the sideboard, where the major-domo had left a china pot filled with flowers. With a slight shrug, the Baroness carried the pot to its usual place — a marble column at the further end of the room:

"It was fortunate I came to see how things were! Antoine is a good fellow, but a hare-brained one too!" thought she.

Madame de Vibray paused a moment: the light from an electric lamp shone on the vase and wonderfully enhanced its glittering beauty. It was a piece of faience decorated in the best taste. On its graceful form the artist had traced the lines of an old colour print, and had scrupulously preserved the picture born of an eighteenth-century artist's imagination, with its brilliancy of tone and soft background of tender grey. Madame de Vibray could not tear herself away from the contemplation of it. Not only did the design and the treatment please her, but she also felt a kind of maternal affection for the artist: "This dear Jacques," she murmured, "has decidedly a great deal of talent, and I like to think that in a short time his reputation. . . ."

Her reflections were interrupted by the servant. The good Antoine announced in a low voice, and with a touch of respectful reproach in his tone:

"Monsieur Thomery awaits the Baroness in the small drawing-room: he has been waiting ten minutes."

"Very well. I am coming."

Madame de Vibray, whose movements were all harmonious grace, returned by way of the gallery to greet her guest. She paused on the threshold of the small drawing-room, smiling graciously.

Framed in the dark drapery of the heavy door-curtains, the soft light from globes of ground glass falling on her, the Baroness de Vibray appeared a very attractive woman still. Her figure had retained its youthful slenderness, her neck, white as milk, was as round and fresh as a girl's; and had the hair about her forehead and temples not been turning grey — the Baroness wore it powdered, a piece of coquettish affection on her part — she would not have looked a day more than thirty.

Monsieur Thomery rose hastily, and advanced to meet her. He kissed her hand with a gallant air:

"My dear Mathilde," he declared with an admiring glance, "you are decidedly an exquisite woman!"

The Baroness replied by a glance, in which there was something ambiguous, something of ironical mockery:

"How are you, Norbert?" she asked in an affectionate tone. . . . "And those pains?"

They seated themselves on a low couch, and began to discuss their respective aches and pains in friendly fashion. Whilst listening to his complaints, Madame de Vibray could not but admire his remarkable vigour, his air of superb health: his looks gave the lie to his words.

About fifty-five, Monsieur Norbert Thomery seemed to be in the plenitude of his powers; his premature baldness was redeemed by the vivacity of his dark brown eyes, also by his long, thick moustache, probably dyed. He looked like an old soldier. He was the last of the great Thomery family who, for many generations, had been sugar refiners. His was a personality well known in Parisian Society; always first at his office or his factories, as soon as night fell he became the man of the world, frequenting fashionable drawing-rooms, theatrical first-nights, official receptions, and balls in the aristocratic circles of the faubourg Saint-Germain.

Remarkably handsome, extremely rich, Thomery had had many love affairs. Gossips had it that between him and Madame de Vibray there had existed a tender intimacy; and, for once, gossip was right. But they had been tactful, had respected the conventions whilst their irregular union had lasted. Though now a thing of the past, for Thomery had sought other loves, his passion for the Baroness had changed to a calm, strong, semi-brotherly affection; whilst Madame de Vibray retained a more lively, a more tender feeling for the man whom she had known as the most gallant of lovers.

Thomery suddenly ceased talking of his rheumatism:

"But, my dear friend, I do not see that pretty smile which is your greatest charm! How is that?"

Madame de Vibray looked sad: her beautiful eyes gazed deep into those of Thomery:

"Ah," she murmured, "one cannot be eternally smiling; life sometimes holds painful surprises in store for us."

"Is something worrying you?" Thomery's tone was one of anxious sympathy.

"Yes and no," was her evasive reply. There was a silence; then she said:

"It is always the same thing! I have no hesitation in telling you that, you, my old friend: it is a money wound — happily it is not mortal."

Thomery nodded:

"Well, I declare it is just what I expected! My poor Mathilde, are you never going to be sensible?"

The Baroness pouted: "You know quite well I am sensible . . . only it happens that there are moments when one is short of cash! Yesterday I asked my bankers to send me fifty thousand francs, and I have not heard a word from them!"

"That is no great matter! The Barbey-Nanteuil credit cannot be shaken!"

"Oh," cried the Baroness, "I have no fears on that score; but, as a rule, their delay in sending me what I ask for is of the briefest, yet no one has come from them to-day."

Thomery began scolding her gently:

"Ah, Mathilde, that you should be in such pressing need of so large a sum must mean that you have been drawn into some deplorable speculation! I will wager that you invested in those Oural copper mines after all!"

"I thought the shares were going up," was Madame de Vibray's excuse: she lowered her eyes like a naughty schoolgirl caught in the act.

Thomery, who had risen, and was walking up and down the room, halted in front of her:

"I do beg of you to consult those who know all the ins and outs, persons competent to advise you, when you are bent on plunging into speculations of this description! The Barbey-Nanteuil people can give you reliable information; I myself, you know . . ."

"But since it is really of no importance!" interrupted Madame de Vibray, who had no wish to listen to the remonstrances of her too prudent friend: "What does it matter? It is my only diversion now! . . . I love gambling — the emotions it arouses in one, the perpetual hopes and fears it excites!"

Thomery was about to reply, to argue, to remonstrate further, but the Baroness had caught him glancing at the clock hanging beside the fireplace:

"I am making you dine late," she said in a tone of apology. Then, with a touch of malice, and looking up at Thomery from under her eyes, to see how he took it:

"You are to be rewarded for having to wait! . . . I have invited Princess Sonia Danidoff to dine with you!"

Thomery started. He frowned. He again seated himself beside the Baroness:

"You have invited her? . . ."

"Yes . . . and why not? . . . I believe this pretty woman is one of your special friends . . . that you consider her the most charming of all your friends now! . . ."

Thomery did not take up the challenge: he simply said:

"I had an idea that the Princess was not much to your taste!"

The eyes of Madame de Vibray flashed a sad, strange look on her old friend, as she said gently:

"One can accustom oneself to anything and everything, my dear friend. . . . Besides, I quite recognise that the Princess deserves the reputation she enjoys of being wonderfully beautiful and also intellectual. . . ."

Thomery did not reply to this: he looked puzzled, annoyed. . . .

The Baroness continued:

"They even say that handsome bachelor, Monsieur Thomery, is not indifferent to her fascinations! . . . That, for the first time in his life, he is ready to link . . ."

"Oh, as for that! . . ." Thomery was protesting, when the door opened, and the Princess Sonia Danidoff rustled into the room, a superbly — a dazzlingly beautiful vision, all audacity and charm.

"Accept all my apologies, dear Baroness," she cried, "for arriving so late; but the streets are so crowded!"

" . . . And I live such a long way out!" added Madame de Vibray.

"You live in a charming part," amended the Princess. Then, catching sight of Thomery:

"Why, you!" she cried. And, with a gracious and dignified gesture, the Princess extended her hand, which the wealthy sugar refiner hastened to kiss.

At this moment the double doors were flung wide, and Antoine, with his most solemn air, his most stiff-starched manner, announced:

"Dinner is served!"

" . . . No," cried she, smiling, whilst she refused the arm offered by her old friend; "take in the Princess, dear friend; I will follow . . . by myself!"

Thomery obeyed. He passed slowly along the gallery into the dining-room with the Princess. Behind them came the Baroness, who watched them as they went: Thomery, big, muscular, broad-shouldered: Sonia Danidoff, slim, pliant, refined, dainty!

Checking a deep sigh, the Baroness could not help thinking, and her heart ached at the thought:

"What a fine couple they would make! . . . What a fine couple they will make!"

But, as she seated herself opposite her guests, she said to herself:

"Bah! . . . I must send sad thoughts flying! . . . It is high time!"

"My dear Thomery!" she cried playfully: "I wish — I expect you to show yourself the most charming of men to your delicious neighbour!"

Ten o'clock had struck before Madame de Vibray and her guests left the dinner-table and proceeded to the small drawing-room. Thomery was allowed to smoke in their presence; besides, the Princess had accepted a Turkish cigarette, and the Baroness had allowed herself a liqueur. A most excellent dinner and choice wines had loosened tongues, and, in accordance with a prearranged plan, Madame de Vibray had directed the conversation imperceptibly into the channels she wished it to follow. Thus she learned what she had feared to know, namely, that a very serious flirtation had been going on for some time between Thomery and the Princess; that between this beautiful and wealthy young widow and the millionaire sugar refiner, the flirtation was rapidly developing into something much warmer and more lasting. So far, the final stage had evidently not been reached; nevertheless, Thomery had suggested, tentatively, that he would like to give a grand ball when he took possession of the new house which he was having built for himself in the park Monceau! . . . And had he not been so extremely anxious to secure a partner for the cotillion which he meant to lead! . . . Then Madame de Vibray had suggested that the person obviously fitted to play this important part was the Princess Sonia Danidoff! Who better!

The suggestion was welcomed by both: it was settled there and then.

"Yes," thought the Baroness, "Thomery's marriage is practically arranged, that is evident! . . . Well, I must resign myself to the inevitable!"

It was about half-past eleven when Sonia Danidoff rose to take leave of her hostess. Thomery, hesitating, looked first at his old friend, then at the Princess, asking himself what he ought to do. Madame de Vibray felt secretly grateful to him for this momentary hesitation. As a woman whose mourning for a dead love is over, she spoke out bravely:

"Dear friend," said she, "surely you are not going to let the Princess return alone? . . . I hope she will allow you to see her safely home?"

The Princess pressed the hands of her generous hostess: she was radiant:

"What a good kind friend you are!" she cried in an outburst of sincere affection. Then, with a questioning glance, in which there was a touch of uneasiness, a slight hesitation, she said:

"Ah, do let me kiss you!"

For all reply Madame de Vibray opened her arms; the two women clung together, sealing with their kiss the treaty of peace both wished to keep.

When the humming of the motor-car, which bore off the Princess and Thomery, had died away in the distance, Madame de Vibray retired to her room. A tear rolled down her cheek:

"A little bit of my heart has gone with them," she murmured. The poor woman sighed deeply: "Ah, it is my whole heart that has gone!"

There was a discreet knock at the door. She mastered her emotion. It was the dignified mistress of the house who said quietly:

"Come in!"

It was Antoine, who presented two letters on a silver salver. He explained that, believing his mistress to be anxiously awaiting some news, he had ventured to bring up the last post at this late hour.

After bidding Antoine good night, she recalled him to say:

"Please tell the maid not to come up. I shall not require her. I can manage by myself."

Madame de Vibray went towards the little writing-table, which stood in one corner of her room; in leisurely fashion she sat down and proceeded to open her letters with a wearied air.

"Why, it's from that nice Jacques Dollon!" she exclaimed, as she read the first letter she opened: "I was thinking of him at this very minute!" . . . "Yes," she went on, as she read, "I shall certainly pay him a visit soon!"

Madame de Vibray put Jacques Dollon's letter in her handbag, recognising on the back of the second letter the initials B. N., which she knew to be the discreet superscription on the business paper of her bankers, Messieurs Barbey-Nanteuil. It was long and closely written, in a fine, regular hand. When she began to read it her attention was wandering, for her mind was full of Sonia Danidoff and Thomery, and what she had ascertained regarding their relation to each other; but little by little she became absorbed in what she was reading, till her whole attention was taken captive. As she read on, however, her eyes opened more and more widely, there was a look of keenest anguish in them, her features contracted as if in pain, her bosom heaved, her fingers were trembling under the stress of some intense emotion:

"Oh, my God! Ah! My God!" she gasped out several times in a half-choked voice.

Silence had reigned for a long while in the smart town house of the Baroness de Vibray in the Avenue Henri-Martin. . . .

From without came no sound; the avenue was quiet, deserted; the night was dark. But when three o'clock struck, the bedroom of Madame de Vibray was still flooded with light. She had not left her writing-table since she had read the letter of her bankers, Messieurs Barbey-Nanteuil. She wrote on, and on, without intermission.

III

UNEXPECTED COMPLICATIONS

At nine o'clock in the morning, the staff of that great evening paper, *La Capitale*, were assembled in the vast editorial room, writing out their copy, in the midst of a perfect hubbub of continual comings and goings, of regular shindies, of perpetual discussions.

A stranger entering this room, which among its frequenters went by the name of "The Wild Beasts' Cage," might easily have thought he was witnessing some thirty schoolboys at play in recreation time, instead of being in the presence of famous journalists celebrated for their reports and articles.

Jérôme Fandor had no sooner appeared on the threshold than he was accorded a variety of greetings — ironical, cordial, fault-finding, sympathetic. But he ignored them all; for, like most of those who came into the editorial room at this hour, he was preoccupied with one thing only — where the caprice of his editorial secretary would send him flying for news, in the course of a few minutes? On what difficult and delicate quest would he be despatched? It depended on the exigencies of passing events, on how questions of the hour struck the editorial secretary, in relation to Fandor.

Just as he had expected, the editorial secretary called him.

"Hey! Fandor, come here a minute! I am on the make-up: what have you got for to-day?"

"I don't know. Who has charge of the landing of the King of Spain?"

"Maray. He has just left. Have you seen the last issue of *l'Havas*?"

"Here it is. . . ."

The two men ran rapidly through the night's telegrams.

"Deplorably empty!" remarked the editorial secretary. "But where am I to send you? . . . Ah, now I have it! That article of yours on the rue Norvins affair, yesterday evening, was interesting — it made the others squirm, I know! Isn't there anything more to be got out of that story?"

"What do you want?"

"Can't you stick in something just a little bit scandalous about the Baroness de Vibray? Or about Dollon? About no matter whom, in fact? After all, it's our one and only crime to-day, and you must put in something under that head! . . ."

Jérôme Fandor seemed to hesitate.

"Would you like me to rake up the past — refer to what happened before?"

"What past?"

"Come now, you must have an inkling of what I refer to!"

"Not I!"

"Ah, my dear fellow, it will not be the first time we have had to mention these personages in our columns! . . . Just cast your mind back to the Gurn affair! . . ."

"Ah, the drama in which a great lady was implicated . . . to her detriment! Lady . . . Lady Beltham?"

"You have got it! These Dollons — Jacques and Elizabeth — did you know it? — happen to be the children of old Dollon, who was murdered in the train — an extraordinary murder! — when on his way to Paris, to give evidence in the Gurn case?"

"Why, of course! I remember perfectly!" declared the editorial secretary: "Dollon, the father, was the Marquise de Langrune's steward! . . . The old lady who was murdered! . . . Isn't that so?"

"That's it! . . . But, after the death of his mistress, he entered the service of the Baroness de Vibray, she who was assassinated yesterday!"

"Well, I must say they have not been favoured by fortune," said the secretary jokingly. "But, look here, Fandor — like father, like son, eh? . . . If this young Dollon has murdered Madame de Vibray, doesn't that make you think that his father was the murderer of the Marquise de Langrune?"

Jérôme Fandor shook his head:

"No, old boy, yesterday's crime was ordinary, even commonplace, but the assassination of the Marquise de Langrune, on the contrary, gave the police no end of bother."

"They did not find out anything, did they?"

"Why, yes! . . . Don't you remember? . . . Naturally enough, it must all seem rather remote to you, but I have all the details as clearly in mind as if they had happened only yesterday. . . . The Gurn affair was one of the first I had a hand in, with Juve . . . it was in connection with that very affair I made my start here on *La Capitale*."[2]

Fandor grew pale:

"And you were jolly proud of it, eh, Fandor? . . . Good Heavens, how you did hold forth about this Juve! And you regularly fed us up with this villain, so mysterious, so extraordinary, who was never run to earth, could not be captured, was capable of the most inhuman cruelties, capable of devising the most unimaginable tricks and stratagems — this Fantômas!"

Fandor grew pale:

2   See *Fantômas*.

"My dear fellow," said he, "never speak sneeringly or jokingly of Fantômas! . . . No doubt it is taken for granted, by the public at any rate, that Fantômas is an invention of Juve and myself: that Fantômas never existed! . . . And that because this monster, who is a man of genius, has never been identified; because not a soul has been able to lay hands on him . . . and because, as you know, this fruitless pursuit has cost poor Juve his life. . . ."

"The truth is, this famous detective died a foul death!"

"No! You are mistaken! Juve died on the field of honour! When, after a terribly difficult and dangerous investigation, he succeeded (by this time it was no longer the Gurn-Fantômas affair, but that of the boulevard Inkermann at Neuilly) in cornering Fantômas, he was well aware that he risked his life in entering the bandit's abode. What happened was that the villain found means to blow up the house, and to bury Juve underneath the ruins. Fantômas has proved the stronger; but, according to my ideas, Juve has had, none the less, the finest death he could desire — death in the midst of the fight — a useful death!"

"Useful? In what way? . . ."

"My dear fellow," cried Fandor, in a tone of vigorous denial, "in the opinion of all unprejudiced minds, the death of Juve has proved, proved up to the hilt, the existence of Fantômas. . . . More, it has forced this villain to disappear; it has restored peace, tranquillity to society. . . . At the cost of his life, Juve has scored a final triumph, he has deprived Fantômas of the power to do harm — pared his claws in fact."

"The truth is he is never mentioned now by a soul . . . for all that, Fandor, only to see you smile! Why —" and the editorial secretary shook a threatening finger at his colleague: "I'll wager you still believe in Fantômas! . . . That one fine day you will write us a rattling good article, announcing some fresh Fantômas crime!"

Jérôme Fandor made no direct reply to this — it was useless to try and convince those who had not closely followed the records of crimes perpetrated during recent years: you could not make them believe in the existence of Fantômas. Fandor *knew*; but, Juve dead, was there another soul who could know the true facts?

All he said was:

"Well, my dear fellow, this does not tell us what we are to fill up the paper with now! . . . If the doings connected with Fantômas are frightful, rousing our feelings in the highest degree, I repeat that yes-

3   See *The Exploits of Juve*.

terday's crime bears no resemblance to them: we can put in a paragraph or so — that is all!"

"No way, is there, of compromising anyone with our Baroness de Vibray?"

"I don't think so! It's a perfectly common-place affair. An elderly woman patronises a young painter, whose mistress she may or may not be, and she ends up by getting herself assassinated when the young man imagines he is mentioned in her will."

"Ah! good! Well, I think you will have to fall back on the opening of the artesian well. That suit you?"

"Oh, quite all right! . . . If you like I can give you my copy in half an hour. I know who are going to speak at the inauguration ceremony, and I can add names this evening! You know I am a bit of a specialist as regards reports written beforehand!"

Fandor had got well on with his article: at the rate he was going he would have finished that morning, he thought with pleasure, and would have a free afternoon. Just then an office boy appeared:

"Monsieur Fandor, you are being asked for at the telephone."

Like most journalists, Fandor was accustomed to reply in nine cases out of ten, in similar cases, that he was not to be found. On this occasion, however, some interior prompting made him say:

"I will come."

A few minutes later Fandor went up to the editorial secretary:

"Look here, old fellow, something unexpected has happened. . . . I must go to the Palais de Justice . . . you don't want me for anything else this morning, do you?"

"No, go along! But what's up?"

"Oh . . . this Jacques Dollon, you know, the assassin of the rue Norvins? Well, this imbecile has gone and hanged himself in his cell!"

At the exit door of *La Capitale*, in the noisy rue Montmartre, crowded with costermongers' barrows, Jérôme Fandor hailed a taxi.

"To the Palais!"

Some minutes later he was crossing the hall of the Wandering Footsteps (as it is called), giving rapid, cordial greetings to all the barristers of his acquaintance — one never knew when they might impart a special piece of information which let an enterprising journalist into the know, or put him early on to a good thing — and finally reached the lobbies of the Law Courts proper. He was saying to himself as he went along:

"He is a good fellow, Jouet! The news is not known yet! He telephoned me first!"

His friend Jouet met him, with a warm handshake:

"You did not seem to be in a good temper at the telephone just now, although I was giving you a nice bit of information!"

"Yes," retorted Fandor, "but information which simply proved how much the administrators of justice, to which you have the misfortune to belong, can make egregious mistakes! When, for once, you succeed in immediately arresting the assassin of someone well known, and are in a position to bring into play all the power and rigour of the law, you are clumsy enough to give the fellow a chance of punishing himself, you let him commit suicide on the very first night of his arrest!"

Fandor had been speaking in a fairly loud voice, as usual, but, at imperative signs made by his friend, he lowered his tones:

"What is it?" he murmured.

His friend rose:

"What we are going to do, old boy, is to take a turn in the galleries! I have something to say to you, and, joking apart, you are not to breathe a word of it to a soul — sh?"

"Count on me!"

Presently the two friends found themselves in one of the corridors of the Palais, known only to barristers and those accused of lawbreaking.

"Come now!" cried Fandor, "your assassin has hanged himself, hasn't he?"

"My assassin!" expostulated the junior barrister: "My assassin! Allow me to inform you that Jacques Dollon is innocent!"

"Innocent?" Jérôme Fandor shrugged a disbelieving shoulder: "Innocent! It is the fashion of the day to transform all murderers into innocents! . . . What ground have you for making such a declaration of innocence?"

"Here is my ground! I have just copied it out for you! Read! . . ."

Fandor hastened to read the paper handed to him by his friend. It was headed thus:

> "Copy of a letter brought by Maître Gérin to the Public Prosecutor, a letter addressed to Maître Gérin by the Baroness de Vibray."

"Oh, it's a plant!" cried Fandor.
"Go on reading, you will see. . . ."
Fandor continued:

"My dear Maître, —
You will forgive me, I am certain of that, for all the inconvenience I am going to cause you; I turn to you because you are the only friend in whom I have confidence.
I have just received a letter from my bankers, Messieurs

Barbey-Nanteuil, of whom I have often spoken to you, who you know manage all my money affairs for me.

This letter informs me that I am ruined. You quite understand — absolutely, completely ruined.

The house I am living in, my carriage, the luxurious surroundings so necessary to me, I shall have to give it all up, so they tell me.

These people have dealt me a terrible blow, struck me brutally. . . .

My dear maître, I learned this only two hours ago, and I am still stunned by it. I do not wish to wait for the inevitable moment when I shall begin to console myself, because I shall begin to hope that the disaster is exaggerated. I have no family, I am already old; apart from the satisfaction it gives me to use my influence on behalf of youthful talent, and to help forward its development, my life has no sense in it, it is without aim or object. My dear maître, there are not two ways of announcing to one's friends resolutions analogous to that I now take: when you receive this letter I shall be dead.

I have in front of me, on my writing-table, a tiny phial of poison which I am going to drink to the last drop, without any weakening of will, almost without fear, as soon as I have posted this letter to you myself.

I must confess that I have an instinctive horror of being dragged to the Morgue, as happens whenever there is some doubt about a suicide. It is on account of this I now write to you, so that, thanks to your intervention, all the mistakes justice is liable to make may be avoided.

I kill myself, I only; that is certain.

No one must be incriminated in connection with my death, if it be not Fatality, which has caused my ruin. I once more apologise, my dear maître, for all the measures you will be forced to take owing to my death, and I beg you to believe that my friendship for you was very sincere:

Signed:

Baroness de Vibray."

"Good for you!" cried Fandor. "Here's a go! What a pretty petard in prospect! . . . Jacques Dollon was innocent; you arrest him; he is so terrified that he hangs himself! Well, old boy, I must say you make some fine blunders on Clock Quay!"

"It is nobody's fault!" protested the young barrister.

"That is to say," retorted Fandor, "it is everybody's fault! By Jove! If you let innocent prisoners hang themselves in their cells, I am no longer surprised that you leave the guilty at liberty to walk the streets at their sweet will!"

"Don't make a joke of it, old boy! . . . You understand, of course, that so far no one in the Palais has seen the letter! It has just been brought to the Public Prosecutor's office by Madame de Vibray's solicitor, Maître Gérin. You came on the scene only a few minutes after I had sent up the original to the examining magistrate. The case is in Fuselier's hands."

"Is he in his office?"

"Certainly! He should proceed with the examination relative to poor Dollon this morning."

"Very well then, I will go up. I shall jolly soon get out of this booby of a Fuselier the information I need to make one of the best reports I have ever written. And you know, I am ever so obliged to you for the matter you've given me! But, mind you, I am going to put together a bit of copy that will not deal tenderly with our gentlemen of the robe — the lot of you! No, it is a bad, unlucky business enough, but it is even more funny — it is tragi-comedy!"

"For my part . . ." began Fandor's barrister friend.

"Yes, yes! Good day, Pontius Pilate!" cried Fandor. "I am going up to Fuselier. . . . We must meet to-morrow!"

Hastening along the corridors, Fandor gained the office of the examining magistrate.

Fandor had known the magistrate a long while. Was not Fuselier the justice who, with Detective Juve, had had everything to do with the strangely mysterious cases associated with the name of Fantômas? In the course of his various judicial examinations he had often been able to give Fandor information and help. At first hostile to the constant preoccupation of Juve and Fandor — for long the arrest of Fantômas was their one aim — the young magistrate had gradually come to believe in what had seemed to him nothing but the detective's hypothesis. Open-minded, gifted with an alert intelligence, Fuselier had carefully followed the investigations of Juve and Fandor. He knew every detail, every vicissitude connected with the tracking of this elusive bandit. Since then the magistrate had taken the deepest interest in the pursuit of the criminal. Thanks to his support, Juve had been enabled to take various measures, otherwise almost impossible, avoid the many obstacles offered by legal procedure, risk the striking of many a blow he could not otherwise have ventured on.

Fuselier had a high opinion of Juve, and his attitude to Fandor was sympathetic.

Our journalist was going over the past as he hastened along:

Ah, if only Juve were here! If only this loyal servant of Justice, this sincerest of friends, this bravest of the brave, had not been struck down, Fandor would have been full of enthusiasm for the Dollon affair; for its interest was increasing, its mystery deepening! But

Fandor was single-handed now! He had had a miraculous escape from the bomb which had blown up Lady Beltham's house on that tragic day when Juve had all but laid hands on Fantômas!

But Fandor would not allow himself to become disheartened — never that! In the school of his vanished friend he had learned to give himself up with single-minded devotion to any task he took up; his sole satisfaction being duty well fulfilled. . . . Well, the Dollon case should be cleared up! . . . To do so was to render a service to humanity! Having come to this conclusion he hastened to interview Monsieur Fuselier.

"Monsieur Fuselier," cried Fandor as he shook hands with the magistrate, "you must know quite well why I have come to see you!"

"About the rue Norvins affair?"

"Say rather about the Dépôt affair! It is there the affair became tragic."

Monsieur Fuselier smiled:

"You know then?"

"That Jacques Dollon has hanged himself? Yes. That he was innocent? Again, yes!" confessed Fandor, smiling in his turn: "You know that at *La Capitale* we get all the information going, and are the first to get it!"

"Evidently," conceded the magistrate. "But if you know all about it, why put my professional discretion to the torture by asking absurd questions?"

"Now, what the deuce are they about on Clock Quay? Don't they supervise the accused in their cells?"

"Certainly they do! When this Dollon arrived at the Dépôt he was immediately conducted to Monsieur Bertillon: there he was measured and tested, finger marks taken, and so on."

"Just so," said Fandor. "I saw Bertillon before coming on to you. He told me Dollon seemed crushed: he submitted to all the tests without making the slightest objection; but he never spoke of suicide, never said anything which could lead one to imagine such a fatal termination."

"Well, he would not cry it aloud on the housetops! . . . When he left Monsieur Bertillon, what then?"

"After! . . . Oh, the police took him to a cell, and left him there. At midnight the chief warder made his rounds and saw nothing abnormal. It was in the morning they found this unfortunate Dollon had hanged himself."

"What did he hang himself with?"

"With strips of his shirt twisted into a rope. . . . Oh, my dear fellow, I see what you are thinking! You fancy that there has been a want of common prudence — that the warders were lax — that they had let him retain his braces, his cravat or his shoe laces! . . . Well, it was not so — precautions were taken."

"And this suicide remains incomprehensible!"

"Well! . . . This wretched youth must have been ferociously energetic, because he had fastened these shirt ropes of his to the iron bars of his bed, and strangled himself by lying on his back. Death must have been long in coming to release him from his agony."

"Can I not see him?" asked Fandor.

"Why not photograph him?" asked the magistrate in a bantering tone.

"Oh, if it were possible! . . ." Fandor stopped short. A youth knocked and entered:

"A lady, who wishes to see you, monsieur."

"Tell her I am too busy."

"She asked me to say that it is urgent."

"Ask her name."

"Here is her card, monsieur."

Monsieur Fuselier looked at the card: he started!

"Elizabeth Dollon! . . . Ah . . . Good Heavens, what am I to say to this poor girl? How am I to tell her?"

Just then the door was pushed violently open, and a girl, in tears, rushed towards him:

"Monsieur, where is my brother?"

"But, mademoiselle! . . ."

Whilst the magistrate mechanically asked his distracted visitor to sit down, Jérôme Fandor discreetly withdrew to the further side of the room; he was anxious that the magistrate should forget his presence, so that he might be a witness of what promised to be a most exciting interview.

"Pray control yourself, mademoiselle," begged the magistrate. "Your brother has perhaps been arrested through a mistake. . . ."

"Oh, monsieur, I am sure of it, but it is frightful!"

"Mademoiselle, the dreadful thing would be that he was guilty."

"But they have not set him at liberty yet? He has not been able to clear himself?"

"Yes, yes, mademoiselle, he has vindicated himself, I even . . ." Monsieur Fuselier stopped short, intensely pained, not knowing how to tell Elizabeth Dollon the terrible news.

At once she cried: "Ah, monsieur, you hesitate! You have learned something fresh? You are on the track of the assassins?"

"It is certain . . . your brother is not guilty!"

The poor girl's countenance suddenly brightened. She had passed a horrible night after her return to Paris, and the receipt of the wire from Police Headquarters.

"What a nightmare!" she cried. "But the telegram said he was injured — nothing serious, is it? . . . Where is he now? Can I see him?"

"Mademoiselle," said the magistrate, "your brother has had a terrible shock! . . . It would be better! . . . I fear that! . . ."

Suddenly Elizabeth Dollon cried:

"Oh, monsieur, how you said that! How can seeing me do him harm?"

As Monsieur Fuselier did not reply, she burst into tears:

"You are hiding something from me! The papers said this morning that he also was a victim! Swear to me that he is not?"

"But . . ."

"You *are* hiding something from me!" The poor girl was frantic with terror: she wrung her hands in a state of despair: "Where is he? I must see him! Oh, take pity on me!"

As she watched the magistrate's downcast look, his air of discomfiture, the horrid truth flashed on Elizabeth Dollon:

"Dead!" she cried. She was shaken with sobs.

"Mademoiselle! . . . Oh, mademoiselle!" implored the magistrate, filled with pity. He tried to find some words of consolation, and this confirmed her worst fears:

"I swear to you! . . . It is certain your brother was not guilty!"

The distracted girl was beyond listening to the magistrate's words! Huddled up in an arm-chair, she lay inert, collapsed. Presently she rose like a person moving in some mad dream, her eyes wild:

"Take me to him! . . . I want to see him! They have killed him for me! . . . I must see him!"

Such was her insistence, the violence with which she claimed the right to go to her brother, to kneel beside him, that Monsieur Fuselier dared not refuse her this consolation.

"Control yourself, I beg of you! I am going to take you to him; but, for Heaven's sake, be reasonable! Control yourself!"

With his eyes he sought for the moral support of Fandor, whose presence he suddenly remembered. But our journalist, taking advantage of the momentary confusion, had quietly slipped from the room.

Evidently some unpleasant occurrence had upset the routine existence of the functionaries at the Dépôt. The warders were coming and going, talking among themselves, leaning against the doors of the numerous cells. The chief warder called one of his men:

"There must be no more of this disorder, Nibet!"

The chief warder was furious: he was about to hold forth to his subordinate, when an inspector approached.

"What is it?" he asked.

"Sergeant, it is Monsieur Jouet. He has a gentleman with him. He has a permit. Should I allow him to enter?"

"Who? Monsieur Jouet?"

"No, the gentleman accompanying him!"

"Hang it all! Why, yes — if he has a permit!"

The sergeant moved away shrugging his shoulders disgustedly.

"Not pleased with things this morning, the chief isn't," one of the warders remarked.

"Not likely, after last night's performance!"

"It's he who will catch it hot over this business!" The warder rubbed his hands, laughing.

Meanwhile, Fandor had appeared at the entrance of the corridor, under the guidance of a warder. He was thinking of the splendid copy he had secured: he was hoping that when Fuselier learned that a journalist had obtained admittance to the Dépôt, and had seen the corpse of Jacques Dollon in his cell, that he would not turn vicious: "But after all," said he to himself, "Fuselier is not the man to give me the go-by out of spite."

Fandor walked up and down the hall of the prison. He had informed the warders that he was waiting for the magistrate. "How strange life is!" thought he. "To think that once again I should be brought into close contact with Elizabeth Dollon, and that there is no likelihood of her recognising me — we were such children when we parted — she especially! Had she any recollection of the little rascal I was at the time of poor Madame de Langrune's assassination?" And, closing his eyes, Fandor tried to call to mind the features of the Jacques Dollon he used to know: it was useless! The body of Jacques Dollon he would be gazing at in a few minutes would be that of an unknown person, whose name alone awakened memories of bygone days. . . .

So to pass the time Fandor continued his marching up and down.

Monsieur Fuselier appeared at the entrance to the Dépôt, supporting the unsteady steps of poor Elizabeth Dollon. Fandor quickly drew back into an obscure corner:

"Better not attract attention to myself just at present," thought Fandor; "I will wait until the cell door is opened. If Fuselier does not wish to give me permission to remain, I can at any rate cast a rapid glance round that ill-omened little cell!"

Fandor followed, at a distance, the wavering steps of the poor girl whom Monsieur Fuselier was supporting with fatherly care.

When they paused before one of the cells pointed out by the head warder, Monsieur Fuselier turned to Elizabeth Dollon:

"Do you think you are strong enough to bear this trial, mademoiselle? . . . You are determined to see your brother?"

Elizabeth bent her head; the magistrate turned towards the

warder:

"Open," said he. As the key was turned in the lock he said: "According to instructions from the Head, we have placed him on his bed again. . . . There is nothing to frighten you . . . he seems to be asleep. . . . Now then!"

But as he opened the door, stretching his arm in the direction of the bed where the body of Jacques Dollon should be, an oath escaped him:

"Great Heavens! The dead man is gone!"

In this cell with its bare walls, its sole furniture an iron bedstead and a stool riveted to the floor, in this little cell which the eye could glance round in a second, there was no vestige of a corpse: Jacques Dollon's body was not there!

"You have mistaken the cell," said the magistrate sharply.

"No, no!" cried the astounded warder.

"You can see, can't you, that Jacques Dollon is not there?"

"He was there a few minutes ago!"

"Then they must have taken him somewhere else!"

"The keys have never left me!"

"Oh, come now!"

"No, sir. He was there . . . now he isn't there! That's all I know! . . . Hey! You down there!" yelled the warder: "Who knows what has become of the corpse of cell 12? . . . The corpse we laid out just now?"

One after the other the warders came running. All confirmed what their chief had said: the dead body of Jacques Dollon had been left there, lying on the bed: not a soul had entered the cell: not a soul had touched the corpse! . . . Yet it was no longer there! Jérôme Fandor, well in the background, followed the scene with an ironical smile. The frantic warders, the growing stupefaction of Monsieur Fuselier, amused him prodigiously. The magistrate was trying to understand the how, why, and wherefore of this incredible disappearance:

"As this man is not here, he cannot have been dead . . . he has escaped . . . but if he wanted to escape he must have been guilty! . . . Oh, I cannot make head or tail of it!"

Seizing the head warder by the shoulders, almost roughly, Monsieur Fuselier asked:

"Look here, chief, was this man dead, or was he not?"

Elizabeth Dollon was repeating:

"He lives! He lives!" and laughing wildly.

The warder raised his hand as though taking a solemn oath:

"As to being dead, he was dead right enough! . . . The doctor will tell you so, too: also my colleague, Favril, who helped me to lay out the body on the bed."

"But how can a dead body get away from here? If he *was* dead, he could not have escaped!" said the magistrate.

"It is witchcraft!" declared the warder, with a shrug.

Fuselier flew into a rage:

"Had you not better confess that you and your colleagues did not keep proper watch and ward! . . . The investigation will show on whose shoulders the responsibility rests."

"But, sakes alive, monsieur!" expostulated the warder: "There aren't only two of us who have seen him dead! . . . There are all the hospital attendants of the Dépôt as well! . . . There is the doctor, and there are my colleagues to be counted in: the truth is, monsieur, some fifty persons have seen him dead!"

"So you say!" cried the impatient magistrate: "I am going to inform the Public Prosecutor of what has happened, and at once!"

As he was hurrying away, he spied Jérôme Fandor, who had not missed a single detail of the scene.

"You again!" exclaimed the irate magistrate: "How did you get in here?"

"By permit," replied our journalist.

"Well, you have learned what there is to know, haven't you? Be off, then! You are one too many here! . . . Frankly, there is no need for you to augment the scandal! . . . Will you, therefore, be kind enough to take yourself off?" And Fuselier, almost beside himself with rage, raced off to the Public Prosecutor's office.

After the magistrate's furious attack, Fandor could not possibly linger in the corridors of the Dépôt. The warders, too, were pressing their attentions on him and on Elizabeth Dollon:

"This way, monsieur! . . . Madame, this way! . . . Ah, it's a wretched business! . . . Here, this way! This way! . . . Be off, as fast as you can!"

Presently Fandor was descending the grand staircase of the Palais, steadying the uncertain steps of poor Elizabeth Dollon.

"I implore you to help me!" she cried: "Help me: help us! My brother is guiltless — I could swear to that! . . . He must — must be found! . . . This hideous nightmare must end!"

"Mademoiselle, I ask nothing better, only . . . where to find him?"

"Ah, I have no idea, none! . . . I implore you, you who must know influential people in high places, do not leave any stone unturned, do all that is humanly possible to save him — to save us!"

Intensely moved by the poor girl's anguish of mind, Fandor could not trust himself to speak. He bent his head in the affirmative merely. Hailing a cab, he put her into it, gave the address to the driver, and as he was closing the door Elizabeth cried:

"Do all that is humanly possible — do everything in the world!"

"I swear to you I will get at the truth," was Fandor's parting promise. The cab had disappeared, but our journalist stood motionless, absorbed in his reflections. At last, uttering his thoughts aloud, he said:

"If the Baroness de Vibray has written that she has killed herself, then she has killed herself, and Dollon is innocent. It's true the letter may be fictitious . . . therefore we must put it aside — we have no guarantee as to its genuineness. . . . Here is the problem: Jacques Dollon is dead, and yet has left the Dépôt! Yes, but how?"

Jérôme Fandor went off in the direction of the offices of *La Capitale* so absorbed in thought that he jostled the passers-by, without noticing the angry glances bestowed on him:

"Jacques Dollon, dead, has left the Dépôt!" He repeated this improbable statement, so absurd, of necessity incorrect; repeated it to the point of satiety:

"Jacques Dollon is dead, and he has got away from the Dépôt!"

Then, in an illuminating flash, he perceived the solution of this apparently insoluble problem:

"A mystery such as this is incomprehensible, inexplicable, impossible, except in connection with one man! There is only one individual in the world capable of making a dead man seem to be alive after his death — and this individual is — Fantômas!"

To formulate this conclusion was to give himself a thrilling shock. . . . Since the disappearance of Juve, he had never had occasion to suspect the presence, the intervention of Fantômas in connection with any of the crimes he had investigated as reporter and student of human nature.

Fantômas! The sound of that name evoked the worst horrors! Fantômas! This bandit, this criminal who has not shrunk from any cruelty, any horror — Fantômas is crime personified!

Fantômas! He sticks at nothing!

Pronouncing these syllables of evil omen, Fandor lived over again all the extraordinary, improbable, impossible things that had really happened, and had put him on the watch for this terrifying assassin.

Fantômas!

It was certain that to whatever degree he had participated in the assassination of the Baroness de Vibray, one must not be astonished at anything; neither at anything inconceivable, nor at any mysterious details connected with the murder.

Fantômas!

He was the daring criminal — daring beyond all bounds of credibility. And whatever might be the dexterity, the ingenuity, the ability, the devotion of those who were pursuing him, such were his tricks, such his craft and cunning, such the fertility of his invention, so well conceived his devices, so great his audacity, that there were grounds for fearing he would never be brought to justice, and punished for his abominable crimes!

Fantômas!

Ah, if life ever brought Jérôme Fandor and this bandit face to face, there would ensue a struggle of every hour, day, and moment — a struggle of the most terrible nature, a struggle in which man was pitted against man, a struggle without pity, without mercy — a fight to the death! Fantômas would assuredly defend himself with all the immense elusive powers at his command: Jérôme Fandor would pursue him with heart and soul, with his very life itself! It was not only to satisfy his sense of duty at the promptings of honour that the journalist would take action: he would have as guide for his acts, and to animate his will, the passion of hate, and the hope of avenging his friend Juve, fallen a victim to the mysterious blows of Fantômas.

In his article for *La Capitale* Fandor did not directly mention the possible participation of Fantômas in the crime of the rue Norvins. When it was finished he returned to his modest little flat on the fifth floor in the rue Bergere. He was about to enter the vestibule, when he noticed a piece of paper, which must have been slipped under his door. He stooped and picked up an envelope:

"Why, it is a letter — and there is no name and no stamp on it!"

Entering his study, he seated himself at his table and prepared to begin work. Then he bethought him of the letter, which he had carelessly thrown on the mantelpiece. He tore it open, and drew out a sheet of letter paper.

"Whatever is this?" he cried. His astonishment was natural enough, for the message was oddly put together. To prevent his handwriting being recognised, Fandor's correspondent had cut letters out of a newspaper, and had stuck them together in the desired order. The two or three lines of printed matter were as follows:

"Jérôme Fandor, pay attention, great attention! The affair on which you are concentrating all your powers is worthy of all possible interest, but may have terribly dangerous consequences."

Of course there was no signature.

Evidently the warning referred to the Dollon case.

"Why," exclaimed Fandor, "this is simply an invitation not to busy myself hunting for the guilty persons! . . . Who has sent this invitation and warning? Surely the sender is the assassin, to whose interest it is that the inquiry into the rue Norvins murder should be dropped! . . . It must be Jacques Dollon! . . . But how could Dollon know my address? How could he have found time between his flight from the Dépôt and the present minute, to put this message of printed letters together, and take it to the rue Bergere? . . . And that at the risk of encountering someone who could recognise him, and might have him arrested afresh? Had he accomplices?"

Fandor was puzzled, agitated:

"But I am mad! . . . mad! It cannot be Dollon! . . . Dollon is dead — dead as a door nail — dead beyond dispute, because fifty men have seen him dead; dead, because the Dépôt doctors have certified his death!"

Daylight was fading; evening was coming on; Fandor was still turning the whole affair over in his mind. Every now and again he murmured:

"Fantômas! Fantômas has to do with this extraordinary, this mysterious affair! Fantômas is in it! . . . Fantômas!"

IV

A SURPRISING ITINERARY

Jérôme Fandor had passed a bad night!

Visions of horror had continually arisen in his troubled mind. Between nightmare after nightmare he had heard all the horrors of the night sound out in the darkness and the glimmering dawn. Then he had fallen into a heavy sleep, which had left him on awaking broken with fatigue. He had given himself a cold douche, and this had calmed his nerves; then he had dressed quickly. When eight o'clock struck he was at his writing-table, thinking things over:

"It's no laughing matter. I thought at first that the Dollon affair was quite ordinary; but I am mistaken. The warning I received last night leaves me no doubts on that head. Since the guilty person thinks it necessary to ask me to keep quiet, it is evident he fears my intervention; if he is afraid of that it is because it must be hurtful to him; if disastrous to him, a criminal, it is evident that it must be useful to honest folk. My duty, then, is to go straight ahead at all costs. . . ."

There was another motive besides this of duty which incited him to follow more closely the vicissitudes of the rue Norvins drama, a motive still indefinite, vague, but nevertheless terribly strong. . . .

Jérôme Fandor had sworn to Elizabeth Dollon that he would get at the truth.

He recalled the girl's entreaty, her emotion; and when he closed his eyes, now and again, he seemed to see before him the tall, graceful, fair and fascinating sister of the vanished artist. . . . All Fandor would admit to himself was a chivalrous feeling towards her — Elizabeth Dollon was worth putting himself out for — that was all!

Our journalist spent the entire morning seated at his writing-table, his head between his hands, smoking cigarette after cigarette, arranging his plans for investigating the Dollon case:

"What I have to find out is how the dead man left the Dépôt. It is the first discovery to be made, the first impossibility to be explained — yes, and how am I to set about it?"

Suddenly Fandor jumped up, marched rapidly up and down his room, whistled a few bars of a popular melody, and in his exuberant gaiety attempted an operatic air in a voice deplorably out of tune.

"There are eighty chances out of a hundred that I shall not succeed," cried he; "but that still leaves me twenty chances of arriving at a satisfactory result — let us make the attempt!"

As Fandor was hurrying off, he called to the portress in passing:

"Madame Oudry, I don't know whether I shall be back this evening or no. Perhaps I may have to leave Paris for awhile, so would you be kind enough to pay particular attention to any letters that may come for me — be very particular about them, please!"

Fandor went off. A thought struck him. He turned back. He had something more to say to the good woman:

"I forgot to ask you whether anyone called to see me yesterday afternoon!"

"No, Monsieur Fandor, no one!"

"Good! If by any chance a messenger should bring a letter for me, look very carefully at him, Madame Oudry. I have a colleague or two who are playing a joke on me, and I should not be sorry to get even with them!"

This time Fandor really went off, having set his portress on the alert. In the rue Montmartre he hailed a cab:

"To the National Library! And as quick as you can!"

"By Jove! It's three o'clock! I've not a minute to lose!" cried Fandor as he got back his stick from the cloak-room of the National Library: he had handed it in there some hours ago. He entered the rue Richelieu. Now for an ironmonger's shop! He caught sight of one and went in:

"I should like fifty yards of fine cord, please; very strong and very pliable," said Fandor.

The shopkeeper stared at the smart young man:

"What do you want it for, sir? . . . I have various qualities."

Without the trace of a smile, and as if it were the most natural thing in the world, he replied:

"It is for one of my friends: he wants to hang himself!"

A shout of laughter was the response to this witticism, and the amused shopkeeper forthwith displayed various samples of cords. Fandor promptly made his choice and left the shop.

"Now for a watchmaker's!" said our journalist. He entered a jeweller's close by:

"I want an alarum clock — a small one — the cheapest you have!"

Provided with his alarum, Fandor looked at his watch again:

"Confound it all! It's half-past three!" he cried. He signalled to a closed cab:

"To the Palais de Justice! As hard as you can lick!"

Directly Fandor was well inside the vehicle, he drew down the blinds; took off his coat; unbuttoned his waistcoat! . . .

The great clock of the Palais de Justice had just struck four, and its silvery tones were echoing harmoniously along the corridors when Jérôme Fandor entered the tradesman's gallery. He turned to the right, and gained the little lobby in which the cloak-room is. He quietly entered it. Barristers were coming and going, full of business, throwing off their gowns, inspecting the letters put aside during the sittings of the Courts. Fandor made his way among the groups with the ease of custom. He seemed to be looking for someone, and finished by questioning one of the women employed in the cloak-room:

"Is Madame Marguerite not here?"

"Oh, yes, monsieur, she is down below."

Madame Marguerite was an old friend of Fandor's. She was head of the cloak-room staff, and by her kind offices she had often obtained an interview for our journalist with one or other of the bigwigs of the bar, who generally object strongly to being questioned by journalists. When she appeared, Fandor told her he only wanted a little bit of information from her.

"Oh, yes, I know all about that! There is someone you wish to see, and you want me to manage it for you!"

"No! Not a bit of it! What I want to know is, where these gentlemen of the Court of Justice robe and unrobe? I mean the Justices of the Assize Courts!"

This seemed to astonish Madame Marguerite considerably:

"But, Monsieur Fandor, if you wish to interview one of the puisne judges, it would be ten times quicker for you to go and see him at his own home: here, at the Palais, it's almost certain he will refuse to answer you. . . ."

"Don't bother about that, Madame Marguerite! Just tell me where these worthy guardians of order, defenders of right and justice, divest themselves of their red robes?"

Madame Marguerite was too much accustomed to our young journalist's ridiculous questions and absurd requests and remarks to argue with him any longer.

"The robing-room of these gentlemen," said she, "is in one of the outer offices of the court, near the Council Chamber."

"There is an assistant in that room, isn't there?"

"Yes, Monsieur Fandor."

"Ah! That is just what I wanted to know! Many thanks, madame," and Fandor, grinning with satisfaction, made off in the direction of the Court of Assizes. He ran up the steps leading to the Council Chamber, and spying the messenger asked:

"Can President Guéchand see me, do you think?"

"Monsieur le President has gone."

Fandor seemed to be reflecting. He gazed searchingly round the room. As a matter of fact, he was verifying the correctness of Madame Marguerite's information. All round the room Fandor saw the little presses where the men of law kept their red robes. Yes, it was the robing and unrobing room of the puisne judges, the magistrates, right enough!

"So the President has gone? Ah, well . . ." Fandor hesitated: he must think of some other name. He noticed the visiting cards nailed to each press, indicating the owner. He read one of the names and repeated it:

"Well, then, could Justice Hubert see me — could he possibly? Will you ask him to let me see him for five minutes?"

"What name shall I say?"

"My name will not tell him anything. Please say it is with reference to the — er — Peyru case — and I come from Maître Tissot."

"I will go and see," said the messenger, moving off.

Whilst he was in sight Fandor walked up and down in the regulation way, murmuring:

"Maître Tissot! . . . The Peyru case! . . . Go ahead, my good fellow! You will have a nice kind of reception down below there — with those made-up names."

Some minutes later, the messenger returned to his post, prepared to inform the importunate young man that he could not possibly be received by Justice Hubert. He stopped short on the threshold: not a soul was to be seen!

"Wherever has that young man got to? Taken himself off, most likely! . . . I expect he was one of those lawyer's clerks — confound them! A nice fool I should have looked if his Honour, Justice Hubert, had said he would receive him!"

With this reflection the messenger went back to his newspaper, not without having ascertained that it was four o'clock, and therefore he had still an hour to wait before he could have his coffee and cigar at the "Men of the Robe."

Through the great windows of the Court of Assizes, carefully closed as they were, not a ray of moonlight filtered into the court room. And this obscurity lent an added terror to a silence as profound as the grave, a silence which, with the falling shades of night, assumed possession of the vast hall, where so many criminals had listened to the fatal sentence — the sentence of death.

When the Court had risen, the assistants had, as usual, proceeded to put the place in order; then the police sergeant had made his rounds, and had gone away, double locking the doors behind him. After this the chamber had gradually sunk into complete repose: a repose which would be broken the following morning when the bustling routine of the legal day commenced once more.

Little by little, too, the many and varied noises, which had echoed and re-echoed the whole day through in the galleries of the

Palais de Justice, had died down, and sunk into silence.

The custodians had made their last round; the barristers had quitted the robing-room; the poor wretches who had slunk in to warm themselves at the heating apparatus in the halls had shuffled back to the cold street, and the whistling blasts of the north wind. The immense pile was entirely deserted.

A clock began to strike.

Then, hardly had the last stroke of eleven sounded, awakening the echoes of the empty galleries, than in the Court of Assizes itself, under the monumental desk, before which the justices sat in state by day, a noise made itself heard, long, strident, nerve-racking — the noise of an alarum clock!

Just as the alarum ceased its raucous call, a loud yawn resounded through the empty spaces of the chamber. The sleeper, who had selected this spot that he might indulge, all undisturbed, in a revivifying sleep, evidently took no pains to smother the sound of his voice, for, after yawning enough to dislocate his jaws, he uttered a loud: "Ah!" He accompanied his yawns with exclamations:

"It's a fact, the Republic doesn't do things up to the scratch! The rugs here are of poor quality! . . . I'm aching all over! . . . The floor is strewn with peach kernels — surely? . . . At any rate, it's a quiet hotel, and one is not disturbed — a truly delectable refuge to have a jolly good snore in!"

The sleeper sat up:

"What's the time exactly? Let us have a light on it!" A match was struck, and a tiny flare of light shone from under the desk of the presiding judge:

"Ten past eleven! I've still five minutes to be lazy in — and I shall need all of it, for I've a rough night before me! I can rest awhile, and think things over!"

The speaker calmly lay down again, trying to find a comfortable position on what he christened mentally: "The administrative peach kernels":

"Let me see, now!" he went on aloud. "At five in the afternoon it was known that Jacques Dollon had committed suicide; was probably innocent, and that his corpse had disappeared. Yesterday, at half-past five, *La Capitale* announced that he had a very pretty sister. . . . To-night at ten past eleven behold me, shut up quite alone in the Palais de Justice, free to proceed to the little investigation I think of making. . . . Jérôme Fandor, my dear friend, I congratulate you! You have not managed badly! . . .

"Yes," went on our journalist, "what a joke it is! Here have I got myself shut up in the Palais without the slightest difficulty! It is true, that if the assistant had been obliged to open, and verify, the contents of all the robing-rooms of all the judges, he would never have finished. As for me, in my cupboard, I followed all the good fellow's movements, and he never suspected my presence. If I am to be congratulated, he cannot be blamed for it! There I was, there I remained, and now I must be off!"

Fandor drew a small wax taper from his pocket and lighted it with a match.

"What's to be done with the alarum?" he went on. "To leave it will be to betray my having passed this way — what of it? . . . In any case, even if this reporting job fails, I shall make a story out of it . . . and how can they accuse me of stealing if I leave my cloak as a gift for his judgeship!"

Laughing, Fandor piled up the law books lying on the desk, and placed the alarum on the top; that done, he went to the principal entrance, the only one with double doors. He seized the heavy iron bar placed across the door and worked it loose. He drew the two leaves of the door towards him; and, although it had been locked as usual, he effected his escape, after a considerable trial of strength.

Out on the stairs, lighted taper in hand, the laughing Fandor closed the two leaves of the door with the utmost care, and went forward whistling a marching tune. His objective was a certain little staircase leading to the top story of the Palais, and this he mounted with vigorous determination. There was no likelihood of chance encounters, for there was not a soul in the vast building: the police were making their rounds outside it. Our adventurous journalist did not make his way upwards with stealthy tread — there was no need for that. Having gained the top floor, he went straight to a corner where an ebony ladder was ensconced, a ladder which had long been the joy and pride of the grand master of this part of the Palais, the amiable Monsieur Peter.

"Pretty heavy!" grumbled Fandor, as he carried it upwards. Under the roof he caught sight of a skylight, rested his ebony ladder against it, and climbed briskly on to the roof.

From thence Fandor had a view that was fairy-like. Spread out in the distance were the sparkling lights of Paris. He was divided from them by the vast mass of roofs about him, by a gulf of empty space, and beyond, by a dark blur — the two arms of the Seine flowing on either side of the Palais de Justice. . . . The mysterious darkness! The fascination of the sparkling points of light! . . . Fandor gave himself a mental shake. . . . This was no moment for dreaming under the stars!

From his pocket he took a tiny, folding dark lantern; from his pocket-book he drew a paper, which he spread out and proceeded to study. As he bent over it, he murmured:

"A bit of good luck that I was able to get hold of a complete and detailed plan of the Palais de Justice! Without it I never could have found my way among these roofs!"

He examined the plan for some minutes; made a note of various landmarks; then refolding it, he gained one of the sloping roofs facing the quay of the Leather Dressers:

"Now," thought Fandor, "I must be just above the Dépôt! And now to find out how Jacques Dollon, dead or living, has got out of the Dépôt! No use thinking of a window, for the cell has not got one! Fuselier has reason on his side when he declares that you do not get out of the cells of the Dépôt, nor out of the Palais! . . . Well, now — to carry off Dollon, dead or living, by way of the Palais Square, or by the boulevard, is out of the question: there are too many people about! . . . To carry him off by one of the exits, on to either of the quays, is equally out of the question: there are the sentries, in the first place, and then comes the Seine — then Jacques Dollon has left the Dépôt, or he has not, or, at any rate, he is still somewhere in the Palais — unless . . ."

Fandor interrupted his cogitations to light a cigarette: smoking helped him to think things out:

"It is equally certain that if Dollon is still in the Palais, he cannot be in the Dépôt, for the Dépôt has been rigorously searched since his disappearance, and he would most certainly have been found, had he been anywhere about the Dépôt. It is also certain that he is not inside the Palais, because the only means of communication between the Dépôt and the Palais is a single staircase, and it is certain that a corpse could not have been taken that way unperceived. . . . Then it follows that Jacques Dollon must have got out by the only ways which are in communication with the Dépôt: that is to say, the drains and the chimneys!"

"How could he have got out, or been got out by the drains? As far as I know, there is no system of pipes large enough to allow of the passage of a man through the pipes which join the main sewers; but, as a set-off to that, there is a chimney — the ancient chimney of Marie Antoinette — which communicates with the Dépôt, and the roof I am now on: it must have been by this chimney that the escape was made! Let us see whether this is so or not!"

By the light of his tiny dark lantern Fandor studied afresh the plan of the Palais, and tried to identify the various chimneys about him. He soon picked out the orifice of Marie Antoinette's chimney. After a considering glance at it, he remarked:

"That's odd! Here is the only chimney whose opening is below the ledge of the roofs! It is certain that unless one had been warned, and had examined this roof from some neighbouring building, the orifice of this chimney would not be noticed. If Jacques Dollon passed out by it, no one would notice his exit!"

Our journalist continued his examination, full of excitement. Surely he was on the right track!

"Ah! Ah! Here are stones freshly scraped and scratched!" he cried delightedly. "And this white mark is just the kind of mark which would be made by a cord scraping against the wall! And look what a size this chimney is! It's not only one Jacques Dollon who could pass out by it, but two! But three! A whole army! Ah, ha, I believe I am on the right track! Now for it!"

Fandor bent over and looked down the interior of the chimney; and, at the risk of toppling over, he managed to reach something he saw shining in the darkness of the opening; he drew himself up, radiant:

"By Jove! There are irons fixed in the walls of the chimney to climb up and down by; and, what is more, they bear traces of a recent passage — the rust has been rubbed off here and there! . . . Yes, it is by this way Dollon has come out! . . . To whom else could it be an advantage to use this as an exit from the interior of the Palais, on to the roofs?"

Fandor was keen on the scent! Here, indeed, was matter for an article which would bring him into notice — good business for a journalist!

"If Dollon had been alive," reflected Fandor, "it is evident that, once on the roofs, he had a choice of three ways to escape: he could do what I have just done, but the other way about; he could break a skylight, jump into a garret, and lie hidden under the tiles, awaiting the propitious moment when he could gain the corridors below and, mingling with the crowd, slip unobserved into the street; or, he could hide among the roofs, and stay there; or, he could search for an opening — one of those air holes which put the cellars and drains in communication with the exterior. . . . But I have come to the conclusion that Dollon is dead! Then his corpse could only remain up here; or, it has been put down into some place where nobody goes. The garrets of the Palais are so incessantly visited by the clerks and registrars that no corpse could remain undiscovered in any of them. Therefore, either Jacques Dollon's corpse is somewhere on the roofs of the Palais, or there is some sort of communication between the roofs and the drains — it is obvious!"

Evidently the next step was to search every hole and corner of these same roofs. Armed with revolver and lantern, Fandor started on his tour of investigation; but prudently, for he was now almost certain that there were a number of accomplices involved in this Dollon affair.

To go carefully over the enormous roof of the Palais de Justice was no light task! One has only to consider the immensity of this monumental pile, its complicated architecture, the numberless little courts enclosed within its vast confines, to understand the difficulties with which our intrepid journalist had to contend. But Jérôme Fandor was not the man to be discouraged in the face of difficulties: he was determined to brave them — conquer them! He examined, minutely, the entire roofing of the Palais; he did not leave a corner or a morsel of shadow unexplored; there was not a gutter which he had not searched from end to end. When, after two hours of strenuous exertion, he returned to his starting-point, the chimney of Marie Antoinette, he was fain to confess that if Jacques Dollon had mounted to the roof of the Palais de Justice he certainly had not remained there.

Fandor unfolded his plan once more. It fluttered in the night breeze, as he carefully numbered all the chimneys opening on to this roof; then, one by one, he identified them with the real chimneys before his eyes. He exclaimed joyfully:

"There, now! It's just what I suspected!"

He had discovered there was one chimney not down on the plan: "Whither did it lead?" At all costs he must find out — make sure. He hastened to this extra chimney. Its orifice was large enough to allow of the passage of a man; also, here again, stones had been recently loosened, and a rope had rubbed against them:

"What the deuce is this chimney?" thought Fandor. "Another mystery! This chimney is not a chimney; there is not a trace of soot on it, even old soot!"

After a moment's reflection, he added:

"Can it be for ventilation only? But a ventilation hole could only communicate with one of the apartments in the Palais itself, and how the deuce could they drop a corpse down there? It would have been in the highest degree imprudent to attempt it! No, it is not by that road they have carried off Dollon's body! But then by what way?"

He glued his ear to the chimney. After a while, Fandor could make out a vague, intermittent sound — could catch a little, far-away, plashing sound.

"Can the chimney communicate with the Seine?" he asked himself. "No, we are too far off it. Why this opening, then? . . . Ah, I have it! It is a drain, a sewer, it communicates with!"

To verify that, there was nothing for it but to descend this chimney, which was no chimney! So be it! . . . Fandor took off his coat, and uncovered the long, fine cord, rolled round and round his middle. Weighting the cord with a flint, he let it slide down the chimney, testing the straightness of the descent by the balanced oscillations of the stone, and so ascertaining the even size of the opening, as far as the line would go. This was the work of a few minutes.

Fandor did not hesitate: he was eager to embark on the descent.

"After all," he murmured, "though I may find myself face to face with a band of assassins — what of it? It is all in the night's risks!"

He fastened the end of the cord to one of the neighbouring chimneys — fastened it firmly; then, his revolver handily stuck in his belt, Fandor seized the cord, twisted it round his legs, and let himself slowly down through the narrow opening.

It was a perilous descent! Fandor did not know whether his cord was long enough, and, lost in the darkness, with only the gleam of light from his lantern to guide him, he was naturally afraid of reaching the end of his rope unawares, and of falling into the black void beneath. But what he observed in the course of his descent excited him so much that he almost forgot the danger he was running. To those at all practised in police detective work, it was clear as daylight that men had passed this way, and recently.

"Here is a dislodged stone," muttered Fandor. "And here are scrapes and scratches — fresh . . . and . . . that mark looks like blood!"

Pushing his knees and his shoulders against the wall to support himself and stay his movements, he examined the mark. There was no doubt possible: Fandor's sharp eyes and the lantern's light had picked out a little red patch, which sullied one of the projecting stones in the chimney walls:

"This," reflected our amateur detective, "only confirms Dollon's death: if the wound which caused this mark had been made by a living body, the mark would have been larger, and there would have been others, for it must come from an abrasion of the skin made during the descent. But this blood mark has resulted from a dead body knocking against the stones of the wall: it is not a mark make by flowing blood, but by blood crushed out."

He descended a few yards further:

"Here's a find!" he cried. He had just perceived some hairs sticking to the rough surface of the stones. Again, with arched shoulders and bent knees, he supported himself against the wall, examined his discovery, left half the hairs where they were, took the rest, and carefully placed them in his pocket-book:

"The police must not be able to say that I have arranged this for their benefit," Fandor remarked. "Cost what it may, if I do not come across Dollon's corpse below, I must find out to-morrow whether these hairs resemble his."

Fandor went on descending, and first in one place, then in another, he saw on the walls of this chimney whitish patches such as might have been caused by the passage of a heavy mass or body, hanging at the end of a rope, and striking against the walls on its way down. Whilst he still believed himself to be some distance off the end of his downward journey, he felt a point of resistance beneath his feet. At first he mistook it for firm ground, much to his surprise. He was about to leave go of his cord when a remnant of prudence restrained him:

"How do I know there is not an abyss depths upon depths below me — down into the very bowels of the earth! I had better take care!"

What Fandor had taken for firm ground was nothing but an iron staple projecting from the wall. Fandor seized it, stopped for a minute or two's breathing space, ascertained, by drawing it up, that of his cord there were only a few yards remaining; but he also perceived, and with what relief, that from where he was resting, downwards the chimney was, as far as he could see by his lantern's light, marked off into regular spaces by these iron staples which are sometimes placed there for the use of chimney cleaners and masons. Fandor found them a most convenient kind of ladder. The descent now became easy, and in a short time our adventurous journalist reached the bottom of the chimney. At first he could not understand where he had got to. In the thick gloom around him his lantern's gleam of light showed him a kind of vaulted wall of massive masonry. He advanced a step or two with noiseless tread, listening, on the alert. Not a sound could he hear: he decided to expose the full light of his lantern.

The brighter light showed him that the chimney from which he was now standing some yards away ended in a kind of sewer, evidently no longer in use; and the plashing sound he had heard on the far up heights of the Palais roofs proceeded from a thin and muddy stream of water flowing in the middle of the sewer channel in the direction of the Seine. Kneeling at the foot of the chimney Fandor could distinguish marks of steps made by human feet; much deeper and very different indentations were visible also:

"Not only have men passed this way but a short while ago," he murmured, "but they were carrying a heavy burden: there are two kinds of footmarks, made by two kinds of shoes, and the heels have made much deeper marks in the soil than have the tips — yes, these men bore a heavy burden!"

Fandor was so pleased that he mentally rubbed his hands over this discovery. His quest was a success so far: he was on the track of Dollon's body! And what copy for *La Capitale*! Then a sad thought came to dim his delight:

"Poor, poor Elizabeth Dollon! I swore to her I would get at the truth — and a lamentable truth it is! Her brother is dead: he died in the Dépôt: he was done to death — it was no suicide!"

Whilst talking to himself Fandor was scrutinising every inch of the ground as he moved forward: there might be fresh clues:

"It's a queer kind of sewer," he went on. "This streamlet is as much mud as water, is almost stagnant. Evidently this underground sewer way is no longer used — has been abandoned!"

A horrid spectacle struck him motionless. His lantern made visible a struggling, heaving mass of rats, fighting tooth and claw, enormous rats devouring some hidden thing!

Fandor's stomach rose at the sight.

Oh, horror! Could it be Jacques Dollon's body?

Fandor snatched up a stone and flung it furiously among the unclean beasts. They fled. On the ground he could distinguish a mass, a red, formless mass, saturated with congealed blood:

"Assuredly, if the corpse has disappeared, it is there the assassins must have cut it in pieces, that they might carry it more easily, and those vile creatures are in the thick of feasting on the poor victim's remains! . . . Pouah!"

Fandor moved on, only to discover another pool of blood almost as large, also besieged by rats:

"Evidently I shall find nothing else," thought Fandor: "the corpse no longer exists!"

He continued his advance, determined to find out what this underground way ended in. His lantern was flickering to a finish when he arrived at the end of the sewer and found, as he had foreseen, that its opening had been cut in the steep bank of the Seine:

"That's a bit of luck! I can get out this way instead of having to climb back the way I came, up to the Palais roof and down again!"

It was still night; darkness reigned save on the far horizon, where a faint, whitish line indicated the early dawn of an April day.

Fandor was just asking himself by what gymnastic feat he could regain the quay, and he was leaning over the opening of the sewer, his body bending far forward over the inky waters of the Seine. Before he had time to turn, before he could regain his balance, a brutal blow from behind half stunned him, and a vigorous thrust precipitated his body into the Seine.

V

MOTHER TOULOUCHE AND CRANAJOUR

"Come along, Cranajour! Let's have a sight of what they've given you for the frock coat and the whole outfit!"

The person thus challenged rummaged in the pockets of his old, much-patched and filthy garments, and after interminable fumblings and huntings, finished by extracting a certain number of silver pieces, which he counted over with the greatest care, finally he replied:

"Seventeen francs, Mother Toulouche."

Mother Toulouche showed her impatience:

"It's details I want! How much for the coat? How much for the whole suit? I've got to know, I tell you! I've got to write it all down, and I've got to see how much I've to hand over to each of the owners of the duds! . . . Try to remember, Cranajour!"

The individual who answered to this odd appellation reflected. After a silence, shrugging his shoulders, he replied:

"I don't know. I can't make myself remember — not anyhow! . . . And it's a long time since I sold the goods!"

Mother Toulouche shrugged in turn:

"A long time!" she grumbled. "What a wretched job! Why, it's only two hours since — barely that! . . . It's true," she went on, with a pitying look at the shabby, down-at-heel fellow, who had spread out his seventeen francs on the table, "it's true that you're known not to have two ha'p'orths of memory, and that at the end of an hour you have forgotten what you've done!"

"That's right enough," answered Cranajour.

"Let's have done with it, then," cried Mother Toulouche.

She held out a repulsive-looking specimen of old clothes:

"Be off with you! Go and pawn this academician's cast-off! When the comrades catch a sight of this bit of stuff to the fore, they'll understand they can come without danger! . . . No cops about the store on the lookout, are there?"

Mother Toulouche took the precaution to advance to the threshold of her store, cast a rapid glance around — not a suspicious person, nor a sign of one to be seen:

"A good thing," muttered she, "but I was sure of it! Those police spies are going to give us some peace for a bit! . . . Likely the whole lot of them are on this Dollon business! Isn't it so, Cranajour?"

As she retreated into her store again Mother Toulouche knocked against that individual, who had not budged: he had hung over his arm respectfully the miserable bit of stuff that had been styled an academician's robe:

"Well, what are you waiting for?" asked she sharply.

"Nothing. . . ."

"What are you going to do with that?"

Cranajour seemed to reflect:

"Haven't I told you," grumbled Mother Toulouche, "to go and stick it up outside? . . . Don't say you've gone and forgotten already!"

"No, no!" protested Cranajour, hastening to obey orders.

"What a specimen!" thought Mother Toulouche, whilst counting over the seventeen francs.

Cranajour was a remarkably queer fish, beyond question. How had he got into connection with Mother Toulouche and her intimates? That remained a mystery. One fine day this seedy specimen of humanity was found among the "comrades" exchanging vague remarks with one and another. He stuck to them in all their shifting from this place to that: no one had been able to get out of him what his name was, nor where he came from, for he was afflicted with a memory like a sieve — he could not remember things for two hours together. A feeble-minded, poor sort of fellow, with not a halfpenny's worth of wickedness in him, always ready to do a hand's turn for anyone: to judge by his looks he might have been any age between forty and seventy, for there is nothing like privations and misery to alter the looks of a man! Faced by this queer fish, with a brain like a sieve, they had christened him "Crâne à jour" — and the nickname had stuck to this anonymous individual. Besides, was not Cranajour the most complaisant of fellows, the least exacting of collaborators — always content with what was given him, always willing to do his best!

As to Mother Toulouche; she kept a little shop on the quay of the Clock. The sign over her little store read:

"For the Curiosity Lover."

This alluring title was not justified by anything to be found inside this store, which was nothing but a common pick-up-anything shop: it was a receptacle for a hideous collection of lumber, for old broken furniture, for garments past decent wear, for indescribable odds and ends, where the wreckage of human misery lay huddled cheek by jowl with the beggarly offscourings of Parisian destitution.

Behind the store, whose little front faced the edge of the quay and looked over the Seine, was a sordid back-shop: here the pallet of Mother Toulouche, a kitchen stove out of order, and the overflow of the goods which were crowded out of the store were jumbled up in ill-smelling disorder. This back-shop communicated with the rue de Harlay by a narrow dark passage; thus the lair of old Mother Toulouche had two outlets, nor were they superfluous; in fact, they were indispensable for such as she — ever on the alert to escape the inquisitive attentions of the police, ever receiving visitors of doubtful morals and thoroughly bad reputation.

Mother Toulouche's quarters comprised not only the two stores, but a cellar both large and deep, to which one obtained access by a staircase pitch dark, crooked, and everlastingly covered with moisture, owing to the proximity of the river. The floor of the cellar was a kind of noisome cesspool: one slipped on the greasy mud — floundered about in it: for all that, this cellar was almost entirely filled with cases of all kinds, with queer-looking bundles, with objects of various shapes and sizes. Evidently the jumble store of Mother Toulouche did not confine itself to the rough-and-ready shop in the front; and, into the bargain, this basement might be used as a safe hiding-place in an emergency, a precious refuge for whoever might feel it necessary to cover his tracks, and thus escape the investigations of the police, for instance!

Mother Toulouche, as a matter of fact, needed such premises as hers: if she took ceaseless precautions it was because she had a reason for her uneasy watchfulness.

Mother Toulouche had already come into involuntary contact with the police; and her last and most serious encounter with them went as far back as those days of renown when the band of Numbers had as their chief the mysterious hooligan Loupart, also known under the name of Dr. Chaleck. She had been arrested for complicity in a bank-note robbery, had been tried, and had been sentenced to twenty-two months' imprisonment.

Not turned in the slightest degree from the error of her ways, and possessing some money, which she had kept carefully hidden, Mother Toulouche had decided to set up shop close to the Palais de Justice, that Great House where those gentlemen of the robe judged and condemned poor folk! She would say:

"Being so close to the red-robed I shall end by making the acquaintance of one or two of them, and that may turn out a good job for me one of these days!"

But this was merely a blind, for other considerations had led to Mother Toulouche renting this shop on the Isle of the City, in opening on the quay of the Clock, a quay but little frequented, her wretched jumble store of odds and ends. She had kept in touch with the band of Numbers, which had gradually come together again as

4   See *The Exploits of Juve.*

soon as the various numbers of it had finished serving their time.

For a while they had lived unmolested, but lately misfortunes had laid a heavy hand on the group. Still, as the band began to break up, other members came to replace those who had disappeared, either temporarily or for good and all.

At any rate, they could safely count on the assistance of an individual more valuable to them than anyone; this was a man named Nibet, who although he intervened but seldom, could, thanks to his influence, save the band many annoyances. This Nibet held an honourable official position; he was a warder at the Dépôt.

Whilst Mother Toulouche, from the back of her store, was watching with a derisive air the good-natured Cranajour fasten up the Academician's robe in a prominent position on the front of her nondescript emporium, someone stepped inside, and warmly greeted Mother Toulouche with a:

"Good day, old lady!"

It was big Ernestine, who explained volubly that for a good half hour she had been prowling about near the statue of Henry IV, keeping the store well in view, but not daring to approach until the usual signal had been displayed. Those who frequented the place knew that when the store was under police observation and Mother Toulouche feared a raid she took care to hang out any kind of old clothes; but if the way was clear, if no lurking police were on the lookout, then the rallying flag would be hoisted, the flag being the old, patched, rusty, musty Academician's robe.

Ernestine had arrived looking thoroughly upset:

"Have you heard the latest?" she cried, "the bad news?"

"What news? Whose news?" questioned Mother Toulouche.

"Why, that poor Emilet has come down a regular cropper!"

"The poor fellow! . . . He isn't smashed up, is he?" Mother Toulouche lifted her hands.

"I haven't heard anything more than what I've told you!"

Consternation was on the faces of the two women.

Their good Mimile! He who knew how to take care of himself without leaving a comrade in the lurch, who stuck to them, working for the common good.

A few years previous to this Mimile, having refused to conform to military law, had been arrested in the tavern of a certain Father Korn during a particularly drastic police raid, and the defaulting youth had

5   See *The Exploits of Juve.*

been straightway put under the penal military discipline adminis- tered to such as he. Instead of making himself notorious by his exe- crable conduct as those in his position generally did, he behaved like a little saint. Having thus made a reputation to trade on, he was twice able to steal the money from the regimental chest without a shadow of suspicion falling on him, and, what was worse, two of his innocent comrades had been accused of the crime, had been condemned and shot in his stead! Owing to his good conduct Mimile had been trans- ferred to a regiment stationed in Algiers, and having a considerable amount of spare time on his hands, he got into close touch with the aeroplane mechanics.

He was very much at home in this branch of work: could not Mimile demolish a lock as easily as one rolls a cigarette? He was daring to a degree, and, as soon as his time in the army was up, he began to earn his living as an aviator, and rightly, for he had become an able airman. Nevertheless, Mimile become Emilet, had aspired to greater things: a humdrum honest livelihood was not to his taste!

He had come to the conclusion that provided he went warily nothing could be easier than to carry on a lucrative smuggling trade by aeroplane: he could fly from country to country under the pretext that he was out to make records in flying. Custom-house officials and police inspectors in the interior would never think of examining the tubes of a flying machine, to see whether or no they were packed with lace; nor would it occur to them to overhaul certain cells fore and aft to discover whether things of value had been secreted in them, such as thousands of matches or false coin.

So, from time to time, Mimile would announce that he was off on a trial trip to Brussels from Paris, from London to Calais, and so on.

For mechanics Mimile had two brokendown sharpers, who served as connecting links between the aviator and the band of smug- glers and false coiners who gathered at the lair of Mother Toulouche under the seal of secrecy. This was why big Ernestine was so anxious when she heard of Mimile's accident. Had the aeroplane been totally wrecked? Would the very considerable prize of Malines lace they were expecting reach its destination safe and sound?

For some time past ill-luck had pursued them, had seemed to pursue implacably these unfortunates who took such pains and pre- cautions to carry through their unlawful operations to a successful issue. Already the Cooper, a member of the confraternity who had had his glorious hour in the famous days of Chaleck and Loupart, had scarcely left prison retirement before he had been nabbed again, owing to the far too sharp eyes of the French custom-house officials on the Belgian frontier. Others of the band were also under lock and key again: it really seemed as if Mother Toulouche and her circle were being strictly watched by the police . . . and now here was Emilet who had come a regular cropper in his aeroplane — no doubt about it!

Mother Toulouche was set on knowing the rights of it:

"But what has happened to Emilet exactly?"

She called Cranajour. The queer fellow came forward from the back store, where he had been loafing: he had a bewildered air.

"Cranajour," said Mother Toulouche, putting a sou in his hand, "hurry off and buy me an evening paper! Now be quick about it! . . . Don't forget. . . . Make a knot in your handkerchief to remind a stupid head!"

"Oh, don't be afraid, Mother Toulouche," declared Cranajour, "I shan't forget!" He nodded to big Ernestine, and vanished as by magic into the darkness, for night had fallen.

Scarcely had Cranajour gone, than a surly looking individual slipped into the store, not by the quay entrance, but through the back store, to which he had gained access by the dark passage leading to the rue de Harlay.

His collar was turned up as though he were cold; his cap was drawn well over his eyes, thus his face was almost entirely hidden.

Having barred the door on the quay side of the store, Mother Toulouche joined big Ernestine and the newcomer:

"Well, Nibet, anything fresh?" she asked.

Removing his cap and lowering his collar Nibet's crabbed visage glowered on the two women: it was the Dépôt warder right enough:

"Bad," he growled between his teeth: "Things are hot right at the Palais!"

"Things to worry about — to do with comrades committed for trial?" questioned big Ernestine.

Nibet shrugged and threw a glance of disdain at the girl:

"You're going silly! It's this Dollon mess-up!"

The warder gave them an account of what had happened. The two women were all ears, as they followed Nibet's story of events which had thrown the whole legal world into a state of commotion: incomprehensible occurrences, which threatened to turn an ordinary murder case into one of the most mysterious and most popular of assassination dramas.

Mother Toulouche and big Ernestine were well aware that Nibet knew much more than he had told them about the details of the Dollon-Vibray affair; but they dared not cross-examine the warder who was in a nasty mood — nor did the announcement of Emilet's accident add to his gaiety!

"It just wanted that!" he grunted: "And those bundles of lace were to turn up this evening too!"

"Who is to bring them?" asked big Ernestine.

"The Sailor," declared Nibet.

"And who is to receive them?" demanded Mother Toulouche.

"I and the Beadle," answered Nibet in a surly tone. "Come to think of it," went on Nibet, staring hard at big Ernestine, "where *is* that man of yours — the Beadle?"

Like someone who had been running at top speed Cranajour, who had been gone about an hour on his newspaper-buying errand, drew up panting before the dark little entry leading from the rue de Harlay to the den of Mother Toulouche. He slipped into the passage; but instead of rejoining the old storekeeper he began to mount a steep and tortuous staircase, which led up to the many floors of the house. He climbed up to the seventh story; turned the key of a shaky door, and entered an attic whose skylight window opened obliquely in the sloping roof.

This poverty-stricken chamber was the domicile of the queer fellow who passed his daylight hours in the company of Mother Toulouche, hobnobbing with a hole-and-corner crew, cronies of the old receiver of stolen goods.

Overheated with running, Cranajour unbuttoned his coat, opened his shirt, sprinkled his face and the upper part of his body with cold water, sponged the perspiration from his brow, and brushed the dust off his big shoes.

It was a clear starlight night. To freshen himself up still more he put his head and shoulders out of the half-opened window. He was gazing at the roofs facing him; suddenly he started, and his eyes gleamed. They were the roofs, outlined against the night sky, of the Palais de Justice. There was a shadow on the roof of the great pile, a shadow which moved to and fro, passing from one roof ridge to another, now vanishing behind a chimney, now coming into view again. Anxiously Cranajour followed the odd movements of the mysterious individual who was making his lofty and lonely promenade up above there.

"What the devil does it mean?" soliloquised the watcher. Whoever could have seen Cranajour at this moment would have been struck by the marked change produced in his physiognomy. This was not the Cranajour of the wandering eye, the silly smile, the stupid face, known to Mother Toulouche and her cronies; it was a transformed Cranajour, mobile of feature, lively of movement, a sharp, keen-witted Cranajour! Veritably another man!

Puzzled by the vagaries of the promenader on the Palais roofs, Cranajour followed his movements intently for a few minutes longer. He would have remained at the window the whole night long had the unknown persisted in his peregrinations; but Cranajour saw him climb to the top of a chimney, a wide one, lower himself slowly into the opening of it, and then vanish from view!

Cranajour waited a while in hopes that the unknown would not be long in coming out of his mysterious hiding-place again. He waited and expected in vain: the roofs of the Palais resumed their ordinary aspect: solitude reigned there.

Not long afterwards Cranajour re-entered the back store.

"What a time you have been!" cried Mother Toulouche: "You've brought the newspaper, haven't you?"

Cranajour looked at the little company with his most stupid expression and then lowered his eyes:

"My goodness, I've forgotten to buy one!" he cried.

Nibet, who had paid but scant attention to the new arrival, continued his conversation with big Ernestine: they were talking about her lover, nicknamed the Beadle.

He was a terrible individual this Beadle! Though his nickname suggested a peaceful occupation, he really owed it to the frightful reputation he had won as a "*bell-ringer*"; but the bells big Ernestine's lover was in the habit of ringing were unfortunate pedestrians whom he would rob and half murder, beating them unmercifully about the head and body. Sometimes he would beat them to within an ace of their last gasp: occasionally he would beat the life out of them altogether if they tried to resist his brutal attacks. The Beadle was an Apache of the first order of brutality.

Big Ernestine finished explaining to Nibet that he must not count on the Beadle that evening, for things were so queer and uncertain, the outlook was so gloomy that no one knew what bad business they might be in for.

Mother Toulouche asked if he had got mixed up in the Dollon affair.

Cranajour cocked his ear at that, whilst pretending to put a great bundle of old clothes in order.

But Nibet replied:

"The Beadle has nothing whatever to do with that business. . . . I know what I know about all that. . . . He's afraid of getting what the Cooper got, so he keeps away. He's not far out either — you've got to be careful these days — queer times!"

Ernestine and Mother Toulouche bewailed the Cooper's fate:

"Poor fellow! No sooner out of quod than back — only a fort-

6   Hooligan.

night's liberty! And with a vile accusation fastened to him — smuggling and coining!"

Nibet tried to relieve their minds:

"Haven't I told you," growled he, "that I'm going to get Maître Henri Robart to defend him? He knows how to get round juries: he'll get the Cooper off with an easy sentence."

Nibet looked at his watch:

"It will soon be half-past two! Got to go down! The boatman will be there before long, at the mouth of the sewer!"

Mother Toulouche, who was always in a flurry when smuggled goods were to be unloaded in her cellars, tried to dissuade Nibet:

"You'll never be able to manage it by yourself!"

Nibet glanced at Cranajour. The warder hesitated, then said:

"Since there's no one else, couldn't I take Cranajour with me?"

At first objections were raised; there was a low-voiced discussion, so that the simpleton might not catch what they were saying: Cranajour had never been up to dodges of this kind: so far he had been kept out of them; besides, he was such a senseless cove, he might give things away, make a hash of it!

Nibet smiled:

"Why, it's just because he is such a simpleton, and because he hasn't a mite of memory that we can use him safely!"

"That's true!" said Mother Toulouche, somewhat reassured.

She called to Cranajour:

"Come along, Cranajour, and just tell us where you dined this evening!"

The simpleton seemed to make a prodigious effort of memory, seized his head between his hands, closed his eyes, and racked his brains: after quite a long silence, he declared emphatically and with a distressed air:

"Faith, I can't tell you now!"

Nibet, who had closely watched this performance, nodded:

"It's quite all right," he said.

The cellars below Mother Toulouche's store were extensive, dark, and ill-smelling. The walls glistened with exuding damp, and the ground was a sticky mass of foul mud, of all sorts of refuse, of putrefying matter.

Nibet, followed by his companion, made his way down to them: it was no easy descent, for they had to climb over cases of all kinds, and over bales and bundles that moved and rolled about. They passed into a smaller cellar, around which were ranged long boxes of tin with rusty covers.

Cranajour, who had been given the lantern to carry, was attracted to these boxes: he lifted the cover of one of them and drew back wonderstruck, for the box was full of shining gold pieces! Nibet, with a jab and thrust in the back, interrupted Cranajour's contemplation of this fortune:

"Nothing to faint over!" he growled. "You're not such a simpleton then! You know the value of yellow boys? All right, then, I'll give you one or two, if you do your job all right! But," continued the warder, leading his companion to the further end of the second cellar, "you will have to look out if you present your banker with one of those pieces, for the little bits of shiny won't pass everywhere — you've got to keep your eye open — and jolly wide, too!"

Cranajour nodded comprehension:

"False money! False money!" he murmured.

There was a very strong big door: an iron bar kept it closed. Nibet raised it with Cranajour's help. Through the door the two men passed into a long dark passage, swept by a sharp rush of air. The floor of it was paved, and at the side of it flowed a pestilential stream, carrying along in its slow-moving water a quantity of miscellaneous filth: it was thick as soup with impurities.

"The little collecting sewer of the Cité," whispered Nibet. Pointing to a grey patch in the distance he put his mouth to Cranajour's ear:

"See the daylight yonder? That's where the sewer discharges itself into the Seine: it's there the boatman and his load will be waiting for us presently."

Nibet stopped dead; drew Cranajour back by the sleeve, and stepped stealthily backwards to the massive doors of the cellar. An unaccustomed noise had alarmed the warder. In profound silence the two men stood listening intently. There was no mistake! The sound of sharp regular steps could be clearly heard coming from that part of the sewer opposite the opening.

"Someone!" said Cranajour, who was all on the alert, as he had been in his attic, watching the shadow and its vagaries on the roofs of the Palais de Justice.

Nibet nodded.

The light from a dark lantern gleamed on the damp, slimy walls of the subterranean passageway.

"Come inside," murmured Nibet, in an almost inaudible voice; and, with infinite precaution, he closed the massive portal between the cellar and the sewer-way.

In safe hiding the two men could watch the approaching intruder: they had extinguished their lantern, and were peering through the badly joined wood of the solid door. Friend or foe? An individual moved into view. The reflected light of his lantern lit up the vaulting of the sewer-way, and showed up his face. The man was young, fair, wore a small moustache!

Hardly had he passed the cellar door when Nibet gripped Crana-jour's arm and growled — intense rage was expressed in grip and tone — "It's he! Again! The journalist of the Dollon affair, of the Dépôt business — Jérôme Fandor! Ah. . . . This time we'll see! . . ."

Nibet's hand plunged into his trouser pocket.

Cranajour was eagerly watching the warder's every movement: he clearly heard the sharp snap of a pocket-knife — a long sharp knife — a deadly weapon!

Giving prudence the go-by, Nibet had opened the door, and dragging Cranajour in his wake had rushed into the sewer-way, hard on the heels of the journalist, who was slowly going in the direction of the Seine. Nibet ground his teeth.

"I have had enough of that beast! Always on our track! Too good a chance to miss! I'm going to make a hole in his skin for him!"

In the twilight of early dawn, which penetrated the sewer near the opening, Cranajour shuddered.

With stealthy step the two men drew near the journalist. Fandor walked on unsuspicious at a slow regular pace, his head lowered. The two bandits came up to within a yard of him. Noiselessly, savagely determined, Nibet lifted his arm for a murderous stroke. At this pre-cise moment Fandor stopped at the verge of the exit, by which the sewer discharged its burden steeply into the Seine.

Yet a moment: Nibet's knife was poised for the rapid and terrible stroke; it was about to bury itself in the neck of the journalist up to the hilt, when Cranajour lifted his foot, as if inspired by an idea on the spur of the moment, gave the journalist a violent kick in the lower part of the back, and sent him flying into space!

They heard his body fall heavily into the Seine. . . . So roughly sudden had been Cranajour's movement that Nibet stood dumb-founded, arm in air, and staring at Cranajour:

Cranajour smiled his most idiotic smile, nodded, but did not utter one word! . . .

It was formidable, the rage of Nibet! Here had that crass fool, Cranajour, kicked away the warder's chance of ridding himself of the journalist for good and all! This hit-and-miss made Nibet foam with rage. Of all the exasperating simpletons, this fool of a Cranajour took the cake!

The two made their way back to the store, where Mother Tou-louche and big Ernestine anxiously awaited results; and now not only had the two men returned stuttering over their statements and with no news of the boatman, who was generally up to time, but they had missed a fine opportunity chance had offered them!

Nibet hated the journalist like all the poisons. Taunts, jeers, abuse were heaped on the silly head of Cranajour, who, all in vain, raised his eyes to heaven, beat his chest, shrugged his shoulders, stammered, mumbled vague excuses:

"He didn't know exactly why he had done it! He thought he was helping Nibet!"

They disputed and contended for two hours. Suddenly Cranajour broke a long silence and demanded, looking as stupid as a half-witted owl:

"What have I done then? What are you scolding me for?"

Mother Toulouche, big Ernestine, and the wrathful Nibet stared at one another, taken aback — then they understood: two hours had gone by, and Cranajour no longer remembered what had happened!

Decidedly he was more innocent than a new-born babe! There was nothing whatever to be done with such an idiot, that was certain!

VI

IN THE OPPOSITE SENSE

When Jérôme Fandor had been precipitated into the Seine so unexpectedly and with such violence he kept control of his wits: he did not utter a cry as he fell head foremost into the darkling river. He was an excellent swimmer: all aching as he was, he let himself go with the current and presently reached the sheltering arch of the Pont Neuf. There he took breath for a minute:

"Queer!" was all he murmured. Then with regular strokes he made for the steep bank of the Seine opposite. Quitting the river, he secreted himself behind a heap of stones which lay on the quay. He took off his soaked garments and wrung the water out of them. This done, and clad in what looked like dry clothes, Fandor walked along the quay, hailed a passing cabman half asleep on his seat, jumped inside, and gave his address to the Jehu.

When he arrived at *La Capitale* on the Friday morning a boy approached him, and whispered mysteriously:

"Monsieur Fandor, there's a very nice little woman in the sitting-room, who has been waiting for over an hour. She wishes to see you. She will not give her name: she declares that you know who she is."

"What is she like?" Fandor asked. His curiosity was not much aroused.

"Pretty, fair, all in black," replied the boy.

"Good. I'll go in," interrupted Fandor.

He entered the sitting-room and stood face to face with Mademoiselle Elizabeth Dollon. She came forward, her eyes shining, her face alight with welcome:

"Ah, monsieur," she cried, taking his hands in hers, a movement of pure gratitude: "Ah, monsieur, I knew you would come to my help! I have read your article of yesterday. Thank you again and again! But, I implore you, since my brother is alive, tell me where I can see him! For mercy's sake don't keep me waiting!"

Surprise kept Fandor silent a moment.

La Capitale had published the evening before a sensational article by Fandor, in which, under the guise of suppositions and interrogations, he had narrated the various adventures as they had happened to himself, concluding with the question — really an ironical one: "If Jacques Dollon, who had disappeared from his cell, where he had been left for dead, had escaped from the Dépôt by way of the famous chimney of Marie Antoinette, had reached the roof of the Palais, had redescended by another passageway to the sewer opening on to the Seine, did it not seem possible that Dollon had escaped alive from the Dépôt?"

Fandor had indulged in a gentle irony, despite the gravity of the circumstances, in order to complicate the already complicated affair, and so plunge the police into a confusion worse confounded: this, in spite of his conviction that Dollon was dead, dead as dead could be!

Now the cruelty of this professional game was brought home to him. His article had raised fresh hopes in Dollon's poor sister! At sight of this charming girl, brightened with hope, Fandor felt all pity and guilt. He pressed her hands; he hesitated; he was troubled. He did not know how to explain. At last he murmured:

"It was wrong of me, mademoiselle, very wrong to write that article in such a way without warning you beforehand. Alas! You must not cherish illusions, illusions which this unfortunate article has given rise to, illusions I cannot believe in myself. I speak with all the sincerity of which I am capable, with the keenest desire to be of service to you: I dare not let you buoy yourself up with false hopes. . . . I assure you then, that from what I have been able to learn, to see, to know, I am convinced that your unfortunate brother is no more! . . . If there have been moments when I have doubted this, I am now morally certain that he is dead. Take courage, mademoiselle! Try, try to forget — to — to . . ."

Fandor was trembling with emotion: he could not continue. Elizabeth bent her head, her eyes full of tears. She could not speak. She was overcome by this cruel dashing to the ground of her hopes. Never, never, to see her brother again!

An agonising silence reigned.

Fandor was profoundly troubled by this mute grief. He sought in vain for some word of comfort, of encouragement.

Elizabeth rose to go. The poor girl realised that nothing could be gained by prolonging the interview. Her one need now was to be alone, for then she could weep.

Fandor was about to accompany her to the door, when a boy entered:

"Monsieur Fandor, there's a man wishes to speak to you!"

"Say I am not here," replied our journalist: he had no wish to see strangers just then.

"But Monsieur Fandor, he says he is the keeper of the landing stage of the passenger boat service, and he comes with reference to the Dollon affair!"

Both Elizabeth Dollon and Jérôme Fandor started. She was trembling. Our journalist said at once:

"Bring him in then!"

The boy went off, and Fandor turned to the trembling girl.

"Tell me, Mademoiselle Elizabeth, do you feel equal to hearing what this man has to tell us? It is not improbable that he has seen something — something it would be best you should not hear — had you not better avoid it?"

Elizabeth shook her head in the negative. She was collecting all her forces: she would not remain ignorant of any detail of the terrible tragedy which had cost her brother so dear:

"I shall be strong enough," she announced firmly.

The boy ushered in the visitor. He looked a good specimen of his class, a man about forty. On his cap were the gold anchors of those in the employ of the Paris boat service.

"Monsieur! . . . Madame! . . . At your service!" The good fellow was very much embarrassed:

"Monsieur Fandor," he went on, "you do not know me, but I know you very well, that I do! . . . I read your articles every day in *La Capitale*. They're jolly good! What I say is . . ."

Fandor cut short his admirer: "Now tell me what brings you here!"

"Oh, well, here goes! I was reading your article yesterday, about how Jacques Dollon, no more dead than you or I, had escaped over the roofs of the Palais de Justice. That made me laugh, because I am the keeper of the landing stage at the Pont Neuf Station. This affair is supposed to have happened in my parts, don't you see? . . . Well, I had just come to the bit where you also suppose that the corpse might easily have been devoured by rats inside the sewer. . . . Well, Monsieur Fandor, I can assure you that it was nothing of the sort. . . ."

The journalist was all eyes and ears. He signed to Elizabeth that she must keep quiet, so as not to intimidate the good fellow.

"Come now, what is it you have seen?"

"What I've seen? . . . Why, I saw Dollon break bounds!"

At this statement Elizabeth grew white as a sheet. She jumped up, and with clasped hands rushed towards the keeper:

"Speak, speak quickly, I implore you!" she cried.

Fandor drew Elizabeth back gently, and whispered a few words to her. He turned to the keeper:

"Mademoiselle has also come to make a statement regarding this affair," he explained. "That is why she is so interested in what you have just told us. . . . But tell us how you saw Jacques Dollon escape!"

"Well, I had got up a bit earlier than usual to see that the anchors and mooring were all right, and I thought I saw what looked like a big bundle fall into the river from the sewer opening — only I was half asleep and didn't take much notice; for, what with all the rain we've been having, there's no end of filthy stuff tumbling out of the mouth of the sewers. But, a few minutes after that, I noticed that the bundle, instead of going with the flow of the current, was drifting across the Seine, plainly making for the bank. There could be no mistake about that!"

Elizabeth Dollon cried:

"And then? And then?"

"Then, my little lady, what if this surprise packet didn't turn off behind an arch of the Pont-Neuf! I didn't see what became of it — but no one will get it out of my head that it isn't some jolly dog who had no wish to show himself — that's what I think!"

The keeper paused, then went on:

"That's all I have to tell you, Monsieur Fandor . . . it might serve for one of your articles some time or other . . . only you mustn't say that I told you. I might get into trouble with my chiefs about it!"

Elizabeth Dollon was no longer listening. She had turned to Fandor, and with shining eyes murmured:

"He lives! . . . He lives! . . ."

Fandor thanked the keeper, and got rid of him. Directly the door closed on him he darted to Elizabeth:

"Poor child!" he cried, full of pity for her.

"Ah! Don't pity me! I don't need your pity now! . . . My brother is alive! . . . That man has seen him!"

Fandor had to undeceive her:

"Your brother is certainly dead," he declared. "If he were the individual in question, it would not have been yesterday morning, but the morning before that, when the keeper saw him; and I do assure you . . ."

"But this good fellow is telling the truth then?"

"I assure you that I have good reasons, the best of reasons, for believing, for being certain, that the swimmer who crossed the Seine was not your brother!"

"Great Heaven! Who was it then?"

Fandor hesitated a moment. . . . Should he divulge his secret? All he said was:

"It was not your brother — I know that!"

So decisive was his tone, so great the sympathy vibrating through his words, that Elizabeth Dollon, once more convinced that Fandor was not speaking at random, bent her head and shed tears of deepest grief and bitter disappointment.

Fandor allowed the sorrow-stricken girl to give way to her grief for a few minutes; then he gently asked her:

"Mademoiselle Elizabeth, shall we have a little talk? . . . You see I simply cannot tell you everything, yet I would gladly help you! . . . But first and foremost, I beg of you to put quite out of your mind this hope that your brother is still alive! . . ."

Sadly Elizabeth wiped away her tears, and in a voice which she tried to steady, said:

"Oh, what is to become of me! I thought I had found in you a support, a help, and now you abandon me! And I had put my faith in your goodness of heart! . . . There are your articles on the one hand, and your attitude on the other — what am I to make of it? It is driving me to despair! And if you only knew how much I need to be supported, encouraged; I feel as if I should go out of my senses — out of my mind . . . and I am alone, so terribly alone!"

The poor girl's voice was broken by sobs, her whole body was shaken by them. Fandor went up to her, and spoke to her in a low tone affectionately: he felt great sympathy and an immense pity for this unhappy young creature, who charmed and attracted him. He tried to console her, and to change the current of her thoughts:

"Come now, Mademoiselle, do try to control yourself a little! I have promised to help you, and I certainly shall — you may be sure of it. But consider now — if I am to be of real use to you, I must know a little about you: you, yourself, your family, your brother; who your friends are, and who are your enemies! I must enter into your existence, not as a judge, but as a comrade who is interested in all that concerns you. Will you not confide in me? Once I know what there is to know we might then unite our efforts to some purpose, and find out what really has happened, since the mystery remains inexplicable."

Elizabeth Dollon felt the young man was sincere, and that what he said in such a gentle voice was true.

This poor human waif asked no more than to be allowed to cling to whoever would take pity on her and be kind. She now spoke to Jérôme Fandor of her childhood without suspecting in the least that the same Jérôme Fandor — Charles Rambert — used to play with her in those days.

She mentioned the assassination of the Marquise de Langrune — the first tragic episode of her life; then had come the horrible death of her father, old Steward Dollon, who had passed from the service of the Marquise to that of the Baroness de Vibray, and then perished, the victim of a criminal.

She explained how Jacques Dollon and she had come to settle in Paris, feeling themselves rich on the savings they had inherited from their parents. Elizabeth had become a dressmaker, and Jacques had become an artist-craftsman. Gradually the young man's talent and

7   See *Fantômas*.

industry had enabled his sister to leave her workroom and come to live with him. His reputation was a growing one, and the two young people looked forward to an existence of honest comfort in the near future. They got to know some people, one or two of whom were rich, and had shown their interest in the brother and sister.

Jérôme Fandor interrupted her:

"You always remained on good terms with the Baroness de Vibray?"

At this question the girl's eyes flashed:

"They have put into print shameful things about this poor dear Baroness, and about my brother also. The papers have represented her as eccentric, as mad; they have said worse things than that, you know that, don't you? . . . They have declared that there was a very intimate relation between her and my brother — I cannot say more — it is too hateful! It is all false — as false as false can be! The Baroness was particularly interested in Jacques, but assuredly that was owing to the long standing relations between her family and ours. . . . The suicide of the Baroness has been a sad addition to my grief, for I was very fond of her! . . ."

Fandor had been listening attentively to Elizabeth's story. He now said:

"You have used the word 'suicide,' mademoiselle: do you then really think, as everyone seems to do, that your patroness killed herself of her own free will?"

Elizabeth reflected a minute before replying:

"That was what she wrote — and one must believe that, nevertheless . . ."

"Nevertheless?"

Elizabeth hesitated, passed her hand over her forehead, then said:

"Nevertheless, Monsieur Fandor, the more I think over this death, the more remarkable it seems. The Baroness de Vibray was not the kind of person to commit suicide, even if she were unhappy, even if she were ruined. I have often heard her speak of her money affairs; she even used to joke about the expostulations of her bankers, Messieurs Barbey-Nanteuil, because she was too fond of gambling. That was our poor friend's weakness: she was a dreadful gambler: she was always betting on horses and gambling on the Bourse."[8]

"Do you know the Barbey-Nanteuils at all, mademoiselle?"

"A little. I have met them once or twice at Madame de Vibray's —

8   Stock Exchange.

when she had one of her little evenings. Once or twice my brother has asked their advice about investments — very modest investments I can assure you — and they got one of their friends, a Monsieur Thomery, to buy some of my brother's art pottery."

"Have you many acquaintances in Paris, mademoiselle?"

"Besides the Baroness we hardly saw anyone except Madame Bourrat, a very nice, kind woman, widow of an inspector of the City of Paris; she keeps a boarding-house at Auteuil, rue Raffet. In fact, I am staying with her now, for I had not the courage to go back to my brother's place: too many dreadful memories are connected with his studio there. I am lucky to find such a sympathetic friend in Madame Bourrat, and such a warm welcome. . . . I am alone now, and life is sad."

Fandor went on with his cross-examination:

"Nevertheless, mademoiselle, I must ask you to return in thought to that tragic home of yours. Please tell me what people you knew in your immediate neighbourhood? Acquaintances?"

Elizabeth considered:

"Acquaintances is the word, because we were not on really intimate terms with our neighbours in the Cité; for the most part they are either art students or work-people. However, we saw fairly often a nice man, a stranger, a Dutchman I think he was, called Monsieur Van Hoeren; he manufactures accordions; and lives in a little house opposite ours, with six children; he has been a widower for years! Also there was a Monsieur Louis, an engraver, who used to take tea with us in the evening sometimes, his wife also: he is employed in the Posts and Telegraphs. We had practically no other acquaintances."

Elizabeth stopped. There was a silence. Fandor asked another question:

"Tell me, mademoiselle, when you entered the studio for the first time after the tragedy, did you notice anything abnormal?"

The poor girl shuddered at the appalling picture before her mind's eye:

"Good Heavens, monsieur," she cried, "I did not examine the studio minutely! I had only one thought — to be with my brother, who had been so unjustly accused, so . . ."

Fandor interrupted to ask:

"Do you not know that at his preliminary examination your brother declared that he had not received a single visitor during the evening preceding the tragedy? How then do you explain the fact that the Baroness de Vibray was found dead in his studio, and at his side, when no one had seen her enter it? Did your brother make a mistake? Please tell me what you think about it!"

Elizabeth gazed anxiously at the young journalist, then fixed her eyes on the floor. Her hands twitched; she began to twist her fingers feverishly:

"Do trust me!" begged Jérôme Fandor. "Please tell me what you think!"

Elizabeth rose, took several steps, and placed herself in front of the journalist:

"Ah, monsieur, there is something mysterious, which I cannot explain! As a matter of fact, someone must have come to see my brother that evening: I cannot assert it as a fact beyond dispute certainly: but in my own mind I feel quite sure about it."

"But you must have more proof of it than that?" cried Fandor.

"But — there is more!" cried Elizabeth, as if enlightened by a sudden discovery: "There is a fact! . . ."

"Tell me, do!" cried Fandor, intensely interested.

"Well, just imagine, then! Among the papers scattered over his table, and close to his book, which was open, I noticed a sort of list of names and addresses, written on our own note-paper, and in the kind of green ink we use — so — well . . ."

"So," interrupted the journalist, "you came to the conclusion that this list had been written at your brother's house?"

"Yes, and it was not my brother's handwriting."

"Nor that of the Baroness de Vibray?"

"Nor that of the Baroness de Vibray!"

"And what did this list contain?"

"Names, addresses, I tell you, of persons we knew. There were also two or three dates. . . ."

"And is that all?"

"That is all, monsieur: I saw nothing else!"

"Little enough," murmured Fandor, disappointed. "Still no detail, however slight, must be ignored! . . . What have you done with that list, mademoiselle?"

"I must have taken it with me when I collected all the papers I could find the day before yesterday, before going to the boarding-house at Auteuil."

"When you have an opportunity, will you bring me that list?" requested Fandor.

The conversation was interrupted. A boy came to tell Fandor that he was wanted on the telephone by someone in the Public Prosecutor's Office.

Later on in the day Jérôme Fandor sent the following express message to Elizabeth Dollon:

"Do not believe a word of the Police Headquarters' version which you will read in this evening's La Capitale."

This despatched, our journalist commenced his article entitled:

STILL THE AFFAIR OF THE RUE NORVINS

Police Headquarters takes a view of this affair which is the very reverse of that taken by our contributor, Jérôme Fandor.

By the Seine sewer, the roofs of the Palace, and the chimney of Marie Antoinette, an inspector has succeeded in reaching the Dépôt.

Police Headquarters is convinced that Jacques Dollon escaped alive!

VII

PEARLS AND DIAMONDS

"Nadine!"

"Princess!"

"Nadine, what time is it?"

The young Circassian, with hair as black as ink, souple and slender, rose from her chair and was hastening from the bedroom to ascertain the time when her mistress recalled her:

"Don't go away, Nadine! Stay with me!"

The dusky Circassian obeyed: she stared with big, astonished eyes into those of her mistress:

"But, Princess, why don't you wish me to go?"

The Princess stammered in a mysterious tone:

"Don't you know then, Nadine, that to-day is the anniversary? . . . and I am frightened!"

Princess Sonia Danidoff was in her bath robe. It must have been a quarter past eleven, or even nearer midnight than that. Although she had lived in Paris for years, she had never been able to make up her mind to settle in a flat of her own. Possessing an immense fortune, she much preferred the American way of living, and had taken a suite of rooms in one of those great palace-hotels near the place de l'Etoile. Though a very smart staff of servants was reserved for her exclusive use, her favourite attendant was a pretty Circassian, in whom she had absolute confidence. This Nadine was a native of Southern Russia. The movement of city life and civilised manners and customs had at first terrified this little savage; but she had learned to adapt herself to her changed surroundings, and was now high in the favour of Princess Sonia. She, and she alone, was authorised to be present when the beautiful great lady took her daily baths. For some years past the Princess had insisted on the presence of a maid when she took her baths: without fail they must either be in the bathroom itself, or in the room next to it, within reach or call. But on this particular evening Sonia Danidoff, more nervous and restless than usual, would not allow Nadine to leave her for a second. As to the time — well, if she did not know the exact time it could not be helped! Really it did not matter to her whether she were half an hour or no, for the ball given in her honour by Thomery, the millionaire sugar refiner: in fact, it would be much better to make her appearance after all the guests had assembled — her arrival would give the crowning touch of brilliancy to this society function.

Sonia Danidoff had pronounced the word "anniversary" in a

tone of anguish so sincere that Nadine was genuinely alarmed. She knew, only too well, what this fatal word meant to her mistress.

She had not forgotten that five years ago to the day, just when the Princess was enjoying her evening bath, a mysterious individual had appeared before her, who, after frightening her, had robbed her of a large sum of money. The adventure would have been little out of the ordinary, for hotel robberies are frequent, had not the audacious bandit been quickly identified as the enigmatic and elusive Fantômas, whose prodigious reputation had only increased with the passage of the years.

Sonia Danidoff, who was not ignorant of the dramatic adventures imputed to this legendary hero, could not bear to think of the position she had been placed in that awful night, when, threatened and robbed by Fantômas, she had escaped death by a series of unknown and unguessable circumstances: the tormenting mystery of it all had preyed insistently upon her mind. Since then Sonia Danidoff had never taken a bath without thinking of Fantômas; and every year when the anniversary of his aggression came round she suffered cruelly: she was seized with wild, unreasoning fears at the idea that she might see this terrifying bandit appear before her again, and that this time he would be merciless.

Nadine knew all this. She also shuddered at the vision this horrible anniversary evoked, but controlling herself, she was anxious to change the current of her dear mistress's thoughts:

"Forget, try to forget, Sonia Danidoff," she counselled in her melodious voice: "You are going to a ball — at Monsieur Thomery's — at your fiancé's house!"

The Princess shuddered:

"Ah, Nadine, my Nadine!" she cried, raising herself, and regarding her maid with a strange look: "I cannot overcome my uneasiness — my alarms! . . . This coincidence of date agitates me. . . . You know how superstitious we are at home — in our Russia — and the life I lead in Paris has not destroyed in me the simplicity of soul of a daughter of the Steppes!"

Nadine did not know what reply to make to this pathetic outburst. The Princess went on:

"And then, do you see, I think it wrong of Monsieur Thomery to even want to give this ball, only a fortnight after the tragic death of that poor Baroness de Vibray! . . . I tried to dissuade him from it. . . . I think the Baroness was his most intimate friend once! . . ."

"So it is said," murmured Nadine.

Sonia Danidoff went on, as if speaking to herself:

"I am not sure of it . . . it is precisely to remove this suspicion from my mind that Thomery was determined to have his ball to-night at all costs! . . . The Baroness de Vibray, so he told me, was no more than a good old friend. . . . I cannot make her death an excuse for putting off the announcement of our marriage . . . that would be to give colour to scandal."

Sonia Danidoff shrugged her beautiful shoulders:

"Hand me a mirror!"

Nadine obeyed. The Princess gazed long and complacently at the marvellously lovely face reflected in the glass.

"Princess," cried Nadine, "you must leave the bath, you will be late otherwise!"

In the adjacent dressing-room, brilliantly illuminated by electric light, the Princess dressed with the aid of Nadine, proud and happy to be the sole assistant of her beloved mistress. The toilet was a triumph: silk of an exquisite blue, draped with silk muslin incrusted with pointe de Venise and bands of ermine: a costly masterpiece of the dressmaker's art. It enhanced the brilliant beauty of Sonia Danidoff, and threw Nadine into raptures.

The Princess opened her jewel-box:

"This evening, Nadine, I shall be pearls and diamonds!" cried the lovely creature, as she fixed two large grey pearls in her ears.

"Oh, how beautiful you are, Princess! And what a lot they must have cost!" cried Nadine.

"Ten thousand francs, my child, on each side of my head!"

Sonia slipped on her fingers three diamond rings set in platinum:

"And here are eight or nine thousand francs more," continued she, as Nadine's eyes grew round with wonder: her mind could hardly grasp all these thousands of francs-worth of diamonds and pearls. There were still more to come; for, rejecting a magnificent bracelet, on the plea that one no longer wore them at balls, the Princess smilingly bade her Circassian fasten round her neck a superb triple collar of pearls. To this was added a sparkling cascade of diamonds. Never had Nadine seen her beautiful mistress so richly dressed. Thus adorned, in Nadine's eyes, Sonia Danidoff was dazzlingly beautiful, exquisitely lovely.

"You look like the Holy Virgin on the icons!" stammered Nadine, kneeling before her mistress, quite overcome by emotion.

"Good Heavens! That is blasphemy! I am only a humble human creature!" said the Princess smiling. Then she once more looked at herself in the mirrors, well satisfied with her appearance, certain of the effect she would produce on her future husband Thomery. She threw over her shoulders a superb mantle of zibeline which was quite needed, for, though it was the middle of April, it was quite cold.

Then, ready at last, she descended to her motor-car, and was whirled away to the ball.

"Cranajour! . . . Cranajour!"

Mother Toulouche shouted herself breathless: she tried to shout louder and louder. It was in vain. She might shout herself hoarse — there was no reply.

The old termagant, who had left the front of her hovel and had gone to call her assistant, shouting in the passage at the back of the store, returned cursing and swearing, and seated herself near the store in the lean-to which did duty as a kitchen:

"Where in the devil's name has that imbecile got to?" she grumbled, whilst sipping with gusts from the bottom of a cup, into which she had poured a small allowance of coffee and a copious ration of rum. It was about eleven in the evening. There was not a sound to be heard.

Having finished her rum and tea the old receiver of stolen goods went to the entrance of the passage:

"Cranajour! . . . Cranajour!" yelled the old termagant.

There was no answer.

"He can't possibly be in his canteen," said Mother Toulouche to herself. "If he was he'd have answered, fool though he is, and would have come down! . . . Sure he's gone to drag his old down-at-heels somewhere — but where? . . . Oh, well, we can manage to do without him!"

The old receiver went back to her store, and was starting on a queer sort of job when the door, which led on to the quay, burst open before a panting, breathless individual. He ran right up the store and stopped short. Mother Toulouche had seized the first thing she could find, and had taken up a defensive attitude. Her weapon was a great ancient cavalry sabre!

But the newcomer intended no harm — quite the contrary! After an instinctive recoil, he leaned against a table and wiped his forehead, breathing in gasps, incapable of pronouncing a syllable.

Mother Toulouche had recognised him:

"Ah! It's you, Redhead! . . . And not a bit too soon either! I've been waiting for you this last half-hour! Ernestine will be there in ten minutes' time! However is it you are so late?"

Redhead was well named! His bullet-head was covered with russet-red hair, cut very short; his complexion was a good match; his bloated cheeks and his potato-shaped nose were covered with red patches; his shaven chin was a tawny red; round his little gimlet eyes was a fringe of red lashes: it was a bestial face.

He was hatless; above his waistcoat with metal buttons he wore a black coat; his trousers had a yellow line down them: he was evidently a servant, wearing the livery of some big house. The fellow was slowly recovering his breath; but he continued to wipe great drops of sweat off his narrow forehead; he was shaking all over, and his morose countenance was twitching and contracting nervously.

"Well, what's your news? Good or bad?" questioned Mother Toulouche in a brutal tone.

Redhead replied almost inaudibly:

"That depends! . . . It's good on the whole."

A gleam of cupidity showed in the old receiver's eyes:

"Got a bit of tin on her back, that woman — eh?"

Redhead nodded a "yes." Thereupon Mother Toulouche went into her back store and returned with a claret glass filled to the brim with rum:

"Shoot that down your throat! That'll put you right!"

When he had swallowed the bumper he seemed to gain courage, and said:

"If I didn't get here sooner it's because I had to wait — but I saw the little thing. . . ."

"What's her name?"

"Nadine," replied Redhead, and added: "A pretty little brat, too! . . . She's got some fire in her eyes!"

"What's that to do with it?" interrupted Mother Toulouche.

"You don't mean to tell me you were able to make her gabble a bit?" she queried contemptuously.

Redhead bridled: "Likely, since I know everything now . . . and I'm her sweetheart, let me tell you!"

Mother Toulouche said in a jeering tone:

"You don't tell me! You!"

"Oh," replied Redhead, "it's just a way of speaking. She's a good little thing — there's nothing to it, you know!"

"So much the worse!" declared Mother Toulouche. "Virtuous sorts aren't any use to our lot! . . . Well — what did she tell you — out with it!"

"Well," said Redhead, "I waited three-quarters of an hour before Nadine joined me. . . . I had no bother in making her talk, I can tell you: without the asking she told me everything . . . she was pretty well flabbergasted with all the jewels her mistress had stuck on her clothes and her skin. . . . Seems there's hundreds of thousands' worth! . . . All pearls and diamonds! Nothing but. . . ."

Mother Toulouche was calculating:

"Real pearls, real diamonds — it's possible there's all that worth!"

Steps could be heard on the pavement just outside.

Redhead began to shake all over:

"Who is it?" he asked. "Someone coming in?"

Mother Toulouche grinned:

"Be easy, then! Haven't I told you there's nothing to fear?"

Nevertheless he asked anxiously:

"There's nothing more I'm wanted for here, is there? I've told you all I know."

"No, no, it's all right!" replied Mother Toulouche, maternal and conciliating, "there's nothing more for you to do here. . . . Still, if you want to see big Ernestine. . . ."

Without waiting to hear the end of her sentence Redhead hurried towards the exit. Mother Toulouche did not try to detain him:

"After all," she said in a low tone to his back as a kind of farewell, "cut your sticks, my lad . . . since you're funky!"

When alone she grumbled aloud:

"What a lot they are! . . . I never did! . . . White-livered, and for nothing at all!"

Mother Toulouche was still muttering when big Ernestine marched in through the back way. She had on a large hat and was heavily veiled. She proceeded to remove both hat and veil:

"Well?" she queried.

"They've got on to it all right! Redhead has just gone! He knows through the little maid that the Princess went off to the ball, dressed up to the nines — hung with jewels like a shrine!"

Big Ernestine uttered a deep sigh of satisfaction: her only reply was to hustle the old receiver:

"Look alive, Mother Toulouche! . . . You've got to give me a beg-gar's outfit: it's up to you to see I'm disguised properly, and there's not a minute to lose either!"

Mother Toulouche was an expert at disguises and make-up of every sort: this was not to be wondered at, considering the queer company she kept, and the fraudulent business she carried on, and the smuggling she was mixed up in!

Big Ernestine, disguised as a poverty-stricken creature and ren-dered unrecognisable, looked exactly like some unfortunate reduced to soliciting alms. She walked into the back store, and helped Mother Toulouche to take from a cupboard some bottles, bandages, and med-icated cotton-wool. By the light of a smoky lamp the two women scrutinised the labels, sniffing the various phials and flasks. Big Ernestine, with the aid of Mother Toulouche, prepared compresses of pomade and cotton-wool, on which she sprinkled a few drops of a yellow liquid, giving out a sickening odour. Besides this big Ernestine put inside her bodice a long phial, after making certain that the mix-ture, with which it was full, contained chloroform. . . .

Then, under Mother Toulouche's watchful eye, Ernestine pre-pared what was called in that world of light-fingered gentry "the mask": a mask of cotton, which is moulded by force on the face of the victim in order to plunge him, or her, into a heavy sleep. Whilst making these sinister preparations the two women talked as they went on with their evil task. Big Ernestine said, in reply to Mother Toulouche's questionings:

"Oh, it's simple enough! It's like this: . . . When the motor-car stops I shall go to the right-hand door and begin to beg . . . likely enough, the Princess won't want to hear what I have to say, but while I attract her attention, Mimile, who will be on the other side, will open the door, and will stick the compress on her mug. . . . She won't struggle — besides, Mimile will have hold of her — and then I'll have had time to see where her jewels are, and how they are fastened, and then I'll soon have them in my pocket — my deep 'un!"

Mother Toulouche nodded:

"It's arranged all right, but how will you arrest the motor?"

"Oh, that's where the others come in; they'll do it all right. . . . I expect they're seeing to it now! . . ."

"But, look here," cried Mother Toulouche, "Mimile isn't in bits then? They said he had fallen from his flier!"

Big Ernestine gave a laugh:

"He fell right enough, poor little fellow, and from pretty high too — but he's not broken a thing . . . not this time . . . a bit of luck I don't think — eh?"

"He's a mascot, I'm certain," declared Mother Toulouche. Then she said: "You spoke of the others? . . . Who are they — the others?"

"But didn't they tell you?" cried the surprised Ernestine, for she thought old Mother Toulouche was in the know: "Why, there's the Beadle — and the Beard. . . ."

"Oh," cried Mother Toulouche, much impressed: "If the Beard's in it, then it's a serious affair!"

"Yes," replied big Ernestine, staring hard at the old receiver of stolen goods: "It's serious all right! If the chloroform doesn't work — oh, well . . . they'll bring the knife into play. . . ."

Big Ernestine looked at her little silver watch to mark the time:

"Past midnight!" she remarked: "I must hurry off and see what they're up to!"

As she was making off Mother Toulouche stopped her:

"Have a glass of rum to start on — it puts heart into you!"

The two women were quite ready for a drink together. When they had swallowed their dose, big Ernestine smacked her tongue:

"Famous stuff! . . . It puts a heart into you and no mistake!"

"Yes, it's the right stuff — the best," agreed Mother Toulouche: "It's what Nibet prefers!" she added. Then she cried: "But Nibet, how . . . isn't he in it?"

Big Ernestine put a finger on her lips:

"Nibet's in it of course — as he always is — you know that, old Toulouche — but he's content to show the way — you know he seldom does anything himself . . . besides, it seems he's on duty at the dépôt to-night!"

Big Ernestine threw an old shawl over her head and went off crying:

"I'm off, and in for it now! . . . Soon be back, Mother Toulouche!"

The magnificent mansion of Thomery, the sugar refiner, overlooked the park Monceau. It was approached by a very quiet little avenue, in which were a few big houses: it opened on to the boulevard Malesherbes, and was known as the avenue de Valois. All the dwellings there are sumptuous, richly inhabited, and if the avenue is peaceful and silent by day, it is no uncommon thing to see it of an evening crowded with carriages and luxurious motor-cars, come to fetch the owners away to dinners and entertainments.

On this particular evening the approaches to the avenue de Valois were full of animation. Motors and broughams succeeded one another in a long file, putting down the guests of Thomery under an immense marquee, covering the steps leading up to the vestibule.

All the smart world had been invited to the reception: all Paris swarmed into the brilliantly illuminated entrance-halls of the mansion.

Two mounted policemen sat as immovable as bronze caryatides on either side of the entrance, whilst a swarm of policemen made the carriages move on, and drove away from the aristocratic avenue de Valois the band of poverty-stricken and ragged creatures who crowded the pavement with the hope of securing a handsome tip by opening a carriage door or picking up some fallen object.

It was no easy matter to keep order. One of the police sergeants accustomed to ceremonial functions remarked to one of his younger colleagues:

"I have seen balls and receptions enough! Well, my boy, this Thomery affair is as fine a set out as if it were at the President's!"

Although it was one o'clock in the morning, both on the boulevard Malesherbes and at the entrance to the rue de Monceau there was movement and activity. If, as seemed likely, there was a crush in the great reception-rooms of the Thomery mansion, it was certain that outside the crowd had to form up in line to get near the counters, where the wine sellers were serving their customers without a moment's intermission — serving them with drinks of every description. Thus there was a hubbub, there was noise and roystering clamour all around. Most of the chauffeurs, coachmen, and servants knew one another.

Mingling with all this aristocracy of the servant class were pick-pockets, mendicants obsequious and wheedling, who offered themselves as understudies to these of the upper ten of the servant world, and these aristocrats were ready to seize this chance of a little liberty, and at the same time play the generous patron to these poor failures in life's battle. In fact they gave more generous tips than their masters; for did they not rub shoulders with misery and thus realise, only too vividly, the measureless horrors of destitution?

Ernestine and Mimile lost themselves in the noisy crowd. They were all eyes and ears for everything going on around them, whilst keeping in view their two accomplices, the Beadle and the Beard. This was more than usually difficult, because they were disguised almost out of recognition. The Beard was muffled in a blue blouse and a big soft hat, which gave him the look of a peasant, who had wandered into a crowd with which he had nothing in common. The Beadle was capitally disguised as a coachman in good service who is out of a situation, but who, from vanity and custom, sports the emblems of office.

He was continually chewing a quid of tobacco; for such is the habit of coachmen who cannot smoke on their seats, and thus console themselves with two sous' worth of roll tobacco.

The Beadle stopped beside a chauffeur who had just got down from his car, a magnificent limousine, lined with cream cloth, while its exterior was a dark maroon in the best taste.

"Why, it's Casimir!" cried the Beadle, going up to the chauffeur with hands outstretched and smiling face.

Mechanically the chauffeur, addressed as Casimir, responded to the offered handclasp. But, after a short silence, he said in a questioning tone, quite frankly:

"I cannot recall you."

"Can't you remember me!" cried the Beadle. "Why, don't you remember César — César who was with Rothschild last year?"

No, Casimir could not remember. But he was quite willing to believe that he knew César, for he had seen and known so many since he had been in the service of Princess Sonia Danidoff, that there was nothing extraordinary about his forgetfulness. Besides, César looked quite a decent fellow, and had a taking face, and one only had to look at that beaming countenance of his to be sure that an invitation to take a drink together would soon be forthcoming!

The Beadle, satisfied that he had so easily made a friend of the chauffeur of Sonia Danidoff, whom he had only known by sight for the last forty-eight hours, did in fact suggest their taking a glass together. The Beadle had indeed come up to expectations!

Drink was Casimir's besetting sin. Excellent chauffeur, solid and serious fellow as he was, he had two defects: he was addicted to tippling, though he never drank to excess, and never got drunk. Also, he was fond of a gossip: he could talk for hours without stopping.

The Beadle had been posted up regarding Casimir's little weaknesses and tastes. Thus nothing was easier than to set trap after trap, into each of which the simple fellow fell as they were set — fell fatally.

The Beadle introduced the Beard to Casimir under the name of Father India-rubber: an old codger, whose trade was to buy and sell tyres to chauffeurs, tyres new and also second-hand. At this moment a young ragamuffin appeared on the scenes: he asked if he might be left in charge of the car. It was Mimile. The young hooligan, who had followed the conversation of the three men, and of Casimir in particular, whilst keeping in the background, now intervened at the right moment. He made his offer just as the chauffeur was looking about him in hopes of finding some poverty-stricken creatures into whose charge he could give his car. Casimir gave him twenty sous as an earnest of what was to follow in the way of coin, saying:

"Take great care of my little shanty! Don't let anyone come mouching around it, and when I return you shall have double what you've just had!"

"Thank you, master!" cried Mimile, bowing low before the chauffeur: "You may rest assured I shall keep a good look out!"

Mimile exchanged signs of understanding with his two accomplices, whilst they, talking as they went, drew the innocent Casimir towards the nearest tavern, which was crowded with wine-bibbers.

Mimile, as faithful guardian of the limousine, soon got bored, although big Ernestine was prowling around, and came to have a minute's talk with him now and again: they dared not be seen together too much for fear of attracting attention. As time went on, Mimile was surprised that neither the Beadle nor the Beard came to report progress. But at long last the majestic outline of the Beard was seen at the corner of the rue Monceau. The pretended seller of india-rubber was coming out of the tavern.

He hastened to Mimile and, in a low, distinct voice, he gave him some hurried instructions, for now there was no time to lose:

"That idiot would never get done with his stories about motor-cars, and all that stuff and rubbish — what's that to us? But — keep your ears open now, Mimile — it seems there are still fifteen litres of petrol in the tank, and that would take it a long way, for the motor consumes very little. . . . But this shanty has got to stop about five hundred yards from here, at the corner of the rue de Monceau and the rue de Téhéran . . . it's by this way Casimir will take his Baroness back from the ball. . . . Well, what you have to do is to take fourteen litres and a half from that tank and pitch them in the gutter! . . . When Casimir finds that his petrol has given out, he will have to go in search of more . . . it's during his absence that we will work the trick on the pretty Princess — we'll perform an operation on her, and amputate her — jewellery — the whole lot!"

The Beard drew from under his blouse an empty bottle, which he had stolen in the tavern:

"Here's your measure! Count carefully fourteen litres and a half — that done, wait quietly till Casimir turns up: your part in the story will be forty sous, and not to rouse his suspicions; then, while he goes up the avenue de Valois to take up the Princess, you and Ernestine have to gallop off to the corner of the rue de Monceau and the rue de Téhéran, then . . . wait!"

Mimile, with the agility of a monkey and the ability of a first-rate chauffeur — for there was nothing he did not know in the way of applied mechanics, as became an aviator — executed to the letter his accomplice's orders.

The Beard meanwhile had returned to the tavern and Casimir.

Suddenly, all was activity in the world of carriages and coachmen! The great ball was drawing to its end. Casimir was once more in possession of his motor, and had generously tipped his understudy: thereupon the hooligan had made off as fast as his legs could carry him. Ernestine joined him at the appointed spot: there the two rogues waited. "Listen!" cried big Ernestine some fifteen minutes later.

She stared in the direction of the boulevard Malesherbes, with neck outstretched and straining eyeballs. At last, after an agonising wait, she and Mimile saw the carriages driving by. "Attention!" cried big Ernestine in a sharp whisper . . . "everybody's on the move at last!"

The Beadle and the Beard, hidden in the crowd which thronged the approaches to the Thomery mansion, awaited the departure of Princess Sonia Danidoff: the idea of this rich prey excited them. Then as they stared at the first outflow of departing guests, the two bandits could not but notice that far from looking gay and animated as people do who have danced and supped well, these guests of Thomery showed pale, dejected faces: in fact, they had all the appearance of people under the influence of some tragic emotion.

"They look pretty down in the mouth, don't they?" whispered the Beard in the Beadle's ear.

"That's a fact! You'd think they were returning from a funeral!"

Then a vague rumour began to circulate; confirmation followed, spread insensibly within the Thomery mansion, was passed on by the lackeys, spread from the pavements to the avenue. People whispered of incomprehensible things incredible, but which little by little took definite shape. It was said that the Thomery ball had just become the scene of an accident, of a drama, of a robbery, of a crime! . . . The police, and of the highest grade, had intervened. . . . The news spread like a train of ignited gunpowder. . . . Nevertheless, if Thomery's guests were cognisant of the details, they did not take the beggars and pickpockets into their confidence: among the light-fingered gentry conjectures were rife.

The Beadle and the Beard, who tried to catch odds and ends of talk separately, joined each other again, looking crestfallen, discomfited. The Beadle broke silence, with an oath, adding:

"I am certain we have been done . . . someone has got in before us — been too smart for us!"

Beard nodded: he was of the same opinion.

But who then could have had the audacity to plan such an attempt and carry it out, too? Who could have had the same idea as he and his comrades, and to realise it successfully? Whoever it was had proved himself the better man. In spite of himself the bandit, in thought, formulated one word:

Fantômas!

VIII
END OF THE BALL

When Sonia Danidoff entered Thomery's ball-room she made a sensation. It was not far off midnight when she appeared in all her brilliant beauty and dazzling array, leaning on the arm of her host and fiancé, who bore his honours proudly. Dancers paused to admire this handsome couple; then the Hungarian band redoubled their efforts, and the whirling, eddying waltz started afresh, more gay, more inspiriting than before.

In a corner opposite the musicians a group of persons were in animated talk: among them Sonia Danidoff, Thomery, and Jérôme Fandor. Music was their theme, some admired Wagner and the classics, others voted for the moderns, for the sugariest of waltzes, for the romantic, the bizarre.

"For the profane like myself," declared Thomery, laughing, "gipsy music has its charms!"

"Oh," cried Sonia Danidoff, "you are not going to tell me that such hackneyed things as *The Smile of Spring* and *The Blush Rose Waltz* are to your taste!"

Her tone was reproachful, but her smile was charming.

Nanteuil, the fashionable banker, who was fluttering about the Princess, hastened to take her side:

"Come now, Thomery, you would not put your signature to that?"

Jérôme Fandor, who had just joined the group, declared:

"For my part, I thoroughly agree with you, my dear Monsieur Thomery!"

Sonia Danidoff looked her surprise.

Thomery replied, with a touch of malice:

"Monsieur Fandor is like myself — the Tonkinoise is more to his taste!"

"More than Wagner's operatic big guns!" finished Fandor.

Then turning to the Princess who still wore her air of surprise:

"Yes, Princess, I confess it — my taste in music is deplorable: it comes from absolute ignorance. I do not understand these modern symphonies — the simple romantic suits me best!"

"And that is?" . . . queried Nanteuil:

"Just some music-hall air or ditty," answered Fandor with a smile as frank as his confession.

The Princess was amused at this little pseudo-artistic discussion. She was about to speak when a couple of waltzers broke into the group and scattered it.

Jérôme Fandor slipped away and wandered through the gorgeous reception rooms. Here and there, when caught up in the throng and forced to halt, or when pressed against the wall of the ball-room, scraps of conversation, mingled with the strains of the Hungarian band, fell on his retentive ears. He took refuge at last in the embrasure of a window; but his retreat was soon invaded by two young men who, he gathered, had run across each other in the gallery, and were continuing their talk about old times and new.

"Come, tell me, dear Charley, what has been happening to you since we left the school?"

"Bah! I go from the Madeleine to the Opera nearly every evening, and then back again; I go to bed late and get up late; I go out a good deal, as you see; sometimes I dance, but very rarely; I often play bridge . . . and that is about all! It's not very interesting; but you, old boy . . . I heard you had got a jolly good billet, my dear Andral!"

"Oh, hardly that, dear fellow; but I am well on the way to one, I fancy. I had the good luck to be introduced to Thomery, and it so happened he was wanting a young engineer for one of his sugar plantations in San Domingo."

"Good Lord! At San Domingo, among the niggers?"

"That's right! Not so bad, though it and the boulevards are a few miles apart! But, on the other hand, I am interested in my work, and I am married to a charming woman — Spanish."

"Won't you introduce me to your wife?"

"When we are nearer to her, old fellow! I came to Paris by myself to talk big business with Thomery. I am only here for a fortnight. . . . Now do point out some of the celebrities — you know everybody!"

Charley adjusted his eyeglass and looked about the room:

"Ah, there's an interesting pair! That old fellow and the young one, who are so extraordinarily alike — the Barbey-Nanteuils, bankers for generations in the financial swim, and mixed up in all sorts of big affairs, sugar, among them. . . . Look here! That's the widow of an iron master, Allouat — she is passing close to the orchestra — not bad looking in spite of her mahogany-coloured hair, granddaughter of a famous French peer, Flavogny de Saint-Ange. . . . Ah, I breathe again! . . . It's a detail, but I am quite delighted! General de Rini's daughters have at last found partners: they are ugly, poor things, and they've dressed themselves in rose-pink as though they were school-girls: a fine name, a distinguished position, but no fortune, and no husband! . . . Ah, now there's someone who looks as if he were in luck — and he is, too — matrimonial luck. The affair is settled this evening, it's whispered. It will interest you particularly, for the lucky fellow is none other than Thomery!"

"What! Thomery?"

"Yes, Thomery! Although he is well over fifty, he means to commit matrimony! I quite envy him his future wife, my Andral! There she is! That stately dame who is going towards the last of the reception rooms all alone, rather haughty, but a noble creature — it's Princess Sonia Danidoff, related to the Tzar in some distant way and with an immense fortune. Just look, dear boy, at those splendid jewels on that beautiful neck of hers! They say she's got on seven hundred thousand francs' worth — and the rest to match — millions to swell the sugar refiner's pouch! She is to lead the cotillion with him, so there's no doubt about the betrothal. By the by, you are going to stay for the cotillion?"

"Hum! I . . ."

"But you must! You simply must! We must sit together at supper, we have still so much to say! . . . Besides, if you hurry off like that, I fancy Thomery won't be best pleased. Oh, I say, there he is, coming our way! There's no denying it, he is a fine figure of a man, though he is in the fifties — but! . . . but! . . . but do look! What is the matter with him? He looks as if he had seen a ghost."

Sonia Danidoff, who had been waltzing with Thomery, was a little out of breath. A quick glance in a mirror showed the lovely Princess that her cheeks were rather flushed:

"I am scarlet," she thought, with that touch of feminine exaggeration characteristic of her! She was a true daughter of Eve!

At that exact moment she felt a slight tug at the bottom of her skirt, and at the same time a black coat was making profuse apologies: it was Monsieur Nanteuil:

"I am in despair, Princess!" cried the banker. "But no one is quite responsible for his movements in such a crush! . . . I am very much afraid that I have stepped on the muslin of your ravishing toilette and have slightly torn it!"

The Princess protested that it did not matter in the least, and the banker moved away, bowing low and pouring out apologies and regrets. As soon as he had left her the Princess showed her annoyance: how could she lead the cotillion with this tear in her dress, slight though it might be — and the cotillion would begin in less than half an hour! Then she remembered that her fiancé had led her, on her arrival, to a little drawing-room, quite away from the reception rooms at the end of the gallery, that she might leave her cloak there, saying:

"Dear Princess, I have prepared this boudoir for you, and *you only*."

Sonia decided to retire to this boudoir at once and repair the damage to her dress. As she passed the cloak-room on her way a maid offered her services. The Princess refused them. If she could not have Nadine, she preferred to manage for herself, besides, she saw that two pins, concealed in the silk muslin, would put her dress to rights; and a touch of powder to her cheeks would bring her colour down to a becoming tint.

She was considerably amused at the veritable arsenal of flasks and boxes of perfumes which Thomery, as became an attentive lover, had placed there in her honour: the little boudoir had been transformed into a comfortable ladies' dressing-room. Everything was provided, down to a glass of sugar and water, down to a little phial of alcohol and mint!

Sonia opened a powder box; then, like all the women of her race, having a passion for perfumes, she took up a scent sprayer and lavishly sprinkled her throat and the lower part of her face with what was labelled, "essence of violets."

The Princess may have suffered from the intense heat of the ballroom, and required rest without realising it, for she felt slightly faint, a little sick — almost a desire to sleep. . . . She slipped down on to a low divan, which occupied a corner of the room: she drew deep breaths, breaking in the perfume, a sweet rather strange scent, from the sprayer.

"This scent is sickly," she thought. "If only I had some eau-de-Cologne!"

Without rising, for she felt a real lassitude stealing over her, she looked round for the eau-de-Cologne she wanted: Thomery's arsenal did not contain any. There was only one sprayer and that Sonia Danidoff held in her hand.

She sprinkled herself a second time, hoping that the perfume would revive her; but, on the contrary, her fatigue increased: her eyes closed for a moment. . . . When she opened them again the room was in darkness.

Sonia tried to rise from the divan. An overpowering torpor, though not disagreeable, was benumbing her whole body, and before her eyes bright lights seemed to float, succeeded by thick darkness. Her head turned round and round . . . she strove to cry out, but her voice stuck in her throat: her body jerked with a feeble convulsive movement. She heard indistinctly an unknown voice murmuring:

"Let yourself go! . . . Sleep! . . . Have no fear!"

Sonia Danidoff essayed a momentary resistance, then she succumbed and lost all consciousness of her surroundings. . . .

Absolute silence reigned in the boudoir Thomery had reserved for the sole use of his beautiful betrothed, when he arrived to lead her to the cotillion. He found the door shut. He knocked discreetly. There was no reply. Repeated knocking evoked no audible answer.

Thomery opened the door. The room was in total darkness. He switched on the electric light: the boudoir was brilliantly illuminated. . . . The sight that met his startled eyes was so moving that he grew livid with horror and rushed to the side of his betrothed.

Sonia Danidoff was extended on the divan motionless and pale as death. A hoarse and laboured breath came from her heaving bosom at irregular intervals: on the exquisite skin of neck and breast were spattered streaks of blood!

Beside himself, Thomery rushed away in search of help.

It was at this terrible crisis that the fiancé of Sonia Danidoff had attracted the attention of Charley, whose friend, the young engineer Andral, was the protégé of the man whose awful pallor and distracted air spelt tragedy.

Thomery, his countenance ravaged by intense emotion, his hands clenched, shaken by nervous tremors, hastened, with unsteady steps, in the direction of the gallery leading to the anteroom.

Suddenly a woman's shrieks broke in on the charming harmonies of a slow waltz, which the orchestra was rendering at the moment. . . . There was an irresistible rush towards the boudoir, where two half-fainting women had collapsed on chairs, and the famous surgeon, Dr. Marvier, was doing his utmost to prevent the crowd from entering the room. The word went round that a tragedy had taken place — a death! Princess Sonia Danidoff was in the room lying dead! The words "crime" and "murder" were freely bandied about: murmurs of "assassin," "robber," "assassination" could be heard.

Some twenty of the guests who had entered the boudoir could give details. The dreadful rumours were true. Sonia Danidoff, they declared, was stretched out on the floor covered with blood, her breast bare, her pearls had vanished — a horrible sight!

The uproar died down; an icy silence reigned. The dancers drew together in groups discussing the terrifying tragedy. . . . Several women were still in a fainting condition; pallid men were opening windows that fresh air might circulate in the overheated rooms; on all sides they were watching for the return of their host.

Thomery remained invisible.

General de Rini called his two daughters to his side and spoke words of affectionate encouragement, for they were much upset. The old soldier marched off with them in the direction of the grand staircase and towards the cloak-room on the landing. As he was preparing to take over his coat and hat, one of the footmen went up to him and said a few words in a low voice:

"What! . . . What!" cried the General. "What's the meaning of this? . . . Not to leave the house! . . . But, am I under suspicion then? . . . It is shameful! . . . I never heard of such a thing!"

A butler approached the irate General and said, very respectfully:

"I beg of you, General, to speak lower! A definite order to that effect was given us ten minutes ago. Directly Monsieur Thomery was aware of the . . . accident he had the entrance doors closed and had the house surrounded by the detectives who were downstairs on duty. The sergeant is there to see this order carried out: you cannot leave the premises! . . . It is not that you are under suspicion, General — of course not — but perhaps in this way they may succeed in finding the guilty person who has certainly not left the house, for no one has gone from the house for at least an hour. . . ."

General Rini had calmed down. He understood why his host had issued the order. He retired to a corner of the gallery with his daughters, Yvonne and Marthe: the poor things seemed stunned.

The reception rooms slowly emptied: the guests crowded on to the verandah and into the smoking-room. There was a buzz of talk — queries, comments, conjectures: it ceased abruptly.

Monsieur Thomery had just appeared at the top of the grand staircase, accompanied by a gentleman, whose simple black coat was in striking contrast to the light dresses and brilliant uniforms of the guests.

Someone whispered:

"Monsieur Havard!"

It was, in fact, the chief of the detective police force. Within a couple of minutes of his frightful discovery, Thomery had rushed to the telephone and had called up Police Headquarters. It was a piece of unexpected good fortune to find Monsieur Havard there at so advanced an hour. He had immediately responded to the call in person.

Whilst crossing the reception rooms Thomery talked to him in a low voice:

"Accept my grateful thanks, Monsieur, for having answered my appeal for help so quickly. No sooner did I discover the body of my Princess than I lost no time in having all the exits from the premises watched. Unfortunately I was obliged to leave my reception rooms for quite a quarter of an hour, so that I cannot tell you what happened there. If only I had been able to remain with my guests, I might possibly have surprised some movement, some gesture, some look, which would have put me on the track of this murderous thief . . . unfortunately . . ."

Monsieur Havard interrupted, smiling:

"That does not matter, Monsieur: if the guilty person is among your guests and has in some way betrayed himself, I shall hear of it. There are, at least, four or five plain clothes men among the dancers, I can assure you of that."

"I can assure you to the contrary!" replied Thomery — "I know my guests — know who have been admitted here!"

"I also am sure of what I say," insisted Monsieur Havard. "There is scarcely a ball, a reception, however select it may be, where you will not find a certain number of our men."

Thomery made no reply to this: they had arrived at the door of the fatal room. The doctor was standing beside the victim. Dr. Marvier reassured Monsieur Havard. He announced that the Princess had been almost literally felled to the ground by a most powerful soporific and was in no real danger: she would certainly regain consciousness in the course of an hour or two. . . . But she must be kept perfectly quiet: that was absolutely necessary.

Monsieur Havard did not question the doctor's statement. After a rapid glance he was able to form his own opinion. There had been no struggle: the victim's wounds were due to the haste with which the thief had torn the jewels from Sonia Danidoff's neck. He next considered the two windows which, with the door opening on to the gallery, were the only means of entrance and exit the room had. There were strong iron shutters behind the windows: these could not be very easily opened: in any case, it was impossible to close them again from the outside. The thief must have been in the house, probably in the ball-room, and had followed the Princess into this little retiring-room. . . . But what had been the Princess's motive for coming here alone? Monsieur Havard had learned that the room had not been thrown open to the other guests. Then he perceived that the lace at the bottom of her dress was undone. He bent down and examined it carefully: two pins, hastily stuck in, kept together a piece of this lace. . . . The conclusion Monsieur Havard came to was, that the Princess having a rent in her dress had wished to be alone for a minute or two in order to repair the damage, and that while she was stooping towards the bottom of her skirt the assassin had thrown her to the ground and despoiled her of her jewels.

The chief of the detective force turned to Thomery abruptly:

"I shall be obliged to follow a course of action which may rather annoy your guests; but they must excuse me. Everything leads me to think that the guilty person is on the premises, since no one has gone away. . . . I must hold an investigation at once. I am going to cross-examine your guests — probe them thoroughly — and I wish to put them through their paces in your office, Monsieur Thomery, one by one. . . . I will begin . . . with you . . . so that your guests take my questioning with a good grace . . . it is only a mere matter of form — a pure formality! . . ."

The investigations were lengthy and trying and led to no result whatever.

Fandor, who was preoccupied by this fresh drama in which he had taken some part — far too slight to please him — was putting on his overcoat when he stopped dead.

A voice — an unrecognisable voice — had murmured in his ear: "Attention! Fandor! . . . It is serious! . . ."

Our journalist turned round in a flash. Ah, this time he would find out who the mysterious unknown was — the unknown, who wished to influence by word written and word spoken, the course of these investigations he had taken in hand:

Anonymous friend?

Concealed adversary?

He must, at all costs, clear up the mystery.

A dozen people were crowding round Fandor, insisting on being attended to in the cloak-room.

No one noticed the journalist. . . .

No one seemed interested in what he was doing. . . .

Fandor examined every one of Thomery's guests who were standing about him. He knew some of them by name, some he knew by sight. He searched their faces with penetrating eyes; but, in vain. . . . Some were common-place looking, others calm, others impenetrable:

"Hang it all," he grumbled. He went off furious and upset.

IX

FINGER PRINTS

After having interrogated all the witnesses of last night's tragedy he could get into touch with, Jérôme Fandor returned to the Palais de Justice.

"All the same," he confessed to himself, "I must admit that, up to the present, I do not know anything very definite about it. This Princess Sonia Danidoff has managed to get robbed in a most extraordinary way. At one o'clock in the morning, Havard declares that the thief can be none other than one of the guests, and thereupon every person present has to submit to being searched — an exhaustive search! Nothing comes of it. Then Bertillon arrives on the scene, and it seems he has obtained very distinct imprints of finger marks. If they are as distinct as all that, the task of the police will be simplified; but, on the other hand, is it likely the guilty person will be so simple as to respond to the summons issued by the Public Prosecutor, a general summons issued to all Thomery's guests to parade in Bertillon's office for the finger-mark test? . . . Not he! Why the moment he heard of it he would make for the train and pass the frontier!"

When his cab arrived at the Palais, Fandor uttered a big sigh of satisfaction:

"There are a good many things I am not clear about: let us hope Bertillon will give me some information."

The entrance to the anthropometric department was under the discreet observation of two detectives:

"Oh," thought Fandor. "They think it probable there will be an immediate arrest, do they? We are going to have some complications, I foresee, in connection with the finger-mark ceremony!"

He sent in his card and a few minutes after he found himself in the presence of Monsieur Bertillon.

"Well, what is it you want me to tell you?" asked this famous man of science.

"Why, dear master, everything that took place last night! Is it true that you have summoned here all Thomery's guests? . . . Have you obtained such perfect reprints that, in your hasty examination, you can be certain of identifying them with those of the persons who will pass through your office to undergo the test?"

Bertillon smiled:

"Oh, my dear fellow, you are of those who do not put much faith in the results of my tests for police purposes! That, let me tell you, is because you are not acquainted with our procedure. The impressions I obtained are distinct — precise as can be; if an arrest is made before long it will be made on sure grounds."

Fandor bowed:

"I accept your statement, dear master! . . . But, do be kind enough to tell me what happened after my departure?"

"Oh, nothing very extraordinary. . . . Of course you know about the affair — how the Princess Sonia Danidoff was discovered? . . ."

"What I know is that Thomery found one of his guests, Princess Sonia Danidoff, in a dead faint in a small drawing-room; that Dr. Du Marvier declared she had been rendered unconscious; that the theft of a pearl necklace worn by the victim had been the motive of this criminal attempt; that Monsieur Havard, called in at once, first made sure that no one had left the house, and then had everyone on the premises searched . . . and that is really all I know about it!"

"Well, Havard did not find anything!"

"No one was caught with compromising jewels in their possession. The last guest gone, the house searched from top to bottom, not a single pearl had been found. . . . I arrived just when the investigations had terminated: at the moment when they were about to take the Princess home. She had regained consciousness by this time and declared she knew nothing except that she had fallen asleep after using a perfume sprayer. This has been seized and chloroform has been found in it; but no one seems to know who filled the sprayer with this stupefying perfume."

"Did Monsieur Havard send for you?"

"Yes, he telephoned. You know, of course, that I am always asked to intervene now in any ticklish affair! . . . Well Dr. Du Marvier, an expert in his way, noticed that the Princess had been half strangled by the thief in his haste to secure the pearl collar, and he wished me to search for finger prints on the nape of the victim's neck — to discover the assassin's signature in fact."

"And there were some?"

"A quantity. The Princess had been slightly wounded in the nape of the neck . . . blood had been pressed on to the skin of her neck, and it was easy to take a cast of one of the fingers."

"Was that sufficient?"

"Yes, and no; such an impression is something; but there is better than that! The thief must have given the neck a violent squeeze with his hands, consequently there is a complete impression of the hand . . . that I had to get. . . ."

Fandor instinctively put his hand to his neck as if he were squeezing it. He said:

"Are such impressions imperceptible?"

"Yes; to the eye, but not to the photographing apparatus. It is thoroughly established that the pattern formed by the innumerable lines which furrow the fleshy part of our fingers is as peculiarly characteristic of each individual as the form of his nose, of his ears, or the colour of his eyes. The curves or rings, the various forms taken by these lines already exist in the newly born and never change to the day of his death. Even in case of a burn, if the skin grows again, the ridges reappear exactly as they were before the accident. Look you, one can obtain by this method — this test — such results as you would never dream of. For example, by taking these imprints I obtained in the early hours of to-day, as a basis, I can tell you, with almost absolute accuracy, the height of the individual. . . ."

"This is marvellous!" cried Fandor. "The service your department renders then is to abolish legal blunders?"

"That is so. Every individual identified, is identified plainly, irrefutably. Unfortunately, we cannot always obtain perfect imprints on the spot where the crime is committed."

"But this night?"

"Ah, as I told you, the impressions were most satisfactory. I have the thief's hand — the whole of it! I will even go so far as to declare that the fellow who committed the crime has already been through my hands. I recognise that hand! You shall see, whether or no I have made a mistake!" . . .

Bertillon pressed a bell, and asked the official who answered it:

"Have you identified the imprints I sent you just now?"

"Yes, sir. This man has already been measured here. It is register 9200."

Bertillon turned to Fandor:

"You see, I was not mistaken! All I have to do is to turn up my alphabetical index, and for this very month, for the number is a recent one, and I shall know the name of the old offender — he must be one, as he is catalogued here — who has committed this assault."

Whilst speaking, Monsieur Bertillon was turning over the leaves of an enormous register:

"Ah! Here is the 9200 series! . . ."

Suddenly the book slipped from his hands, and he exclaimed: "The guilty man is . . ."

"Is who?" questioned Fandor.

"Is Jacques Dollon! . . . The hand that has robbed Princess Sonia Danidoff is the hand of Jacques Dollon!"

"But it is impossible!"

Bertillon shrugged his shoulders.

"Impossible? . . . Why, since the proof of it is there?"

"But Jacques Dollon is dead!"

"He was the thief of yesterday's crime."

"You are making a mistake! . . ."

"I am not making a mistake! . . . Jacques Dollon is the thief I tell you!"

This was too much for Jérôme Fandor: he could not contain himself.

"And I tell you, Monsieur Bertillon, that I know that I am certain — positively certain, that Jacques Dollon is dead! . . . Now, then! . . ."

The man of science shook his head.

"I, in my turn, say, you are making a mistake! Look at the two imprints I have here! That of Jacques Dollon taken a few days ago, and this made from the impressions obtained this very night, or, to be exact, in the early morning hours of to-day! They are identical — one can be exactly superposed on the other! . . ."

"Coincidence!"

"There is no such coincidence possible — besides" — Monsieur Bertillon took up a powerful magnifying glass — "look at these characteristic details! . . . Just look at the lines of the thumb, all out of shape! . . . The presentment of the thumb itself is not normal either; it denotes habitual movement in a certain direction: it is the thumb of a painter, of a potter! . . . Oh, it is all as clear as daylight — believe me — there is no doubt about it! Jacques Dollon is the guilty person!"

"But," repeated Fandor obstinately: "Jacques Dollon is dead! I swear to you he is dead! . . ."

This assertion made no impression on the man of science.

"As to whether Jacques Dollon is alive or dead — that is for the police to decide! . . . For my part, I can declare that the man who committed the theft yesterday evening is the identical man who passed through my hands some days ago — and that man is certainly Jacques Dollon!"

Jérôme Fandor left Monsieur Bertillon. The young journalist was perplexed. . . . If the finger-prints on the neck of Princess Sonia Danidoff were, beyond dispute, those of Jacques Dollon — then the mystery surrounding this affair, and not this affair only, but a series of incidents, so far from being cleared up, was more impenetrable than ever!

But Fandor was obsessed by the idea of Fantômas, of Fantômas in the depths of mystery, presiding over this series of dramatic occurrences.

"Yes, Fantômas is certainly in this!" he cried. . . . But Dollon has left traces of himself here — has, as it were, put his signature, his identification mark to this crime! . . . But Dollon is not Fantômas . . . besides Dollon is dead! . . . I have proofs of it — yes, he is dead! . . . Well then? . . .

What to make of it?

Fandor could not make anything of it!

X

IDENTITY OF A NAVVY

"The Barbey-Nanteuil bank is certainly gorgeous!" thought Jérôme Fandor as he traversed the hall on the ground floor, where the massive mahogany furniture, the thick carpets, the deep, comfortable chairs, the sober elegance of the window curtains breathed an atmosphere of luxury and good taste. "And decidedly banking is the best of businesses!" added our young journalist.

An attendant advanced to meet him.

"What do you want, monsieur?"

"Will you take in my card to Monsieur Nanteuil? I should be glad to have a few minutes' talk with him."

The attendant bowed.

"On a personal matter, monsieur?"

"A personal matter? . . . Yes."

Jérôme Fandor wanted to interview the Barbey-Nanteuils on the subject of the recent occurrences, which had roused Paris opinion to the highest degree — mysterious occurrences on which no light seemed to have been thrown so far. . . . Not only were the Barbey-Nanteuils the bankers of the Baroness de Vibray, but they had been present at Thomery's ball, when the attack on Princess Sonia Danidoff had taken place. . . . Would they allow themselves to be interviewed? Fandor decided that they certainly would, for they were business men, and was he not going to give them a free advertisement?

The attendant — a stately individual — returned.

"Monsieur Nanteuil is sorry he cannot see you, he is taking the chair at an important committee meeting; but Monsieur Barbey will see you for a few minutes, that is to say, if he will do instead of Monsieur Nanteuil."

"In that case, I will see Monsieur Barbey," said Fandor, rising.

Following the attendant, Fandor traversed the whole length of the bank, and passing the half-open door of Monsieur Nanteuil's office — the name on the door told him this — he noticed that it was empty.

Monsieur Barbey received him coldly and with a solemn bow. Fandor's reply was a pleasant smile.

"I know," said he, "that your time is precious, Monsieur Barbey, so I will come straight to the object of my call. . . . You must be aware of the profound impression caused by the double crimes recently committed on the persons of Madame de Vibray and the Princess Sonia Danidoff?"

"It is true, monsieur, that I have followed, in the papers, the account of the investigations regarding them: but, in what way? . . ."

"Does it concern you?" finished Fandor. "Good heavens, monsieur, is it not a fact that the Baroness de Vibray was your client? And were you not present at Monsieur Thomery's ball?"

"That is so, monsieur; but if you are hoping that I can supply you with further details than those already published, you will be disappointed. I myself have learned a good deal about these crimes only from reading your articles, monsieur."

"Can you confirm the statement that Madame de Vibray was ruined?"

"I do not think I am betraying a professional secret if I say that Madame de Vibray had had very heavy losses quite recently."

"And Princess Sonia Danidoff?"

"I do not think she is one of our clients."

"You do not think so?"

"But, monsieur, you cannot suppose that we know all our clients? Our business is a very extensive one, and neither Nanteuil, nor I, could possibly know the names of all those who do business with us."

"You know the name of Jacques Dollon?"

"Yes. I knew young Dollon. He was introduced to me by Madame de Vibray, who asked me to give him a helping hand, and I willingly did so. I can only regret now that my confidence was so ill placed."

"Do you believe him guilty then? . . . Not really?"

"I certainly do! . . . So do all your readers, monsieur. Is that not so?"

But, whilst Monsieur Barbey was regarding Fandor with some astonishment because of his half-avowal, that he himself was not sure of Dollon's guilt, the door was flung open with violence, and Monsieur Nanteuil, out of breath, looking thoroughly upset, rushed into the room, followed by five or six men unknown to Jérôme Fandor, and showing traces of fatigue and emotion also.

"Good Heavens! What is it?" cried Monsieur Barbey, rising to meet his partner. . . .

"The matter is," cried Monsieur Nanteuil, "that an abominable robbery has just been committed. . . ."

"Where?"

"Rue du Quatre Septembre! . . ." Still panting, he began to give details. . . .

Fandor did not wait to hear more. He rushed from the Barbey-Nanteuil bank and made for the place de l'Opéra at top speed.

In consequence of the extraordinary occurrence which Monsieur Nanteuil had hastened to report to his partner, a considerable crowd had flocked to the scene of the accident; but barriers had been quickly erected, and the crowd, directed by the police, were able to circulate in orderly fashion when Fandor arrived on the scene.

The agile young journalist had made his way to the front row of the curious, and was bent on entering the stone and wood yards of the works forbidden to the public; the usual palisade no longer existed owing to the landslip.

Just as he was searching in his pocket for the precious identification card, which the police grant to the reporters connected with the big newspapers, Fandor was jostled by an individual coming out of the yards. It was a navvy all covered with mortar, white dust, and mud; he was without a hat and held his right hand pressed against his cheek; between his fingers there filtered a few drops of blood.

The glances of the man and the journalist met, and Fandor felt as though someone had struck him a blow on the heart! The navvy had given him so strange a look. Fandor thought he had read in his eyes a threat and an invitation.

Whilst our journalist hesitated, troubled by this sudden encounter, the man moved off, forcing his way through the crowd. Then Fandor caught sight of some of his colleagues, stumbling about amidst the ruins and rubble in the stone-yard. This reassured him; if he followed the navvy, and he had the strongest inclination to do so, he could telephone to some reporter friend who would supply him with the necessary details for his article on the accident. He had got some facts already: a sudden collapse of stones and mortar had buried a hand-cart, in which were large bars of gold belonging to the Barbey-Nanteuil bank. But the precious vehicle had soon been rescued, and they were taking it to the bank under escort.

Satisfied as to this, Fandor followed with his eyes this strange navvy who was going further and further away.

Fandor had an intuition — a very strong feeling — that he must follow the trail of this man and make him talk. It was of the utmost importance — something told him this was so.

The navvy was not simply going away, he had the air of a man in flight.

Fandor, who was following now and keenly observant, noticed the hesitating movements of the man — then there was an astonishing move on the navvy's part: he hailed a taxi and got in. Fandor had the good luck to find another taxi at once; jumping in, he said to the driver:

"Follow the 4227 G.H. which is in front of you: don't let it outdistance you . . . you shall have a good tip!"

The chauffeur, a young alert fellow, understood there was a chase in question, and amused at the idea of pursuing a comrade through the crowded streets of Paris, he set off. He adroitly cut through a file of carriages and caught up taxi 4227 G.H. He then proceeded to follow closely in its track.

Fandor, keen as a bloodhound on the scent, kept watch over their progress to an unknown destination.

They rolled along the avenue de l'Opéra: they cut across the rue de Rivoli. Then, when they were going at a good pace through the place du Carrousel, Fandor felt much moved by memories of past times, those days of great and wonderful adventures, when he would follow this very route to keep some exciting appointment with his good friend, Juve. How frequent those appointments used to be, when the famous detective was alive and so actively at work — the work of unearthing criminals — those pests of society! Off Fandor used to set when the longed for summons came, and would meet Juve in his little flat on the left side of the Seine. Ah, those were times, indeed!

When a lad, Fandor had been practically adopted by the famous detective. Young Jérôme Fandor had served a kind of apprenticeship with Juve, and this had brought him into close touch with the ups and downs of a number of crime dramas: he and Juve together had even been the voluntary, or involuntary, heroes of some of them! Then the tragic disappearance of Juve had occurred, when Fandor had escaped death by a kind of miracle!

After that dreadful date, our journalist had found himself alone, isolated, with not a soul to whom he cared to confide his perplexities, his anxieties, his hopes! Fandor shuddered at the thought of this.

The taxi had just crossed the bridge des Sainte Pères, had followed the quay for a few minutes, then rounding the Fine Arts School they entered the old and narrow rue Bonaparte. . . .

What was this? Of course, it could only be a coincidence . . . but still . . . rue Bonaparte — why that only brought the memory of Juve more vividly to mind! For Juve had lived in this street; and now, a few yards further on, they would pass before the modest dwelling where, for years, the detective had made his home, keeping jealously hidden, from all and sundry, this asylum, this secret retreat.

Ah, what happy hours, what jolly times, what tragic moments, too, had Fandor not passed in that little flat on the fourth floor! How they had chatted away in the detective's comfortable study! Then Fandor, full of spirit, would come and go from room to room, unable to sit still, all fire and activity; and Juve would remain in one place, calm, full of thought, sometimes sunk in a reverie, often silent for hours at a time, his eyes obstinately fixed on the ceiling, smoking methodically, mechanically even, his eternal cigarette. Oh, those good, good days gone for ever!

After the disastrous disappearance of Juve, Fandor had not gone near the rue Bonaparte for six months. It was all too painful, to find again the familiar rooms and no Juve! It was too painful.

However, one fine day, he determined to go and see what had happened to his friend's old home. . . . Alas, in Paris, the lapse of half a year suffices to alter the most familiar scene! In rue Bonaparte, the former house porters had left; their place had been taken by a stout, sulky woman who gave evasive replies to Fandor's questions. He extracted from her the information that the tenant of the fourth floor flat had died, that his furniture had been cleared out very soon after his death, and the flat had been let to an insurance inspector. . . .

Fandor was roused from this retrospect: he grew pale, his heart seemed to stop its beating: the taxi he was pursuing had slowed down — had drawn up beside the pavement — had stopped in front of Juve's old home!

Fandor saw the navvy descend from the taxi, pay his fare, and enter the house, still keeping his right hand pressed to his cheek. Without a moment's reflection, Fandor leapt from his taxi, flung a five-franc piece to his driver, and without waiting for the change he rushed into the house, whose passages and stairs were so familiar.

The navvy was swiftly mounting the stairs in front of our excited young journalist, who was close on his quarry's heels: the two men were panting as they went up that dark staircase.

At the fourth floor, Fandor was nearly overcome by emotion, for the man entered Juve's old flat as if he had a right to do so.

He was on the point of shutting the door in the face of his pursuer, but Fandor had foreseen this. He slipped through with a forceful push and caught the navvy by his jacket.

Quick as lightning the navvy turned, and the two men stood face to face. . . . The result was startling!

Speechless they stared at each other for what seemed an interminable moment; then, with a strangled cry, Fandor fell into the man's arms, and was crushed in a strong embrace. Two cries escaped from their lips at the same moment:

"Juve!"

"Fandor!"

When he came to himself again, Fandor found he was lying in one of the comfortable leather arm-chairs in Juve's study. His temples and the lobes of his ears were being bathed with some refreshing liquid: the commingled scent of ether and eau-de-Cologne was in the air.

When he opened his eyes, it was with difficulty that he could credit the sight that met them!

Juve, his dear Juve, was bending over him, gazing at him tenderly, watching his return to consciousness with some anxiety.

Fandor vainly strove to rise: he felt dazed.

"Fandor!" murmured Juve, in a voice trembling with emotion. "Fandor, my little Fandor. My lad, my own dear lad!"

Oh, yes, this was Juve, his own Juve, whom Fandor saw before him! . . . He had aged a little, this dear Juve of his — had gone slightly grey at the temples: there were some fresh lines on his forehead, at the corners of his mouth, too; but it was the Juve of old times, for all that! . . . Juve, alert, souple, robust, Juve in his full vigour, in the prime of life! Oh, a living, breathing, fatherly Juve: his respected master and most intimate friend — restored to him, after mourning the irreparable loss of him and his incomprehensible disappearance!

While Fandor slowly came to himself, Juve had lessened the disordered state of his appearance; he had taken off his workman's clothes, and also the red beard which he had worn, when he ran up against the journalist in the place de l'Opéra.

As soon as Fandor was himself again, not only did he feel intense joy, a quite wild joy, but he also knew the good of a keen curiosity. Now he would know why the detective had felt obliged to disappear, officially at any rate, from Paris life for so long a period.

Protestations of faithful attachment, or unalterable affection poured from Fandor's excited lips, intermingled with questions: he wanted to know everything at once.

Juve smiled in silence, and gazed most affectionately at his dear lad.

At last he said:

"I am not going to ask you for your news, Fandor, for I have seen you repeatedly, and I know you are quite all right. . . . Why, I do believe you have put on flesh a little!"

Juve was smiling that enigmatic smile of his.

Fandor grew impatient, on fire with curiosity. Ah, this was indeed the Juve of bygone days, imperturbable, ironical, rather exasperating also!

However, Juve took pity on Fandor, who was still under the influence of the shock he had received.

"Well, now, dear lad, did you recognise me, a while ago?"

Fandor pulled himself together.

"To tell you the truth, Juve, I did not . . . but, when our glances met, I had an intuition, a kind of interior revelation of what I had to do, and without any beating about the bush — I knew I had to follow you, follow you wherever you went."

Juve nodded his approval.

"Very good, dear fellow; your reply gives me infinite pleasure, and on two counts: in the first place, I perceive that your remarkable instinct for getting on to the right scent, strengthened by my teaching, has improved immensely since we parted; and, in the second place, I am delighted to know that I made my head and face so unrecognisable that even my old familiar friend, Fandor, did not know me when we were brought face to face!"

"Why this disguise, Juve?" demanded Fandor, his countenance alight with curiosity. "How was it I came across you at the very spot where the Barbey-Nanteuil load of gold had been submerged, for the moment, under bricks and mortar? And, with regard to that, Juve, how comes it . . ."

Juve cut Fandor short.

"Gently! Fandor! Gently! You are putting the cart before the horse, old fellow; and if we continue to talk by fits and starts, never shall we come to the end of all we have to say to each other, and must say. Are you aware, Fandor, that we have been drawn into a succession of incomprehensible occurrences — a mysterious network of them? . . . But I have good hopes that now we shall be able to work together again; and I like to think that if we follow the different trails we have each started on, we shall end up by . . ."

It was Fandor's turn to interrupt:

"Hang it all, Juve! I partly understand you, of course; but there's a lot I don't know yet. . . . What are you after, dear Juve? Are you, as I am, on the track of Jacques Dollon?"

There was a pause, then Juve said:

"I shall reserve the details for our leisure. What matters now is, that I should make clear to you the principal lines my existence has followed during the past three years or so. A few minutes will suffice to put you in possession of the main facts. Now, listen."

The narrative went back to the time when Juve, aided by Fandor, was close on the heels of their mortal enemy, the mysterious and elusive Fantômas. The detective and the journalist had succeeded in cooping up the formidable bandit in a house at Neuilly, belonging to a great English lady, known under the name of Lady Beltham. This Englishwoman was the mistress and accomplice of the notorious Fantômas. But at the precise moment when Juve was about to arrest him, a frightful explosion occurred, and the building, blown up by dynamite, collapsed in ruins, burying the two friends and some fifteen policemen and detectives.

9   See *The Exploits of Juve*.

Rescuers were on the spot in a very short time, and uninterrupt-edly, for forty-eight hours, they searched among the ruins for the vic-tims of the disaster, dead or alive.

By a miraculous piece of good fortune, Fandor had been but slightly hurt, and at the end of a few days he was as well as ever. But the poor fellow had lost his best friend — Juve!

The search for Juve had been a useless one. Several corpses could not be identified owing to the injuries they had sustained; and, as it seemed incredible that the detective could have escaped, they had concluded that one of the unrecognisable bodies must be his.

Juve, however, was not one of the dead!

Saved in as miraculous a fashion as Fandor had been, less injured even, a few seconds after the frightful crash, he had been able to rise and make his escape. The distracted detective had raced away from the scene of disaster in search of Fandor, and also in pursuit of Fantômas, for he believed that both had made their escape.

After wandering about for some hours, he had returned to mingle with the crowd of rescuers, and had learned that Fandor had been found, and was not dangerously hurt: on the other hand, there were those present who declared that he, Juve, was killed!

This unexpected announcement gave him an idea: for an indefi-nite period he would accept this version! For, more than ever set upon catching his enemy, the detective said to himself, that if Fantômas could feel certain that Juve no longer existed, the pretended dead would have a far better chance of catching the living bandit!

Thereupon, Juve had submitted his project to his chief, Mon-sieur Havard; and the head of the police secret service had consented to ignore Juve's presence among the living.

Juve knew that Lady Beltham had escaped to England.

Supposing that Fantômas would rejoin her without delay, the detective left Paris, crossed the Channel. He then went to America. For scarcely had he arrived in London when he learned that the ban-dits had gone off to the United States.

Juve travelled from place to place for some months. It was a vain quest: Fantômas had vanished, leaving not a trace behind, and the disgusted detective, now convinced that he had followed a false trail, returned to France.

He determined to set himself to study anew the prison world; he was all the more interested in it because, before his supposed death, Juve had effected the arrest of several members of a band of which Fantômas was the leader. Among these were the Cooper, the Beard, and old Mother Toulouche.

Then, at the prison connected with the asylum, Juve had come across a warder, who, some years previous to this, had been the warder in charge of a man condemned to death, one Gurn, who had not been guillotined because a substituted person had been executed in his stead. Juve was convinced that the condemned criminal was none other than Fantômas. Juve strongly suspected that this warder, Nibet by name, knew a great deal about this old affair. But soon Nibet passed to the Dépôt. The accomplices of Fantômas, having served the time of their respective sentences, some at Melun, others at Clermont, all this nice collection of criminals would meet once more on the pavements of Paris. Juve, therefore, had imperious reasons for mingling with this charming crowd! . . .

Fandor had followed Juve's rapid narrative with the most intense interest.

"And then, Juve, what then?" insisted Fandor.

"And then," said the detective, "to make an end of it — for we must not be forever going over the past adventures — let me tell you, that after many and diverse happenings, a band of smugglers and false coiners, among whom are to be found individuals already known to you, notably the Beard, the Cooper, and also that wretch of a Mother Toulouche, one fine day made the acquaintance of a poor sort of creature, simple-minded, and anything but sharp-witted — an individual who goes by the name of Cranajour!"

"Cranajour?" queried Fandor, "I don't in the least understand."

"Yes, Cranajour," repeated Juve. "Here is how it came about. You remember when Fantômas got an unfortunate actor named Valgrand executed in his stead? Well, our mysterious Fantômas, the better to mislead and bamboozle those who might suspect this atrocious jugglery, our bandit of genius — for Fantômas has genius — took the personality of Valgrand for several hours, and dared to go to the theatre where the real Valgrand was playing. However, as Fantômas was not capable of playing the part to a finish, he conceived the idea of making those about Valgrand believe that he had been suddenly afflicted with loss of memory, and from that moment could not remember anything whatever: Fantômas, the false Valgrand, could thus pass for the true Valgrand, and be taken as such by the true Valgrand's intimates! . . . I humbly confess, Fandor, that I copied Fantômas by creating Cranajour. . . ."

Juve, then rapidly explained to the journalist the origin of this nickname, and also told him how the bandits treated him as one of themselves; how, as soon as they were convinced that he could not remember anything he had seen or heard for two hours together, they talked freely before him of their plans and doings!

The detective went on:

"I must add, my dear Fandor, that no very sensational revelations have come to me, so far, through my intimacy with this set of criminals. It seemed to me I was in the midst of common thieves, who smuggled and circulated false coin; but one thing did puzzle me — puzzles me still: these folk succeed in selling a considerable number of pounds sterling, false coin, of course, and that without my being able to discover, so far, where they sell them — who makes their market. They also sell lace smuggled from Belgium; that, however, interests me but little, and I was prepared to leave to the lower ranks of the service the duty of clearing Paris of this common-place brood of criminals; already, indeed, the regular police had arrested one of the smugglers, the Cooper, and two of his subordinate confederates; I was about to turn my back on this crew in order to give all my attention to a new trail which might put me on the track of Fantômas once more, when the Dollon affair blazed forth; and then suddenly, I meet again my Fandor, braver than ever, more perspicacious also, adroitly taking the affair in hand, bravely thrusting himself into the breach!

"Is there any connection between the Dollon affair and my band of smugglers?"

"You will appreciate the importance of this question and the reply to it in a minute, my Fandor, when you learn that the Dépôt warder, Nibet, is one of the most valuable confederates of the coiners, of Mother Toulouche, of that hooligan, the Beard. . . ."

"Is it possible!" cried Fandor. "Ah, Juve, all this is so strange that I believe you are really on Fantômas' track, once more!"

Juve shook his head; then he continued:

"I have still a great deal to tell you, but I must pause a moment to say, that I ought to apologise to you for a fairly brutal act I committed on your behalf — in your best interests, as you will see. . . ."

And to Fandor, who opened his eyes in astonishment, the detective related, in humorous fashion, the history of the famous kick he had administered — a kick wherewith Juve had removed his friend from the immediate and certain danger of assassination, at the hand and by the knife of Nibet.

Fandor could not get over it! He grasped Juve's hands and pressed them warmly.

"My friend! My good friend!" murmured he, moved almost to tears. "If I had had the least suspicion! . . ."

Juve interrupted him.

"There are many more things, Fandor, you never suspected, things you ought to know. . . . And what is more, you seem to me to be neglecting your work badly at this very moment, Mr. Reporter! It is already one o'clock in the afternoon; and if they are counting on you to supply them with information about this affair of the place de l'Opéra. . . ."

Fandor leapt to his feet.

"It's true!" he cried. "I had quite forgotten it! . . . But it is of no importance by the side of . . ."

Juve interrupted.

"*The affair is serious, Fandor, attention!* . . . Do you remember? It is the formula I employed on two or three occasions, when warning you, after the assassination of Jacques Dollon, after the attack on Sonia Danidoff at Thomery's house. . . ."

"What! It was you, Juve!" cried Fandor.

"Yes, it was . . . but let us pass on! Time presses. I am going to disappear anew; but you now know where to find me, in future, and under what form, should occasion require it. Cranajour I am; Cranajour I remain — for the time being, at any rate. As to you, Fandor, be off with you at once . . . and go and hatch out that article of yours!"

Our journalist rose mechanically; but Juve, thinking better of it, caught him by the arm, drew him back and pointed out the writing-table.

"Come to think of it, you know nothing about the affair, and I do: there are things which should be said, above all things, to be hinted at . . . do you wish me to give you information? . . . Sit yourself there, my lad: I am going to dictate your article to you!"

Our journalist, understanding the gravity of the situation, and well knowing that if Juve took this course, he had important reasons for so doing, did not say one word. He simply brought out his fountain pen, screwed it ready for action, and, with his hand resting on a pile of white paper, he waited.

Juve dictated.

"First of all, put this as your title:

An Audacious Theft

"That does not tell the reader anything, but it awakens his curiosity. . . . Let us continue!

"Write."

XI

AN AUDACIOUS THEFT

Two hours after Juve had dictated his article to Fandor, our journalist was reading it, in proof, in the offices of *La Capitale*. His article ran thus:

"By a fortunate coincidence we found ourselves, this very morning, in the directorial office of the Barbey-Nanteuil bank, chatting with Monsieur Barbey himself, when Monsieur Nanteuil arrived, breathless, and announced to his partner that a sensational robbery had just been committed in the rue du Quatre Septembre, a robbery involving a sum of twenty millions representing a clearance recently effected by the Federated Republic.

"It seems that at ten o'clock this morning, Monsieur Nanteuil accompanied the little hand-cart used for transferring the bullion and paper money to the station, from whence it was to be despatched. According to custom, six of the bank clerks and three plain clothes men went with Monsieur Nanteuil. But, at the very moment when the hand-cart passed out of the place de l'Opéra and turned the corner of the rue du Quatre Septembre, that is to say, at the precise moment when it was passing the palisade, surrounding the works on the Auteuil-Opéra Metropolitan line, a formidable explosion was heard, and the hand-cart, as well as the men who were drawing it, and escorting it, including Monsieur Nanteuil himself, disappeared in a deep excavation caused by the explosion, whilst a water pipe which had burst at the same moment, poured out torrents of water, flooding the surrounding pavement and roadway.

"It was then about eleven o'clock in the morning, and the rue du Quatre Septembre presented a very animated appearance. At the noise of the explosion, the passers-by were glued to the spot, dazed, stupefied. Then exclamations broke out on all sides.

"'An accident?'

"'A bomb?'

"The explosion had created a veritable chasm. The first moment of stupefaction past, policeman 326 quickly organised the rescuers, and sent notice to the nearest police station. Some minutes later, the firemen arrived on the scene armed with ladders and ropes. Meanwhile, the crowd of curious onlookers was increasing with amazing rapidity.

"Monsieur Nanteuil was the first to be drawn up from the pit; by a miracle he had escaped injury; unfortunately, the clerks of the Barbey-Nanteuil bank had not got off so well; bruises, contusions, cases of severe shock, more or less serious, had to be attended to by neighbouring chemists.

"Monsieur Nanteuil, reassured as to the fate of his clerks, turned his attention to the hand-cart and its millions of bullion, and the police in charge were given to understand that it must be drawn up without delay.

"Into the pit the firemen once more descended; at first they were surprised not to find the hand-cart and its millions! No doubt, it had been covered by the mass of fallen bricks and mortar! But fireman Le Goffic, who had advanced some yards along the railway line, caught sight of it. The cart was lying upside down; but, except for a few scratches, it was found to be unbroken.

"It was immediately hauled up to the roadway. Monsieur Nanteuil at once ascertained that the seals were intact. He then gave orders that it was to be taken back to the Barbey-Nanteuil bank without delay. As the train, which was to have borne away the bullion, had left the station hours ago, Monsieur Nanteuil decided to break the seals, and place the bullion in one of the bank's safes for the night.

"Monsieur Nanteuil's stupefaction can be imagined when, having unsealed and opened the hand-cart, he realised that the sacks of gold had been replaced by sacks of lead!

"It was at this moment that Monsieur Barbey was informed of the fact by his half-frantic partner. We were witnesses of this dramatic scene.

"Every second was of value: instant action was the thing! Police headquarters was warned at once; and, but a few minutes had elapsed, when Monsieur Havard arrived in a taxicab to take charge of the investigations.

"Thanks to the courtesy of Monsieur Havard, we were allowed to accompany him to the stone-yards of the Metropolitan: the police were convinced that it was hereabouts that the robbery had been accomplished. We reached the spot about an hour after the explosion. The first investigations produced no result; but Monsieur Havard pursued his solitary search up one of the sidings, and had his reward. His exclamation was heard, and we hastened to the spot. . . . He had just found a second hand-cart, in all points similar to that he had recently examined in the courtyard of the Barbey-Nanteuil bank!

"Monsieur Havard at once realised that he had before his eyes the original hand-cart, and that the hand-cart he had seen in the bank courtyard was a clever substitute! It need scarcely be said that there is no trace of the stolen millions to be found in the original hand-cart, cast away in a siding of the Metropolitan. . . .

"Our readers know something of the appearance presented by these lines, in course of construction on the Metropolitan railway. We have repeatedly published in La Capitale details regarding the way in which the engineers and workmen supervise and execute the cutting of the passageway on the underground. The operations in the place de l'Opéra are on an enormous scale, for there is a junction here, and the soil is more undermined than elsewhere on the railway.

"At the precise spot where the explosion occurred, there are four galleries in course of construction: one is the future Auteuil-Opéra line, the others either lead to existing lines, or are galleries made for the convenience of the workmen. Hand-cart number one, that is to say, the substituted hand-cart filled with sacks of lead, was found in the passageway of the Auteuil-Opéra line, which is perfectly accessible, and would naturally be visited by the rescuers.

"The original hand-cart was hidden away in one of the lateral galleries, which are small and narrow, and not likely to be visited and examined, except as a last resource. It is, therefore, clear that the affair has been carefully arranged: a premeditated robbery. The presence of the two hand-carts would establish this — the hand-carts used by the bank for the transport of bullion and other forms of money are of a particular make — unique, in fact. Their respective positions show that the robbers had carefully prepared their drama, and it was skilfully arranged.

"Thanks to Monsieur Havard's kindness, we were permitted to approach the original hand-cart. It was in a lamentable condition: the body of it was nearly smashed to pieces! Of course, no traces of the seals were to be found. The only remark we see fit to make in this connection is, that Monsieur Nanteuil, his clerks, and those who witnessed the accident, must have been greatly excited and upset, otherwise they would naturally have been much astonished at finding the substituted hand-cart practically uninjured after an accident of so crushing a nature.

"We have carefully examined the soil round the original handcart, in the hope of finding some clear footprints of the thieves, or their accomplices; but it was impossible to draw any conclusion from this examination — the footmarks are intermingled, superimposed, undistinguishable. It must be admitted the soil of the Metropolitan, hereabouts, has been very much trampled over and beaten down so that it is difficult to believe that researches, with the object of discovering the robbers' footmarks, are likely to have any clear result.

"At the moment these lines have been written, the investigation in the Metropolitan passageways still continues, and will, in all probability, be continued late into the night. So far, the police admit that results are meagre. Monsieur Havard considers it certain that the deed is a premeditated one, carefully prepared, and that, consequently, the explosion which caused the catastrophe was a deliberate act of violence. On the other hand, Monsieur Nanteuil declares that outside the parties interested, that is to say, the Barbey-Nanteuil bank and the Comptoir d'Escomptes, who were to receive the bullion, not a soul could know of the transfer on that particular morning. But the staffs of the bank and of the Comptoir National d'Escomptes are absolutely trustworthy: their honour has never been questioned.

"It is evident that such a daring and desperate deed, carried through so successfully in the galleries of the Metropolitan, in the sight of all Paris, at eleven o'clock in the morning, could only be the work of a band of criminals, numerous and perfectly organised.

"'Are we returning to the days of — Fantômas?'

"Let us add, that owing to the number of individuals probably involved, and the daring nature of the crime, Monsieur Havard considers that it will be extremely difficult for the guilty persons to escape from the police."

Jérôme Fandor had just finished correcting this sensational article, when slips from the Havas Agency arrived at *La Capitale*.

Our journalist cast his eyes over them, thinking he might find some piece of news which had come to hand at the last minute. As he read he grew pale. He struck his writing-table a violent blow with his fist.

"For all that, I am not mad!" he cried.

And, holding his head between his hands, spelling out each word, he reread the following telegram from the Havas Agency:

Affair of the rue du Quatre Septembre

"At the last moment of going to press, a bloody imprint has been discovered on hand-cart number 2. Monsieur Bertillon immediately identified this imprint: it was made by the hand of Jacques Dollon, the criminal who is already wanted by the police for the murder of the Baroness de Vibray, and the robbery committed on the Princess Sonia Danidoff."

"But I am not mad!" cried Fandor, when he had read these lines. "I declare I am not mad! By all that's holy, Jacques Dollon is dead! . . . Fifty persons have seen him dead! But, for all that, Bertillon cannot be mistaken!"

After a minute or two, Fandor took up his pen again, and added a note to his article, entitled: —

Sensational development. The police say: "It is the late Jacques Dollon who has stolen the millions!"

This note showed clearly that Jérôme Fandor did not believe that Jacques Dollon could possibly be involved in this affair, or in either of the other crimes in connection with which his name had been mentioned.

XII

INVESTIGATIONS

A man jumped quickly out of the Auteuil-Madeleine tram.

It would have been difficult to guess his age, or see his face. He wore a large soft hat — a Brazilian sombrero — whose edges he had turned down. The collar of his overcoat was turned up, so that the lower part of his face was so far buried in it that his features were almost hidden. Then, during the entire journey, seated at the end of the tramcar he had kept his back turned on the other passenger: he seemed to be absorbed in watching the movements of the driver. At the end of the rue Mozart, where the rues La Fontaine, Poussin, des Perchamps meet, he had quitted the tram with real satisfaction.

Then, in the silence of the evening, the clock of Auteuil church had slowly struck eight silvery strokes.

The listening man murmured:

"Oh, there's no hurry after all. I've a two good hours' wait in front of me!"

Leaving the frequented ways, he plunged into the little by-streets, newly made and not yet named, which join the end of the rue Mozart with the boulevard Montmorency. He walked fast, at the same time taking his bearings.

"Rue Raffet? . . . If I don't deceive myself, it lies in this direction!"

He reached the hilly and lonely road bearing that name, which, on both sides of its entire length, is bordered by attractive private residences.

Swiftly, silently, stealthily, this individual approached one of these houses. He glanced through the garden railing, scrutinising the windows which were lighted up.

"Good! Good! Decidedly good!" he said, in a low tone of satisfaction. . . . "But there's two hours to wait . . . they are still in the dining-room, if I am to go by the lighted windows."

The watcher now inspected the rue Raffet. The house which interested him so much, was situated just where the rue du Docteur Blanche opens into the street at right angles. Auteuil is certainly not a frequented part, but, as a rule, the rue Raffet is generally more lonely than any of the streets in Auteuil: no carriages, no pedestrians.

From an early hour in the evening, that hilly road was, more often than not, quite deserted, so was the rue du Docteur Blanche, still surrounded by waste land, and more especially at the rue Raffet end.

A glance or two sufficed to show the man the lie of the land. He noted the feeble glimmer of the street lamps; he made certain that not one of the neighbouring houses could perceive his actions, mark his movements. He repeated in a theatrical tone of voice with a note of amusement in it.

"Not a soul! Not a solitary soul! Well, it is no joke to wait here; but, after all, it is a quiet spot, and I can count on not being disturbed in the job I have in hand to-night. . . ."

This individual traversed the rue Raffet, gained the rue du Docteur Blanche, and, wrapping himself up in his voluminous black cloak, ensconced himself in a break in the palisades bordering the pavement. He stood there motionless; anyone might have passed within a few yards of him without suspecting his presence, so still was he, so imperceptibly did his dark figure blend with the blackness of the night.

He started slightly. The church clock struck nine, its notes sounding silvery clear through the tranquil night . . . in the distance some convent clock chimed an evening prayer, then a deeper silence fell on the darkness of night. . . .

Suddenly, the front door of the house, which the stranger had watched with scrutinising intentness, was thrown wide open, showing a large, luminous square in the darkness. Two women were speaking.

"Are you going out, my darling?" asked the elder.

"Don't be anxious, madame," replied a girlish voice. "There is no need to wait for me. I am only going to the post. . . ."

"Why not give Jules your letter?"

"No, I prefer to post it myself."

"You would not like someone to go with you? There are not many people about at this hour. . . ."

The same fresh, young voice replied:

"Oh, I am not frightened . . . besides it's only rue Raffet which is deserted; as soon as I reach rue Mozart there will be nothing more to fear!"

The luminous square, drawn on the obscurity of the garden, disappeared.

The mysterious stranger, who had not lost a word of this conversation, heard the door of the vestibule close, then the gravel of the garden crunch under the feet of the girl coming down the path. Very soon the gate of the garden grated on its badly oiled hinges, and then the elegant outline of a young girl was visible on the badly lighted pavement. She was walking fast. . . .

The stranger remained stationary until the girl had gone some way; then pressing against the wall, concealing his movements with practised ability, he followed her at a discreet distance. . . .

"There can be no doubt about it," he murmured. "I recognised her voice directly! . . . It's the very deuce! . . . It's going to complicate matters! . . . A lover's meeting? Not likely! . . . She must be going to the post, as she said. . . . She will return in about a quarter of an hour, and then . . . then! . . ."

The girl was far from suspecting that she was being followed. She had walked down rue Mozart, turned into rue Poussin, posted her letter, and then walked quietly back to the house.

The stranger had not followed her into the more frequented streets: he awaited her return in a dark and deserted side street. When she came into view again, he sighed a sigh of great satisfaction.

"Ah, there is the dear child! . . . That's all right. . . . Now we shall have some fun! . . . or, rather, I shall!"

Anyone seeing his face, whilst making these significant exclamations, would have been frightened by his sneering chuckle, his hideous grin.

A few minutes later, the girl re-entered the little garden of the house in the rue Raffet. A stout woman opened to her ring.

"Ah, there you are, darling." There was relief in her tone.

"Yes, here I am, safe and sound, madame!"

"Nothing unpleasant — no one molested you, Elizabeth?"

Elizabeth Dollon, for she it was, shook her head and smiled a smile both sad and sweet.

"Ah, no, madame! . . . I was sure you would be waiting for me — I am so sorry!"

"No, not at all! . . . Tell me, Elizabeth. . . . Jules has told me that you would not be going out to-morrow. The poor fellow is so stupid that I ask myself if he has not made a mistake?"

"No," said Elizabeth. "It is quite true. . . . I do not think I shall go out, either in the morning or the afternoon."

"You expect a caller?"

"It is possible someone may come to see me. . . . If by any chance I have to go out for a few minutes, to get something or other, I must warn Jules: he must make the visitor wait: I shall not go far in case . . ."

"All right! That's settled then, darling. Now, good night, I am going to my room."

"Good evening, madame, and good night!"

Leaving stout and kindly Madame Bourrat, owner of this private boarding-house where Elizabeth Dollon had found a refuge, the poor girl, still with a smile on her pale lips, made her way upstairs, entered her bedroom, and carefully locked the door. She lit the lamp. Her face now wore a tragic look: its expression was wild and desperate. . . .

"If only he would come!" she sighed. . . . "Ah, I am afraid! I am afraid! . . . I am terribly afraid!"

Elizabeth stood motionless — a frozen image of fear — all but her eyes: they were casting terrified glances about her. . . .

And no wonder! Elizabeth was neatness personified, and her room was kept with exquisite care — but now, everything was in the greatest disorder. . . . The drawers of her chest of drawers were piled one on top of the other in a corner of the room; their contents were thrown down in heaps a little way off; books had been cast pell-mell on a sofa; a great wicker trunk, wherein Elizabeth had packed numerous papers belonging to her brother, was overturned on the floor, the lid open.

Its contents were scattered near — a confused mass of documents and crumpled papers.

Elizabeth stared about her for a long minute, and again she cried:

"Oh, if only he would come! What is the meaning of all this? . . ."

She regained her self-control. Her usual expression of serene gravity returned.

"To go to sleep," she murmured. "That is the best thing — tomorrow will come more quickly so — and, oh, I am so sleepy, so very, very tired!"

Soon Elizabeth blew out her lamp — darkness reigned in her room.

It was about half-past ten o'clock, and the light in Elizabeth Dollon's room had been extinguished for some little while, when the front door of the little house was opened again. . . .

Noiselessly, with infinite precautions, with searching and suspicious glances, taking care to keep off the gravel of the paths, tiptoeing on the grass edging the flower beds, where his steps made no sound, a man left the house and went towards the garden gate.

He quickly reached it; and there he commenced to whistle a soft, slow, monotonous, and continuous whistle.

Second succeeded second; then another whistle, identical in rhythm, replied: soon a voice asked:

"It's you, Jules?"

"It is I, master!"

The man whom Jules named "master," was the stranger, who, for two weary hours, had kept strict watch over the goings and comings of the house. . . .

"All well, Jules?"

"All well, master!"

"And nothing new? . . ."

"I don't know about that, master: she has written a letter. . . ."

"To whom? . . ."

"I couldn't say. . . . I could not see the address, master. . . ."

"You red-headed idiot!"

The servant protested.

"No, it was not my fault! . . . She did not write in the drawing-room, but in her own room. . . . I couldn't get a squint at her paper. . . ."

"Did she not say anything?"

"Nothing."

"Did she look upset?"

"A little."

"No one suspects anything?"

"I hope not, master! . . . Gods and little fishes, if anyone suspected!"

The visitor's voice grew harsh, imperious.

"Enough," said he. "We have no time to lose!"

"How? No time. . . ."

"That's it! We must set to work. . . ."

"Work? . . . Now? . . . This very night? . . . Oh, master, surely not!"

"Don't I? Do you imagine that I arranged a meeting only for the pleasure of talking to you? . . . Come on, now! . . . March!"

"What are we to do?"

A moment's silence.

"I cannot see the house very well, because of the branches: listen — look! . . . Isn't there a light? . . . Someone still up?"

"No. They've all gone to bed."

"Good. And she?"

"She, too."

"You did what I told you?"

"Yes, master."

"You were able to pour out the narcotic?"

"Yes, master."

"And then?"

"What do you mean by then?"

"Have you carried out all my orders . . . the last?"

"Yes, it is all right! . . . I went into her room and blew out the lamp."

"Good! Now for it! . . ."

A slight brushing sound, along the low stone wall of the garden, was barely perceptible to a listening ear. The wall was topped by railings, and the gate had sheets of iron fastened to it. In a twinkling, the stranger leaped down beside Jules.

"It's child's play to vault that gate," he said.

By the uncertain light of the stars, Jules could see the individual who had just joined him. His appearance was fantastic, and the wretched Jules started and trembled in every limb. The stranger, who had thus invaded Madame Bourrat's domain, who a short while before had been wearing a long cloak and immense sombrero, wore them no longer. Probably he had rid himself of them by casting them among the bramble bushes on the waste ground around rue Docteur Blanche. . . . Now he was clad in a long black knitted garment moulded tightly to his figure, a sinister garment, by means of which the wearer can blend with the darkness so as to be almost indistinguishable. His face was entirely concealed by a long black hood, a movable mask, which prevented his features being seen: through two slits gleamed two eyeballs: they might have burned a way through like glowing coals.

"Master! . . . Master!" murmured Jules. "What are you going to do now?"

This spectral figure replied in a low tone:

"Fool! . . . go on in front — or no — better follow me! And not a sound — it's as much as your skin is worth! . . . Take care — great care!"

The two men advanced in silence. But, while Jules seemed to take exaggerated precautions to prevent being heard, his companion seemed naturally shod with silence.

He advanced noiselessly, almost invisible in his black garment.

The two accomplices were soon at the front-door steps of the house.

"Open," commanded the master.

Jules slipped a key into the lock: noiselessly the door turned on its hinges.

"Listen," whispered the cloaked man. "Half-way up the stairs, you must stop: I do not wish you to go right up. . . ."

"But . . ."

"Do as I say! You must keep watch. . . . If, by chance, you should hear a noise, if I were to be taken by surprise, you must go downstairs, making a great noise and shouting at the top of your voice: 'Stop him! . . . Stop him! . . .' Thus, in the first moment of confusion, everyone will rush after you, and that will give me time to choose my way of escape."

Jules, whatever his fears, did not dare to question his instructions.

"Very good, master," he breathed. "I'll do as you say."

"I should think you would," scoffed his master, almost inaudibly.

Leaving his accomplice on the stairs, the masked man went forward. He seemed to know the ins and outs of the house, for he turned into the corridor and, without a moment's hesitation, walked towards the door of Elizabeth Dollon's room. He put his ear against it.

"She sleeps," he murmured.

He had inserted a key in the lock: there was an obstacle to its easy entrance.

"Confound it! The girl has left her own key in the lock!" he said softly. . . . "What the deuce am I to do now? What did Jules do when he got in and put out the lamp? . . . Why, of course, he took off the screw that fixes the staple — a simple push will suffice." With a push of his shoulder the door yielded. The stranger entered and carefully closed the door. He walked to the window and drew the curtains, muttering:

"That fool should have thought of this just now."

Taking a small electric torch from his pocket he turned on the light. Calmly, collectedly, he approached a couch at one side of the room. . . . On it lay Elizabeth Dollon in a deep sleep. She looked white as death.

"An excellent narcotic," he muttered, bending over the unconscious girl. "When one thinks that she took it at dinner, then went out, and that then it produced its effect! . . ."

Moving away from Elizabeth, he crossed the room to where the contents of the overturned trunk lay.

"Damnable papers!" he growled low. "To think! . . . It is too late now to continue the search. . . . Bah! By shutting the mouth of an informant . . . that's the way to settle it . . . the best way too! . . . Now for it! . . ."

Without apparent effort, the man in the hooded mask seized Elizabeth Dollon in his muscular arms.

"Come, mademoiselle," he said in a jeering tone. "Come to bye-bye! Sleep better than on this sofa! You will sleep a longer sleep, that's certain!" An evil smile punctuated these sinister remarks.

He laid the poor girl's body on the floor in the middle of the room; then, approaching a little gas stove, he detached the india-rubber tube and slipped the end of it between his victim's teeth.

He turned the gas tap. . . .

"Perfect!" he said, as he straightened himself.

"To-morrow morning, early, at eight o'clock, or at nine, the excellent Madame Bourrat will open the meter. The narcotic this child has taken will prevent her from waking, so that, without suffering, without cries, quite gently — pfuit! . . . sweet Elizabeth will pass from life to death! . . . But it will not do to linger here . . . let us find Jules and give him the necessary instructions!"

The stranger went out into the corridor closing the door. The thing had been well managed; the screws keeping the bolt case in position were put back in their holes — the key remained inside — no one would suspect that only a slight push was necessary to get into the room.

With a chuckle, the stranger bent down and pushed a tassel under the door.

The servant must not discover the trick when she is sweeping the passage: now with this wedge, the door cannot be opened without a violent push.

With a last glance up and down the passage, illuminated for a moment by his electric torch, the stranger made sure that there was no one about to see him; then, with silent tread, he began to go downstairs. . . .

Half-way down, his accomplice awaited him.

"Well, master?" questioned Jules in a low, trembling voice.

In a calm, quiet voice, the man in the hood mask replied:

"It is done — is successful. . . . I have wedged the door to. You will be careful when you are sweeping to-morrow."

Jules lowered his head.

"Yes . . . yes. . . . Have you? . . ."

The stranger put his hand on the servant's shoulder.

"Listen," whispered the stranger, "I do not repeat my orders twenty times over, . . . have I not already told you that I do not allow myself to be questioned? . . . try to remember that! . . . You wish to know whether I have killed her? . . . Well, I will tell you this: I have not killed her. But I have so managed things that she will kill herself! . . . A suicide, you understand. . . . One piece of advice: to-morrow, keep anyone from going to her room as long as you can . . . if Madame Bourrat, or anyone else asks for her, you must say that you saw her leave the house — that she has gone out. . . ."

"But," protested Jules, "it is impossible, what you tell me to say, master! It just happens that she is expecting visitors to-morrow! . . . She told me that, on this account, she meant to stay indoors all day!"

The man with the hood mask ground his teeth.

"You idiot! What does that matter? . . . You are to say: Mademoiselle Elizabeth has just gone out, but she told me that she was not going far, and that she would return in about twenty minutes. . . . If anyone should ask for her again, you are to answer that she has not come in yet! . . ."

"But . . . master . . . when they find out what's happened really? . . ."

"Ho! When it is discovered, it will seem quite natural that a person who means to commit suicide — for she will have committed suicide, you understand — should have taken precautions not to be disturbed . . . you grasp this?"

"Yes, master . . . yes! . . ."

They had returned to the garden: the man in the hooded mask

was preparing to get over the gate. . . .

"Farewell! Be faithful! Be intelligent! . . . You know what you have to gain? . . . You also know what risks you run? . . . Eh! . . . Now go!"

"You will return to-morrow, master?"

The man with the hooded mask looked his accomplice up and down.

"I shall return when it pleases me to do so."

Then, with marvellous agility, without making a spring for it, with a quite extraordinary muscular flexibility and power, the stranger leaped on to the little wall, cleared the gate, and disappeared into the night. . . .

Jules, with bent head, much moved, terribly anxious, slowly walked back to the house. . . .

XIII

RUE RAFFET

Maray, second reporter of *La Capitale*, shook hands with Fandor.

"Are you in a good humour, dear boy?"

"So — so. . . ."

"Ah! Well, here is something which will cheer you up, I'm sure! . . . Here's a letter from a lady for you. . . . I found it in my pigeon-hole by mistake!"

Fandor smiled.

"From a lady? . . . You must be mistaken! . . . How do you know it is?"

"By the handwriting, the paper, and so on — I'm not mistaken — am I ever? . . ." Laughing, Maray threw down on Fandor's table a small envelope with a deep black border.

"Yes, it is a letter from a woman," said Fandor, as he picked it up: "from whom? . . . Ah, . . . why yes! . . ."

With a hasty finger, he tore open the envelope whilst his colleague withdrew making a joking remark.

"Dear boy, I leave you to this tender missive: I should be annoyed with myself were I to interrupt your reflections!"

Fandor's friend would have been surprised, if he could have seen the gloomy expression which the perusal of this so-called love-letter produced. Jérôme had turned to the signature — *Elizabeth Dollon.*

"What does she want with me?" he asked himself. "After the extraordinary affair of rue du Quatre Septembre, one must suppose that she has arrived at some conclusion regarding the possible guilt of her brother . . . so long as she does not let her imagination run away with her, and, like the police, fancy that Jacques Dollon is still in the land of the living? The position the poor thing is in is a very cruel one!"

Fandor had met Jacques Dollon's young sister repeatedly; and, every time, he had been more and more troubled by the poor girl's touching grief, as well as by her pathetic beauty, which had made a great impression on him. . . . He began to read her letter.

"Dear Sir,
    You have been so good to me in all my troubles, you have shown me such true sympathy, that I do not hesitate to ask your help once more.
    Such an extraordinary thing has happened to me which I cannot account for at all, which, nevertheless, makes me think, more than ever, that my poor brother is living, innocent,

and kept prisoner, perhaps by those who compel him to accept the responsibility for all those horrible crimes you know about.

To-day, whilst I was in Paris on business, some people, of whom I know nothing, I need hardly say, whom not a soul in the private boarding-house where I am saw, these persons entered my room!

I found all my belongings turned upside down; my papers scattered over the floor, every drawer and trunk and box ransacked from top to bottom!

You can guess how frightened I was. . . .

I do not think they had come to do me any personal harm, not even to rob me, for I had left my modest jewellery on the mantelpiece and found them still there: those who entered my room did not covet valuables.

Then, why did they come?

You are perhaps going to say that my imagination is playing me tricks! . . . Nevertheless, I assure you that I try to keep calm, but I cannot keep control of myself, and I am terribly afraid!

I have just said that nothing was stolen from me; I think, however, it right to mention one strange coincidence.

I was convinced that I had left, in a little red pocket-book, the list I spoke to you of, which had been retrieved at my brother's house on the day of Madame de Vibray's death. It was, as I have told you, written in green ink by a person whose handwriting I do not know. I can hardly tell why, but amidst all the disorders in my room I immediately searched for this list. The little pocket-book was on the floor amongst other papers, but the list was not to be found in it.

Am I mistaken? Have I packed it in somewhere else, or, allowing for the fact that everything had been turned upside down, has this paper slipped among other papers, which would explain why I had not come across it again?

In spite of myself, I must confess to you that the thieves, I fancy, had only one aim in view when they entered my room, and that was to get hold of this list.

What is your opinion?

I feel that perhaps I am about to show myself both inconsiderate and injudicious, but you know how miserable I am, and you will understand how the position I am in gives me grounds for being distracted. I am bent on talking this over with you, on knowing what you think of it. Perhaps even, knowing how clever you are, you might be able to find something, an indication, some detail, in my room? I have not touched anything.

I shall stay indoors all to-morrow in the hope of seeing you; do come if you possibly can. It seems to me that I am forsaken by everyone, and I trust only you. . . ."

Jérôme Fandor read and reread this letter, which had been written with a trembling hand.

"Poor little soul!" he murmured. "Here is something more to add to her troubles! It is really terrible! It seems to me as if we should never come to the end of it; and I ask myself, whether the police will ever find the key to all these mysteries! . . .

"Did someone really break into Elizabeth Dollon's room to steal this paper? It is rather improbable. Judging from what she told me, there is nothing compromising in it. But then, why this search? . . . She is right so far: if the intruders had been merely thieves, they would have carried off her jewellery! . . . Then it is for that paper they came? Besides, ordinary burglars would have had considerable difficulty in getting into her room, where she is remarkably well guarded, by the very fact of there being other boarders in the house. . . .

"No, the very audacity of this attempted theft seems to prove, that it is connected with the other affairs which have brought the name of Jacques Dollon into such prominence!

"I see in this the same extraordinary audacity, the same certainty of escape, the same long and careful preparation, for it is a by no means convenient place for a burglary in open day: comings and goings are perpetual, and the guilty persons ran a hundred risks of being caught. . . ."

Fandor interrupted his reflections to read Elizabeth's letter once more.

"She is dying of fright! That is evident! . . . In any case she calls to me for help. Her letter was posted yesterday evening. . . . I will go and see her — and at once. . . . Who knows but I might find some clue which would put me on the right track?"

Jérôme Fandor did not feel very hopeful.

After having gone carefully over every point connected with, and pertaining to, the affair of rue du Quatre Septembre, he had almost come to the conclusion, optimistic as he was regarding the police, that chance alone would bring about the arrest of the guilty parties.

"To lay these criminals by the heels," he had frankly declared, "requires the aid of very favourable circumstances, and without them, neither I nor the police will get at the truth of it all."

Fandor made a definite distinction between the opinion of the police and his own, because two different theories now obtained with regard to the two affairs: that of the attack on the Princess Sonia Danidoff, and that of the robbery of rue du Quatre Septembre, where the imprints of Jacques Dollon's fingers had been found.

The police and Fandor coupled Monsieur Havard with Monsieur Bertillon under this definition; the police held it for certain that Jacques Dollon was alive, very much alive, and the probabilities were great that he was guilty of the different crimes attributed to him.

In an interview granted to a press rival of *La Capitale* Monsieur Bertillon had stated:

"We base our assertion that Dollon is alive, and consequently guilty, on material facts: we have found his signature attached to each of the crimes, and it is a signature which cannot be imitated by anyone. . . ."

For his part, Fandor held it as certain that Jacques was dead.

"I maintain that, since fifty persons have seen Jacques Dollon dead, it is infinitely more likely that he is dead than that he is alive! The imprints of his fingers, his hand, are equally visible, it is true, and seem to prove that he is alive. But the conclusive nature of this test is nullified by the fact that, before the discovery of these imprints, before these imprints had been made, Jacques Dollon was dead!"

And in his articles in *La Capitale*, Jérôme Fandor, with a persistency which finished by disconcerting even the most convinced partisans of the police contention, continued to maintain that Jacques Dollon was dead, dead as dead, and, to use his own expression, "as dead as it was possible for anyone to be dead!"

Jérôme Fandor had just rung the bell at the garden gate of Madame Bourrat's private boarding-house in Auteuil.

Jules hastened to answer this ring, and was met by the question:

"Is Mademoiselle Elizabeth Dollon at home?"

"No, monsieur. She went out not an hour ago!"

"And you are certain she has not returned?"

"Absolutely, monsieur. . . . There are two visitors waiting for her already."

"She will be in soon, then?"

"Certainly, monsieur: she will not be long. . . ."

Fandor looked at his watch.

"A quarter past ten! . . . Very well, I will wait for her."

"If monsieur will kindly follow me?"

Fandor was shown into the drawing-room. He had advanced only a step or two when he was greeted with:

"Why! Monsieur Fandor!"

"I am delighted to see you!" cried Fandor, shaking hands with Monsieur Barbey and Monsieur Nanteuil. Both gave him a pleasant smile of welcome.

"You have come to see Mademoiselle Dollon, I suppose?"

"Yes. We have come to assure her that we will do all in our power to help her out of her terrible difficulties. She wrote to us a few days ago to ask if we would act as intermediaries regarding the sale of some of her unfortunate brother's productions, also to see if we could get her a situation in some dressmaking establishment. . . . We have come to assure her of our entire sympathy."

"That is most kind of you! They told you, did they not, that she had gone out? I think she will not be absent long, for I have an appointment with her. But, if you will allow me, I will go to the office and ask if they have the least idea of which way she has gone, for I have little time to spare, and if we could go to meet her, it would save, at least, a few minutes. . . ."

Jérôme Fandor rose and went towards one of the drawing-room doors.

"You are making a mistake," said Monsieur Nanteuil, "the office is this way," and he pointed to another door.

"Bah! All roads lead to Rome!" With that, Fandor went out by the door he had approached first. . . .

"They are nice fellows," said Fandor to himself. "If Elizabeth Dollon is really not in! . . . but . . . Is she really not in the house? I am by no means sure. . . . If she feels timid at the idea of seeing the bankers — their visit may have made her nervous, considering the state she is in . . . she might have sent to say she was not at home in order to have time to add some finishing touches to her toilette."

Fandor, who knew the house, mounted the little staircase leading to the first floor. Elizabeth's room was on this floor. Before her door he stopped and sniffed.

"Queer smell!" he murmured. "It smells like gas!"

He knocked boldly, calling:

"Mademoiselle Elizabeth! It is I, Fandor!"

The smell of gas became more pronounced as he waited.

A horrible idea, an agonising fear, flashed through his mind.

He knocked as hard as he could on the door.

"Mademoiselle Elizabeth! Mademoiselle!"

No answer.

He called down the stairs:

"Waiter! . . . Porter!"

But apparently the one and only manservant the house boasted was occupied elsewhere, for no one answered.

Fandor returned to the door of Elizabeth's room, knelt down and tried to look through the keyhole. The inside key was there, which seemed to confirm his agonising fear.

"She has not gone out then?"

He took a deep breath.

"What a horrible smell of gas!"

This time he did not hesitate. He rose, stepped back, sprang forward, and with a vigorous push from the shoulder, he drove the door off its hinges.

"My God!" he shouted.

In the centre of the room, Fandor had just seen Elizabeth Dollon lying unconscious. A tube, detached from a portable gas stove, was between her tightly closed lips! The tap was turned full on. He flung himself on his knees near the poor girl, pulled away the deadly tube, and put his ear to her heart.

What joy, what happiness, he felt when he heard, very feeble but quite unmistakable beatings of Elizabeth's heart!

"She lives!" What unspeakable relief Jérôme Fandor felt! What thankfulness!

The noise he had made breaking the door off its hinges brought the whole household running to the spot. As the manservant, followed by Madame Bourrat, followed in turn by Monsieur Barbey and Nanteuil, appeared in the doorway uttering cries of terror, Jérôme called out:

"No one is to come in! . . . It is an accident!"

Then lifting Elizabeth in his strong arms, he carried her out of the room.

"What she needs is air!"

He hurried downstairs and out into the garden with his precious burden, followed by the terrified witnesses of the scene.

"You have saved her life, monsieur!" cried Madame Bourrat in a tragic voice. She groaned. "Oh, what a scandal!"

"Yes, I have saved her," replied Fandor as, panting with his exertions, he laid Elizabeth Dollon flat on a garden seat. . . . "But from whom? . . . It is certainly not attempted suicide! There is some mystery behind this business: it's a regular theatrical performance arranged simply for effect, and to mislead us," declared Fandor. Then, turning to the bankers, he said courteously but with an air of command:

"Please lay information with the superintendent of police at once . . . the nearest police station, you understand!"

"Madame," he said, addressing the overwhelmed Madame Bourrat, "you will be good enough to look after Mademoiselle Dollon, will you not? . . . Take every care of her. There is not much to be done, however! I have seen many cases of commencing asphyxia: she will regain consciousness now, in a few minutes."

Then, looking at the manservant, he said in a sharp tone:

"Come with me! You will mount guard at the door of Mademoiselle Elizabeth's room, whilst I try to discover some clues, before the police arrive on the scene."

To tell the truth, our young journalist felt embarrassed at the idea that Elizabeth Dollon was about to regain consciousness, and that he would have to submit to being thanked by her, when she knew who had saved her.

Accompanied by the manservant, he went quickly upstairs and into Elizabeth's room.

"You must not enter Mademoiselle Dollon's room on any account!" said Fandor sternly. "It is quite enough that I should run the risk of effacing the, probably very slight, clues which the delinquents have left behind them. . . ."

"But, monsieur, if the young lady put the tubing between her lips, it must have been because she wished to destroy herself!"

"On the face of it you are right, my good fellow. But, when one is right, one is often wrong!"

Without more ado, Fandor started on a minute inspection of the room. Elizabeth had but stated the truth when she wrote that it had been thoroughly ransacked. Only her toilet things had been spared; but some books had been taken from their shelves and thrown about the floor, their pages crumpled and spoilt. He noticed the emptied trunk: its contents — copy books, letters, pieces of music — had been roughly dealt with. On the mantelpiece, in full view, lay Elizabeth's jewellery — some rings and brooches, a small gold watch, a purse.

"A very queer affair," murmured Fandor, who was kneeling in the middle of the room, rummaging, searching, and not finding any clue. He rose, carefully examined all the woodwork, but found nothing incriminating. He examined the lock of the unhinged door, which had subsided on the floor. The lock was intact, the bolt moved freely: the screws only of the staple had given way.

"That," thought Fandor, "is probably owing to the force of my thrust!"

The window fastening was intact: the window closed.

"If the robbers," reflected Fandor, "got into a closed room, they must have used false keys."

Having examined the means of access to the room, Fandor started on a still more minute examination of the interior. He scrutinised the furniture and the slight powdering of dust on each article: in vain! . . . Then the washstand had its turn: nothing! . . . He scrutinised the soap.

"Ah! This is interesting!" he cried. The manservant had made himself scarce; and Fandor, unobserved, could wrap up the piece of soap in his handkerchief and hide it in the lowest drawer of the chest of drawers, under a pile of linen. He was whistling now.

"That bit of soap is interesting — very!" he cried. "Let the police come! I am not afraid of their blundering! . . . Now to see how Elizabeth is getting on!"

When he reached her side, he found she had recovered full consciousness, and was preparing to answer the questions of a police superintendent, who, summoned by the bankers, had hastened to the scene of action. He was a stout, apoplectic man, very full of his own importance.

"Come now, mademoiselle, tell us just how things happened from beginning to end! We ask nothing better than to believe you, but do not conceal any detail — not the slightest. . . ."

Poor Elizabeth Dollon, when she heard this speech, stared at the pompous police official, astonished. What had she to conceal? What had she to gain by lying? What did he think, this fat policeman, who took it upon himself to issue orders, when he should rather have tried to comfort her! Nevertheless, she at once began telling him all that she knew with regard to the affair. She told him of her letter to Fandor: that her room had been visited the evening before: by whom she did not know . . . that she had not said a word about it to anyone, fearing vengeance would fall on her, frightened, not understanding what it all meant. . . .

Then she came to what the police dignitary called "her suicide." As she finished her recital with a reference to her rescue by Fandor, she looked at the young journalist. It was a look of great gratitude and a kind of ardent tenderness, with a touch of fear in it.

"Strange, very strange!" pronounced the superintendent of police, who had been taking notes with an air of great gravity. "So very strange, mademoiselle, that it is very difficult to credit your statements! . . . very difficult indeed! . . ."

Whilst he was speaking, Fandor was saying to himself:

"Decidedly, it is that! . . . Just what I was thinking! It is quite clear, clear as the sun in the sky, evident, indisputable!" And he refused, very politely of course — for one has to respect the authorities — to accompany the superintendent, who, in his turn, went upstairs to Elizabeth's room, in order to carry out the necessary legal verification. . . .

XIV

SOMEONE TELEPHONED

The nuns of the order of Saint Augustin were not expelled in consequence of the Decrees. This was a special favour, but one fully justified, because of the incalculable benefits this community conferred on suffering humanity. The vast convent of rue de la Glacière continues to serve as a shelter for these holy women, and as a sort of hospital for the sick. For close on a hundred years, generation after generation of those living near its walls have heard the convent clock sound the hours in solemn tones; so, too, the convent chapel's shrill-voiced bells have never failed to remind the faithful that the daily offices of their church are being said and sung by the holy sisters within the hallowed walls.

In the vast quarter of Paris, peopled with hospitals and prisons, the convent shows a stern front in the shape of a high, blackened wall. A great courtyard gate, in which a window with iron bars and grating is the only visible opening to the exterior world.

About half-past six in the morning, slightly out of breath with his rapid walk from the Metropolitan station, Jérôme Fandor rang the convent door bell. The sound could be heard echoing and re-echoing in the vaulted corridors, till it died away in the stony distance. There was a silence: then the iron-barred window was half opened, and Fandor heard a voice asking:

"What do you want, monsieur?"

"I wish to speak to Madame the Superior," replied Fandor.

The window was closed again and a lengthy silence followed. Then, slowly, the heavy entrance gate swung half open. Fandor entered the convent. Under the arched doorway, a nun received him with a slight salutation, and turned her back.

"Kindly follow me," she murmured.

Fandor followed along a narrow passage, on one side of which were cells, whilst on the other, it opened by means of large bays, on a vast rectangular cloister quite deserted. A door-window in the passage was ajar: the nun stopped here and said:

"Kindly wait in this parlour, and be good enough to let me have your card. I will inform our Mother Superior that you wish to see her."

The room in which our journalist found himself was severely furnished: its walls were white, on them hung a great ivory crucifix, and here and there, a simple religious picture framed in ebony. A few chairs were ranged in a circle about an oval table: on the floor, polished till it shone like a mirror, were a few small mats, which gave a touch of common-place comfort to the icy regularity of this parlour, set apart for official visits.

What emotions, what dramas, what joys, have had this parlour for a setting! It is there that the life of the cloister touches mundane existence; it is there the nuns receive their future companions in the religious life and their weeping families; it is there the parents of those in the convent infirmary come to hear from the doctor's lips the decrees of life or death; for the convent is not only a retreat, it is an asylum for the sick, the ailing, recommended to their patients by the most eminent doctors, the most prominent surgeons.

Accustomed though he was to every kind of human misery, Fandor shuddered at the thought of all these walls had seen and heard. His reflections were broken by the arrival of a little old lady, whose eyes shone strangely luminous in her pale and wrinkled face — a face showing the highest distinction.

Fandor made a deep bow: it might have expressed the reverence of the world to religion.

"Madame la Supérieure," murmured he, "I have come to pay my respects to you and to ask for news of your boarder."

The Mother Superior, in a gay tone, which contrasted with her cold and reserved appearance, replied at once:

"Ah, you preferred to come yourself! You had not the patience to wait at the telephone? I quite understand. Would you believe it, while the sister, who has charge of this young girl, was being sent for, the communication was cut off. That is why we could not give you any information."

Fandor stared.

"But I do not understand, madame?"

The Mother Superior replied:

"Was it not you then who telephoned this morning to ask for news of Mademoiselle Dollon?"

"I certainly did not do so!"

"In that case, I do not understand what it means, either! But it does not matter much: you shall see your protégée now."

The Mother Superior rang: a sister appeared.

"Sister, will you take this gentleman to Mademoiselle Dollon! She was walking in the park a short while ago, and is probably there now. . . . Monsieur, I bid you good day."

Gliding swiftly and noiselessly over the polished floor, the Mother Superior disappeared. The nun led the way and Fandor followed: he was very much upset by what the Mother Superior had just told him.

"How had Elizabeth's place of refuge been so quickly discovered? . . . Who could have telephoned to get news of her?"

The nun had led Fandor across the great rectangular courtyard; then by corridors, and many winding, vaulted passages, they had come out on to a terrace, overlooking an immense park, which extended further than the eye could see. Here were bosky dells, ancient trees, bowers and grooves, meadows where milky mothers chewed the cud in the shade of blossoming apple trees. It might have been in Normandy, a hundred leagues from Paris!

The nun turned to the admiring Fandor.

"The young lady you seek, monsieur, is coming along this path: there she is! . . . I will leave you."

Fandor had seen Elizabeth's graceful figure moving towards him, thrown into charming relief by the country landscape flooded with sunshine. In her modest mourning dress, with her fair shining hair, she appeared prettier than ever: a touching figure of sorrowing beauty!

Elizabeth pressed Fandor's hands warmly.

"Oh, thank you, monsieur, thank you!" she cried, "for having come to see me this morning. I know how little spare time you have! I feel vexed with myself for putting you out so . . . but you see" — Elizabeth could not repress a sob — "I am so alone . . . so desolate . . . I have lost everything I cared for . . . and you are the only person I can trust and confide in now! . . . I feel like a bit of wreckage at the mercy of wind and wave; I feel as though I were surrounded by enemies: I live in a nightmare. . . . What should I do without you to turn to? . . ."

Our young journalist, moved by such great misfortune so simply, so candidly expressed, returned the pressure of Elizabeth's hands.

"You know, mademoiselle," he said softly, but in a voice vibrating with sympathetic emotion — the only sign of feeling he permitted himself to show — "you know that you can count absolutely on me. In getting you to take a few days' rest in this retreat, I felt I was doing what was best for you. You are not solitary; but your surroundings are peaceful and friendly, and should you have enemies, though I am loath to think it, you are sheltered here beyond their reach. With reference to that, have you given your address to anyone, since yesterday?"

"To no one," replied Elizabeth. "Has anyone by chance? . . ."

She looked troubled, and gave an anxious questioning glance at Fandor.

He did not want to frighten the much-tried girl, but he wished to solve the mystery of the unaccountable telephone call.

"Oh, I just wished to know, mademoiselle. . . . Now, tell me, have you quite recovered from . . . your experience of the other day?"

"Ah, monsieur, I owe my life to you!" cried Elizabeth. "For, I am certain that someone wished to get rid of me . . . don't you agree with me? . . . I must have been dosed with some narcotic, just as they dosed my poor brother, for I am now absolutely convinced that he also was sent to sleep and poisoned. . . ."

"And that he is dead! Is that not so?" asked Fandor in a low voice.

Without hesitation, in a tearful voice, Elizabeth repeated:

"And that he is dead. You have given me so many proofs that it is so, that I can no longer doubt it, alas! But I will take courage, as I promised you I would. I ought to live, that I may strive to rehabilitate his memory, and restore to him his reputation as a man of probity, of honour, to which he is entitled. But directly I begin to think about the horrible mystery in which I am involved, my very reason seems to totter — you can understand that, can you not? I don't understand, I don't know, I can't guess . . . oh! . . ."

"But," interrupted Fandor, "we must seriously consider the situation in all its bearings. It may cause you atrocious suffering, but you must summon all your courage, mademoiselle. We must discuss it."

Fandor and Elizabeth had moved away from the terrace, and were now in the leafy solitudes of the park.

Fandor began:

"There is that paper with its list of names, written in green ink, mademoiselle! It was a mistake on your part not to attach any importance to it until you fancied, and perhaps rightly, that someone had tried to steal it from you. Come now, can you tell me whether this list is still in your possession, or not?"

Elizabeth shook her head sadly.

"I do not know, I cannot tell! My poor head is so bewildered, and I find it all the trouble in the world to collect my thoughts. I told you, the other day, that this list had disappeared from a little red pocket book, that I had put on the chimney piece of my room at Auteuil. But the more I think it over, the more doubtful I am. . . . It seems to me now, that this list ought to be, must be still — unless it has been stolen since — in the big trunk, into which I threw, pell-mell, the papers and books my brother left scattered about his writing table. To be quite sure about this, we must return to Auteuil. . . . But perhaps it is useless; because when I wanted to send it to you some forty-eight hours ago, I searched everywhere for the wretched thing, and in vain! . . . I am not even sure now that I brought it away with me from rue Norvins!"

Fandor gently comforted the distracted girl whose eyes were full of tears.

"Do not be disheartened. Try rather to put together in your memory what was written in this paper! You told me, surely, that there were names in this list of persons you knew, or had heard of? Search your memory a little, mademoiselle."

"I don't know! I cannot remember!" cried Elizabeth nervously.

"Come now," said Fandor encouragingly, "I know an excellent way of assisting the memory. The eyes are like a sensitive photographic plate: what the brain does not always retain, the mirror of the eye registers: do not try to remember, but try, as it were, to read on white paper what your eyes saw! . . ."

"Let us sit down a minute and I will help you to do it!" Fandor pointed out a rustic seat, under the trees, in front of which was a garden table. They sat down together and Fandor drew from his pocket a sheet of white paper and his fountain pen.

Elizabeth's arm touched his shoulder.

As though electrified by this contact, the two young people trembled, their eyes met in a glance full of troubled emotion — a feeling new to both — whose immense significance neither understood. Fandor remained speechless, and Elizabeth blushed.

They gazed at each other, embarrassed, not knowing what to say for themselves; and their embarrassment was only relieved by the appearance of the sister who attended to the turning box at the entrance gate. She stood at the top of the steps leading down to the park and called Elizabeth.

"Mademoiselle! Mademoiselle! There is someone on the telephone who wishes to speak to you!"

Fandor rose.

"Will you allow me to accompany you, mademoiselle? I am very curious to know whether the person now asking for you is identical with the person who asked for you a little while ago?"

The young couple hurried to the big parlour, and Elizabeth went to the telephone.

"Hullo? . . ."

Elizabeth had handed one of the receivers to Fandor. He heard a voice — an unknown voice, but beyond question masculine — who said, over the wire:

"Hullo! . . . Is it really Mademoiselle Dollon to whom I have the honour of speaking?"

"Yes, monsieur. Who is speaking to me?"

But just as Elizabeth was about to repeat her question, Fandor thought he heard whoever had called up Elizabeth, hang up the receivers. No reply reached them! . . .

Elizabeth cried impatiently:

"Hullo! . . . Hullo! . . . Who is speaking to me?"

But there was no one at the end of the line!

Fandor swore softly to himself, then seizing the two receivers he called:

"Hullo! Come, monsieur, reply! . . . Whom do you want? Who are you?"

He could not obtain any reply.

Fandor rang up the central office. When the telephone girl answered, he called:

"Mademoiselle, why have you cut me off?"

"But I have done nothing of the kind, monsieur!"

"But I cannot get any reply!"

"It is because the receivers have been hung up by whoever called you. I assure you that is so."

"What was my caller's number?"

"I cannot tell you that, monsieur — the rules forbid it."

Fandor knew this quite well, so he did not insist further. But, as he turned away from the telephone, a dull anger smouldered within him.

"Who was this mysterious individual who had called Elizabeth twice over the telephone, and then, no sooner put into communication with her, had refused to talk to her?"

Fandor felt nervous, anxious, exasperated by this incident; but it would never do to trouble his young friend to no good purpose. He led her back to the garden.

"Where were we in our talk, monsieur?" asked Elizabeth.

With a considerable effort, the journalist collected his thoughts.

"We were discussing the mysterious paper found at your brother's, mademoiselle."

In agreement with Elizabeth, Jérôme Fandor determined the approximate size of this list of addresses. He tore from his note-book a sheet of white paper.

Elizabeth looked fixedly at the white sheet for a long time, as though, by concentrated will power, she could force the mysterious names which she read some days before on the original paper, to rise up in front of her eyes. Certainly it seemed to her that on this list figured the name of her brother, that of the Baroness de Vibray, lawyer Gérin's also: then she remembered a double name, a name not unknown to her, which had appeared in the list.

"Barbey-Nanteuil!" she suddenly cried. "Yes, I do believe those two names were on it!"

Fandor smiled. Encouraged by his smile and the results of this semi-clairvoyant attempt, Elizabeth allowed her thoughts free play.

"I am sure of it: there was even a mistake in spelling: *Nanteuil* was spelled *Nauteuil*: the bankers were third or fourth on the list, and I am certain now that the Baroness de Vibray's name headed the list. . . . There was also a date, composed of two figures — a 1 . . . then — wait a minute! . . . a figure with a tail to it . . . that is to say, it could only have been a 5, a 7, or a 9. . . . I cannot remember which. Then there were other names I had never heard of."

"Try, mademoiselle, to remember. . . ."

There was a silence. Fandor was puzzling over the figures he had written down in the order Elizabeth had mentioned them — fifteen — seventeen — nineteen — but what could he deduce from them? . . . Ah! . . . The mysterious robbery of rue du Quatre Septembre was committed on May 15th! There may be a clue there! The thread of Fandor's reflections were abruptly broken by a cry from Elizabeth.

"I have recalled a name — something like . . . Thomas! . . . Does that tell you anything?"

"Thomas?" repeated Jérôme Fandor slowly. . . . "I don't see. . . ."

But suddenly he saw light!

He jumped up:

"Isn't it Thomery?" cried he, intensely excited. "Are you not confounding Thomas with Thomery?"

Elizabeth, taken aback, confused, tried hard to remember: she threshed her memory with knitted brows.

"It may be so," she declared. "I see quite clearly the first letters of the word — Thom . . . written in a large hand, . . . then the rest is indistinct . . . but I have the impression that the end of the word is longer than the last syllable of Thomas."

"Perhaps you are right!"

Fandor was no longer listening to her. He had left the rustic bench, and without paying any attention to Elizabeth, he began walking up and down the shady path, talking to himself in a low tone, as was his habit when he wished to reduce his thoughts to order.

"Thomas — that is Thomery; Jacques Dollon, the Baroness de Vibray, Barbey-Nanteuil, lawyer Gérin — but they are all the victims of the mysterious band that plots and plans in the shade! . . . It is incomprehensible — but we shall find a way to get to the bottom of it all!"

Fandor returned to Elizabeth.

"We shall get to the bottom of these mysteries," cried he, with so triumphant an air, his face shining with joy, that Elizabeth, in spite of her torturing anxieties, could not help smiling.

They were alone in these green and flowery spaces. A great peace was all about them. The birds were singing, the breeze lightly stirred the trees and bushes with caressing breaths. . . . Fandor gazed tenderly at Elizabeth, very tenderly. . . . The young girl smiled tremulously, as she met this glance of lover-like tenderness.

"We shall get to the bottom of it," repeated Fandor. "You will see, I promise you. . . ."

Their glances mingled in a mute communion of thought and feeling. . . . Spontaneously, their hands met and clasped. . . . They were standing close together, and theirs the consciousness of living through an unforgettable moment: they felt most vividly alive together. How young they were! How intoxicating, a moment! . . . The world of outside things ceased to exist for them. . . . They were enwrapt in a glowing world of their own! . . . Fandor's hand slid to Elizabeth's shoulder; he leaned towards the unresisting girl, and with closed eyes, their lips met in a long kiss — a kiss all ecstasy. . . .

It was a moment's mutual madness! . . . The instant past, both knew it. Torn from this momentary dream of bliss, they gazed at each other, embarrassed, greatly moved: for that very reason they wished to part. Ah, this was not the moment to speak of love, to dream of happiness and mutual joy! Dark, dreadful mysteries enclosed them: it was a sinister net they struggled in: as yet they could see no clear way out! . . . They had no right to be themselves until the mysteries were cleared away. . . . They could not belong to each other now!

Fandor, when taking leave of Elizabeth, expressed a wish that she should not accompany him to the convent; and she, still shaken with emotion, had not insisted on doing so.

As he was on the point of stepping into the street, a sister came up to him.

"You are Monsieur Jérôme Fandor?"

"Yes, sister."

"Our Mother Superior wishes to speak to you."

Our journalist bowed acquiescence.

Some minutes later, the Mother Superior joined him in the large parlour.

"Monsieur," she began, "I must apologise for having sent for you, but I wished to have a necessary talk with you."

Fandor interrupted the saintly nun.

"And I must apologise, reverend Mother, for not having come to pay my respects to you before leaving. Had I not been much troubled, I should never have dreamt of leaving without thanking you for the help you have been good enough to give me."

The nun looked at him questioningly. Fandor continued:

"In agreeing to receive Mademoiselle Elizabeth Dollon as a boarder, you have done a deed of true charity: this poor girl is so unhappy, so tried, so unfortunate, that I really do not know where she could have found a better refuge than in this convent under your sheltering care. . . . I . . ."

But the nun would not allow Fandor to continue.

"It is precisely about Mademoiselle Dollon that I wish to speak to you. . . . Of course, I should be glad to help and comfort one suffering from a real misfortune; but I must confess, that when Mademoiselle Dollon presented herself here as a boarder, I was ignorant of the exact nature of the scandal in which she is involved."

Fandor was taken aback at the harsh tone of the nun's speech.

"Good Heavens, madame, what do you mean to insinuate?"

"I have just been informed, monsieur, of the exact nature of the relations which existed between the criminal, Jacques Dollon, and Madame de Vibray."

Fandor stiffened with indignation.

"It is false!" he cried. "Utterly false! You have been misinformed!"

He stopped short. The nun signified by a movement of her hand that further protests were useless.

"In any case, whether false or not, it is quite certain that we cannot keep this girl here any longer, for her name will, in the end, do harm to the respectability of this house."

Fandor was astounded at this extraordinary statement.

"In other words," said he, "you refuse to keep Mademoiselle here any longer as a boarder?"

"Yes, monsieur!"

The journalist moved a step or two, then, with bent head, seemed to be turning something over in his mind.

"It comes to this, madame, you are not giving me your true reasons for . . ."

Again the nun interrupted the young man with a gesture.

"True, monsieur, I should have preferred not to mention my real and very definite reasons which make it an imperative duty that I should request Mademoiselle Dollon to seek another refuge. Nevertheless, since you insist, I will tell you that Mademoiselle Dollon's attitude just now — her behaviour — is what we cannot possibly allow. . . ."

"Good Heavens! What do you wish to insinuate now, madame?"

"You kissed her, monsieur. I regret that you have forced me to go into details. I regret that you have compelled me to put into words this — I will not allow you to turn this religious house into a lover's meeting place! Am I clear?"

Before Fandor had time to protest, the nun gave him a curt bow, and prepared to leave him.

The young journalist recalled her. He was angry; all the more so, because he knew that the Mother Superior had some justification for the attitude she had taken up. Alas! All his protestations were vain!

"Very well, madame," he said at last. "You are utterly mistaken; but I recognise that your attitude has some colour of justification, and I bow to your decision, based on misinformation and a mistake though it be. Kindly allow me two days' grace, that I may find another refuge for Mademoiselle Dollon!"

With a movement of her head the nun signified her assent; then, with a final bow, she left the parlour.

Crestfallen, but full of angry resolve, Jérôme Fandor turned his back on the convent.

XV

VAGUE SUSPICIONS

Fandor was talking to himself — an inveterate habit of his — as he sat in the cab which was carrying him to the Palais de Justice.

"Beyond question, I ought to have examined that paper they have stolen from Mademoiselle Elizabeth. I should have looked through it at the first opportunity. That sequence of names; those dates, which seem to almost coincide with the different criminal attempts, probably relate to the mysterious plan which the assassins are carrying out systematically. . . . But, that means there are to be more victims, and we shall witness fresh tragedies! . . . I am not at all easy about Elizabeth either! . . . Who the deuce could have telephoned to her at the convent? . . . Perhaps what I am going to do is stupid, but no chance must be neglected. . . . I wonder if I shall learn anything worth knowing at the court to-day? . . .

"When they arrested these smugglers, five months ago, I recollect perfectly that Monsieur Thomery's name was mentioned in connection with the business. . . . If I only held the connecting link of interest in my hands, which would make it clear why all these people — Jacques Dollon, the Baroness de Vibray, Princess Sonia Danidoff, Barbey-Nanteuil, and even Elizabeth Dollon — have been the victims of the horrible band I am pursuing. . . . The motive? Evidently robbery! But there must be some other reason, for — and it is a significant fact — all these people know one another, meet one another, or at least are either clients of the Barbey-Nanteuil bank, or are friends of Monsieur Thomery. . . . It's the devil's own mystery!"

Jérôme Fandor had arrived at the Palais de Justice. He crossed the great hall des Pas-Perdus and entered the Assize Court.

The trial of the Cooper and his accomplices was a small affair, and had not attracted many listeners, for these smuggling and coining cases were apt to be dull. As a matter of fact, there would not have been a soul present, if the accused had not had the most popular of counsels to defend them — Maître Henri Robart!

Fandor joined a group who were on familiar terms evidently, and, although he had not seen her for many a day, he at once recognised Mother Toulouche by her remarkable appearance and grotesque get up. He had had so many other irons in the fire, that he had not followed this smuggling case at all closely: he was surprised, therefore, to see Mother Toulouche in the little passage adjoining the court, for he had the impression that the old receiver of stolen goods had been under lock and key for some weeks. . . . She was now being interviewed by one of his colleagues. Fandor went up to them.

Though she had not been accused of anything so far, the old storekeeper was vehemently protesting her innocence.

"Yes," she declared to her interviewer, "it is abominable, when such things are discovered all of a sudden!"

Mother Toulouche went on to explain that on Clock Quay she rented a small shop for the sale of curiosities: that she was an honest woman, who had never wronged a soul by as much as a farthing: all she asked was to be left in peace to earn a decent living, so that she could retire from business some day or other. . . . Everyone had a right to ask as much as that! . . . Her store consisted of two rooms and an underground cellar, in which she had put a quantity of old odds and ends, when she had moved to her present abode. . . . She never descended to this cellar, never at all: she was far too much afraid of rats to venture down there! Not she! But, one day, if you please, when she was quietly engaged in mending some old clothes, the police had suddenly burst into her store! . . . And they had accused her of receiving smuggled goods and false money, and she didn't know what more besides! . . .

The police, not content with this, had made her go down to the cellar to find out whether or no there were such things in the second cellar belonging to her store! . . . Who had been most surprised then? Why who but Mother Toulouche, who, until that very minute, had not known that this second cellar existed! How then was she to know that it communicated with the sewer, still less that the sewer opened on to the Seine, and that by the Seine arrived bales of smuggled goods, which were concealed in her cellar by the smugglers? . . . Fortunately, the judges had understood this, and after twenty-four hours' detention on suspicion, Mother Toulouche had been set at liberty!

At first, she had declared that she did not know the accused persons summoned to appear that day, the Cooper in particular; to tell the truth, she had made a mistake; she did know them, through having met them a long time ago, when she lived near la Capelle; so long ago was it that she had forgotten all about it! Anyhow, she wanted to have done with the business!

From the very beginning of the trial, Mother Toulouche had been disagreeably struck by the inquisitorial glances and pointed questions of the Public Prosecutor throughout the proceedings. Now, in her turn, the old storekeeper was questioning her audience, trying hard to find out what would be the probable attitude of the magistrate, when she herself should be summoned to the witness-box.

"Witness! . . . Mother Toulouche!"

Fandor smiled as he listened to the loquacious old storekeeper, for he knew how much faith was to be put in her veracity and respect-ability! . . . It was pretty clear that she was every whit as guilty as the handcuffed individuals now in the dock. As she had not been arrested, it simply meant that, in Juve's opinion, this was not an opportune moment to put a stopper on the nefarious activities of this bad old woman.

At this precise moment, Fandor recognised Juve. He was leaving a group of barristers and officials, who had been hugely entertained by his stupid answers and remarks. Yes, it was Juve, so admirably made up and disguised that Fandor had difficulty in recognising him. Here was Cranajour on the scene! He approached Mother Toulouche and stood there — a Cranajour who was the picture of gaping imbe-cility!

"You, too?" cried Mother Toulouche, looking askance at him. "Are you one of the witnesses?"

Cranajour's reply was a comical grimace. He scratched his beard, remarking finally:

"I have forgotten! I don't know!"

His audience burst into roars of laughter: Fandor laughed loudest of all!

One of Maître Henri Robart's juniors whispered in Fandor's ear, with an air of giving the journalist a piece of information worth having.

"A simple-minded soul, that! — a kind of idiot! You can guess that, at the preliminary inquiry, they soon found that out! . . . He may be heard — or he may not?"

Fandor nodded. He found it difficult not to laugh.

"Thanks many for the information," he stammered. The young barrister did not understand the ironical tone of our journalist.

Mother Toulouche was envying Cranajour.

"You're in luck, you are — to be too silly to go and talk to those inquisitive fellows in there! Eh?"

Conversations stopped. The little low door, giving entrance to the court, had just opened: an usher announced:

"The case is resumed! . . . Witnesses this way! . . . The woman Toulouche? . . . It is your turn! . . ."

They jostled and pushed their way through the narrow entrance in order to get into the court room quickly.

Fandor, however, instead of following the crowd, had grasped the simple Cranajour by the shoulder, and shouted loud enough to be heard by those who might have been surprised at his action.

"You duffer of a Cranajour! Go along with you! You're the man for my money, old fellow! Here's something for a glass — but come with me for five minutes: I want to interview you and make a jolly good article out of it!"

Fandor went off, followed by the detective. When they were quite away from everyone, Fandor turned quickly to his friend.

"Well, Juve?"

"Nothing, so far. . . ."

"You have not run in the whole gang?"

"Not I!" replied Juve. "These are only the supernumeraries, and there are some of them out of my reach! . . . Look here, Fandor," continued Juve in a low tone. "You will see someone in court presently whose presence will astonish you — it is an aviator — the aviator Emilet. . . . Well, my boy, I have a notion that this fellow is no stranger to all these goings-on! . . . But patience! . . . besides, you know, Fandor, it's not my way of doing things to put the bracelets on mediocrities such as he: I fly higher! . . . Good-bye. Shall see you later on!"

Fandor asked, in a low tone:

"Shall I remain for the sitting?"

"Yes," said Juve. "It is quite likely that I shall not be present; and it would be a good thing if you were to get a general idea of this affair: you may pick up some useful information."

"Juve, I very much wish to have a longer talk with you — there are things I want to say — to tell you!"

Steps could be heard coming in their direction: the two men separated at once; but Juve had just time to say:

"This evening then, at eight, I shall come to your place, Fandor. Expect me!"

Half an hour later, Fandor entered the court room. . . .

The speech for the Crown had just been concluded.

The arrest of these smugglers, now on their trial, had made some stir, about five months ago. Public opinion had been aroused almost to fever pitch, when it became known that the accused had, for nearly two years past, succeeded in getting through into Paris, without having paid town dues, quantities of the most highly taxed articles, and thus had accumulated a large store of riches in contraband goods and money. They owed their arrest to the betrayal of a wretched dealer, who was dissatisfied with his remuneration.

The journalists had, after their manner, amplified all the details, had exaggerated the realities, and had given a romantic colouring to the various incidents in the varied lives and adventures of this daring band of smugglers.

They had been represented as perfect gentlemen, who had formed themselves into a marvellously organised Black Band, led by a chief having right of life or death over them: a band fertile in tricks and extraordinary stratagems, who massed their plunder in immense vaults and cellars under the very heart of Paris, in the Isle of the Cité, and communicating with the river, which, under the eyes of the police, served to bear the barges laden with their booty.

Cellars and vaults in the Isle of the Cité!

"Well," thought Fandor, "men organised into such a powerful association in this part of Paris might well put one on the track of strange discoveries regarding the mysterious events connected with the Jacques Dollon affair!"

Then, having spoken to his colleagues on the press, Fandor turned in the direction of the jury and set himself to follow attentively Maître Henri Robart's speech for the defence.

XVI

DISCUSSIONS

The portress rang up Fandor on the telephone.

"Monsieur Fandor! There is a stout little lady down here! She wants to see you! Should I let her go up?"

Fandor's first impulse was to say "no." He glanced at the time-piece: it was exactly two minutes past eight and Juve might be here at any minute. He was sure to keep his appointment.

After an instant's hesitation, Fandor decided on a "yes." He called down to the portress:

"Let her come up!"

Fandor had an idea: perhaps this person knew something about the appointment made that afternoon at the Palais de Justice! It would be well to find out the why and wherefore of this call. In any case, it was best for a journalist to see all comers, if possible.

There was a discreet ring, announcing that the stout little lady had already mounted the five flights of stairs and was now on Fandor's landing.

Our journalist went to open the door, standing well back in the shadow, so that his visitor might show herself first, as she passed into the little hall.

Yes, she was certainly stout, short, and also elderly. She wore a bonnet with strings, perched on a thick crop of grey curls, yellowish at the tips. This elderly dame wore glasses; she was wrapped in a large brown shawl, and she supported herself, as she walked, with a crook-handled stick.

Whilst the puzzled Fandor closed his front door, the visitor made straight for the little sitting-room, where our journalist usually sat, surrounded by his books and papers.

"Ah, she seems to know my flat!" thought Fandor. The next moment he jumped back; for, no sooner had the visitor got well into the room, than she straightened her bent back, threw off her shawl, and dropped her stick! Then, tearing off her grey curls and her spectacles, the visitor revealed herself as — Juve!

Fandor burst out laughing.

"Juve! Well, I never!"

"It's Juve, all right, my boy!" cried the smiling detective, as he rid himself of the feminine get-up which impeded his movements. "I was pleased to see, my lad, that you did not suspect my identity until I had thrown off this second-hand wardrobe I bulked myself out with!"

"Oh!" cried Fandor, "that's only because I hardly looked at you. If I had, Juve, you may be sure I should have recognised you!"

"Possibly! But what do you think of the disguise?"

"Not so bad, Juve; but why did you change your sex this evening?"

"Oh, for the fun of it, and to keep my hand in . . . besides, the more precautions we take when we meet, the better. Admit for a moment that our enemies are keeping a watch on you here: what will they recollect about your doings this evening? Why, that Fandor, the journalist, had a call from a lady, and that she did not leave in a hurry either!"

"Hang it all! I've no objection to a Don Juan reputation, but I may say, without offence, that, as a woman, there's nothing particularly attractive about you, Juve, in the garb you've just discarded!"

"Bah!" replied Juve. "You mustn't be so particular, my dear boy — as if dress mattered — or appearance either!"

Juve was lighting a cigarette as he walked about the room, examining the books and other objects with which Fandor had surrounded himself.

"A charming home!" murmured the detective. . . .

Then, he inspected the contents of a little show-case, in which Fandor had collected what he called his "Circumstantial Evidence"; in other words, various objects relating to cases he had been engaged on, such as scraps of clothing, blood-stained weapons, broken locks: these records of crimes, new and old, were carefully labelled. Juve began questioning Fandor about these sinister relics. Five minutes of jokes and laughter, then Fandor became serious. He drew his friend to a corner settee.

"Juve," said he, in an impressive tone, "I have found the connecting link!"

"By Jove! You have, have you!" cried Juve in a bantering tone, and with a quizzical look. "Let us see it! . . . Explain! . . ."

Regardless of his friend's scepticism, Fandor proceeded to expound his theory.

"I did as you suggested. I was present at the trial of the smugglers: I listened to Counsel's speech for the defence, but judged it useless to stay to the end. When Maître Henri Robart began a disquisition on the facts, I left. Here is what I have noted:

"Someone owns a house in the Isle of the Cité; a house which is a meeting place for receivers of stolen goods, ruffians, robbers, and vagabonds: a house possessing underground cellars of no ordinary kind. Now, this Someone never mentions this strange house of his, though he must be aware of its existence; then this Someone knows intimately several, at least, of the people more or less involved in the Jacques Dollon affair, and — one may boldly assert it — the Dollon plot was hatched in a cellar, in a sewer of the Cité.

"One of two things! . . .

"Either this personage is timorous, is afraid of being compromised, and does not consider in what an awkward position this coincidence places him — if that be so, he is a singularly thick-headed individual — or — well — Monsieur Thomery . . . you are the most rascally scoundrel it has been my lot to admire, up to now! But I assure you, we know how to get even with you! From the moment we have established, in the first place, a connection between all these affairs — that they indubitably hang together; secondly, that you, Monsieur Thomery, are the connecting link. . . ."

"No," interrupted Juve, sharply. . . .

"What is that you say? . . ."

"I say — *no.*"

"What?" cried Fandor, taken aback. He stared at Juve, who continued to smoke his cigarette, unmoved. But Fandor was obstinately set on stating his point of view.

"The primary cause of the Dollon affair seems to be the suicide of the Baroness de Vibray, a suicide probably owing to a love disappointment — the old lady had been forsaken by her lover — Monsieur Thomery! . . ."

"No."

Juve's denial slightly annoyed Fandor, but did not stop him.

"I ask: was the man who robbed Sonia Danidoff one of the guests? It is very unlikely; for, not only were the clothes of all those present searched, but all Thomery's guests were known, well known! . . ."

"No!"

Fandor bit his lip.

"It's true, Juve! You were there yourself, and no one penetrated your disguise, and discovered who you really were! My last argument is, therefore, worthless . . . but I fancy your attitude, your way of receiving my deductions, hides something. Have you got new information! Fresh facts to go on? You know who stole the jewels?"

"No."

"Good Heavens! How aggravating you are, Juve! . . . But this time you will simply have to agree with me! Listen! . . . When we first met, after our long separation, you admitted that one thing bothered you — the ease with which your nefarious band of villains of the Isle of the Cité were able to get rid of considerable sums of false money; and you were trying to find their market — by what means these wretches were able to rid themselves of the coin; when, apparently, they were not acquainted with any influential people in the business world, or in the circles of high finance. . . . Well, I have discovered their channel of distribution — it is none other than the proprietor of this house properly, the ground floor and basement of which are occupied by Mother Toulouche — obviously, it is Thomery! . . ."

"No!"

Fandor lifted hands to heaven in despairing fashion and sat silent. He was deeply mortified. There was a long pause, during which Juve calmly smoked on. At last, Fandor asked in a hopeless sort of tone:

"Well? . . . What do you think?"

Slowly, as if awakening from a dream, Juve began to speak.

"We know nothing for certain so far, my lad, except that the Baroness de Vibray has committed suicide; that Princess Sonia Danidoff has recovered from the shock of her jewel robbery, and is to marry Thomery next month . . . there is nothing extraordinary in that . . . just as there is, perhaps, nothing surprising or extraordinary in the series of robberies, nor even in the crimes occupying our attention at the present moment!"

Fandor jumped up. "Nothing!" he shouted. "You are joking, Juve! It is absurd what you say! Do just think a minute, my dear fellow! Why, all these affairs are closely connected, from the Jacques Dollon affair, up to . . . up to . . ."

Fandor stopped short. Juve, who had been listening to him with seeming inattention, now appeared wholly anxious to hear the end of the sentence: he stared hard at Fandor.

"Go on! Go on! I want to make you say it! . . ."

And Fandor, as though in spite of himself, finished with:

"Up to Fantômas!"

"Yes, at last we have got it!" cried Juve.

The two men gazed at each other; once more the logic of deductions, the chain of circumstances had inevitably led him to pronounce the name of the formidable bandit, of whom they could not think without a shudder; whose memory they could not evoke without immediately feeling themselves surrounded by sinister gloom, lost in a thick fog of mystery, of what was strange, hidden, occult!

Fandor's countenance cleared suddenly as he gave utterance to the idea which had just crossed his mind.

"Juve, do you not think that this mysterious prison warder, called Nibet, might very well be an incarnation of Fantômas, because in so many circumstances . . ."

Juve interrupted Fandor with a gesture of denial.

"No, old fellow," said he gravely. "Don't start on that trail, it is assuredly a bad one: Nibet is not Fantômas. Nibet does not count for much, one might say, for nothing at all; he can scarcely be called a tiny wheel even in the great machine driven on its diabolical course by our fiendish enemy . . . we must look higher than that!"

"Thomery?" insisted Fandor, who still held to his idea, and was determined to turn Juve to his way of thinking. . . .

But Juve still said "no!" to that.

"Let us drop Thomery, my lad! As to Fantômas, how do you think we can identify him in this haphazard fashion, basing our idea on pure supposition? . . . For, who is Fantômas — the real Fantômas, among so many probable Fantômas?

"Can you tell me that, Fandor?" continued Juve, who was getting excited at last. . . . "I grant you that we have seen, in the course of our chequered existence, an old gentleman, like Etienne Rambert, a thickset Englishman like Gurn, a robust fellow like Loupart, a weak and sickly individual like Chaleck. We have identified each one of them, in turn, as Fantômas — and that is all.

"As for seeing Fantômas himself, just as he is, without artificial aid, without paint and powder, without a false beard, without a wig, Fantômas as his face really is under his hooded mask of black — that we have not yet done. It is that fact which makes our hunt for the villain ceaselessly difficult, often dangerous! . . . Fantômas is always someone, sometimes two persons, never himself!"

Juve, once started on this subject, could go on for ever, and Fandor did not try to stop him: when the course of conversation led them to talk of Fantômas the two men were as though hypnotised by this mysterious creature, so well named, for he was really "Fantômatic," a spectral entity: the two friends could not turn their minds to any other subject. They discussed Fantômas up and down, in and out, and round about! . . .

It was getting on towards one o'clock when Fandor saw Juve off as far as the staircase. The detective had resumed his disguise, but neither man was in a joking mood now. Fandor had given Juve an account of the annoying, yet rather absurd incident at the convent, when he and Elizabeth were unsuspectingly bidding each other a passionate farewell under the watchful and scandalised eye of a nun! Fandor had thought it better to take Juve into his confidence on the point, though it went against the grain, for he was bashful with regard to his feelings.

Juve had openly laughed at first, but when he understood that Elizabeth, requested to leave the convent, would again be without a safe shelter, he became serious, reflected for a minute or two, then gave his dear lad a piece of advice, advice which Fandor had seemingly taken objection to, and had finished by agreeing to. . . .

They parted with these words:

"The more you think it over, dear lad, the better you will like my idea," said Juve.

Fandor had not said "No" to it!

XVII

AN ARREST

The day after his memorable talk with Juve, Fandor was summoned to appear before the police magistrate, because he could give evidence regarding the rue Raffet affair, and had saved Elizabeth Dollon's life.

It was about four in the afternoon, and he had just entered the passage leading to the offices so familiar to him, when he met Elizabeth. Behind her came several persons whom he recognised: among them were the Barbey-Nanteuil partners, Madame Bourrat, and the servant, Jules. They were together and were talking. The moment she saw him, Elizabeth went up to him.

"Ah, monsieur!" she cried, with a reproachful look. "We had given up all hope of seeing you. . . . Just imagine, the magistrate has finished his enquiry already! Twice he asked if you had come!"

Fandor seemed surprised.

"The summons was for four this afternoon, was it not?" he asked, taking from his pocket the summoning letter. A glance showed that he was not mistaken: he gave Elizabeth the letter to read. She smiled.

"You were summoned for four o'clock, I see; but we had to appear earlier: I was examined as soon as I arrived, and I was summoned to appear at half-past two."

Fandor was annoyed with himself: he might have guessed it! He was vexed because he had not been on the watch in the passage whilst this examination was proceeding. He was moving towards Monsieur Fuselier's room, the magistrate in charge of the Auteuil affair, and he must have looked his vexation, for Elizabeth said:

"I am a little to blame, perhaps, that you had not due notice, but what could I do! Yesterday evening when you telephoned to the convent to ask for news of me, I was just going to tell you at what time I was summoned, but when I went to the telephone. . . ."

"What's this you are telling me?" asked Fandor, staring hard at Elizabeth. "I never telephoned to you yesterday evening. Who told you I had been asking for you on the telephone?"

"Nobody said so; but I supposed it was you! Who else would be so kindly interested in my doings?"

Fandor made no reply to this. Here was the telephone mystery again — an alarming mystery. Elizabeth had not given her address to anyone: Fandor had been careful not to give it to a soul. . . . Clearly, this poor girl, even in the heart of this peaceful convent, was not secure from some unknown, outside interference; and Fandor, optimist though he was, could not help shuddering at the thought of these mysterious adversaries, implacable and formidable, who might work harm to this unfortunate girl, whose devoted protector he now was. . . . Besides . . . did he not feel for Jacques Dollon's pretty sister something sweeter and more tender than pure sympathy? . . . Whenever he was near her, did he not experience a thrill of emotion? Fandor did not analyse his feelings, but they influenced him unconsciously.

He turned to Elizabeth.

"Since you cannot remain any longer at the convent, where do you think of staying?"

"Well, monsieur, I shall go back to the convent this evening, though it is painful to me — very, very painful — to be obliged to accept their icy hospitality . . . as for to-morrow!"

Fandor was about to make a suggestion, when the door of Monsieur Fuselier's room opened half-way. The magistrate's clerk appeared, and, glancing round the passage over his spectacles, called, in a dull tone:

"Monsieur Jérôme Fandor!"

"Here!" replied our journalist. "I am coming!"

Then, taking a hasty farewell of Elizabeth as he went towards the magistrate's room, he whispered:

"Wait for me, mademoiselle; and, for the love of Heaven, remember this — whatever I may say, whatever happens, whether we are alone, together, or in the presence of others, whether it be in a few minutes, or later on, do not be astonished at what may befall you, even though it be my fault — be absolutely convinced of this — whatever I may do will be for your good — more than that I must not say!"

Elizabeth had not a word to say, but his words were humming and buzzing in her ears when Fandor was in the magistrate's room.

With a cordial handshake, Monsieur Fuselier began by congratulating him on having saved Elizabeth Dollon's life.

"Ah," said he, smiling, "you journalists have all the luck; and, between yourselves, I envy you a little, for your lucky star has led you to the discovery of a drama, and has enabled you to prevent a fatal ending to it. Now, do you not think, as I do, that this Auteuil affair is not a case of suicide, but of attempted assassination?"

"There is no doubt about it," replied Fandor quietly.

The magistrate drew himself up with a satisfied air.

"That is also my opinion — has been so from the start."

The clerk now interrupted the two men, who were talking as friends rather than as magistrate and witness, asking, in nasal tone:

"Does His Honour wish to take the evidence of Monsieur Jérôme Fandor?"

"In four lines then. I do not think Monsieur Fandor has anything more to tell us than what he has already told us in the columns of *La Capitale*. That is so, is it not?" asked the magistrate, looking at Fandor.

"That is correct," replied our journalist.

The clerk rapidly drew up the deposition of Monsieur Jérôme Fandor, in due form, and read it aloud in a monotonous voice.

Fandor signed it. It did not compromise him at all. He was about to leave when Monsieur Fuselier caught him by the arm.

"Please wait a minute! There are one or two points to be cleared up: I am going to ask the witnesses a few questions: we will have a general confrontation — we will compare evidence!"

Then, the journalist's friend, now all the magistrate, asked the assembled witnesses certain questions, in an emphatic and professional tone.

Fandor, seated a little apart, had leisure to examine the faces of the different persons whom circumstances had brought together in this room.

His first look was for Elizabeth: energy and courage were plainly marked on her pretty, sad face. Then there was the proprietor of the Auteuil boarding-house: an honest, vulgar creature, red-faced, perpetually mopping her brow and raising her hands to heaven; ready to bewail her position, deploring the untimely publicity given to this affair, a publicity which threatened discredit to her boarding-house.

As he was seated directly behind the manservant, Jules, Fandor had a view of his broad back, surmounted by a big bullet head and ruffled hair. This witness spoke with a strong Picardy accent, and there was nothing remarkable about his answers: he seemed the conventional second-rate type of servant. He did not seem to have understood much of what occurred on the famous day: when questioned as to the order of events, his answers were vague, uncertain.

Then, seated beside Fandor were the bankers: Barbey, a grave-looking man, no longer young, judging by his beard, which was going grey; he was decorated with the Legion of Honour: the other, Nanteuil, looked about thirty, elegant, distinguished, lively. These two were well known in the highest Parisian society as representing finance of the best kind. They were highly thought of.

The magistrate asked the bankers a question.

"Why," asked he, "did Messieurs Barbey-Nanteuil call on Mademoiselle Dollon? Was it to bring her some help, as has been stated?"

Elizabeth blushed with humiliation at the magistrate's question. Monsieur Nanteuil answered:

"There is a slight distinction to be made, your Honour, and Mademoiselle Dollon certainly will not object to our mentioning it. It never entered our minds to offer Mademoiselle Dollon charity —

charity she never asked of us, be it clearly understood. Mademoiselle Dollon, with whom we had previously been acquainted, whose misfortunes have inspired us with deep sympathy, wrote to ask us if we could find her some employment. Hoping to find some post for her, we came to see her, to talk with her, to find out what her capabilities were. That is all. We were very glad it so happened, that we were able to aid Monsieur Fandor in restoring her to life."

"Can you tell me, Monsieur Fandor, did you notice anything suspicious in Mademoiselle Dollon's room when you entered it? You wrote, in your article, that at first you had thought it simply an attempted burglary, followed by an attempted murder?"

"That is so," replied Fandor. "Directly the window was opened, I leaned out: I wanted to see if there was anything suspicious on the wall of the house. I also looked behind the shutters."

"Why?" asked the examining magistrate.

"Because I had not forgotten the close of the Thomery drama — the same Monsieur Thomery mentioned in the Assize Court yesterday — oh, in all honour, of course; but you have not forgotten — although that examination was not in your hands, and I regret it, because I am of the opinion that there are points of connection interlinking all these mysterious affairs — you have not forgotten, I am sure, that when the investigations were over and Monsieur Thomery's guests had been allowed to leave the house, that a thread of flax was discovered hanging to the window fastening of the room in which Princess Danidoff had been found unconscious. This flax thread was very strong, and was broken at the end: it is easy to conclude that the stolen pearls had been temporarily fastened to it. This led me to think that the aggressor, or aggressors, had remained in the reception rooms during the whole course of the investigations, since it is proved that no one left the house. . . .

" . . . But, after all, we are not here to investigate the Thomery affair. . . . I wished to explain why I had examined the window and shutters Of Mademoiselle Dollon's room: I wanted to ascertain whether the procedure of the would-be murderer of Mademoiselle Dollon was similar to that of the robber in the Danidoff-Thomery case."

"And what conclusion did you come to?" asked the magistrate.

"Window and shutters bore no traces that I could see," said Fandor. "I could not come to any conclusion."

Here Monsieur Barbey intervened.

"If I may be allowed to say so" — he glanced at the magistrate for the required permission, which was given with a smile and gesture of assent — "I quite agree with Monsieur Jérôme Fandor. I also am convinced that, even if there is not a close connection between the

Thomery affair and the Auteuil affair, at least there exists such a connection between the Auteuil affair and the terrible drama of rue Norvins."

"I would go even further than that," declared Monsieur Nanteuil. "The robbery of rue du Quatre Septembre, of which we are the victims, is also connected with this same series of mysterious cases."

The magistrate asked a question.

"It is a matter of twenty millions, is it not? It must have been a terrible blow to you?"

"Fearful, monsieur," replied Monsieur Nanteuil. "Our credit was shaken: it affected a considerable number of our clients, Monsieur Thomery among them, and we consider him one of our most important clients. You are aware, of course, that in financial matters confidence is almost everything! . . . Our losses have just been covered by an insurance, but we have suffered other than direct material losses. Still" — the banker turned towards Elizabeth, who was wiping tears from her eyes — "still, what are our troubles compared with those which have struck Mademoiselle Dollon blow upon blow? Assassination of the Baroness de Vibray, mysterious death — — "

"The Baroness de Vibray was not assassinated, she committed suicide," interrupted Fandor sharply. "Most certainly, I do not wish to make you responsible for that, gentlemen; but when you wrote, announcing her ruin, you dealt her a very hard blow!"

"Could we have done otherwise?" replied Monsieur Barbey, with his customary gravity of manner and tone. "In our matter of fact business, where all must be clear and definite, we do not mince our words: we are bound to state things as they actually are. What is more, we do not share your point of view, and are convinced that the Baroness de Vibray was certainly murdered."

Monsieur Fuselier now expressed his opinion, or at least, what he wished to be considered as his opinion:

"Gentlemen, consider yourselves for the moment as not in the presence of the examining magistrate, but as being in the drawing-room of Monsieur Fuselier. In my private capacity, I will give you my opinion regarding the rue Norvins affair. I am decidedly less and less in agreement with Monsieur Fandor, though I recognise with pleasure his fine detective gifts."

"Thanks," interrupted Fandor ironically. "That is a poor compliment!"

Smiling, the magistrate continued:

"I am of the same opinion as Messieurs Barbey-Nanteuil: I believe Madame de Vibray was murdered."

Fandor could not control his impatience.

"Be logical, messieurs, I beg of you!" he cried. "The Baroness de Vibray committed suicide. Her letter states her intention. The authenticity of this letter has not been disputed. The disastrous revelations, contained in Messieurs Barbey-Nanteuil's communication, proved too severe a shock for the poor lady's unbalanced brain: the news of her ruin, abruptly conveyed, drove her to desperation. The death of the Baroness de Vibray was voluntary and self-inflicted."

There was a dead silence. Then Monsieur Barbey asked a question.

"Well, then, Monsieur Fandor, will you explain to us how it happened that the Baroness de Vibray was found dead in the studio of the painter, Jacques Dollon?"

Fandor seemed to expect this question from the banker.

"There are two hypotheses," he declared. "The first, and, in my humble opinion, the more improbable, is this: Madame de Vibray at the same time that she decided to put an end to her life, wished to pay her protégé a last visit; all the more so, because he had asked her to come and see his work before it was sent in to the Salon. Perhaps the Baroness intended to perform an act of charity, in this instance, before her supreme hour struck. Perhaps she miscalculated the effect of the poison she had taken, and so died in the house of the friend she had come to see and help: her death there could not have been her choice, for she must have known what serious trouble it would involve the artist in, were her dead body found in his studio.

"Here is the second hypothesis, which seems the more plausible. The Baroness de Vibray learns that she is ruined, she decides to die, and by chance or coincidence, which remains to be explained, for I have not the key to it yet, some third parties interested in her fate, learn her decision. They let her write to her lawyer; they do not prevent her poisoning herself; but, as soon as she is dead, they straightway take possession of her dead body and hasten to carry it to Jacques Dollon's studio. To the painter himself they administered either with his consent or by force — probably by force — a powerful narcotic, so that when the police are called in next day they not only find the Baroness lying dead in the studio, but they also find the painter unconscious, close by his visitor. When Jacques Dollon is restored to consciousness, he is quite unable to give any sort of explanation of the tragedy; naturally enough, the police look upon him as the murderer of her who was well known to have been his patroness. . . . How does that strike you?"

It was now Monsieur Fuselier's turn to hold forth.

"You forget a detail which has its importance! I do not pretend to judge as to whether she was poisoned by her own free act or not; but, in any case, we have this proof — an uncorked phial of cyanide of potassium was found in Jacques Dollon's studio. It seemed to have been recently opened; but, when the painter was questioned about it, he declared that he had not made use of this ingredient for a very long time."

Fandor replied:

"I can turn your argument against you, monsieur. If the Baroness de Vibray had been poisoned, voluntarily or not, with the cyanide of potassium in Dollon's studio, he would have taken the precaution to banish all traces of the poison in question. It would have been his first care! When questioned by the police inspector, he would not have declared that he had not made use of this poison for a very long time! the contradiction involved is proof that Dollon was sincere; therefore, we are faced by a fact which, if not inexplicable, is, at least, unexplained."

Monsieur Barbey now had something to say:

"You criticise and hair-split in a remarkable fashion, monsieur, and are an adept in the science of induction; but, let me say without offence meant, that you give me the impression of being rather a romancing journalist than a judicial investigator! . . . Admitting that the Baroness de Vibray was carried to the painter Dollon's studio after her death, and that seems to be your opinion, what advantage would it be to the criminals to act in such a fashion?"

Jérôme Fandor had risen, his eyes shining, his body vibrating with excitement.

"I expected your question, monsieur," he cried; "and the answer is simple. The mysterious criminals seized the Baroness de Vibray's body and brought it to Dollon's studio to create an alibi, and to cast suspicion on an innocent man. As you know, the stratagem was successful: two hours after the discovery of the crime, the police arrested Mademoiselle Dollon's unfortunate brother!"

With a dramatic gesture Fandor pointed to Elizabeth, who, no longer able to contain her grief, was weeping bitterly.

The audience had risen, moved, troubled, subjugated, in spite of themselves, by the journalist's eloquent and persuasive tones. Even Monsieur Fuselier had quitted his classic green leather arm-chair and had approached the two bankers: Madame Bourrat was behind them, and the servant, Jules, with his smooth face and staring eyes.

Fandor continued:

"This is not all, messieurs! . . . There is still something that must be said, and I beg of you to listen with all your attention, for what the result of my declarations will be, I do not know! It is no longer my reason that speaks, instinct dictates my words! Listen! . . ."

It was a poignant moment! All the witnesses, the magistrate included, were thrilled with the certainty that the journalist was about to make a sensational revelation.

Taking his time, Jérôme Fandor walked slowly, quietly up to Elizabeth who, distraught with grief, was in floods of tears.

"Mademoiselle," he said, in a clear level voice, which was in strange contrast with his recent persuasive and authoritative tones. "Mademoiselle, you must tell us everything! . . . You are here, not in the presence of a judge, and of enemies, but amidst friends who wish you nothing but good. . . . I understand your affectionate feelings, I know what an unreasoning, but quite natural, attachment you have for your unfortunate brother — but, mademoiselle, it is now imperatively necessary that you should do violence to yourself — you must tell us the truth, the whole truth!"

Interrupting his appeal to Elizabeth, Fandor turned to the magistrate with a smile so enigmatic that his audience could not tell whether he was speaking sincerely or was acting a part.

"I have contended in my articles up to now that Jacques Dollon was dead, dead beyond recall; but when confronted with recent facts my theory seems to fall to the ground." Fandor turned once more to Elizabeth, resuming his authoritative tone and manner: "Since the affair of the Dépôt, the legal authorities have recognised indelible traces of Jacques Dollon's hand in the series of crimes which have been recently perpetrated. Up to the present, I have determinedly denied such a possibility. But, mademoiselle, I put it to you: you have forgotten to tell us something of the very utmost importance, something quite out of the range of ordinary happenings, something phenomenal. Now here is the staggering fact I am faced with! The other day, between two and three in the afternoon, at the Auteuil boarding-house where you are staying, you received a visit from your brother, Jacques Dollon, the supposed robber of the Princess Sonia Danidoff's pearls, the suspected author of the robbery of rue du Quatre Septembre; and, lastly, the fratricide, for what other explanation of the attack on you can be given — an attempted murder beyond question — and I add . . ." Fandor could not continue. His eyes were fixed on those of Elizabeth who, at the first words addressed to her by the journalist, had started up, trembling from head to foot. . . . Their glances met, challenging, each seeking to quell, to subjugate the other. . . . It seemed to the onlookers that they were witnessing an intense struggle between two very strong natures separated by a deep, a fathomless gulf; that a veil, dark as night, hanging between them had been rent asunder, giving passage to an illuminating flash; that this luminous ray carried with it all the revelations and the key to the fantastic mystery!

But to a calm, perspicacious observer of the two beings standing face to face, it would have been clear that Jérôme Fandor's real attitude was both suppliant and persuasive, and that Elizabeth Dollon's was one of overwhelming surprise.

Monsieur Fuselier, carried away by the journalist's startling and extraordinary statements, did not perceive this. Suddenly, he saw in Jérôme Fandor the denunciator, and in Elizabeth Dollon, the accomplice unmasked. Nevertheless, he said quietly:

"Monsieur Fandor, you have just uttered words of such gravity that you are bound to confirm them by indisputable evidence. Do you mean to persist on these lines?"

Fandor looked away from the stupefied Elizabeth and her questioning glance: he answered the magistrate at once.

"The proof of what I advance, you will find by searching Mademoiselle Dollon's room. . . . I would rather not say more than that. . . ."

"Allow me to state, monsieur, that I cannot arrange for such an investigation until to-morrow morning!"

Then, addressing the astounded Madame Bourrat, the two bankers, and the manservant, Jules.

"Madame, messieurs, will you be kind enough to withdraw? Madame, I advise you, under pain of the most serious consequences, not to allow anyone whatever to enter your premises, nor go into Mademoiselle Dollon's room, before this matter has been fully sifted by the legal authorities. Be good enough to wait in the passage — all of you!"

Having witnessed their exit, the magistrate walked up to Fandor, and looking him straight in the eyes said:

"Well! . . . Out with it!"

"Well," replied the journalist, "if you institute a search in the place I have indicated, you will find, in the chest of drawers, under a pile of Mademoiselle Dollon's personal linen a piece of soap wrapped up in a cambric handkerchief. Take this soap to Monsieur Bertillon's department, and after the scientific tests have been applied to it, you will be able to say that it bears distinct impressions of Dollon's hand!"

"Dollon's?"

The magistrate gasped.

Elizabeth Dollon had fallen back into the arm-chair, from which she had risen all trembling. Her tears had ceased. She stared at the two men with wide open, terrified eyes. All the time, the clerk in spectacles wrote steadily on at his table, noting down the details of the scenes he was witnessing.

There was a palpitating silence.

Monsieur Fuselier had returned to his writing table.

Jérôme Fandor seemed to have recovered his composure, an ironic smile curved his lips beneath his small moustache, whilst his hand sought that of Elizabeth: it was the only way he could, at the moment, express the sympathy he had never ceased to feel for her.

Monsieur Fuselier filled in a printed paper and pressed an electric bell.

Two municipal guards appeared.

Monsieur Fuselier rose and signing to the soldiers to wait, he faced Elizabeth Dollon.

"Mademoiselle, have you any objections to make to the statements of Monsieur Jérôme Fandor? Will you say whether or no you received a visit from your brother?"

Elizabeth, tortured by intense emotion, her throat contracted, strove in vain to pronounce a word; at last, by a supreme effort, she murmured in a strangled voice:

"Oh! Why, you are all mad here!"

As she gave no direct reply to his question, Monsieur Fuselier, after a pause, announced in a grave voice:

"Mademoiselle! Until I have more ample information, I am under the cruel necessity of ordering your arrest! . . . Guards, arrest the accused!" cried the magistrate sternly.

Elizabeth Dollon made a movement of revolt, when she saw herself surrounded and felt her arms seized by the two representatives of authority. She was about to cry out in protest, but a glance — it seemed to her a tender glance — from Fandor restrained her. . . . She stood speechless, inert. After all, had she not confidence in him, although she could not understand his attitude! Had he not been her staunch defender up to now? Had he not warned her that she must not be astonished at anything that occurred — that she must be prepared for anything? . . . Nevertheless, Elizabeth Dollon felt her brain reeling — she was astounded beyond words. . . . The surprise was too strong for her. . . .

About a quarter of an hour after this tragic scene, Fandor was pacing up and down the asphalt of the boulevard du Palais, plunged in thought, when someone clapped him on the shoulder. He turned. It was Monsieur Fuselier.

"Well, my dear fellow!" cried the magistrate, resuming his customary tone of good fellowship. "Well, what an adventure! You have been playing some fine tricks! I never expected such a stroke as that, the deuce if I did!"

"Ho, ho!" laughed Fandor, "I think that a week from to-day we shall know a good many things!"

"Well," replied the magistrate, "I have had the girl placed in solitary confinement — that makes them willing to speak out!. . . ."

Fandor looked the magistrate up and down.

"Ah!" murmured he, with a scarcely perceptible note of contempt in his voice:

"You think you will extract information from that quarter, do you?"

"But why not? Why not?" interrupted the dapper Monsieur Fuselier, in a sprightly tone; and, leaving Fandor abruptly, he leapt into a passing tramcar.

Fandor watched Fuselier cross the road and climb to an outside seat. Whilst the magistrate waved a friendly farewell from the top of the disappearing car, Fandor shrugged disdainful shoulders, and, with pitying lips, muttered one word:

"Fool!"

XVIII

AT THE BOTTOM OF THE TRUNK

After Monsieur Fuselier's departure, Fandor rejoined Madame Bourrat on the boulevard. The good woman was very much upset by the dramatic scene she had witnessed. She had sent off her manservant, and was preparing to take the tram back to Auteuil. Fandor asked if he might accompany her, and Madame Bourrat was only too delighted to have a chance of further talk with the journalist, for she had a lively desire to learn all she could about the extraordinary drama in which she found herself involved.

When they arrived at Auteuil, Madame Bourrat had learned nothing definite, for the journalist had given only evasive answers to her questions. Still, one point was obvious: Madame Bourrat considered Monsieur Jérôme Fandor as the most amiable man in the world, and she was disposed to help him to the utmost of her powers, in defence of any interests he wished to safeguard. . . .

Madame Bourrat was absolutely set on receiving Monsieur Fandor in her private apartments. She then seized the opportunity to complain of the trouble this affair had brought into her regular and peaceful existence. Certainly, in summer, her boarders were less numerous; their numbers being, in fact, reduced to two or three.

This season there had been fewer than usual; but the accident, or attempted assassination of Mademoiselle Dollon, had undoubtedly brought discredit on the house. An old paralysed gentleman, who had been in residence on the day of the drama, had departed the day after. There was not a single boarder in the house: it was empty.

Having made certain that her manservant, Jules, and her cook, Marianne, had retired to their respective rooms, Madame Bourrat conducted Fandor as far as the door of her dwelling. They had been so interested in their talk, that they had forgotten all about dinner: their experiences of the past few hours had left them with little appetite. It was about nine o'clock; night had fallen: house and garden were wrapped in a mantle of darkness.

"Can you find your way?" asked Madame Bourrat. If she accompanied the journalist to her garden gate she would have to grope back to the house in the dark, and alone! Her nerves were shaken by recent events. She did not wish to venture forth and back in the mysterious gloom of night, even on the familiar path of her garden. What might that darkness not hide! What robbers, what murderers might there not be lurking near!

Fandor laughed.

"Why, of course I can, madame! To find the points of the compass, to cultivate the sense of locality, is part of a journalist's profession."

"Do not forget to draw to behind you — it needs a strong pull — the gate which separates us from the street: once shut, no one can open it from outside."

Fandor, shaking hands with the boarding-house keeper, promised to close the gate. As the sound of his steps on the gravel grew less and less, as the gate fell to with a loud noise, and an absolute silence followed, Madame Bourrat felt sure that her guest had left the garden — had gone away.

But he had done nothing of the sort!

Fandor had shut the gate noiselessly, but he had remained inside the grounds. He stood motionless, holding his breath, wishing neither to be seen nor heard. He remained so for a long twenty minutes. Then, being assured that Madame Bourrat had retired for the night — she had closed her shutters and put out her light — he rubbed his hands, murmuring:

"Now we shall see!"

Stepping gingerly along by the side of the wall, he reached the main building of the boarding-house: luckily, it was empty as far as boarders were concerned. He recognised Elizabeth Dollon's window on the first floor and was glad to see that it was half open. Chance favoured him — there was even a gutter pipe running down the wall and passing close to the window. Providence had favoured him with a fine staircase; there would not be much difficulty in climbing that!

No sooner thought than done! Accustomed as he was to exercise and games, Fandor, agile as a young man in good training can be, squirmed up the pipe as far as Elizabeth's window. He caught hold of the sill, recovered his balance, jerked himself up, and, two seconds after, had landed in the room.

Dared he strike a light! He remembered pretty accurately the position of the various pieces of furniture, but he would like to study the room more in detail. His luck still held, for a ray of moonlight suddenly shone out from behind a cloud. He saw the moon sailing in a clear sky. There would be sufficient light from the moon rays to enable him to pursue his investigations.

It was an essentially modern room; the white walls were painted with ripolin, and were as bare of ornament as a nun's cell. An iron bedstead stood in the middle of the room: a wardrobe, with a mirror panel in front, and locked, occupied one of the corners; behind a folding screen was a toilette table, a Louis XV bureau, two chairs, an arm-chair: that was all.

After making this rapid inventory, Fandor considered:

"The situation is growing complicated," said he to himself. "I am quite persuaded that this room will shortly receive a visit from some individuals who will not court recognition — their interests are all against that — and they certainly will not be anxious to meet me here! These individuals assuredly know, at this minute, that the examining magistrate is going to make a thorough investigation here to-morrow morning. . . . How do they know it? It's very simple. The prime mover in the attempted murder, or one of his accomplices, was assuredly among the witnesses this afternoon. Is it the amiable Madame Bourrat? Is it that doltish Jules, who looks an absolute fool, but may be masking his game! Suppose the serious Barbey pops up? Or the elegant Nanteuil? But I do not think so — they are rather victims than attackers — everything leads me to that opinion. But — all this does not tell me whether the place has already been visited or not!"

Fandor unlocked the drawer, searched for the piece of soap under the pile of Elizabeth's linen, and had the extreme satisfaction of finding the soap had not been moved.

"Good! I am here first! Ah, we shall see our men presently! Which, and how many?"

Fandor seated himself and let his imagination work. He tried to picture the faces of the mysterious individuals he was determined to track down — but, so far, in vain! . . . Then with strange, uncanny persistence, one face rose again and again before his mental vision, clear, vital — the face of the enigmatic Thomery, with his silver white hair, his red face, his light blue eyes, that Yankee head of his, well set on his robust torso. . . .

"Thomery!" cried Fandor almost aloud. "The fact is, everything leads me to think . . . but don't let us anticipate! Concealment is the next item on the programme!"

Fandor realised that to hide under the bed was impossible: he would be discovered immediately. . . . The screen was no better! . . . There was Elizabeth's trunk! . . . Why, it was a kind of monument in wicker work! The very thing! It was quite big enough to hold him — it was one of those enormous trunks beloved of women! . . . To hide in it would be an excellent trick — a real joke! Let me burrow in there, and see the stupefaction of these estimable characters when they open it to rummage about among Elizabeth's belongings and find themselves face to face with me! They will see besides my sympathetic countenance the stern mouth of my revolver! . . . Let us see whether it is a possible hiding place!

Fandor raised the cover and lifted out a top compartment, in which were scattered, among objects of feminine apparel, papers, books, and all sorts of things which had evidently belonged to the unfortunate painter. The distracted Elizabeth, in the hurry of departure from rue Norvins, must have thrust them in pell-mell. The lower division of the trunk was empty.

"Another bit of luck!" thought Fandor. "Now to sample my little hide-hole!"

Fandor found he could get into a fairly comfortable position. Then he calculated, that with the compartment back in its place and the cover open, all he had to do to close it was to shake the trunk transversely. He could certainly remain inside for several hours without intolerable discomfort.

Raising the cover, Fandor slipped out.

The interminable hours crawled by. To smoke was out of the question. Fandor's pride in his exploit was sinking to zero: was he passing a wretched night to no purpose? A violent ring sounded. Someone was ringing at the garden gate — ringing loudly, insistently — an imperative summons!

Instantly Fandor was on the alert. Useless to slip to the window and peer cautiously out, for Elizabeth's window did not face the gate: even by leaning out he could not catch any glimpse of any visitors, either coming to the house or passing along towards Madame Bourrat's apartments in the annex. . . . Besides, Fandor feared to make a noise, and the polished boards of the floor cracked and creaked at the least movement!

"The one thing for me to do," thought he, "is to creep back into my retreat and wait. Now who can it be at this time of night?"

Fandor's curiosity was rapidly satisfied — after a fashion! The call of the bell had been answered by noises and hurried footsteps, whisperings, an outburst of voices, then silence. . . . A few minutes after, Fandor clearly heard some persons entering the ground floor of the house.

He listened intently: he could hear his own heartbeats.

Then a voice said:

"In Heaven's name! Is it possible? Why do you come to upset people at this time of night? As if we had not had enough to put up with during the day! It is a dreadful business! There's no doubt about it! Are we never to be left in peace?"

"Why, it's Madame Bourrat's voice!" said Fandor. "Poor woman! What's up?" He listened. Someone said:

"The law is the law, madame, and we are it's humble executors. As the examining judge has ordered me to make an investigating distraint, we are compelled to carry out his instructions to the letter. Be good enough to tell your servant to lead us to the actual spot where the crime was attempted."

"Now what is all this?" asked Fandor. "And from whence comes this police inspector? It only wanted that! He won't know what to make of it when I tell him who I am — and how am I to explain my presence here? Anyhow, wait, and see what happens!"

"Someone was coming upstairs — more than one!"

"This way, messieurs!" said a hoarse voice. "The room the young lady occupied is at the end of this passage!"

"This time I recognise my fine fellow!" thought Fandor. "It is that imbecile of a Jules. But what a triumphant tone! And how different his voice sounds to what it did, this afternoon, at the examination!"

Then Fandor all but jumped from his hiding place.

"Oh! What an egregious fool I am! Why, there is not a police inspector in France who would come at this hour to carry out an investigation — and a distraint to boot! What the devil does it mean? Can they be the fine fellows I am lying in wait to meet?"

The dubious individuals who had roused the house at such an unholy hour entered the room. Someone turned on the electric light.

Though Fandor could obtain a sufficient supply of air through the openings in the wickerwork, he could not see what was going on: he could only listen with all his ears.

Madame Bourrat accompanied her strange visitors.

"It is here," she exclaimed, "that the journalist, Jérôme Fandor, found my boarder stretched out on the floor. . . . You see, in this corner, is the gas stove with its tubing! They have forgotten to refix it to the pipe; but there is no danger, the tap is turned off and so is the meter."

The personage who had given out that he was a police inspector, whose voice was probably an assumed one, replied only by monosyllables. Fandor did not recognise his voice. But there was another speaker, who also had very little to say for himself; and Fandor thought he recognised certain tones as belonging to a man who had been much in his thoughts of late.

"Thomery!" thought he. "Is it Thomery?"

But he only knew the sugar refiner by sight, and had heard him speak but once or twice at the ball: that was not enough to go on, for Fandor had not paid special attention to the distinguishing tone and quality of his host's voice. Nevertheless, he could not get out of his head the idea that the celebrated sugar refiner, honoured by all Paris, esteemed by everybody, was standing only a step or two away from him now in this house of strange happenings, and under very peculiar circumstances. "Was he a burglar — an assassin? One of a nefarious band?"

For Fandor was now convinced that these were not police emissaries bearing a legal mandate to search and distrain: no, they were robbers, criminals! He was preparing to rise from his hiding place and appear before the bandits: he would fire a few shots and make the deuce of a row and rouse the neighbourhood. He would also save poor Madame Bourrat, who was certainly not their accomplice. Just then he heard the pretended police inspector say:

"Will you provide us with writing materials, madame? We must write an official report."

"Why, certainly, monsieur," replied Madame Bourrat. "I will go downstairs and get what you require."

Fandor heard her leave the room. No sooner had she gone than a hurried conversation began in low tones. Clearly Jules was guilty, for the pretended police inspector asked:

"No one this evening? Nothing happened?"

"No," replied Jules in a servile tone. "The journalist brought the mistress back and then went off at nine o'clock. . . ."

"No news of Alfred?" asked the voice.

The third person answered:

"Why, no. You know very well he is always at the Dépôt."

"Let us set to work!" said voice number one.

Fandor felt that the decisive moment had arrived: someone opened the cover of the trunk and feverish hands were turning over the confused mass of objects in the top compartment.

"Didn't you find anything?" asked the voice of Jules.

"No, no, monsieur! I searched everywhere; but as I do not read easily, it's difficult for me. . . ."

"Imbecile!" murmured the voice.

"Ah!" said Fandor to himself. "This fellow pleases me! He has the same opinion of this dolt of a Jules as I have!"

Revolver in hand, Fandor was on the alert. The moment they lifted up the compartment out he would jump. Just then, Madame Bourrat could be heard approaching.

"Confound it! We shall not have time to go through everything!" muttered a voice. The trunk cover was hastily closed.

Fandor heard Madame Bourrat enter the room with slow, heavy step.

"Here are ink and paper, messieurs!" she said.

Then the pretended police inspector made a statement that startled the concealed Fandor.

"Madame, we have no time, nor are we able to make a minute investigation now. Besides, with one exception, there does not seem to be anything suspicious about the room; but here is a trunk which contains papers of great importance. We are going to take it to the police station."

"As you please," replied Madame Bourrat. "I ask only one thing and that is to be left in peace. I do not want to hear anything more about this abominable affair!"

A rapid turn of the key given to each of the locks and Fandor knew that he was now a prisoner! Brave as he was, he felt a rush of blood to his heart and a cold sweat broke out on his forehead.

"Dash it all! I am in an awful position! Impossible to move! If these brutes suspected they had me tight in here they would pitch me into the river as sure as Fate! Then good-bye to *La Capitale*!"

Then, before Fandor's mental vision rose a sweet consoling figure, the figure of the girl for whom he was braving danger, for love of whom — he certainly did love her — he had placed himself in such a serious position.... Then all that was optimistic in his nature — and that was much — rose to the surface, and declared the dilemma was not as serious as it seemed. . . . How could the bandits know of his presence in the trunk? They never would think Jérôme Fandor so stupid as to shut himself up in the trap!

"Jules and I might shake hands as equals in folly!" concluded Fandor.... Just then the trunk began to move. They were trying to lift it. Whilst trying to preserve an unstable equilibrium, he said to himself in a satisfied way:

"And just to think now that they have not rummaged in the chest of drawers, nor have they seized the tell-tale piece of soap! . . . It's true that Fuselier alone knows of its being there — I was careful not to tell anyone else. . . . But, where the deuce are they going? It's the stairs, of course! It might be a rough precipice by the shaking up they're giving me!"

XIX

CRIMINAL OR VICTIM?

At the bottom of his trunk Jérôme Fandor was foaming with rage, furious at being caught in the trap and uneasy as to how this adventure would end.

Whilst he was realising that his unknown porters were carrying their heavy weight with difficulty to the pavement of rue Raffet, he made up his mind to a definite course of action: regardless of consequences, he was going to shout, move about, make a regular disturbance, rouse the attention of the passers-by — if there happened to be any — but, at all costs, he meant to get out of the trap! . . . He saw a ray of hope: Madame Bourrat had accompanied her visitors as far as the gate. In presence of such a witness, they would, at least, hesitate to do him serious bodily harm when he made his presence unmistakably known, furious though they would be. He would take every advantage of the situation. . . .

Fandor was about to act: a second more and he would have started, when he heard them speaking. He kept quiet.

"We must have a taxi, or at the very least a cab to transport this big trunk. Do you know where one is likely to be found?"

"I doubt if one will be passing at this hour, monsieur. We retire early in these parts; but, if you like, Jules can go to the station."

"That's settled. Let him go as fast as he can!"

"Well, that is reassuring," thought Fandor. "If these fine fellows take a cab, it is not with the intention of chucking my cage and me into the river — and that is what I feared most. They may be going to leave me in a cloak-room till called for; or they may pack us off as luggage to some destination unknown! . . . Oh, well, I shall only be a traveller without a ticket and I shall be sure to find some way out of the difficulty! And then, what stuff for an article I shall have when I get back to *La Capitale*! . . . What must they be thinking at the offices! It's forty-eight hours since I put foot in them! Never mind! When they know! . . ."

Fandor was listening with all his ears; but the bandits had little to say; and, when they did speak, their voices were plainly disguised. Was it as a general precaution, or was it on account of Madame Bourrat? . . . But, unless they were known to her, why the necessity? If, however, she knew one or more of them personally, why, they must have disguised their faces and figures as well as their voices! . . . If only he could have a peep at them!

The sound of wheels made him suppose that Jules had succeeded in getting a cab at the Auteuil station. Then the trot-trot-trot of a horse became audible: a few moments later a cab drew up at the edge of the pavement.

A hoarse voice was heard.

"It's not a long journey, I hope!" said the hoarse, grumbling voice of the cabman.

"To Police Headquarters," replied the pretended police inspector.

"We shall see about that!" thought Fandor. "That address is to throw dust in Madame Bourrat's eyes. They will change their destination on the way. I bet on it! . . ."

"The brutes! Are they going to jam my cage and me on to the seat?" Fandor asked himself, for they had seized the trunk and were beginning to lift it up. . . . "Am I to be stuck upside down beside the driver? I don't fancy so! . . . We must weigh at least ninety kilos, as I weigh seventy myself!"

Fandor's mind was soon made easy on that score. After a fruitless attempt to hoist the trunk to the box seat, they decided to put it on to the back seat of the Victoria. One of the bandits planted himself on the little folding seat opposite the trunk: the other bandit mounted to the box seat next the driver.

The two bandits took leave of Madame Bourrat. The rickety old vehicle started off. Presently, Fandor heard what he had expected to hear: one of his captors told the driver to take them to some other address than Police Headquarters. Owing to the rattling of the ramshackle cab — it lacked rubber tyres — Fandor, though listening with ears astretch, could not hear one word distinctly.

Soon pale gleams of light began to filter through the wickerwork: dawn was near.

"Ah, we shall soon reach our destination," thought Fandor. "I don't fancy my trunk lifters will wish to be seen with this turnout in broad daylight! Now, where the deuce are we going?"

In vain did Fandor strive to follow the route taken by the bandits! He had noted each shock and counter-shock produced by cobbled streets and smooth roads, by bumping against pavements, by crossed tram lines and sharp turnings! . . .

The cab stopped with a jolt and a jerk. The two men got out. The trunk was lifted down to the pavement. The driver was paid. He rattled off.

"Now trunk and I are in for it!" thought Fandor.

A bell pealed. A courtyard entrance gate was thrown open. The two men lifted the trunk, cursing under their breath at its weight.

In passing under the archway they called some name unknown to Fandor and so unintelligible that he could not remember it; then it was a painful ascension: up a staircase they went with prodigious effort, stopping on two landings.

"Two floors," counted Fandor. "We are coming to the end, and, all said and done, I would rather be in a house than at the bottom of the river!"

A key turned in a lock; the trunk was pushed rapidly inside; then the noise of a door being shut.

Fandor was in a room; no doubt, alone with the two bandits, and at their mercy! He was plunged into complete darkness. Evidently the shutters were still closed. The noise made by footsteps on the floor showed that it was uncarpeted. Judging from the sound, there seemed to be little furniture and no hangings in the room.

"Am I and my cage in an ordinary room, in a studio, or in a hall?" wondered Fandor. In any case, the fellows who had brought him there seemed anxious to avoid making a noise.

Then he felt the cover of the wickerwork trunk bend slightly and heard it creak. For a moment, he thought the two men were about to open his prison. He had his revolver ready: every inch of him was on the defensive! Then he realised that his captors had merely seated themselves on the trunk to rest!

They began to talk.

"This," thought Fandor, "is splendid! I shall hear everything they say. Why, it is a conversation in my honour! What luck!"

Fandor was delighted: thanks to his position he would hear some interesting secrets. He listened. Alas! He could hear every word they uttered, but he could not understand what they were saying! Fandor swore strictly to himself. The two wretches were conversing in German.

To the best of his judgment, a good hour had passed since the false police inspector and his acolyte had left the room. They had simply drawn to the door behind them, not troubling to lock it, much to the joy of Jérôme Fandor.

Absolute silence reigned.

Fandor attempted some discreet movements as a test. The wickerwork creaked as he gently shook the trunk at short intervals. Not an answering sound came from outside! Menaced with cramp, Fandor felt that the moment of escape had arrived.

He was, certainly, the only living soul in the place: listen as he might, and his sense of hearing was acute, he could not hear any sound of breathing. Yes, the time to quit his prison had come!

Fandor had with him, besides his revolver, a box of matches, and a hunter's knife consisting of several blades, and a little saw. Getting out his knife with some difficulty, he began to hack at the wickerwork. Dry and pliant, the interlaced rods did not long resist the saw's steel teeth. It took him a bare ten minutes to make an opening, sufficiently large to push his head and shoulders through: the rest of his body followed easily. Such was his haste to be free, that he tore, not only his clothes, but his elbows and hands, on the jagged ends of the broken wickerwork: large drops of blood fell on the flooring.

"Bah! I've got off cheaply!" cried Fandor, standing up to relax his cramped muscles and stretching his aching legs and arms.

"Unless I am jolly well mistaken, I am lord of all I survey. I am alone in my glory! There's not a soul in the place! Good luck indeed!"

He turned for a last look at his broken prison house, the cage in which he had spent such exciting hours. He suddenly stiffened and drew back: a nervous trembling seized him — the nervous trembling due to sudden shock. Between the trunk which had been dumped down in the centre of a large square room, without a scrap of furniture in it, and the window, through whose shutters the rays of morning sunshine shone, Fandor had caught sight of a body lying on the floor — a man's body! Fandor leapt forward. Was this same cunning criminal feigning sleep for some evil purpose? Standing over that motionless figure, Fandor bent and touched one of the man's hands: it was ice-cold and rigid. The man was dead!

To see his face was imperative: it was turned towards the floor. With difficulty Fandor raised the head and shoulders, for they were unusually large and strongly built. Fandor glanced at the face and suddenly withdrew his hand: the corpse fell back on the floor with a thud!

"Thomery!" murmured Fandor. "Why, it's Thomery!"

It was the well-known sugar refiner's body. The face was purple, the tongue protruding. Round his neck was tied a tricoloured scarf, the scarf of a police inspector! Was this the murderer's ironic touch?

Fandor sank down quite overcome. He tried to collect his thoughts.

"A disgusting joke this! If someone should take into his head to enter the room at this moment, what kind of explanation could I give? Here I am, alone with the dead body of a man I know, and in a room I don't know, in a neighbourhood whose whereabouts I know no more than the man in the moon."

"Where am I? . . . In whose house? . . . For what purpose? . . . Have those beauties of last night no suspicion of the truth? . . . Did they leave me in this lair of theirs of set purpose, knowing I was cooped up inside the trunk?"

Just then, Fandor felt a slight moisture on the palm of his hand: it was all red: the scratches, made by the jagged edges of the wickerwork, were still bleeding.

"Better and better I declare!" murmured Fandor. "If I don't look like a little holy Saint John! A corpse, and a man with blood on his hands seated beside the dead body of this murdered man! Nothing more is required to jail me with all the power of the law! . . . To go to prison under such suspicious circumstances is serious! . . . The police, who are floundering about in a maze of investigations, without any result so far, will be only too delighted to kill two birds with one stone — to suppress a journalist and discover a criminal! . . . I have got to get out of here; that is plain as a pikestaff! . . . Get away? Yes, but with the honour of war! . . . I must establish an alibi — that is absolutely necessary. . . . I like to think that my false police inspector and his accomplice have cut and run for some time; at any rate, that they will be in no hurry to come back to see what is happening where they have so neatly and nicely left the corpse of this Thomery. . . . What part did this fellow play in the drama? . . . Criminal or victim?"

Fandor had reached the door of the hall opening on to the main staircase. He was listening. . . . He had explored the flat. It was empty. He had found water in the kitchen, had washed his face, and removed every trace of blood from his person. It was a flat suitable for a middle-class household. There were three large rooms, decorated with a certain amount of luxury.

Fandor looked at his watch. It was seven o'clock. He stood listening. Someone, a man, was coming downstairs: someone, a woman, was coming up. They met on the landing just outside.

"Monsieur Mercadier, here are your letters! I was bringing them up to you!"

"It was hardly worth while, my good lady. I have to come down, you see, so you can save yourself five flights of stairs!"

"Oh, no, monsieur! I have to come up to go down my stairs."

Monsieur Mercadier continued to descend, and the portress continued to mount.

Fandor's heart beat faster when he realised that she was approaching the door. Would she come in and find him there? Had the new tenants left a key of the flat with her? No, the portress dusted the landing quickly and continued her ascent: he heard her going up and up. . . .

He made up his mind to slip out on to the landing. Despite his efforts, he could not prevent his shoes creaking: it was spring-time, and already the stair carpet had been taken up. He was on the point of going downstairs, when he heard the portress calling from above:

"Who's there? . . . What do you want?"

Had she heard him leave the flat? Was he to be stupidly caught, just as he was escaping? . . . He must act at once. He went up a step or two of the next flight of stairs and called out:

"Is Monsieur Mercadier at home?"

"Ah, no, monsieur! He has just this minute gone out! I am surprised you did not meet him! . . ."

"Very good, madame. I will come another time!"

Fandor turned on his heel, and, whistling, with hands in pockets, he gained the ground floor, passed the entrance gate, and found himself in the street. He mingled with the passers-by, and learned from the first plaque he came to with the name of the street on it, that he was in rue Lecourbe, Vaugirard. . . .

XX

UNDER THE HOODED MASK

What had happened? By way of what mysterious adventures had the corpse of sugar refiner Thomery reached that empty room in rue Lecourbe, where Jérôme Fandor had come across it?

Two days previous, on the afternoon of Elizabeth Dollon's arrest, Monsieur Thomery was working in his study, when a servant came to tell him that a lady wished to speak to him.

"Did she give you her name?" asked Thomery.

"No, monsieur, this person said her name would tell you nothing; but she was sure monsieur would see her, for she would only detain him a minute or two. . . ."

Piles of papers were stacked on the great sugar refiner's study table: typists were laying numerous letters before him, which awaited his signature. Thomery thought to himself:

"I have still a good half-hour's work before me . . . deuce take this importunate visitor!" He was on the point of saying he could not see any one, when the servant added:

"This person declares she comes with reference to Madame the Princess Danidoff."

Though he was a man of business, Thomery was a gallant man also; and very much in love; his approaching marriage with the Princess, which had been kept secret, was now known. The name of Princess Danidoff settled the question.

"Very well, let her come in!"

The manservant disappeared a minute, then ushered into the study a very unassuming woman of uncertain age and quite ordinary looking.

Thomery rose to meet her, pointing pleasantly to one of the large arm-chairs in the room. The visitor was profusely apologetic.

"I am so exceedingly sorry, Monsieur Thomery, to disturb you at such an hour, when you must certainly have a great deal to occupy your attention; but the matter I have come about will not wait, and I am sure it will interest you. . . ."

This little person seemed very intelligent, and Thomery was favourably impressed by her manner, which was both simple and decided.

"Madame, I am listening to you. In what way can I be of service to you?"

"I am not here, monsieur," she protested, "to pester you with any wants and wishes for myself. I am a diamond broker and . . ."

She had not finished her sentence when Thomery, smiling but

firm, rose, and said sharply:

"In that case, madame, I can guess the motive of your call. . . ."

"But, monsieur . . ."

"Yes! . . . That is so! . . . Ever since my approaching marriage has been announced, I have received, every day, a dozen visits from jewellers, goldsmiths, upholsterers, and so on . . . I regret to have to tell you that you will not be able to persuade me to buy . . . that my betrothed has received so many wedding presents that there is no room for more. . . . I do not require one single thing. . . ."

Although Thomery had spoken in a tone which did not admit of any reply, although he had risen the better to mark his intention of cutting short the call, the diamond broker had remained seated, leaning back in her arm-chair. . . . She gave no sign of being ready to go away.

"Consequently, madame," continued Thomery. . . .

His visitor laughed.

"Monsieur, you have very quickly made up your mind that I have nothing interesting to offer you! I have not come to offer you ordinary jewels. . . ."

It was Thomery's turn to smile slightly.

"I quite understand, madame, that you should think your merchandise exceptional. . . . But once more . . ."

The broker interrupted the sugar refiner with a movement of her hand.

"Do listen to me a moment, monsieur! . . . Though I am a diamond broker, diamonds are not what I have come to ask you to purchase . . . it is a question of something quite different. . . ."

She paused deliberately: Thomery gazed at her without saying a word.

"You know, monsieur," continued the broker, "that in such a business as mine, one is obliged to see a great many jewellers every day; well, in the course of my peregrinations, I found at a jeweller's — you must allow me to withhold his name — some pearls, which I am certain you will find are a wonderful bargain. . . ."

"For the last time, madame, I do not want a wonderful bargain!"

The agent smiled curiously.

"There are some things which simply do not allow themselves to be refused," she declared. . . . She now drew from her pocket a little jewel-case; and, notwithstanding Thomery's unconcealed impatience, opened it, and selected two pearls which she held out to him.

"Do examine these jewels! You are going to tell me that they are perfectly beautiful, are you not, Monsieur Thomery?"

The diamond broker offered them so naturally that Thomery gave way. He examined the pearls: he was a connoisseur.

"In truth, madame, these pearls are superb; unfortunately I am not enough of an expert to buy them without taking competent advice, that is if I thought of acquiring them eventually, but I repeat, I have no wish to acquire such things!"

"Deuce take it!" thought Thomery. "This broker won't take 'no' for an answer! Since I cannot rid myself of her by being pleasant, I shall make myself disagreeable!"

But the would-be seller still insisted.

"Monsieur, you really cannot be a connoisseur, otherwise I am sure you would not return these pearls to me."

"But, madame! . . ."

"And I am convinced that if Princess Sonia Danidoff had had them in her hand instead of you, she would have been greatly taken with them!"

The broker had emphasised her words so strangely that, suddenly, Thomery hesitated.

What did this mysterious visitor mean? What was it she considered so "extraordinary" about the jewels she had just submitted to him? . . . A suspicion flashed across his mind.

"Whence come these pearls, madame?"

But, at this question, the broker got up.

"Monsieur Thomery," declared she, "I should be very vexed with myself were I to make you lose your evening . . . your time is precious; besides, in order to give you a proper answer to your question, I should have to make certain of facts I only now guess at. . . . Still, I think that without having told you anything definite, I have made you sufficiently understand what is in my mind, . . . you will not now doubt the interest that the Princess Sonia Danidoff would have, were she able to examine these jewels. . . ."

"Is that so?"

"Consequently, Monsieur Thomery, I am going to ask you if you will kindly show these pearls to the Princess; and then if you will be good enough to let me know what decision you come to, jointly with her. . . . If you were a buyer, I fancy I might let you have these jewels on quite exceptional terms."

Thomery visibly hesitated. . . . He was looking at the pearls, which he was still holding in his hand, and he thought.

"One might swear that these are two of the pearls stolen from Sonia at my ball!"

Thomery did not reply at once. The broker was looking at him with a smile; she seemed to guess his thoughts. Thomery, on his side, was examining the woman.

"Is she simply a police informer?" he asked himself. "One of these women who apparently are dealers, but are really in the pay of the police, and frequent jewellers for the purpose of tracing stolen jewels?"

He was on the verge of asking her who she was, but he refrained.

If this woman had not presented herself under her true colours, evidently she wished to pass for an ordinary dealer. It was possible that she was really a receiver of stolen goods!

Thomery came to a decision.

"I shall have the privilege of seeing the Princess Danidoff to-morrow afternoon; will you therefore leave the pearls with me? . . . I will show them to her. Should she express the slightest wish to possess them, I might possibly come to terms with you. . . ."

"Dearest, it is sweet of you to make no objection to the way in which I obtained this jewel for you to see, and to choose for your own, if you will. . . . The correct thing would have been to ask you to accompany me to some well-known jeweller, instead of which, I frankly confess, that these pearls were offered to me on very advanta-geous terms. If they please you, it will give me the greatest pleasure to see them adorning your graceful neck."

Princess Sonia laughed.

"My dear, for Heaven's sake, don't worry about such a thing as that! . . . A pearl is not less beautiful because it comes from some unpretentious jeweller's shop. I am too fond of jewels for their own sake, to trouble about the casket that enshrines them!"

Thomery bowed, well pleased.

"Here then, dear Sonia, are the two pearls entrusted to me as samples . . . please, dearest, examine them carefully, very carefully . . . and if you like them, tell me so frankly. . . ."

The Princess took the two pearls from the betrothed, and, crossing the great drawing-room, she approached one of the bay win-dows, lifting the thin hangings that she might the better examine the pearls.

"They are marvellous!" she cried.

"Dear Sonia, you think these gems rarely beautiful?"

"Indeed I do! Their lustre is superb; their quality, their shape, perfect! . . . Why, my dear, these are the most splendid pearls I have ever seen — with one exception — the only pearls to equal them are those that were stolen from me! . . . The loss of them has been a bitter grief . . . they came to me, you know, from my dear mother! . . . I never thought to find pearls of such quality again. . . ."

"You consider these to be of as pure a quality then, dear?"

Sonia Danidoff continued to examine the two pearls.

"It is really extraordinary," she cried suddenly. "Do you know, my dear, there are certain peculiarities about their lustre, . . . yes . . . I could swear that these very pearls you are offering me are two of those stolen from me! . . ."

Thomery appeared to have been impatiently awaiting these very words.

"You really, truly believe, Sonia, that they resemble the pearls stolen from you that unlucky evening?"

"I repeat — they are identical!"

Thomery looked smilingly at Sonia.

"Well, then, my dear one, I do not think you are mistaken! . . . I have all sorts of reasons for supposing that they really are two of your own pearls you are now holding in your hand. . . ." And, then and there, Thomery told his fiancée all about the strange visit he had received the evening before, as well as his hope that he would be able to recover the stolen triple collar in its entirety.

"That intriguing dealer," said he finally, "must be a police informer. . . . In any case, I am persuaded that, before long, she will take me to some receiver or other who is in possession of your pearl collar."

"Oh, tell me you are not going among such people, all alone?" cried Sonia, with a note of sharp anxiety in her voice.

"But, why not?"

"If they are, as you think, thieves?"

"Well?"

"Well! Don't you see, my dear, that if you go to buy the pearls, they will count on your bringing a large sum of money with you! . . . Why, it would be a most imprudent thing to do! . . ."

Thomery shrugged his shoulders.

"Really, that's nonsense, Sonia! If these assassins meant to set a trap for me, they have a thousand other means of doing so . . . besides, it would be remarkably daring of them to advise me to show you these pearls, and draw my attention to the question of their being stolen ones! . . . No, Sonia, this dealer is not the emissary of a band of robbers and assassins: she is a police informer, who has taken precautions. I run no dangerous risks by accompanying her! Reassure yourself on that point! . . ."

But Sonia Danidoff was not reassured by Thomery's arguments.

"All that only frightens me!" said she. . . . "If you do not really think you are running any risk, will you let me go with you? . . . My dear, we will go together to identify those pearls, will we not?"

Thomery rose to take his leave, laughing and protesting.

"Why, dear Sonia, it would be in the highest degree improper on my part, were I to agree to such a proposition! . . . One of two things: either there is no danger, and I should be very sorry that I had let you go out in such shocking weather; or, if there is danger, I should be still more distressed were I to drag you into it with me. . . . I do beg of you, Sonia, do not insist on it. . . . I am not a child! . . . And I will be very careful — very wary! . . ."

Shortly after this, Thomery took leave of Sonia Danidoff. He went straight to the Café de la Paix, where he had arranged to meet the diamond broker. . . .

She was punctual. She greeted Thomery with her most winning smile.

"I am persuaded, monsieur, that Madame Sonia Danidoff was interested by the offer you made her?"

"Quite so," replied Thomery. . . . "Should we go to your jeweller's, without further loss of time?"

"If you really wish to do so, monsieur! Indeed it would be the best thing to do. . . ."

Thomery hailed a cab. He and the diamond agent entered it together, and she gave the driver an address. Twenty minutes later they left the cab and were standing before the house where the present possessor of the pearls was to be found. Thomery knew no more now about the person he had come to interview, than he did when he started: that is to say, practically nothing.

The diamond broker had cleverly evaded giving any direct answers to the sugar refiner's questions: she had confined herself to stating what would be the probable price demanded for the pearl collar — which question interested Thomery least of all!

They mounted, in single file, a rather poor sort of staircase: on the second floor the woman stopped. A narrow door faced them. . . . The woman rang. . . . They waited. . . .

"Someone is coming!" said the woman. "I hear footsteps."

The door was opened half-way.

"Who is it?" asked a man's voice.

"I, dear friend," answered the woman.

The door opened wide: the same voice said:

"Come in, monsieur."

Thomery had barely stepped inside the room, when the diamond broker, who was close behind, flung a long silk scarf round his neck, and, pushing his knee into his victim's back for a support, he attempted to give, with Herculean force, the famous stroke of Father Francis Vigozous; energetic, Thomery did not lose his presence of mind. . . . He knew that to resist such a pull by simple force was impossible. . . . Quickly he threw himself backwards, thus giving to the strangling pull and falling on top of the woman, who had played this dastardly trick on him. From his constricted throat came a hoarse "Ah!" like a death rattle.

As he was falling, for one flashing second, it seemed as though he were going to escape from the vise which was crushing in his throat . . . then, out of the shadow, there had appeared the fantastic vision of a man in a tight fitting sort of black jersey, which covered him from head to foot. . . . His face was concealed by a hooded mask. . . .

This man had leapt out of the shadow.

He held a dagger in his hand.

Before Thomery had time to make a movement, the masked man had pierced his chest with a single stroke! . . . The sugar refiner was naught but a convulsive corpse.

"Ah, well!" declared the so-called diamond broker, who had got to his feet and was kicking Thomery's body aside. "Ah, well, he is a dead weight this fellow! . . . By Jove, master, I fancied he was going to crush me, and that I should have to let him free! . . . You did well to come to the rescue!"

The masked man remarked in an indifferent tone:

"It really does not matter in the slightest! . . . Tell me, does anyone suspect?"

"No one, master. He came like a sheep to the slaughter."

"Princess Danidoff?"

"Ah, as for her — she must be waiting for the return of her beloved friend. . . . I do not advise you to pay her a visit!"

"Be silent, chatter-box!" ordered the masked assassin sharply. "Get rid of your clothes. . . . We must hurry! . . . We have work to do!"

"This evening?"

"This evening!"

And, whilst the diamond broker rid himself rapidly of skirt and bodice and regained his masculine appearance — for this diamond broker was a man — the masked assassin added:

"Nibet, you have played your part perfectly, and I will pay you to-morrow the sum we agreed on; but, I repeat, we have work before us this evening — so, be quick!"

There was a short silence, then the bandit asked:

"You have arranged to put among this fool's papers the rent receipts, which will enable the police to find this flat?"

"Yes, master!"

"Good! Now all we have to do, is to get away from this room, which we shall not see again . . . until this evening at any rate!"

XXI

IN A PRISON VAN

In one of the rooms reserved for readers of *La Capitale*, Jérôme Fandor was gravely listening to Madame Bourrat's account of what had occurred at her boarding-house during the night. She had rushed off to tell him and to ask his advice.

"What you tell me, madame, is truly extraordinary!" said Fandor, with an air of profound astonishment. . . .

"How did you discover that the police inspector who seized the trunk and carried it away was not a genuine policeman?"

"Why, through the arrival of Monsieur Xavié, the police inspector of our district! I know him. . . . There was no mistaking who and what he was; and when I told him that the trunk had been carried off the preceding evening, rather in the dead of night, he guessed everything. . . ."

"And what did he say? . . ."

"Oh, he made us all come to the police station; and I can assure you that he looked far from pleased!"

"You must admit, dear madame, that his annoyance was not without reason! . . . The police were made fine fools of in this affair. . . . But afterwards? . . . Whom did he take back with him to the police station?"

"He took me and my manservant."

"And when you got to the police station?"

"Well, Monsieur Fandor, when we reached the police station, he made us come into his office, and there he put us through a regular examination, . . . just as though he suspected us!"

"But there must have been an accomplice in your house who let the robbers in," said Fandor. "I do not suppose the false police inspector forced the door open!"

"Ah, but, Monsieur Fandor, here is something I do not understand, nor does anybody else! . . . No, they did not try to hide themselves — not the least in the world! They rang the bell; they asked to see me; they told me what they had come for; and, accompanied by my manservant, carried away the trunk, and had it put on the cab — all in the most open and bare-faced manner!"

"It was your manservant who accompanied them?"

"But most certainly . . . and that very fact turned against Jules, in a very nasty manner. . . . Poor Jules! Just imagine, the police inspector finished by ordering my house to be thoroughly searched from top to bottom! And when the policemen returned, without a why or wherefore, they took Jules away to another part of the police station!"

"I say! I say!"

"Oh, it was all explained! As soon as Jules had gone, the police inspector told me that they had found keys in his rooms, keys which could be made to fit any kind of lock whatever. Monsieur Xavié was convinced that my poor Jules was a burglar — imagine it!"

"And you, yourself, madame, are convinced of the contrary?"

"Oh, assuredly! Why, I have known Jules a very long time! And in many little ways on many occasions, he has shown himself to be strictly honest."

"But those false keys?"

"Those false keys, Monsieur Fandor, why I myself made Jules buy them, hoping to find among them one that would open my coach-house."

"So that? . . ."

"So that, Monsieur Fandor, the police inspector was obliged to agree with me that Jules was honest!"

"And he released this servant of yours?" asked Fandor.

His tone expressed annoyance.

"No, and that is why I am so distressed. He said, that provisionally, at least, my servant, Jules, was to be considered as under arrest! What ought to be done to get him let out?"

"But, madame! . . . He will be set free to-morrow, you may be certain of it! . . ."

"No doubt he will! . . . All the same, there is my house turned upside down, and I need Jules to help me to-night! . . . I really do not know what I shall do without him! Poor fellow! . . . I simply cannot imagine how it is they suspect him!"

Fandor said, with mock gravity:

"Ah, madame, Justice is sometimes so stupid — so wrong-headed! . . . Look here now, would you like a bit of good advice? . . . Telephone to Messieurs Barbey-Nanteuil. They are well known and powerful — perhaps they would exert their influence in your servant's favour? He might be set free this evening! I, you see, am but a journalist, and without a scrap of influence!"

Madame Bourrat thought this a good idea. Fandor rang for an attendant.

"Take madame to the telephone!"

Left to himself, the reporter could not help rubbing his hands.

"I must get rid of this excellent woman, who is certainly the most foolish person it has ever been my lot to meet. Good hearing! That servant of hers is under lock and key — things are going in the right direction . . . but they are not going well for me! . . . If he confesses, to-morrow, when he is had up for examination, then the police will have the information before me! . . . Then, too, they are such duffers —

such bunglers — that they are quite capable of giving that Jules his liberty! . . . What the deuce must I do to prevent his being let loose, and how am I to stop the judicial interrogation? . . . What a dog's life a journalist's is!"

Madame Bourrat reappeared.

"Monsieur Nanteuil is not there," she said. "But I got into communication with Monsieur Barbey. . . . He advised me to wait till to-morrow: he said it was too late in the day to do anything. . . ."

"But, will he not intervene to-morrow?"

"I don't know. To tell the truth, I am sure Monsieur Barbey thought it very inconsiderate of me to disturb him about a matter in which he takes not the slightest interest."

"That's a fact. What possible interest can the bankers take in such a matter? . . . My advice was absurd!"

Fandor rose. As he was seeing his visitor out, he said:

"In any case, dear madame, count on me to-morrow morning. I shall call at your house about eleven. If there is anything fresh, we can talk it over! . . ."

"Oh, here's Janson-de-Sailly College! . . . Oh, what detestable remembrances you conjure up! . . . But — this won't do! . . . Go it, my boy! . . . I must play the part!"

The plumber, who had just given utterance to these remarks, glanced sharply about him. When he had made sure that there was no one close on his heels, he stepped into the roadway, and started on a zigzag course which seemed likely to upset his balance. Crossing the avenue Henri-Martin, going straight, towards the town hall at the corner of the rue de la Pompe, the good plumber, who was staggering more than a little, began to stutter and stammer in a drunken voice:

"It is the final struggle!"

The passers-by looked round.

"They sing the *Internationale* in the streets now, it seems!" remarked a severe-looking gentleman.

The workman turned to this correct personage.

"What of it? . . . Don't you think it a jolly fine thing then?"

In a thick voice he continued to sing:

"Let us gather, and on the morrow . . ."

The severe and correct personage spoke.

"My friend, you would do better to hold your tongue! . . . You forget that there is a police station close by! . . ."

But the incorrigible plumber caught the correct personage by his coat tails.

"If I sing the *Internationale*, it's because I'm a free man — ain't I? . . . A free man can sing if he likes, can't he? Eh! . . . Why don't you sing then? . . . Eh! . . ."

The correct personage drew himself up stiffly: tried to push the obnoxious plumber away. . . . The workman had now reached that stage of drunkenness when discussions tend to become interminable.

The gentleman pushed the drunken man aside, saying:

"Come! Come! Go away! . . . Leave me alone!"

But the maudlin plumber was attracting the attention of the passers by his gestures. He addressed the world at large.

"Would you believe it — that fellow there don't want me to sing! . . . No! Well, I'm going to!" and he started triumphantly.

"It is the — the — final . . . strug-gle!"

A policeman came out of the station with a solemn air. He put his hand on the tipsy plumber's shoulder in paternal fashion.

"Go along with you, my friend! . . . Come now — pass along — pass along!" But he could not make the plumber budge before he had finished his verse, any more than he could teach him to walk straight on the spur of the moment! . . . Leaving hold of the gentleman's coat tails, the worthy plumber seized the policeman's arm.'

"Oh, you, you're a brother! . . . I have education, I have! You're a workman too, I know! . . ."

As the police inspector pushed him off, trying to make him go on his way, the plumber put his arm round him.

"No! No! . . . show you're a workman! Sing with me!"

"It is the final . . ."

The scandal could no longer be tolerated! Street-corner idlers were gathering, people were laughing at the policeman: strong measures were necessary.

"Come now," said the policeman. "Yes, or no! Will you be off, and go home? . . . Eh! . . . Or shall I take you to the station? . . ."

"You take me? . . . You take me? . . . Why, it would take four of you to take me! . . ."

There was no shilly-shallying after this! Wounded in his vanity, the servant of the law did not hesitate.

"All right!" said he; and seizing the plumber by the collar, although there was no attempt at resistance, he dragged his prisoner towards the town hall of the district, for the police station was there also.

"Some more game for the Dépôt!" said the policeman as he passed the guard. . . . "A fellow I can't get rid of! Are the cells full up?"

Other policemen came up. An arrest in a peaceful district gives interest to the dull routine of the men on duty.

"The cells full? Go along with you! There's only a small shop-keeper who had no papers."

Thereupon the unfortunate singer, who continued to stagger

about, was quickly pushed into the dark room called "the detention room."

An ordinary every day incident of the streets, this arrest of a drunkard!

"I shall have to write out a report for this fellow!" said the policeman, who had arrested the songster . . . "and the 'Salad Basket'⁰ passes in an hour's time! . . . I shall just do it!"

"Have you anyone for the Dépôt to-day?" asked the driver from his high seat on the prison van. He was on a collecting journey as is usual every evening, when the Salad Baskets, as they are vulgarly called, pass to the various police stations of Paris to pick up the individuals arrested during the day.

"Two of 'em," answered the police sergeant on duty. Whilst official papers were being interchanged and forms were being filled in according to rule, policemen went to the cells to bring out the two prisoners to be despatched to the Dépôt.

The first to pass out was the costermonger. He was straightway put into one of the narrow compartments in the Salad Basket. Then it was the turn of the tipsy and obstreperous workman, who was now silent, moody, and apparently sober.

"Hop it now!" cried the policeman. "Come along with you, you miserable drunk! . . . March now! . . . Foot it!"

As the "drunk" hit against the partition of the narrow passageway running up the middle of the Salad Basket, the policeman, with a shove, pushed him into one of the compartments, carefully shutting the little door on him and fastening it.

"My word!" he exclaimed. "That fellow wouldn't have been capable of walking three steps in an hour's time!"

As the driver climbed to his seat on the van, the policeman called out, with a laugh:

"You have a traveller inside who doesn't detest wine! . . . It's a pity to see a man in such a hoggish state!"

This same policeman would have been surprised, could he have seen the bibulous one's face when the Salad Basket cast loose from her moorings and started off in the direction of the Point-du-Jour police station, the last on the round to be visited!

The "drunk" whom one push had sufficed to plant on his seat, had briskly drawn himself upright and was smiling broadly, a wide, noiseless smile!

10   Prison van.

"What a joke! . . . And what a jolly good actor I should have made!" thought Jérôme Fandor, giving himself a mental hug of satisfaction. . . . "Ah! They arrest the individuals I want to set talking! . . . The police imagine they are going to push in first and find out the answer to the riddle! . . . We shall see!"

Fandor was listening intensely and trying to discover from the movements of the Salad Basket what street they were passing along.

"Smooth going . . . evidently we are still in the rue de la Pompe, so I have about a quarter of an hour more of it!"

Fandor examined the tiny cell in which he had been imprisoned of his own free will.

"Not much to be said for it!" ran his thoughts. "There is scarcely room to sit . . . impossible to stand up or turn around . . . nearly dark . . . and precious little air comes in through those wooden shutters! . . . I shouldn't think there ever had been an escape from these vans! . . ."

Fandor smiled broadly.

"Even if I don't succeed, it is worth while making the attempt! . . . But I shall succeed — see if I don't! . . . I settled it in my mind that I was to leave the cells after this costermonger: he is in front of me, therefore the cell behind me is empty. It will be deucedly queer if, at Auteuil police station, they don't put that confounded Jules in it, whom I intend to interview under the nose of the police! . . . I shall start talking to him by tapping on the partition in prisoner's language. The fellow is pretty sure to be an old offender, so he will know the system. . . . If he doesn't, when we get to the Dépôt, I will push up to him somehow and get a few words with him. . . . If the Dépôt is full, we shall be stuck into the common cell until morning. . . . So, I take it as certain that my interview with this true and faithful servant will come off, and I shall get to know a good deal about the mystery! . . ."

As an afterthought, it occurred to Fandor that probably there had never been such a light-hearted occupant of this cell as he. . . .

"Ah, that's the sound of the trams! . . . One jolt! Two jolts! Good! . . . The rails! . . . We are crossing rue Mozart! We are going faster — in five minutes we shall be at the Auteuil police station, and there we can start our little operations!"

There was one thing that attracted Fandor's attention, which was keenly on the alert. There was a violent jolt, and he had a distinct impression that the vehicle turned to the right.

"Why, where the deuce are they taking us?" Fandor asked himself. "To the boulevard Exelmans station? . . . We had not reached the end of the rue Mozart, surely! . . . Where did we turn then? Rue du Ranelagh? . . . No, there is a channel stone at the entrance, and I should have felt it! . . . Rue de l'Assomption! . . . Again no. The roadway is up: I should be knocked about more than this on my wooden seat. We are going over a perfectly kept road, which cannot have much traffic! . . . Why, of course, it is rue du Docteur-Blanche! . . . Isn't rue Mozart barred at the end? Yes. The driver must be going round by the boulevard Montmorency. . . . Ah, well! I am in no hurry! There will be time enough for me to pay my respects to the illustrious Jules!"

Just as Fandor was thus congratulating himself, he was thrown against the side of his cell! The van seemed to have come into violent collision with some object and had tilted over to a considerable extent.

Muffled oaths came from neighbouring cells; a stifled exclamation reached Fandor's ears; then louder still, came the intermittent humming and snorting of a motor-car.

"Confound you! . . . can't you pay attention to where you are going? . . . Keep to your right!"

Slightly stunned, Fandor heard some one knocking.

A voice asked:

"Are you hurt?"

"No, but . . ."

Already the questioner had moved away.

"Evidently," thought Fandor, "the driver wants to know whether his human packages are damaged or not! We have collided with another vehicle! . . . Cheerful!"

Fandor's cell was now at such an angle that he could only suppose that the Salad Basket had had one of its wheels broken.

"What a nuisance!" he murmured. "Before they have finished their palaver as to how the accident happened and have repaired the damage, we shall have been here a full half-hour. . . . Jules will be in a temper!"

Minute succeeded minute, long, interminable minutes, and Fandor could not hear clearly what was said, what was being done to put the Salad Basket on its legs again. . . . The atmosphere in the little cell was becoming intolerable; for the movement of the vehicle had driven fresh air inside the shutter, and now that the Salad Basket was stationary, the air was becoming almost unbreathable.

Fandor's nerves were on edge.

"It cannot be that they are going to leave us stranded here!" thought he. . . . "Ah, now they have started repairs!" Fandor noticed that his cell was gradually regaining its ordinary level. . . . A lifting-jack must have been slipped under the vehicle, for there was a melancholy creaking sound. They must be putting the wheel on again! . . .

"No," thought Fandor, after some time had passed. "Never would I have supposed that it could have taken so much time to repair a Salad Basket! . . . Why we shall soon have been stuck here for two mortal hours! . . . I hope it won't make any difference to our going to the Dépôt, nor stop my getting into close touch with that villain Jules!"

There was a further period of waiting. Then our exasperated journalist heard the driver pass down the centre of the van. The van door slammed. . . . Once more the Salad Basket was loosed from its moorings.

"Something queer is going on!" said Fandor suddenly. He felt certain the van had turned completely round and was going in the direction it came from.

"Now where in the world are we going? . . . By what kind of a route are we making for that blessed police station?"

There were spaces of asphalt, succeeded by wood pavement, then by hard stones, then asphalt and wood again, and turning succeeded turning, whilst a new Tom Thumb was doing his possible to guess the route the Salad Basket was taking. Presently Fandor gave it up. He had to admit that he was completely lost. . . . Which way the Salad Basket was going he knew no more than the Man in the Moon!

"We have been trotting along for more than half an hour; therefore we cannot be going to the boulevard Exelmans police station . . . the distance from the rue du Docteur-Blanche to the Point-du-Jour is not great. . . ."

As Fandor was murmuring these words, the van slowed down, turned round; then, with a bump and a jolt, it mounted the footpath.

"Now for it," said Fandor. "This is certainly not the Point-du-Jour station! . . . We are passing under an archway — now we are turning again. . . . Ah, we draw up, at last! . . . Not too soon!"

The van did stop.

Again a wait. Fandor cocked both ears; he wondered who was going to enter the cell next his. Then a man approached the door of his little cell, where he was indeed "cribbed, cabined and confined"; inserted a key in the lock, opened, and shouted in a brutal tone:

"Out with you! . . . March! Quick now!"

Fandor had no choice but to obey the orders hurled at him. But no sooner had he descended the steps of the prison van than he exclaimed:

"By Jove! The Dépôt!"

This was not the moment to express all the surprise he felt at being landed at Police Headquarters in this fashion. . . . All round the Salad Basket the police were ranged in irregular order. They shouted to him to be quick.

"Come on with you! Hurry there!"

Fandor, followed by the costermonger, was pushed towards a

little open door in the grey wall which led into a kind of office, where an old frowning man was already looking through the papers, which had been respectfully handed to him by a warder.

"So you have brought only two of the birds?" remarked the frowning official.

"Yes, superintendent."

"Good, that will do! . . ."

Turning to the warders, the frowning little superintendent ordered: "Take them away! . . . Cell 14. . . . Useless to rouse the whole place!"

Once more the warders pushed Fandor before them, as well as the poor costermonger: they were driven into a dark corridor on to which a row of cells opened.

The head warder opened a door.

"In with you, my merry men! You will be put through your paces to-morrow!"

As the door fell to with a resounding clang, Jérôme had inspected the place by the light of a lantern.

"Empty! . . . No luck! . . . My plan has been spoiled: I shall not be able to interview Jules!"

Philosophically, Jérôme Fandor was preparing to go to sleep on the plank bed which decorated one end of the cell, when the little costermonger, roused from his torpid condition, began to moan and groan.

"Oh, what a misfortune! . . . To think I am innocent! Innocent as an unborn babe! . . . What's to be done! . . . Oh, what's to be done!"

The last thing Fandor wished to do was to start a conversation with his lamenting companion. He tapped the costermonger on the shoulder.

"Good Heavens, man, the best thing you can do is to go to sleep! Take my word for it!"

Without puzzling his brains any further over the enigmas he wished to get to the bottom of, Fandor stretched himself on his plank bed, and was soon sleeping the sleep of the innocent.

Monsieur Fuselier looked perplexed.

"You, Fandor! You arrested! . . . But am I going mad?"

Our journalist had been taken from his cell at eight in the morning, and had been conducted to the office of the Public Prosecutor. Here, the acting magistrate, in conformity with the law, wished to put him through the examination which would establish his identity. All arrested persons have to submit to this interrogation within twenty-four hours of their arrival at the Dépôt.

Jérôme Fandor had given his name at once, and, in order to prove the truth of his statements, he had asked that Monsieur Fuselier should be sent for, so that the magistrate might vouch for his identity and say a word in his favour.

Monsieur Fuselier had hastened to the Dépôt, had taken Fandor to his office, and had anxiously questioned him. Why, he asked, had the police been obliged to arrest him for drunkenness in the open thoroughfare?

When Fandor had concluded his statement, the magistrate exclaimed:

"Your ruse is inconceivable! . . . I must compliment you highly on your ability and your detective gifts!"

"I wish I could agree with you," replied Fandor in a depressed tone. "In spite of everything, I have not got into communication with Jules. But, Monsieur Fuselier, have you interrogated him yet?"

The magistrate shook his head.

"Alas, my poor friend, you have no idea of the extraordinary events of the past night; evidently, notwithstanding the fact that you played a passive part in them!"

"I played a part? . . . Extraordinary events? . . . What the deuce do you mean?"

"I mean, dear Fandor, that all Paris is laughing over it. The police have been tricked! You have been tricked! Did you not tell me, just now, that your prison van had had an accident? Do you know what really happened?"

"I ask you to tell me."

"Your vehicle was run into by a motor-car. The driver was extremely clumsy . . . or very capable!"

"What's that?" Fandor leaned forward, keen as a pointer on the scent.

"It was like this," replied Monsieur Fuselier. "Your Salad Basket was very badly knocked about by the collision. The driver could not possibly repair it single-handed. He telephoned to Headquarters. Help was sent at once, and he had orders to drive to the Dépôt as soon as he could: he was not to trouble about the boulevard Exelmans station; that, for once, could be cleared the following morning. Unfortunately the telephone messages and replies had taken up a certain amount of time. When they telephoned to the boulevard Exelmans station, from Headquarters, to warn them not to expect the injured Salad Basket, the Dépôt man who was telephoning was extremely surprised to hear that the Salad Basket had already passed on to the Auteuil station and had taken away the arrested individuals there, notably this famous Jules! . . ."

"I never calculated on this!" cried Fandor.

"The truth is, my dear fellow, that Salad Basket of yours was not knocked out of action by an unlucky accident — the knock-out was intentional — was carefully planned! It was done to stop your van from reaching the Auteuil station! . . . While your Basket was being repaired, another Basket appeared at the Auteuil clearing station! This, if you please, had been stolen! It was standing before the Palais de Justice. Two accomplices took possession of it and drove away. The daring rascals were suitably disguised, of course! They produced false papers at Auteuil, got them endorsed, went through the regular forms, and carried off the men from the detention cells, under the very nose and eyes of the superintendent himself!"

"What became of the stolen Basket?" snapped Fandor.

"It was found at dawn near the fortifications, and, need I say — empty!"

"So that Jules has escaped?"

"As you say! . . ."

"And the car which intentionally knocked my Salad Basket out of action — whose was it?"

Monsieur Fuselier smiled.

"Oh, it's a queer affair, in fact, it may lead to the wind-up of all the Dollon business — we may now get to the bottom of that series of crimes! . . . You will never guess who is the owner of that car, Fandor? . . ."

"No, I am no good at guessing riddles just now . . . besides, I hate them!" Fandor was nettled, exasperated!

"We got the number of the car from a witness of the smash-up; and we have verified its correctness. Well, my dear fellow, the owner of that car is — Thomery!"

"Thomery!" gasped Fandor.

"Yes. I have summoned him to appear before me — the summons has just been issued. Between you and me, I think Thomery is guilty. When he appears here, in, say an hour from now, I shall issue a writ of arrest against this sugar refiner financier, and we don't know what else!"

But, no sooner had Monsieur Fuselier finished his statement — a statement which he fully expected would strike his young reporter friend dumb with amazement — than Fandor threw himself back in his chair and roared with laughter.

The magistrate was taken aback! . . .

"But . . . what the devil do you find to laugh at in that?"

Fandor had already checked his hilarity.

"Oh, it's nothing! Only, Fuselier, I ask myself, if really and truly, Monsieur Thomery, who is a very big fellow solidly built, has been able to discover a dodge, by means of which he can leave Jacques Dollon's imprints here, there and everywhere!"

"But he does not leave Jacques Dollon's imprints, because Dollon is living, because he came to see his sister — why, you admitted that yourself!"

"Why, of course! It's true! . . . Jacques Dollon is alive. . . . I had forgotten. . . . Thomery can only be his accomplice then!" declared Fandor. And as Monsieur Fuselier stared at him, astonished at the way he had received the sensational news of the night, Fandor rose to take his leave.

"My dear Fuselier, will you allow me to express my opinion? . . ."

Monsieur Fuselier nodded.

"Well, I am sure, that with regard to this affair, there are more surprises in store for us: you have not got the answer to the riddle — not yet!"

With that, Fandor smiled and bowed, and left the magistrate's room. He quitted the Palais, half-smiling, half-serious. . . . What was he going to do next?

XXII

AN EXECUTION

"Not much water about, is there?"

"That's so, old 'un. . . . If I'd known, it's boats I'd have taken to!"

"Bah! Your shoes are big enough. That's not saying it's weather for a Christian to be out in!"

"Don't you grumble, old 'un! The more it comes down cats and dogs, the fewer stumps will be stirring out doors! . . . But a comrade or two will be on the prowl, eh?"

"Right-o, old bird! . . . Keep a lookout! . . . Sure he'll come this way?"

"You bet your nut he will! . . . He got my bit of a scrawl this morning. . . ."

"What then?"

"Shut up! Shut up! Folks coming!"

The night was inky black. Rain fell with sudden violence, threshed and driven by icy gusts of wind. The hour was late: the rue Raffet deserted save for the two men who had ventured out into the tempestuous darkness. They advanced with difficulty, side by side, speaking low. Rough customers to deal with. Their faces were emaciated from excessive drinking: their eyes gleamed, their voices were hoarse: a brutal pair! But their movements were souple and lively: they walked with that ungainly swagger affected by the light-fingered gentry and the criminals of the underworld of Paris.

"And what did you say in your scrawl?"

"Oh, medlars! Take-ins! You know! . . . I didn't put my fist to it, though!"

"Who then?"

"You ask that?"

"I'm no wizard! If it wasn't your fist, whose then?"

"My woman. . . ."

"Ernestine?"

"Yes. Ernestine."

They struggled on through the squally darkness. Then one of the two broke the silence.

"You're not jealous, Beadle, making your girl write letters to such folk?"

That sinister hooligan, the Beadle, burst out laughing.

"Jealous? Me? Jealous of Ernestine? You make me laugh, you really do, old Beard!"

But Beard did not share his companion's mirth. He leaned

against a palisade to take breath, while a little sheltered from the fierce onslaughts of the wind.

"I tell you what," he said in a gruff and threatening voice: "I don't like such dodges — like those of this evening. . . ."

"Why so, monsieur?"

"Why, because, after all, it's a comrade!"

"But he's betrayed — a traitor he is!"

"What do we know about it?"

The Beadle nodded; reflected.

"What does anyone know about it?" he said at last. . . .

"Why, when the comrades told us, weren't they surprised, one and all? Nibet, Toulouche, even Mimile — they didn't hesitate, not one of them! . . . Well then, old 'un, as all the pals were of one mind, why hesitate? What's the use of discussing! . . . but, between you and me, I don't relish it either — it bothers me to go for a pal! . . ."

Just then the tempest redoubled its fury: it seemed to the cowering men as though all the devils of the storm were galloping down the wind. Somewhere there was a moon, for scurrying clouds were dancing a witches' saraband across a faintly clearer sky. The unseen moon was mastering the obscurity of this midnight hour.

By now, the two sinister beings were nearing the rue du Docteur-Blanche. They were passing a garden, in which tall poplars, caught by the squall, took fantastic shapes: they were nightmare trees, terrifyingly strange.

"No more to be said," remarked the Beadle. "The scene is set! . . . Where is the meeting place?"

"A hundred yards from there — a little before the corner of the boulevard Montmorency. . . ."

"Good! And the trap?"

"It waits for us a little further off."

"Who's aboard it?"

"Mimile."

"That's good."

The two men were now half-way along rue Raffet. The watch had begun. Gripped by the cold they waited in silence. . . . The minutes passed slowly, slowly, in the deserted street . . . The Beard put his hand on the Beadle's shoulder. . . . A vague sound could be heard in the distance: the steps could be distinguished; some pedestrian was coming up the rue Raffet in their direction.

"It is he!" whispered the Beadle.

"It is he!" affirmed the Beard. "He's not oversteady on his feet!"

"Perhaps he's ill shod!"

The two spoke low and in a jesting tone: it relieved the painful tension of the moment — a comrade was marching to meet his death, and theirs the hands to deal that death — but not yet: it was a reaction against their sense of the looming tragedy of this dark hour!

Now a man's advancing figure could be discerned. He came nearer. He was plainly, by the cut of his garments, an indoor servant. The collar of his coat was turned up: he had his hands in his pockets: he walked fast.

"Hey! You down there! The gang!" cried the Beard, hailing the oncoming figure.

"Ah, it's you?"

"Yes, it's me, comrade."

"And you too, Beadle?"

"As you say. . . ."

"What do you want of me? Since my arrest and escape from the Salad Basket, I'm not anxious to stroll about this neighbourhood — out with it!"

The Beard said in a joking tone:

"You don't suspect, then? Speak out, Jules! . . ."

Jules — for it was indeed he — shook his head.

"My word, I have no idea what you want! . . . Who wrote to me this morning? Ernestine?"

Neither the Beadle nor Beard replied.

The three men stood talking in the deserted street, bending their heads and backs under the rain, which was now pouring harder than ever.

"Come on then! Make haste!" said Jules. "Come now, tell me what's the point — what's up — spit it out, comrades! . . . I don't want to be soaked to the skin, you know!"

The Beadle forced the pace: he lifted his great hairy sinewy hand, brought it down heavily on Jules' shoulder, and in a changed voice, harsh, rough, imperative, he commanded:

"You must follow us!" Already he had his man fast. The unsuspicious Jules did not grasp the situation in the least.

"Follow you?" he asked. "As to that, certainly not! . . . No more walking for me in such weather. Wait for a sunny day, say I! . . . But whatever is the matter with you — eh? . . . What? . . . Why are you sticking out your jaws at me like this? Out with it, my lambs! . . . Where am I to follow you? . . . You won't say, Messieurs Beadle and Beard?

"You won't say? . . ."

Beard moved a step and got behind Jules unnoticed. He repeated in the same tone, harsh, threatening:

"You've got to follow us, I tell you!"

Instinctively Jules tried to turn round. The Beadle's strong grip kept him motionless. Then he understood. He was afraid.

"What's come to you?" he cried in a trembling voice.

The Beadle cut him short.

"Enough! Will you follow us? Yes or no?"

Jules was going to say "no!" but he had not the time! Quick as lightning the Beadle flung a long scarf round his neck, stuck his knee into his victim's back, and pulled!

Jules uttered a faint groan; but, half stifled, nearly strangled, he had not the strength to attempt the slightest self-defence.

Directly he was flung backwards on the ground, where he measured his length and lay nearly stunned, Beard jumped on him, knelt on his chest, and pinioned him. Jules lay motionless.

The Beard now began tying up the legs of their victim.

"Pass me a scarf!"

"There it is, old 'un!"

"Very good, I am going to apply a 'Be Discreet.'"

The "Be Discreet" of the Beard was a gag, which he rolled round the servant's head in expert fashion.

"Feet firm?" asked the Beard.

"Oh, jolly fine!" said the Beadle. He turned his man over as though he were a bale of goods. Now he tied his victim's hands behind his back.

"Is it far to go to the jaunting car?"

"No — for two sous, that's it!"

A motor-car was indeed coming slowly and noiselessly along rue Raffet: it was a sumptuous car!

"And if it is not he?"

"Stick him up against the bank . . . dark as it is, there's every chance he won't be seen."

Rapidly, the doughty two stuck Jules against the bank at the side of the road: the unfortunate creature had fainted. Then they took out their cigarettes, and going a few steps away, they pretended to be sheltering themselves in order to strike a light.

They need not have taken this precaution.

The car stopped in front of them. The familiar voice of Mimile was heard:

"Got the rabbit then?"

"Yes, old 'un!"

"Pitch it into the balloon then!"

"The balloon?" questioned the Beadle. "Whatever's that?"

Emilet laughed.

"At times, my brothers, your ignorance, mechanically speaking, is crass! . . . The balloon is the back part of my car, I'd have you know."

The Beard sniggered.

"Good! . . . Pick it up! Now, Beadle!"

The two seized the body of Jules by shoulders and feet, and flung it brutally into the limousine.

A rug, negligently flung over the body of the trussed Jules, hid him from observation.

"Now we'll embark," announced Emilet.

As a precaution, the young hooligan asked:

"The bloke snores?"

"Yes," replied the Beadle. "He is travelling in No Nightmare Land. . . ." The Beadle laughed.

But Emilet was alarmed.

"You haven't snuffed him out, have you?"

"No danger of it! He's only shamming!"

"Off, then!" said Emilet.

They rolled away at top speed.

The bandits' lair had been well chosen by their chiefs. It was a vast cellar, with a vaulted roof, and earthen walls bedewed with an icy humidity. Axes, mattocks, shovels, rakes, and watering cans lay scattered on the ground: these were worn out tools: they had not served their purpose for many a day.

The lantern, a kind of cresset protected by a wire globe, was suspended from the roof by a string. It shed a faint and wavering light, creating weird shadows in that far-stretching space, too vast for the insufficient illumination.

Directly beneath the cresset lantern, inside the circle of light it threw upon the ground, a fantastic group of human creatures pressed close to one another, drinking, shouting, chattering, singing.

A clean-shaven man, whose suspicious little eyes were perpetually blinking, turned to a young woman.

"Look here, Ernestine, my beauty, are you certain the Beadle understood that we should be waiting for him here?"

Big Ernestine, who was crouching on the ground and warming her hands at a wood fire, throwing up clouds of smoke, shrugged her shoulders.

"Stop it, do! You say things over and over again, like a clock, Nibet! . . . Since I've told you *yes* — *yes* it is — there now, and be hanged to you! . . . You don't by chance fancy the Beadle has been made a mouthful of, do you?"

Roars of laughter greeted this. Nibet was not one of the inner circle; he was not much of a favourite in the band of Numbers. It is true that they reckoned him a comrade, useful, faithful, that they felt safe with him; but they bore him a grudge because of his regular employment, because of his position, because he was an official. . . . And, first and last, his warder's uniform impressed the jail birds unpleasantly.

But Nibet was not the man to allow himself to be intimidated.

"All the same," said he, "I ask where the three of them have got to? . . . If they know the mushroom bed, they should have been back long ago!" He shouted to an old woman.

"Eh, Toulouche, tell us the time!"

But Mother Toulouche shook her head.

"I haven't a watch!"

There was a murmur of protestation. The seven or eight hooligans assembled there awaiting the return of the Beard and the Beadle, sent with Emilet to kidnap Jules, could not believe that. Mother Toulouche had told the truth.

The Sailor caught the old woman by the shoulders and shook her, and went on shaking her.

"Liar! Aren't you ashamed to be in a funk with us? . . . Ever since this blessed Mother Toulouche has sold winkles and many other things, ever since she began to make a little purse for herself, which must be a big purse by now, a purse everyone here has sweated to fill to the brim, she has always distrusted us! . . . You say you haven't a watch! I tell you, you've got dozens of 'em! . . ."

Big Ernestine interrupted.

"It's a half-hour over the hour agreed. . . ."

A shudder ran through the assembly: Nibet, finger on lip, made a sign that they were to listen.

Then, in the mushroom bed, no longer in use, which the band of Numbers had recently adopted as their meeting place, a profound silence fell. . . .

"There they are!" said Nibet.

Big Ernestine leaped up, left the fire, advanced to the far end of the cellar, and imitated the cry of a screech owl to perfection. There was a similar cry in response.

"It's all right. They're here!" she said. She returned to the fire and sat down. But Nibet seized the girl and forced her to get up again.

"Go along with you! Quick march!" he said roughly.

She protested. Nibet stopped her.

"Oh, we can't stand listening to you! . . . Ho there, Sailor! . . . Come here! . . . Sit down on this plank! You, the Beadle, and me — we're to be the judges. . . . Beard makes the accusation: and, if her heart tells her to, Ernestine will defend him."

"I'd rather spit at the tell-tale! . . . You can tear him to bits as far as I'm concerned!" cried the girl. "There's nothing disgusts me so much as a tell-tale!"

The hooligans crowded round big Ernestine. They applauded her ironically; for they all knew that, once upon a time, she had been strongly suspected of having dealings with, what they called, "The dirty lot at the Bobby's Nest."

Silence fell once more. They could hear the rasp of the rope unrolling from a hand windlass attached to an enormous bucket. This was the primitive lift.

Moments passed. The hooligans had formed a circle beneath the black hole where the bucket moved up and down.

"It goes, old Beard?" questioned Nibet, gazing upwards.

"It goes, old bloke!"

"Brought the game?"

"That's what we're sending down now! . . ."

"That's a bit of all right!"

Sailor now seized the trussed Jules from the bucket and flung him on the ground.

"Damaged goods, that — eh?" he laughed evilly.

The Beadle, Beard, and Emilet were coming down in turn. The group below bent curiously over the prisoner.

"He's soft — that sort is!" cried Ernestine. And tapping him on the face with her foot, big Ernestine tried to make Jules show signs of life. Beard dropped out of the bucket and stopped the game.

"Let's see, Ernestine? . . . Stop it now!"

After gripping the hand of each comrade in turn, after hugging a bottle and draining it in a long draught, emptying it to the dregs, Beard flung it aside.

"Let's get to work — no time to waste! . . . If we finish him off, we'll have to get rid of him before morning!"

Sailor lifted Jules with the aid of two comrades. They propped him against a massive pillar of wood which supported the cellar roof. They bound their wretched victim to it with strong cords.

Meanwhile, Ernestine was unwinding the gag.

"Take your places on the tribunal!" commanded Nibet.

"And you others, a glass of pick-me-up for the fellow!"

The pick-me-up intended to restore Jules to consciousness was brought by Mother Toulouche, under the form of a large earthen pot full of cold water. She dashed the water in the prisoner's face.

Jules slowly opened his eyes and regained his wits, amidst an ominous silence. The band watched his return to life with evil smiles: they quietly watched his pallid face turn a livid green with terror.

The wretched creature could not utter a syllable. He stared wildly at those about him, his friends of yesterday, at those seated on the mock judgment bench who, crouching forward, were observing him with sardonic smiles.

Nibet put a question.

"You hear and understand us, Jules?"

"Pity!" howled the victim.

Nibet was indifferent to the cry.

"He understands! . . . For my part, I am all for keeping to a proper procedure. . . . I would not have agreed to sit in judgment on him if he had been unable to defend himself. . . . We don't act that way down here!"

Turning to his acolytes for signs of their approval, he continued:

"Beard! The word is with you! Let us hear why he has been brought up to judgment! . . . Tell us what he is accused of! . . . Bring up all there is against him!"

Beard, who was marching up and down between the hooligan tribunal and the accused, who was half dead, and incapable of making a rational statement, stopped, squared himself with an air of satisfaction, and began his speech for the prosecution.

"Jules, has anyone ever done you any harm here? . . . Has anyone played cowardly tricks on you? . . . Set traps to catch you in? . . . Have you ever been cheated out of your fair share of the spoil? . . . Is there anything you can bring up against us? . . . No? . . . Well, here's what we have against you . . . it's not worth while lying about it either! . . . You are the one who has taken the wind out of our sails over the Danidoff affair . . . do you confess that?"

In a voice barely intelligible Jules gasped out:

"Beard . . . I don't understand you! . . . I have done nothing — nothing. . . . What have you against me? . . ."

Beard took his time.

Planted before the prisoner, with hip stuck out and hand in pocket, the other hand raised in tragic invocation towards his comrades:

"You have heard? . . . Monsieur does not understand! . . . He has not the pluck to be open and aboveboard!"

Turning again to the wretched captive, he continued:

"Well, I'm going to explain . . . it was you, wasn't it, who had to put through the robbery of the lady's jewels? . . . Well, do you know what you did? Do you want me to tell you? . . . Instead of lending us a hand as was promised and sworn, you kept the cake for yourself! . . . In other words, you, and some of your sort, serving at the ball, put your heads together, and shut up the lady in the room they found her in; and that way, you got out of sharing with us! . . . So we have been done in the eye over that deal! . . . The proof that you have comrades we know nothing about is, that yesterday when you were done in, they found a way to get you out of the Salad Basket! . . . It wasn't us! . . . But to return to the Danidoff robbery . . . oh, you must have laughed then! . . . But everyone has his turn . . . you are going to laugh on the wrong side of your mouth now! . . . Do you know what they call it — what you've done — dared to do?"

In the same strangled voice, Jules managed to get out the words:

"But it's not true! . . . I swear to you . . ."

Beard did not listen.

"There's not one of our lot who would give me the lie! . . . To behave like that is treachery! . . . You have betrayed the Numbers. There it is in a nutshell! . . . What have you to reply to that?"

For the third time, Jules repeated in a hoarse whisper, for he felt life was gradually leaving him: an awful fear gripped him, he saw he was completely done for.

"I swear I did not do that! . . . I didn't rob the princess. . . . I don't even know who did!"

Jules was, perhaps, speaking the truth, but he took the worst way to defend himself. . . . If he had had pluck and wit enough to take the Beard's accusation with a high hand, if he had met threats with violent denial and assertion, it is quite possible he might have made an impression in his favour; but he cried for pity and for mercy from men who were pitiless!

He was afraid! . . . His fear was shown by the convulsive trembling which agitated his wretched body, by his ghastly pallor, by the cold drops of sweat rolling down his forehead. . . . He was no longer a man: it was a lamentable bit of human wreckage the hooligans had before them! . . . And the more lamentable this wreck showed itself to be, the less worthy of their interest it seemed!

When Jules gasped out once again:

"I swear to you it was not I! No! . . . I did not do it!"

The hooligans, moved by a common impulse, rose, indignant, furious, mad with rage.

"That's a good one, that is!" yelled Nibet, who, beside himself with rage, suddenly forgot his avowed respect for judicial forms.

"Since he is determined to tell lies, and hasn't the pluck to say what he's done, there's only one thing for us to do, and that's to stop his mouth up! . . . Ernestine, put the plug back!"

And as the girl once more rolled the scarf round and round the head of the miserable Jules, Nibet turned to his comrades.

"Now then? One hasn't any need to waste more time over it! . . . We know all the story — not so? . . . It's settled, I tell you! . . . A fellow who has done what he has done, what does he deserve? . . . You answer first, Mother Toulouche, since you are the oldest? . . ."

Mother Toulouche stretched out a trembling hand, as though calling on Heaven to witness an oath.

"I," said the old woman, with a wicked gleam in her eyes. "I don't hesitate! . . . Comrades who flinch, sneaks who betray, get rid of them, say I! . . . I condemn him to death! . . ."

The old woman's sentence was greeted with loud applause.

Nibet resumed.

"It is said! . . . It is unanimous! . . . Make a quick finish, my lads! . . . Since each has been injured, let each take his revenge! I say: Death by the hammer!"

In that smoke-thickened air rose a chorus of hate and of vengeance.

"Death by the hammer! Death by the hammer!"

In that noisome lair of the bandits a horrible scene ensued.

Mother Toulouche went groping in a dark corner. She searched for, and found, a blacksmith's hammer. She lifted it with trembling hands, and planting herself in front of the victim, more dead than alive, she said in a menacing voice:

"You did harm to the Numbers! You wronged them! Here goes for that then!"

The hammer described a quarter of a circle in the air and descended in a smashing blow on the wretched victim's face!

The awful punishment had begun!

According to age, one after another, the hooligans passed on the hammer, and, in a blind passion of hate, beat followed beat on the agonising body of Jules!

At last the terrible agony was over and done! The passion of hate, the lust for revenge had burnt themselves out. Jules had expiated the crime they had imputed to him!

The band were the victims of a paralysing fatigue. Emilet flung the blood-stained hammer into a far corner of their den.

"Well done!" said he. "He has paid the price!"

Emilet's eyes fell on Nibet. He was leaning against the wall, and, with folded arms, was watching the scene in which he had taken no part. Walking up to the warder, Emilet demanded:

"Ho! Ho! You backed out of it, did you, my boy? . . . You didn't have a throw, did you? . . . No? . . ."

Nibet grinned sardonically.

"Don't talk rubbish, Emilet! . . . If I have stood aside, I had my reasons for doing so. . . . We haven't done with Jules yet! . . . Not by a long chalk! . . . Now that he's been killed, he's got to be got rid of — isn't that true? . . . Look at yourselves, my lambs! You are covered with red! . . . It will take you all of an hour to make yourselves presentable! . . . Now, look at me! I'm neat and clean . . . and I have a plan . . . a famous plan to rid us of that corpse there! Now, just you stir your stumps, Emilet! . . . I am going off to make preparations! . . . I'll give you ten minutes to make yourself fit to be seen . . . it's we two are to be the undertakers; and I swear to you, that we will give them no end of trouble to the curiosity mongers at Police Headquarters!"

XXIII

FROM VAUGIRARD TO MONTMARTRE

On the boulevard du Palais, Jérôme Fandor looked at his watch: it was half an hour after noon.

"The hour for copy! Courage! I will go to *La Capitale*."

Scarcely had he put foot in the large hall when the editorial secretary called:

"There you are, Fandor! . . . At last! . . . That's a good thing! . . . Whatever have you been up to since yesterday evening? I got them to telephone to you twice, but they could not get on to you, try as they might. My dear fellow, you really mustn't absent yourself without giving us warning."

Fandor looked jovial: certainly not repentant.

"Oh, say at once that I've been in the country! . . . But seriously, what did you want me for? Is there anything new? . . ."

"A most mysterious scandal! . . ."

"Another?"

"Yes. You know Thomery, the sugar refiner?"

"Yes, I know him!"

"Well — he has disappeared! . . . No one knows where he is!"

Fandor took the news stolidly.

"You don't astonish me: you must be prepared for anything from those sort of people! . . ."

It was the turn of the secretary to be surprised at Fandor's calmness.

"But, old man, I am telling you of a disappearance which is causing any amount of talk in Paris! . . . You don't seem to grasp the situation! Surely you know that Thomery represents one of the biggest fortunes known?"

"I know he is worth a lot."

"His flight will bring ruin to many."

"Others will probably be enriched by it!"

"Probably. That is not our concern. What we are after are details about his disappearance. You are free to-day, are you not? Will you take the affair in hand then? I would put off the appearance of the paper for half an hour rather than not have details to report which would throw some light on this extraordinary affair."

Then, as Fandor did not show the slightest intention of going in search of material for a Thomery article, the secretary laughed.

"Why don't you start on the trail, Fandor? . . . My word, I don't recognise a Fandor who is not off like a zigzag of lightning on such a reporting job as this! . . . We want illuminating details, my dear man!"

"You think I haven't got any, then? . . . Be easy: this evening's issue of *La Capitale* will have all the details you could desire on the vanishing of Thomery."

Thereupon, Fandor turned on his heel without further explanation, and went towards one of his colleagues, who went by the title of "Financier of the paper." The Financier had an official manner, and had an office of his own, the walls of which were carefully padded, for Marville — that was his name — frequently received visits from important personages.

Fandor began questioning him on the subject of Thomery's disappearance.

"Tell me, my dear fellow, what is happening in the financial world, now that Thomery has disappeared."

"What do you mean?"

"Where is the money going — all the coppers?"

"The coppers?"

"Why, yes! I fancy that when an old fellow like that does the vanishing trick, there are terrible results on the Bourse? Will you be kind enough to explain what does happen in such a case?"

Very much flattered by Fandor's request, Marville cried:

"But, my boy, you are asking for nothing less than a course of political economy — but I cannot do that — on the spur of the moment! . . . State precisely what you want to know."

"What I want to know is just this: Who loses money through Thomery's disappearance?"

The Financier raised his hands to Heaven.

"But everybody! Everybody! . . . Thomery was a daring fellow: without him his business is nothing! . . . There was a big failure on the market to-day."

"Good, but who gains by it?"

"How, who gains by it?"

"Yes. I presume Thomery's disappearance must be profitable to someone? Can you think of any people to whose interest it would be that this old fellow should disappear?"

The Financier reflected.

"Those who gain money by the disappearance of Thomery — only the speculators, I should say. Suppose now that a Monsieur Tartempion had bought Thomery shares at ninety francs. To-day these shares would not be worth more than seventy francs: Tartempion loses money. But let us suppose some financier speculates on the probable fall of Thomery shares, and has sold to clients speculating on the rise of these shares; these shares to be delivered in a fortnight, at a price of ninety francs. If Thomery was still there, his shares would be worth, possibly, the ninety francs, possibly more. In the first case, the financier's deal would amount to nothing: in the second case, his deal would be a deplorable one, because he would be obliged to deliver at an inferior price, and would be responsible for the difference. . . ."

"Whilst Thomery dead . . ."

"Dead — no! But simply in flight, his shares fall to nothing, and this same financier may buy at sixty francs which he must deliver at ninety francs in fifteen days. In that case he has done excellent business."

"Excellent, certainly . . . and . . . tell me, my dear Marville, do you know if there has been any such deal in Thomery shares on a large scale?"

"Ah! You ask me more than I can tell you now . . . but that would be known at the Bourse."

No doubt Jérôme Fandor was going to continue his interrogation, but there was a great disturbance in the editorial room near by. They were shouting:

"Fandor! Fandor!"

The editorial secretary entered the Financier's room, and, catching sight of Fandor, he cried:

"What's the meaning of this? What are you up to here? I told you this Thomery affair was important. . . . Be off for the news as quick as you can. . . . Here is the *Havas*. It seems they have just found Thomery's body in a little apartment in the rue Lecourbe."

Fandor forced himself to appear very interested.

"Already! The police have been quick! . . . I also had an idea that that Thomery had more than simply disappeared!"

"You had that idea?" asked the startled secretary.

"Yes, my dear fellow, I had — absolutely!"

After a silence, Fandor added:

"All the same, I am going out to get news. In half an hour's time, I will telephone details of the death. Does the *Havas* say whether it is a crime or a suicide?"

"No. Evidently the police know nothing."

"Monsieur Havard, I am delighted to meet you! . . . Surely now, you will not refuse me a little interview?"

"Not I, my dear Fandor! I know only too well that you would not take 'no' for an answer."

"And you are right. I beg of you to give me some details, not as regards Thomery's death, for I have already made my little investigation touching that; but as to how the police managed to find the poor man's body."

"In the easiest way in the world. Monsieur Thomery's servants were very much astonished yesterday morning, when they could not find their master in the house.

"After eleven, Thomery's absence from the Bourse gave rise to disquieting rumors. He had some big deals to put through, therefore his absence could only be accounted for in one way — he had had an accident of some sort.

"Naturally enough, they warned Headquarters, and at once I suspected there might be a little scandal of some sort. . . . You guess that I immediately went myself to Thomery's house? . . . I examined his papers; and I found by chance three receipts for the rent of a flat, in the name of Monsieur Durand, rue Lecourbe. One of them was of recent date. I, of course, sent one of my men to ascertain who lived there! This man learned from the portress that there was a new tenant there, who had not yet moved in with his furniture; but who, the evening before, had brought in a heavy trunk. . . . My man went up to this flat, and had the door opened. You know under what conditions he found Thomery's dead body."

"And you did not find indications which went to show why Monsieur Thomery committed suicide?"

"Committed suicide? . . . When a financier disappears, my Fandor, one is always tempted to cry 'suicide'; but, this time, I confess to you that I do not think it was anything of the kind! . . ."

"Because?"

"Because" — and Monsieur Havard bent his head. "Well, when I reached the scene of the crime I immediately thought that we were not face to face with a suicide. A man who wishes to kill himself, and to kill himself because of money affairs, a man like Thomery, does not feel the necessity of committing suicide in a little flat rented under a false name, and in front of a trunk, which you know, do you not, belonged to Mademoiselle Dollon! One might swear that everything was arranged expressly to make anyone believe that Thomery had strangled himself, after having stolen the trunk, for some unknown reason!"

"You did not find any kind of clue?"

"Yes, indeed! And you know it as well as I do, for I have no doubt the extraordinary event has been the gossip of the neighbourhood. On the cover of the trunk we have once again found an imprint, a very clear impression — the famous imprint of Jacques Dollon! . . ."

"And you found nothing else?"

"Yes, in the dust on the floor, we found the marks of steps, numerous foot marks: we have made tracings of them."

"My steps, evidently," thought Fandor. But what he said was:

"What, in short, is your view of the general position, Monsieur Havard?"

"I am very much bothered about it. For my part, I think we are once again faced by another of Jacques Dollon's crimes. This wretch, after having attempted to assassinate his sister, has learned that we were going to search mademoiselle's room. He then made arrangements to steal this trunk, by pretending to be a police inspector, as you know; then he brought the trunk to this flat, examined its contents thoroughly, and having some special interest in the sugar refiner's death, he managed to get him to come to the flat, and there assassinated him, leaving his dead body in front of this trunk, where it was bound to be seen; all this he did in order to tangle the traces and perplex those on his track. . . ."

"But how do you explain the fact of Jacques Dollon being so simple as to leave the imprints of his hand everywhere? . . . Deuce take it, this individual is at liberty: he reads the papers. . . . He knows that Monsieur Bertillon is tracing him! . . . So great a criminal would certainly be on his guard!"

"Of course! Such a successful criminal as Dollon has shown himself to be, must have resources at his disposal, which allow him to laugh at the police. He does not trouble to cover his tracks; it is enough for him that he should escape us."

As Fandor could not suppress a smile, the chief of the detective force added:

"Oh, we shall finish by arresting Dollon, have no fear! So far he has quite extraordinary luck in his favour, but the luck will turn, and we shall put our hand on his collar!"

"I certainly hope you may. But what are you going to do now?"

The two had stopped on the edge of the pavement, and were talking without paying any attention to the passers-by who rubbed shoulders with them. The well-known journalist and the important police official were unrecognised.

Monsieur Havard took Fandor's arm.

"Look here, come along with me, Fandor? Just the time to telephone to a police station, and then I will take you with me to make a fresh investigation."

"Where!"

"At Jacques Dollon's studio. I have kept the key of the house, and I wish to see whether I can find any other rent receipts made out in the name of Durand. Though I can see how Dollon inveigled Dollon into a trap, I do not understand how it came about that Thomery paid the rent of that trap. There is some subtle contrivance of Dollon's here; I want to get to the bottom of it. . . . Will you come to rue Norvins?"

"I jolly well will!" cried Fandor.

The chief of the detective force telephoned to Headquarters, whilst Fandor got into communication with *La Capitale*. He sent on a report of the Thomery case up to that moment.

Quitting the police station, the two men hailed a cab, and were driven to the rue Norvins.

As far as they could tell, the artist's house had not been entered since Elizabeth Dollon's departure.

The neglected garden, with its rank growth of grass and weeds, gave an added air of melancholy to the deserted house.

Monsieur Havard put the key in the lock of the front door.

"Don't you think, Fandor, it gives one a queer feeling to enter a house where an unaccountable crime has been committed?" The key grated in the lock, and Monsieur Havard added:

"In spite of oneself, there is the feeling that some terrifying spectre is lurking within!"

"Or a ghost!" said Fandor.

And as the door was unlocked and opened, our journalist asked:

"Where shall we start this domiciliary visit?"

"Let us begin with the studio," replied Monsieur Havard, mounting to the first story.

No sooner had they entered the room, than a double cry escaped from the two men.

"Oh! . . ."

"Great Heaven! . . ."

In the very middle of the studio, there was the rigid body of a man hanging.

They rushed forward. . . .

"Dead!" was Monsieur Havard's cry.

"Horribly dead!" echoed Fandor.

"Shall we never lay hands on those wretches?" Monsieur Havard stared, horrified, at the hanging corpse. He brought a chair, grasped the strong sharp knife he always carried about him, and, aided by Fandor, he cut the rope, laid the hanged man flat on the floor, and proceeded to examine the miserable remnant of a human being.

The face was swollen, gashed, crushed. . . .

"The hands have been dipped in vitriol — they did not want finger prints taken — it is — it is Jacques Dollon!"

Fandor shook his head.

"Jacques Dollon? Of course, it isn't! . . . If it were Dollon, he would not hang himself here. . . . Why should he hang himself?"

Monsieur Havard remarked:

"He has not hanged himself. Again the stage has been set! . . . I could swear the man had been killed by blows from a hammer and hanged afterwards! . . . It seems to me, that if death had been caused through strangulation, there would have been marks round the neck. . . . But see, Fandor, the rope has hardly made a mark."

"No, the man was dead when they strung him up."

"It is of secondary importance!" remarked Fandor, who was pre-occupied.

"You are mistaken: it matters a great deal! It decidedly looks as if Dollon had accomplices, who wished to be rid of him."

Fandor shook his head.

"It is not Dollon! It cannot be Dollon!"

"Look at the vitriolised hands — that was a precaution."

"I say, as you did just now: it's like a set piece — a bit of slag assassins' stage craft."

"I say, in Dollon's house, we have found Dollon at home!"

Fandor was not convinced. He felt certain Dollon had lied in the Dépôt.

"Well, Elizabeth Dollon can settle the question for us. There may be some physical peculiarity, some mark by which she can identify her brother's body!"

But Fandor was examining the body very carefully. Suddenly he rose from his stooping posture, exclaiming:

"I know who it is!"

"Who?"

"Jules! None other than Madame Bourrat's servant, Jules! . . . That is to say, an accomplice whom the bandits we are after wanted to be rid of. He might give them away when brought up for examination. That was why they managed his escape: they killed him afterwards, because he had served their turn, and was now an encumbrance."

"Your explanation is plausible, Fandor; but how about the truth of it?"

"This proves the truth of it!" cried Fandor, pointing to a cicatrice on the back of the neck of the murdered man: it was the clear mark of where an abscess had been.

"I am certain I noticed a similar mark on the neck of Jules. He sat in front of me the other day, and I particularly noticed this mark. The dead man is Jules. I am certain it is Jules!"

Monsieur Havard was silent. Presently he said:

"If it is Jules . . . it must be admitted that we are no further forward!"

Fandor was about to utter a protest, when there was a knock on the studio door. Startled, the two men looked at each other anxiously.

"It can only be one of the force," murmured Monsieur Havard. "I told them I was coming here with you, and that they were to send for me if necessary."

The two men walked to the door. Monsieur Havard opened it. There stood a cyclist member of the police force. He saluted respectfully, and told his chief that he had come with a message from Michel.

"The message?"

"That the arrest is successful, chief."

"Which?"

"That of the band of Numbers, chief."

"Good! Whom have you bagged?"

"Almost the whole lot, chief!"

"That is to say?"

"Mother Toulouche, Beard, Mimile, otherwise Emilet, and the Cooper — and a few more whose names are not known."

Fandor said, laughing:

"Not Cranajour, I am certain."

"No. Cranajour has escaped," answered the policeman.

Turning to Monsieur Havard, he asked:

"You have no instructions, chief?"

"No. Tell me, how did the capture go?"

"Perfectly, chief. They were assembled in Mother Toulouche's store. They went like lambs."

"Good! . . . Good!"

Monsieur Havard gave the policeman some orders. The cyclist leaped into the saddle and disappeared.

"How did you guess that Cranajour was still at liberty?" asked Monsieur Havard.

Fandor smiled.

"Good business! You take me to be more stupid than I am. It is Cranajour's information which has enabled you to arrest the band of Numbers. Consequently! . . ."

"Cranajour's information? You are mad, Fandor! . . . Whatever makes you imagine that Cranajour belongs to our force?"

Fandor looked Monsieur Havard straight in the eye and said coolly:

"Juve has never told me that he had sent in his resignation!"

Monsieur Havard looked searchingly at our journalist, before remarking:

"Come now! What is this you are telling me? Poor Juve? . . ."

Fandor wished to save the chief of the detective department from telling useless falsehoods.

"Monsieur Havard! Monsieur Havard! Interrogate the members of the band of Numbers, and don't trouble about how I got my information . . . but, be sure of one thing, there are dead men of whom I could tell tales, of whose existence I am as well aware of as you yourself!"

As the chief stared at the journalist, looking more and more astonished, Fandor added:

"And I do not refer to Dollon! I am referring to Juve, to my dear friend Juve, the king of detectives!"

XXIV

AT SAINT LAZARE

"Hop along there! See if you can't hurry up a bit!"

The warder opened the door of Elizabeth's Dollon's cell and pushed in an old woman — a horrid looking creature.

"In with you!" commanded the warder in a harsh tone. "You are to stay here till to-morrow. We will find another place for you when we get instructions. . . ."

Poor Elizabeth Dollon stared miserably at this strange companion which Fate, in the person of a warder, had thrust on her.

The old woman stared with no little curiosity at the pale, sad girl. . . . Silence fell for a few minutes, then the new prisoner asked, in a tone of rough familiarity:

"What's your name?"

"I call myself Elizabeth!"

"Don't know it! . . . Elizabeth, who? . . ."

"Elizabeth Dollon. . . ."

The old woman rose from the corner of the mattress she had seated herself on.

"True? You're Elizabeth Dollon? . . . Well, that's funny! Have you been nabbed long? . . ."

"You ask if it is long since I was . . . ?"

"Nabbed! . . . Taken! . . . Arrested! . . . Eh?"

Elizabeth nodded in the affirmative. It seemed to her that an infinity of time had passed since her imprisonment at Saint Lazare.

"I was nabbed last night. If you want to know my name, I'm called Mother Toulouche. They say I'm one of the band of Numbers, and that I receive stolen goods! Lies! That's well understood!"

Elizabeth had no desire to go into such an unsavoury question. This horrid old woman rather frightened her; but, such had been her distress and fears since she had been a prisoner, that it was a relief not to be quite alone; to have even this old creature to speak to was better than solitary confinement.

In her character of old jail-bird, Mother Toulouche made herself quickly at home.

"Moved to-morrow, they say I'm to be! Pity! At bottom you're not one of the scurvy sort, but you must be here to play spy on me, for all that! . . . When do you go out? Are you long for Saint Lago?" Alas, how could Elizabeth tell?

"I like being a barrister," thought Fandor, as he entered Saint Lazare. "For the last hour I have felt a different person, much more serious, more sure of myself, not to say, more eloquent! . . . I must be eloquent, since I have succeeded in persuading my friend, Maître Dubard, to get himself appointed officially as Mademoiselle Dollon's counsel; then to obtain a permit of communication, and to hand this same permit over to me, so that his identification papers, safely tucked away in my portfolio, make of me the most indisputable of Maîtres Dubard!"

Fandor might well congratulate himself! By means of this ruse — his own idea — he was enabled to see Elizabeth, not in the prison parlour, but in a special cell, and without a witness. As Fandor crossed the threshold of the sordid building, he said to himself:

"I am Maître Dubard, visiting his client, in order to prepare her defence!"

He easily accomplished the necessary formalities, and, at last, he saw himself being conducted by a morose warder to a little parlour, scantily furnished with a table and a few stools.

"Please be seated, maître," said the surly fellow. "I'll fetch your client along!"

Fandor put down his portfolio, but remained standing, anxious, all aquiver at the thought that he was about to see his dear Elizabeth appear between two warders, just like a common prisoner!

"In a moment she will be here," thought he. . . . But she must on no account recognise him on entering! By an exclamation she might betray his identity and complicate things! Therefore, Fandor feigned to be absorbed in a newspaper he unfolded and raised, so as to hide his face from the approaching pair. The door opened.

"Come now! Go in! . . ." growled the warder. "Maître, when you wish to leave, you have only to ring."

The door fell to, heavily, behind the warder.

Fandor made a sharp movement. He stood revealed. He hurried up to Elizabeth.

"Oh, tell me how you are, Mademoiselle Elizabeth!" he cried.

But the girl was struck dumb: she grew suddenly pale, and made no reply.

"Elizabeth! Elizabeth! Will you not give me your hand even? You do not understand why I am here? I had to see you, speak to you without a witness . . . that's why I have passed myself off as an advocate!"

The startled girl was regaining her self-control. Fandor was gazing at her with frankly admiring eyes.

"Poor Elizabeth! How I have made you suffer!"

The poor girl's eyes filled with tears.

"Why have you betrayed me?" she demanded in a voice trembling with restrained emotion. "Oh, how could you get me arrested? You, who well know I am not guilty?"

"You really believe I have betrayed you? You actually credited me with that?"

These two young people, meeting in a prison parlour under such tragic circumstances, were hurt and even angry with each other.

Elizabeth Dollon went on:

"Why did you not tell me that you had found on that piece of soap traces of my brother's finger-marks? Why did you accuse me of having received a visit from him, when you yourself had proved that he was dead?"

Fandor took Elizabeth's two little hands in his and pressed them long and tenderly.

"My dear Elizabeth, when I engineered this theatrical stroke in the presence of the examining magistrate, in order to secure your arrest, believe me, I had no time to warn you of what I meant to do. . . . Ah, if I could have warned you — but it would have only disturbed you to no good purpose, besides — your being really taken by surprise was a help — there could not be any idea of collusion. . . . Of course, you want the answer to this riddle? You shall have it — that is why I am here. . . . Don't you remember, Elizabeth, that on the evening before the fatal day you told me that I had twice rung you up on the telephone? And that each time you answered the call you could not find me at the end of the line? . . . You cannot imagine what I felt when I heard you say that! I never telephoned! I never telephoned to the convent!

"The obvious conclusion was, that the individuals who, for some reason, did not wish to make themselves known, did wish to keep track of you, and to assure themselves that you were still at the convent, rue de la Glacière. . . ."

Fandor's voice trembled a little, as he went on:

"And I was at once afraid, my poor child, that these people who were pursuing you, might be the very same who had got into Madame Bourrat's house, and had tried to kill you. . . . Ah, do you not see how greatly it hurt and troubled me to think that I had taken you to the convent, and had there placed you in security — as I thought — but where you were far from being safe?"

Again Fandor took Elizabeth's hands in his.

"You do understand now, dear child, why I had you arrested? . . . I felt you would be safe here. . . . You see, I could not get your persecutors imprisoned and so prevent them from getting at you. To imprison you was the alternative: you are better guarded here than elsewhere."

Elizabeth smiled a little smile when she saw how moved Fandor was.

"But," replied she, "there is the other point! You certainly told me that you were sure my brother was killed in prison — in his cell!"

"Certainly, I did! The assassination of your brother was premeditated. If the criminals have had accomplices at the Dépôt, and such there certainly were, they have been bought over little by little. . . . The fact of your brother's murder is fresh in the memory of the police, of all, therefore, a special watch is kept over you. I ascertained that it would be so, and Fuselier himself assured me of it: there is a warder specially told off to keep a close guard over you, a safe man, known to be beyond suspicion. . . . No, Elizabeth, do believe me, if I was the cause of your horrified surprise the other day, and then of your imprisonment, I wished to be sure that you were as safe as it was possible to be; then, freed from such intense anxiety, I felt I should be at liberty to continue my investigations. . . . Do say you forgive me!"

All Elizabeth could say was:

"But why not have warned me? . . . I still can't quite see! . . ."

"Why, because, I only thought of the plan at the last moment! Also, because I feared you might not be able to act surprise naturally enough! . . . It was absolutely — yes, absolutely necessary — that everyone should take your arrest seriously. . . . Surely, Elizabeth, you can understand that!"

He repeated his plea.

"Do, do say you forgive me, Elizabeth!"

The smile returned to Elizabeth's lips: she was much moved.

"Indeed, I do . . . You are always my very good friend: you think of everything, and you watch over me as if . . ."

Intimidated, blushing hotly, she stopped short, then changed the conversation.

"Do tell me if you have heard anything fresh!"

Fandor returned to his normal self also. He had sworn to himself that he would not tell Elizabeth he loved her, until he had succeeded in unravelling the tangled skein of the terrible Dollon affair.

"I shall speak," thought he, "when she is once more at peace and free, when she is out of danger. I do not want her to consent to love me just because I have devoted myself to her brother's case. Elizabeth shall be my wife, please God; but only if I deserve her, if I can win her."

And Jérôme Fandor told her the story of the famous wicker trunk — but he did not mention Thomery's death, nor did he speak of the horrible murder of Jules. . . . What was the use of saddening Elizabeth, of adding needlessly to her terrors? Instead, he thought it better to learn what he could from her.

"I have not found that famous list!" said he.

"Oh, I beg your pardon!" cried Elizabeth. "I was so worried! . . . Just imagine that, I found the list after all, and I thought I had lost it! It was in one of my little handbags. I had put it there to bring to you. Here it is: they were quite willing to let me keep it!"

Fandor eagerly took the paper from Elizabeth and proceeded to examine it. Yes, it certainly was a page torn from a note-book of medium size. An unknown hand had traced the following words in bold writing. The names succeeded one another in the form of a list.

Baroness de Vibray, April 3. Jacques Dollon.
Dep. . . . idem
Sonia Danidoff, April 12.
Barbey-Nanteuil, May 15.
Gérin . . . ?
Madame B . . . ?
Thomery, during May.
Barbey-Nanteuil, end May.

Fandor could not find anything more on the paper. Whilst Elizabeth sat silent, Fandor reflected:

"Baroness de Vibray, April 3. Jacques Dollon . . . these correspond exactly with the commencement of this mysterious affair: the two first deaths, and the date of their death. . . . What does *Dep.* signify? The initials of a name — or — yes, Dep . . . Dépôt idem — yes, *Dépôt the same day!* That's it! *Sonia Danidoff, April 12* . . . the full name, the exact date. *Barbey-Nanteuil, May 15*: the affair of rue du Quatre Septembre occurred May 20; that's pretty near. Two more names, and one date which exactly tallies. *Gérin? . . . Madame B. . . . ?* Who are they? Why no date? Ah, Gérin, lawyer of Madame de Vibray, a crime planned, without date, perhaps because he was not indispensable . . . and *Thomery!* Thomery, who died in the middle of May, as this plan indicates! But, how about the last line? *Barbey-Nanteuil, end of May?* Oh, beyond a doubt the bankers were to be victims of some fresh aggression on the part of the mysterious author of these lines!"

"*Barbey-Nanteuil, end of May!* We are at the 28th of the month: only three more days before the sinister date falls due! Are they to be attacked, or is it their money? How to defend them? How organise a trap for the mice?"

Suddenly, Fandor looked up, saw Elizabeth's anxiety, and said quietly:

"Well, this list agrees in every particular with the description you gave me of it, and I don't quite see what fresh information we are likely to get from it. However, will you leave it with me?"

Fandor rose.

"Ah, there is one point which has just occurred to me" — Fandor's voice trembled a good deal — "Do you know for a fact that your brother had bought Thomery shares?"

"He had very few, three or four. I think the Barbey-Nanteuil got them for him."

"And your brother had to pay for them by a certain date?"

"Yes."

Fandor now felt he must tear himself away. He was deeply moved.

"Elizabeth! . . . Elizabeth!" he cried. "I swear to you we shall clear up these dreadful mysteries amidst which we live, and more, you and I! Only have confidence, I implore you! Grant me a week's grace, less even!" Fandor pressed Elizabeth's hands as though he could never let them go! Such little hands, and so dear!

It was not a farewell he took — it was a veritable flight he took from the girl who now meant so much to him!

Leaving the prison, Fandor walked straight ahead, thinking aloud.

"It is clear — evident! The Barbey-Nanteuils have sold Thomery shares to be paid up on a certain date. Thomery was murdered so that his shares should fall to zero, and so that the Barbey-Nanteuils should realise enormous sums at their monthly clearance. Next Saturday, the coffers of the Barbey-Nanteuil bank will be full of gold, and this same Saturday is the last day of May, the fatal day inscribed on the list. Yes, this coming Saturday, they will pillage the Barbey-Nanteuil bank!"

XXV

A MOUSE TRAP

Jérôme Fandor had been ringing Juve's door bell in vain: the great detective was not at home.

"What the deuce is he doing? What has become of him? Never have I needed his advice as I need it now! . . . His support, encouragement — what a comfort they would be! . . . It is possible he would have dissuaded me against the attempt — or, he might have joined forces with me! Hang it all! It was a jolly bad move on Juve's part to make himself scarce at such a critical moment for me! . . . It is a long time, too, since I had news of him! Were I not certain that he has sound reasons for his absence — Juve never acts haphazard — I should be desperately anxious!"

Fandor consulted his watch — four o'clock! He had time then! He could think over all the dramatic events in which he had been involved during the past weeks, beginning with the rue Norvins affair, and ending — how, and when?

At last, our journalist arrived before the immense building which forms the corner of the rue de Clichy. He saw, in front of him, the tall windows of the flat occupied by Nanteuil: on the ground floor were the bank offices.

"Well," thought Fandor, "I certainly am going to do an unconventional thing. If my summing up of them is right, these bankers are balanced, calm, cold, without imagination, and distrusting it in others. I shall have to be eloquent to convince them, to make them listen to me and get them to do what I want. Will they show me the door, as though I were an intriguer or a madman? . . . I shall not let them do it! . . . Ah, they will owe me a fine candle if I have the good luck. . . . Whether there will be good luck for my venture, and gratitude from the bankers, remains to be seen. . . . Here goes! . . ."

Seated behind their large and important looking writing table, as though judges behind a judgment seat, Messieurs Barbey and Nanteuil, in their immense reception office, separated from the rest of the world by a number of padded doors, had just said to Fandor, who was standing in front of them:

"We are listening to you, monsieur."

Fandor had asked to see the bankers, and to see them only, stating that he would wait if they were engaged. He had been shown into a handsomely furnished room, then into another, then into a third; finally, he had been ushered into the office of the partners. He had waited there for a few minutes alone. He recognised it as the same room in which he had interviewed Monsieur Barbey a few weeks earlier. Again he saw the same hangings, the same fine rugs, the same velvet arm-chair of classic design.

Then Barbey, solemn, and Nanteuil, elegant, a rose in his buttonhole, had entered the room, their manner stiff-starched, showing no surprise, accustomed as they were to receive visitors of all sorts and kinds: they were polite, but not cordial.

Fandor, accustomed to society as he was, and audacious as he had to be in the exercise of his profession, was intimidated, for a moment, by the calm simplicity of the two men — these strictly conventional bankers, to whom he was about to say such strange things, and make a most unexpected proposition!

First of all, he made excuse on excuse for having disturbed the bankers at their post time. Then anxiety overcame every consideration of conventional propriety. Full of persuasive ardour, he went straight to the point.

"Messieurs," declared he, "you are more deeply involved than you might think in the mysterious affairs occupying the attention of the police at this moment. So far, they have not got to the bottom of them. I, myself, through the necessities of my profession, and owing to other circumstances, have been drawn into an investigation, conjointly with the detective department, an investigation which has had definite results: it has enabled me to discover clues of the highest importance. I learned, too late, alas, to prevent the tragedies, that certain persons were the chosen victims of these mysterious criminals. Madame de Vibray, the Princess Danidoff were condemned beforehand; the robbery of your gold was carefully arranged. Now to my point! Messieurs, you yourselves are sentenced: the execution of the sentence to be carried out three days hence. Do you believe me?"

Fandor had drawn nearer the two bankers: only the immense mahogany writing-table stood between them!

The partners had listened with cold attention: nevertheless, a slight trembling of Monsieur Barbey's lips betrayed hidden feeling. Noticing this, Fandor was emboldened to proceed.

Monsieur Nanteuil, in a slightly sneering tone, but with a perfectly correct manner, replied to the ardent young journalist:

"We are greatly obliged to you, monsieur, for the sympathy you have shown us by coming to give us information regarding the mysterious assassins, whom the police are so zealously trying to round up. Believe me, we are accustomed to take our precautions, seeing that we have the handling of enormous sums of money. We are none the less grateful to you for your interest in us, and for your warning."

"It is not a question of gratitude," interrupted Fandor sharply. "We have to deal with very strong opponents. I say 'we' because I have become more and more personally involved in all these crime-tragedies. Believe me, I speak from five years' experience as a reporter, who has had to report, on an average, one crime a day! . . . Up to now, nothing, absolutely nothing has hindered the criminals from executing their plans; but, warned in time, we may be able to thwart them."

"But," interrupted Monsieur Barbey, who had grown more and more serious. "What are you aiming at?"

Fandor felt that the decisive moment had arrived. Bending across the table, his face almost touching the faces of the two men, he said slowly and distinctly:

"Messieurs, I have asked *La Capitale* to grant me three days' leave. I have brought a little travelling bag with me: here it is! Leaving home as I did about half an hour ago, I consider I have arrived at the end of my journey! . . . Will you offer me hospitality for the next forty-eight hours? . . . I know that you, Monsieur Nanteuil, live above your offices, whilst Monsieur Barbey goes home every evening to his place at Saint Germain. I ask you to give up your room to me, for I am determined not to leave here for an instant!"

Fandor, in his eagerness, had spoken faster and faster, and his heart was beating violently. He stared fixedly at the two men; he quite expected that his demand would excite astonishment; that objections would be raised; and he was ready with a crowd of arguments by which to convince them and carry his point. . . . But, the surprise was his, for the bankers did not seem particularly astonished.

They consulted each other with a look. Then, as Barbey opened his mouth to reply, Nanteuil began to speak, rising politely at the same time.

"Monsieur Fandor, your last statements and remarks are too serious to be passed over lightly. Your offer is too generous to be rejected without consideration. Will you allow us to retire for a minute or two: my partner and I will discuss the question."

For about ten minutes Fandor marched up and down the sumptuous room. Then one of the padded doors opened silently, and Barbey entered more solemn than ever: Nanteuil was smiling.

"Monsieur," said Barbey, in weighty tones, "my partner and I, in view of the exceptional seriousness of the situation, for your words carry conviction — have come to a decision: we beg of you to consider yourself our guest from this moment, and to consider this house as your own!"

"And it is understood, of course, that you dine with us this evening!" added Nanteuil with friendly graciousness. "Monsieur Barbey will be of the party, and will pass the night in our company . . . and you can count on it, that we shall drink a good bottle of Burgundy to enable us to await with patience and serenity the audacious individuals you say we are to expect. . . . Dear Monsieur Fandor, here are some illustrated papers with some gay sketches of dear little women to exercise your patience over, whilst we sign our outgoing letters as fast as possible. . . ."

XXVI

IN THE TRAP

The servant had retired, leaving the three men to their fruit and wine. His hosts turned to Fandor in mute interrogation. . . . But Fandor continued to peel a superb peach with the utmost coolness: he did not seem disposed to talk.

Barbey broke the silence.

"Tell me, now that your first day on guard is ended, and you have not left us for a moment — have you noticed anything at all suspicious?"

Fandor shook his head. "Nothing whatever."

This was not strictly true; for he had noticed an individual in the bank, occupied in repairing the telephone. He had made discreet inquiries, and had been told that he was a workman sent by the State, at the request of the bankers, to see that the lines were in good working order. This explanation had at first set his mind at rest regarding the comings and goings of this individual.

But, just when he was going in to dinner at seven o'clock, Fandor had come across the man in the vestibule of the bank making preparations to depart. It had been a painful surprise for Fandor. He recognised the man, but could not remember exactly who he was, or where he had seen him. . . .

Was this workman one of the mysterious band of criminals who, he was more and more convinced, meant to strike a blow at Monsieur Barbey, and his partner, Nanteuil?

If Fandor had had anything to go upon, he would have had the man shadowed. But he had no sure ground for his suspicions; besides, sent by the State, the man was most probably what he seemed. As he was working for the Government, he could easily be traced should such a step be found necessary. But to make certain that all was as it should be, Fandor had examined the work done by this individual during the day. There was nothing wrong with it: beyond a doubt, the man was an expert. Therefore, Fandor had felt justified in saying that he had noticed nothing suspicious during the day.

"So much the worse," remarked Monsieur Barbey, with a shrug. . . . "Probably the individuals who are threatening us, have been warned of your presence here, and are on their guard. I rejoice as far as we are concerned; but, as regards the general interest, I almost regret it: that your trap should prove effective, is what we must wish."

"Have no fear, dear Monsieur Barbey, it will not be laid in vain! Knowing the cunning, the cleverness of my adversaries, I have not the least doubt they know I am here; but I also know that the audacity of these criminals is such, that my presence here would not deter them from making their attempt. They believe themselves the stronger, but I hope to undeceive them."

"What is your plan of campaign to-night?" asked Monsieur Nanteuil.

"Before replying to that, will you show me all the means of access to the house?"

"With the greatest pleasure."

The three men left the dining-room: then went into the vestibule.

"Our courtyard gate is at the far end of the house, on the right," said Nanteuil. "On the left, there are the Bank offices: they occupy this ground floor. The only entrance to them is through this vestibule. This door closed, it is impossible to get in."

"Not by the windows looking on to the street?" asked Fandor.

"No, those windows have heavy iron bars before them. To remove them would be difficult — very . . . As to the windows looking on to the garden, they are closed every evening — you can see for yourself — by strong wooden shutters fastened on the inside."

"So the Bank offices are perfectly protected?" said Fandor.

"We believe so. Now, come upstairs to the floor above! . . . Here is a large corridor, and that door, on the right, opens into a library. The two rooms which come next, are my own room and a dressing-room. The other rooms are unoccupied."

"Does your room face the street or the garden?" asked Fandor.

"The garden."

"And the windows?"

"The windows?"

"Yes. Would it be difficult, or impossible to climb up to them?"

"It would be difficult, but not impossible. No one ever enters the garden. If absolutely necessary, a ladder could be placed against them, a square of glass could be cut out, and the fastening could be undone . . . but come and see the room, you can then judge for yourself."

Fandor inspected the room most carefully. The banker was right. It would be comparatively easy to get into the room by the window; but the other entrances to the room could be easily watched; they resolved themselves into one door, which opened on to the corridor.

Monsieur Nanteuil's room was lightly furnished: he evidently favoured the modern method: it was a bare apartment, but it was hygienic.

"Ah," said Fandor, "the bed has its back to the door, and faces the window. Very right. You have electric light, I see, near the fireplace, and above your bed. Then it is possible to switch on a bright light at any time. . . . Valuable, that!"

Having finished a minute inspection of the room, and, to the amusement of the bankers, having looked under the bed to make sure that no one had hidden himself beneath it, Fandor declared:

"I am decidedly pleased with this room, and if you see no objection, I wish to stay here and await the visitors of to-night."

"You think of sleeping here alone?"

"Alone! Decidedly, I do! It is pretty certain that these men know every inch of your flat; and if they are the sort I take them to be, they will make certain that everything here is as usual before attempting to attack the Bank. I do not wish them to be frightened off by finding a companion at my side, and I particularly wish them to mistake me for you. . . ."

"But that is frightfully dangerous, surely?" objected Nanteuil.

"Reassure yourself, monsieur, I do not run any great risk. They won't know I am watching them; but I shall have this advantage over them — I am on the lookout for the rascally assassins and robbers, and I do not fear them in the slightest."

Fandor was not going to own that he knew there was danger; but he was keenly set on running this particular risk, for, by so doing, might he not discover the truth?

When the bankers left him for the night, Fandor again examined every corner of the room, and all it contained. He tested the electric light switch; he took a mental photograph of the situation of the pieces of furniture. He got into bed, half dressed, and lay quietly, grasping his revolver, fully loaded.

He switched off the light, and in that large room, veiled in darkness, he awaited the events of the night. Noises from the street reached him indistinctly. The silence about him was menacing: something was going to happen here, something sudden, unforeseen, perhaps irremediable.

Minute by minute, time went by, interminable, monotonous, casting a soft veil of sleep over the eyes of Fandor. But thoughts were rising within him: more and more keenly he was realising the horrible danger he was exposing himself to. Beneath closed eyes his brain was active, his imagination afire.

"Elizabeth Dollon must be avenged," was his persistent thought. "Consequently, I must run some risks to achieve that!"

A definite fear tormented him. He thought of the curious sleep Elizabeth had fallen victim to in the boarding-house.

"Provided I have not taken some narcotic without knowing it! . . . Suppose the villains are going to inject into the room some gas which would suffocate me, and I should not know I was breathing it in? Suppose I lose consciousness and slip into death?"

But Fandor drew himself together; he stiffened his will.

Do they know I am in this room waiting to entrap them? Do they think they will find Nanteuil here defenceless? Who was that workman? . . . I ought to be able to put a name to that familiar face?

How slow, how deadly slow, the tic-tac, tic-tac, of the timepiece? Centuries passed between the striking of the hours! . . . Would it be to-night? . . . To-morrow night? . . . Or . . .

On the corridor carpet outside the room, a slight rustling sound, continuous, barely perceptible, caught Fandor's listening ear. . . . Who was it? . . . Was it anyone at all? . . . Was it imagination? He listened intently . . . not a sound now. . . . But, yes . . . the same rustling sound . . . it was nearer — moving along the wall. Fandor closed his eyes an instant, so vividly did he feel that someone was looking at him through the wall!

Seconds beat by — seconds that might culminate in a moment of horror — seconds passing steadily by in regular succession, sinking into nothingness. . . .

Had someone moved? Were there steps by the door? . . .

Fandor thought he heard strange sounds all around him, in the room itself! His nerves were tensely strung: he was overwrought. Someone was certainly walking in the corridor! . . . He had felt a movement along the wall against which his bed stood!

Impossible to hesitate longer! The door knob, which he could not see in the darkness, must have moved. . . . Fandor sensed this movement as surely as though he himself had placed his hand on the knob. . . .

Yes, the door was going to open! . . .

It was ajar . . . it was turning on its hinges — it was open. . . . Someone was coming in. . . . Who? . . .

Fandor lay still — he dared not move an eyelid; but in his mind he said:

"Come in, then! Take the trouble to come in!"

Thus Fandor, who believed Death was entering the room, dared to welcome the grim visitor — with a smile!

Nothing was happening. . . . Fandor's feverish excitement sank down to depression. . . . He must have deceived himself — no one was entering the room — nothing untoward was happening! He had simply imagined the noises outside in the corridor, for nothing happened — nothing . . . and once more he was following the eternal tic-tac, tic-tac of the timepiece!

The head of Fandor's bed was near the door. He could not, in the dense darkness, fix the point where he supposed the enemy would find him, and he had the agonising conviction that they were very much at their ease — that they knew exactly where he was, and were quietly preparing their attack.

But had these unknown assassins entered the room? . . . Yes, it was certain — there were men behind him — bending over him with outstretched hands to strangle him! . . . He could hear the sound their fingers made in passing through the air to grip his throat, to squeeze his life out! . . .

Though he lived a hundred years, never could Fandor forget the agonising thrill when he sensed that hidden danger! He held his revolver ready to fire. He thought:

"In whatever way I am attacked, I must not let slip this unique chance to learn the truth! I must seize the attacker at all costs, and leap to the electric switch, turn on the light — and I shall be saved! Saved! . . ."

Without a cry, without a warning sound, without a moment's time to cope with the violence of the attack, Fandor felt a cloth over his face, strong hands on his throat, a heavy weight crushing his chest.

"I am lost!" flashed through his mind.

"I mean to find out the truth!" his will declared.

With all the force of resistant muscle and will he disengaged himself from the power crushing him to death; seized an arm by chance, hung on to it, gripped it, threw off the man, ran to the switch, shouting:

"Help!"

Again, Fandor thought he was done for: the switch acted, but no light flashed forth!

They had cut the wire!

Men were holding on to him: their grip was tightening!

A voice gave a strangled cry.

"Help!"

A strange voice! Whose?

Fandor was weakening. His right hand seemed to be caught in a vise which would break and crush it: it was growing tighter and tighter: it was wrenching his arm, was dragging him backwards: it would fracture his shoulder blade! Who? . . . Who? . . .

By a miraculous effort he freed himself. He leaped away; sprang to the mantelpiece; seized a pocket electric torch he had placed there — clac — a light flashed out! . . . Fandor saw, recognised his attacker! . . .

Ah! The form he had seen before — a slim figure, clothed in black! . . . Ah, this murderer, whose face was concealed by a hooded mask!

Fandor shouted at him.

"Fantômas! It's you and I, Fantômas!"

But, already, this mysterious bandit, unmasked by the unexpected light, had rushed on our journalist.

The electric torch was extinguished.

The struggle recommenced, fierce, formidable, desperate! Fandor was seized by the throat in a strangling grip: he was choking!

His right arm, so twisted, so bruised, was powerless — and in that hand, now so deadened and helpless that it seemed detached from his body, was his revolver. He must shoot, though almost powerless in the formidable grip of the bandit. He must shoot if he was to be saved. He managed to pull the trigger.

There was a loud report.

Fandor felt himself flung towards the wall. The vise loosed its grip. There was a terrific din. The window panes were shattered, a heavy piece of furniture was pushed aside, oscillated, fell with a crash; then a sudden silence; but a silence broken by gaspings, loud breathings, hoarse sounds, an agonising death rattle.

The dead pause seemed interminable. . . . Fandor was about to shoot again, when a voice close to him cried:

"He is escaping! . . ."

Jérôme Fandor recognised that voice! . . .

Another voice said:

"We must have a light!"

A wax match flamed and flared.

By its wavering light Fandor could distinguish three men in the room. . . . Their clothes were torn: there was blood on their faces, they were panting: they stared at one another.

Fandor recognised them instantly.

Leaning against the bed, a gash in his cheek, was Monsieur Barbey.

Lying on the floor, apparently half dead, was Monsieur Nanteuil.

Calmly lighting a candle was the telephone workman. He alone seemed unmoved.

Fandor threw down his revolver and, coolly marching to the door, locked it.

Monsieur Barbey followed the journalist with a look. He made a gesture of discouragement and pointed to the window: its panes were smashed to pieces.

"We are tricked — done!" he said. "The assassin has got away!"

But Fandor, with a shrug, marched up to the window, returned, and said in a matter-of-fact tone:

"It is impossible that Fantômas could have made his escape that way!"

The workman nodded gravely.

"Monsieur Fandor," said he, "I am entirely of your opinion."

XXVII

THE IMPRINT

"Monsieur Fandor, I am entirely of your opinion!"

Hearing these words, Fandor, who had regained his self-possession, and was ready to start fighting again if necessary, looked at the individual who had made this statement — the individual whose face was oddly familiar.

"Who are you?" he asked.

The individual smiled broadly.

"Don't you recognise me?" he asked.

He removed his wig, threw the candle light on himself, and smilingly announced his style and title.

"Sergeant Juve, once of the detective force; formerly dead: now amateur policeman!"

"You! You, Juve!" cried Fandor. "And to think I suspected you. . . ."

But the two bankers interrupted at one and the same moment.

"What are you doing here?"

Juve smiled.

"The art I practise brought me! Since my interest in the Dollon affair is so keen, I follow it up, I wish to find the secret of it, just through love of my art. I dabble in it nowadays."

"But Juve — how did you get here?" questioned Fandor.

"Ah, ha! If you have made some psychological discoveries: if reasoning has landed you here, now facts have led me here! . . . You know I was shadowing the band of Numbers. You know that in the skin of Cranajour I was intimate with those rascals. To my astonishment I found that my wretched companions had dealings with the Barbey-Nanteuil bank, who, of course, had no suspicion of it! Are you surprised then that I felt it incumbent on me to visit this bank? . . . Besides, yesterday, I saw you enter here; but you never came out again! You had reasons for acting so. I determined to be near you, in case you needed my help. I therefore passed myself off as a workman come to attend to the telephone installation. It was easy enough, for I am a good electrician. . . . Well, when I found that you were preparing to pass the night here, I laid my plans accordingly. I pretended to leave the premises, but really I hid myself in the house. Just now, when you called for help, I came to your aid as quickly as I could, naturally!"

"Just as we did!" remarked Monsieur Barbey, looking at his partner.

Monsieur Nanteuil contented himself with a nod. He added:

"Alas, once again that criminal has escaped! Fantômas, since it was Fantômas who was here, just now, Fantômas has got away!" And Nanteuil pointed to the broken window by which it would seem the criminal, taking advantage of the noise, had escaped.

But both Fandor and Juve shrugged doubtfully.

"You believe then, Monsieur Nanteuil, that Fantômas has left this room?" questioned our young journalist.

"What the devil do you mean?" asked Nanteuil.

Juve demanded.

"Which way did he make his escape?"

Nanteuil pointed.

"Why that way! By this window . . . where else? . . . You can see quite well that he has broken the panes! . . . Why, look! His hooded cloak has got caught on the window latch! . . ."

Fandor lay back in an arm-chair. He seemed much amused. He silenced Juve with a gesture, and turned to Nanteuil.

"I can assure, dear Monsieur Nanteuil, that Fantômas has not left the room by this window! . . ."

"Because? . . ."

"Because this window has been broken by means of this chair: this chair, which he flung against the panes to put us on the wrong scent, and make us believe he had escaped that way! . . . Just look at this chair! It is still strewn with broken bits of glass . . . look, there is even a little bit stuck into the wood!"

"But that proves nothing! . . . Fantômas has broken the window panes as best he could, and then made his escape!"

"In that case," insisted Fandor, "dear Monsieur Nanteuil, can you explain how it was he troubled to remove his cloak, hood and all; and, after that, how is it he has left no footprints in the flower-beds beneath the window? When day dawns you will see for yourself that my statement is correct, though I have not verified it! The flower-beds are too wide, too big, for a man jumping from here, to jump clear of them! And the earth is soft enough to take and retain the footprints of a man who leaps down on to them from this height! . . . Nevertheless, such footprints are conspicuous by their absence!"

Monsieur Barbey seemed overwhelmed — aghast.

"If Fantômas did not escape by the window, how then did he get away?" he asked.

Fandor said in clear, distinct tones:

"Fantômas was not able to escape! . . ."

"But he cannot be in the room? . . . Where, then, can he have hidden himself?"

In a hard voice, Fandor made answer.

"He is not hidden in the room. . . ."

"You think then that he has hidden himself somewhere in the house?"

Speaking in the same hard, decisive tone, Fandor asserted:

"He is not hidden in the house! In the very height of the struggle, I kept a strict watch on the direction taken by the man who was doing his utmost to strangle me. I am positive I had my back against the door when I fired, so that exit was barred! Neither by door nor window did Fantômas escape!" Fandor's tone was one of absolute assurance.

"If you are certain of that," said Nanteuil, "can you tell us how Fantômas did escape?"

Fandor's reply was to rise from his arm-chair. He took the candlestick from the table where Juve had placed it and walked towards a large mirror. He carefully examined his neck.

"Very curious!" said he, in a low voice . . .: "Now, monsieur, the man who tried to strangle me was Fantômas — we have seen him. . . . Well, this man had a wound on his thumb, or, more probably, he wounded me, anyhow he has left on my collar the mark of his thumb in blood — you guess what this thumb-mark is?"

Simultaneously, Barbey, Nanteuil, and Juve rushed towards the young journalist. . . . Fandor showed them a little red mark, clear cut on the white surface of the collar; it was a finger-print so characteristic, that the two bankers cried in a trembling voice:

"Again the imprint of Jacques Dollon!"

Silence fell — a pregnant silence. The four men gazed at one another. Fandor soon started whistling a popular air. Juve smiled: Monsieur Barbey was the first to speak:

"Good Heavens! Do you mean to say that Jacques Dollon was here — in this room! . . . It is certain, you say, Monsieur Fandor, that he did not get away either by door or window — for pity's sake explain the mystery!"

But Fandor contented himself with a smile and a question.

"Do you really think, then, that I know it? . . ."

Nanteuil stamped with impatience.

"But hang it all! If you don't know anything, don't let us waste time! Let us begin the search! Hunt through the house! Search the garden from end to end! . . ."

Fandor went on — his tone was ironic.

"And warn the police? Well, no, Monsieur Nanteuil, we will not make any search whatever, you can rely on that! . . . For the last three months we have been striving and struggling to solve a maddening mystery: we never could reach a certain solution of it: we have been vainly pursuing an assassin, who for ever escaped us . . . and now, when for once, we get hold of a definite fact, an indisputable reality, are we going to risk muddling up the whole business? . . . Not if I know it!"

"What do you mean?" demanded Monsieur Barbey.

"Listen!" replied Fandor: "Some minutes ago, I was alone in this room; Jacques Dollon entered the room, because I bear on my neck the imprint of his thumb. Jacques Dollon was Fantômas, because he declared it himself when he believed he would emerge victorious from the struggle. Jacques Dollon — Fantômas — has not left this room, either by door or window. On the other hand, you have entered the room — you Monsieur Barbey, you Monsieur Nanteuil, and you Juve. Since these individuals have entered the room, and no one has left it, it necessarily follows that the personage, Jacques Dollon — Fantômas, must have entered among you, and that he has remained here, between these four walls."

Simultaneously, Barbey and Nanteuil raised protesting voices: but Juve continued to smile.

"Do you believe then? . . ."

But Jérôme Fandor did not allow him to finish.

"I do not *think* anything," said he. "I *know* that I, Jérôme Fandor, am I, and that I am not Jacques Dollon! . . . Juve knows that he is Juve, and that he is not Jacques Dollon. You, Monsieur Barbey; you, Monsieur Nanteuil, you know who you are, and who you are not! None of us can leave imprints similar to those of Jacques Dollon. But, I also know, that Jacques Dollon has entered this room, and that he has not left it — this is all that I know!"

To this extraordinary declaration, Monsieur Nanteuil, with an incredulous shrug of the shoulders, exclaimed:

"This is downright madness, monsieur!"

But Juve congratulated Fandor.

"That's logic, my boy! You are going it strong, lad!"

Fandor continued.

"It follows, that if Jacques Dollon has not left the room, he must be here in this room. He must be arrested. In order to arrest him, we must beg Monsieur Havard to come here as fast as he possibly can! Jacques Dollon is Fantômas, or I should say, Fantômas is Jacques Dollon. Monsieur Havard will not hesitate to put himself to any inconvenience in order to effect such a capture! I am going to call him up at once, messieurs, thanks to this telephone!"

And profiting by the bewilderment of his hearers, Fandor, then and there, telephoned to Police Headquarters; he spoke to one of the officials, who undertook to inform his chief that he was wanted at the telephone on most urgent business.

A minute or two later, Fandor was telling Monsieur Havard what had happened. He terminated his narrative thus:

"I myself had locked the door of the room in which the struggle took place. No one left the room, nor shall anyone leave it before your arrival, I give you my word of honour on that! Come, post-haste. It is of the utmost urgency. Bring a locksmith. He must open the great door of the house. He will have to force open the door of the room in which we now are. I must keep an incessant watch over this room. I do not see Fantômas — Jacques Dollon — in this room; but in this room he must inevitably be — he *is* in it!"

Fandor, listening to Monsieur Havard's answer, repeated it to his companions.

"In a very short time, the chief will be here; in a very short time, messieurs, we shall witness the arrest of Fantômas, that is, of the most inhuman monster that has ever existed!"

"It seems to me you are going too fast!" remarked Monsieur Barbey. "All is mystery — yet you talk of making an arrest!"

"But what do you consider mysterious now?" asked Fandor, laughing.

"Why, everything! Take one thing: do you know what were the motives of the different Fantômas-Dollon crimes?"

Juve replied to this:

"Oh, as for that, perfectly! The motives are clear as crystal! . . . Madame de Vibray was ruined, and really committed suicide because — you will pardon me, I am sure — because the Bourse transactions you advised were not successful. . . . She poisoned herself, and went to Jacques Dollon's studio to die: perhaps she felt for him a secret attachment! Fate willed it that the assassins should choose this very evening to make their way into the painter's studio . . . by means of this first corpse they created an alibi for themselves, and prepared the scene which was bound to mislead justice and make lawyers and police believe in the murder of Madame de Vibray and the suicide of her murderer. . . . Unfortunately for them, Dollon was discovered before the poison they administered had done its deadly work on him, and Dollon was arrested. . . . You can imagine the fury, the distracted state of the guilty! Dollon had seen them — he was going to speak at the legal interrogation — very well, then — they will kill him — and they do kill him. . . ."

"But Jacques Dollon lives, since his imprints are found here, there and everywhere! . . ." cried Monsieur Barbey.

Fandor replied:

"They kill Jacques Dollon, since it has been formally established that Jacques Dollon was seen dead; and once they have killed Dollon, they think that a dead man cannot be arrested by the police, and *they accept this dead man as one of their band.* . . . He, they decide, shall steal the pearls of Princess Danidoff! . . ."

"This is raving lunacy!"

"All that is pretty clearly proved, Monsieur Nanteuil! . . . It is he also who stole the millions in the rue du Quatre Septembre, a sensational robbery which would have ruined your bank, had not this issue of bullion been well covered by an insurance: this insurance signified that you were no losers by this robbery — in fact, owing to an ingenious combination of insurances, you have actually gained by the robbery! As we are on this subject, I might add that were I a member of the Band I should propose restoring to you the vanished ingots — robbers find bullion somewhat difficult to put into circulation: you might buy them back; then turn them into false coin, for instance — that would be all profit — for you! . . ."

"I wonder at you — making such a joke as that!" remarked Nanteuil.

"Please wonder at me! . . . To continue! . . . Having carried out their plan successfully, these robbers remembered something they had forgotten — a compromising paper, or something like it, which had been left in Elizabeth Dollon's possession. Thereupon, they send the dead man — Jacques Dollon — to look for it: he attempts to murder his sister: I arrive just in time to open the windows before she is past all human aid. . . . Meanwhile a series of cleverly arranged deals on the Bourse are brought off, so that if Thomery disappeared the Barbey-Nanteuil Bank would rake in important profits . . . in haste the assassins get rid of an accomplice who is in their way — that duffer of a Jules, the rue Raffet servant, and they send Dollon to kill Thomery. After that they decide to rob your Bank which is stuffed with gold; for, were it not for this theft, it would be your Bank, burdened as it is, with Thomery shares, which would pay out to speculators the differences in value between past and present prices — which amounts would have to come out of the money paid in the day before. Messieurs, with regard to this, Thomery's death did you a great service. . . . Without his death, which enriched you, you would have had to settle up your sales by a certain date, and you would have lost more than you gained at the moment, owing to the sole fact of his disappearance! . . . I think you are very grateful to Jacques Dollon because of what he has done for you."

Monsieur Nanteuil, on hearing these last words, rose. He walked up to the journalist and said, in a voice quivering with some emotion:

"For my part, Monsieur Fandor, I think your way of explaining the Dollon affair is a very strange way! . . . You assert that this painter is dead, and you make him behave as if he were alive! . . . Besides, I have understood your words! In truth, what you say is senseless: you make wild statements! You have involved our Bank in every one of the Dollon crimes! . . . You have shown us as interested parties in all these robberies!"

Fandor said quietly:

"Nevertheless, it is unquestionably true that you are the gainers by these crimes: beginning with Madame de Vibray and ending with Thomery. Madame de Vibray might have brought an action against you for the loss of her fortune, owing to your risky speculations and bad management. Thomery's murder brought down his shares with a run, and you found that a most advantageous state of affairs — you gained by it! . . . But, of course, this is coincidence, since you are not Fantômas, since you are not Jacques Dollon, since you cannot imitate the imprint of his thumb! . . . I have only said this to show . . ." Fandor stopped short.

"Hark! . . . Someone is coming upstairs! Here is Monsieur Havard!"

As the bankers were hurrying impatiently to the door, Fandor said in a bantering tone:

"Do not stir a step further, I beg of you! Not a step! Let us receive the chief of the detective force exactly in the position we were, not an hour ago, when we encountered him whom the chief has now come to arrest!"

Barbey and Nanteuil returned to their former positions. Those in the room could hear voices on the other side of the door exchanging brief remarks. The lock was being picked. Monsieur Havard entered and hurried up to the journalist.

"Well, my dear Fandor, I have followed all your instructions to the letter! . . . Ah! you here, too, Juve! Well? . . . Speak! Anything fresh since your extraordinary telephone communication? . . . What were you telling me?"

"I was saying, Monsieur Havard, that the assassin had entered this room, and assuredly had not left it — that he was here! . . ."

"Here?"

Monsieur Havard had recognised the bankers at the first glance. . . . His question betrayed a certain incredulity which piqued Fandor.

"Here! Yes! That is absolutely so, because it is impossible that he can have left the room! Besides, you shall convince yourself of that! . . . Monsieur Nanteuil, will you do me a small service? Will you draw a plan of the first floor of your house?"

The banker rose and seated himself at his writing-table, which was placed in a corner of the room.

"I am at your disposal." And he began to trace a plan, a pretty rough one, of the various rooms which made up the first floor of his house.

"Is that what you want?" he asked.

Jérôme Fandor rose quickly and went towards Nanteuil.

The journalist's nerves must have been out of order — in a jumpy state, despite his apparent calm, for, in approaching the writing-table, he suddenly staggered, nearly fell, tried to regain his balance, and that so clumsily that he upset the contents of a large ink-pot on the writing-desk. . . .

"Take care!" said Monsieur Nanteuil, who, to save himself from coming into contact with this inky inundation, threw himself back in his chair, and lifted his hands above the flood of ink. . . .

The banker repeated:

"Take care! . . . Here is a fresh catastrophe! . . ."

But he did not finish what he intended to say! Quick as thought, Fandor steadied himself, and before anyone could guess his intention he seized the banker's right hand, pushed it forcibly into the wide-spreading ink, then, immediately after, pressed it on to a sheet of blotting paper which took the hand's imprint quite clearly. . . .

This imprint he glanced at but a moment. . . . Like a flag, he waved it above his head!

"It is the Jacques Dollon imprint!" he shouted. "The hand of Monsieur Nanteuil, whose characteristics are known in the anthropometric section, has just left the imprint of — Jacques Dollon! . . ."

The journalist's action created a momentary stupour!

Juve rushed to him.

"Bravo! Bravo!" he cried.

But Monsieur Havard had gone quite pale. He said in a low voice:

"I don't understand!"

Barbey and Nanteuil retained their self-possession!

Then Monsieur Barbey rose. He looked fixedly at his partner. He spoke in a tone of sad finality:

"I suspected this! . . . Farewell. . . ."

A shout of horror answered him: he had drawn a sharp dagger from inside his coat, and had plunged it in his heart up to the hilt!

Juve knelt by the fallen man. Monsieur Havard kept a sharp eye on Nanteuil.

"Here, then, is Jacques Dollon, the dead-alive! . . . Here is the elusive Fantômas!" said the chief of the detective force.

But the bandit brazened it out as he recoiled before the chief.

"Why do you arrest me because of this imprint?" he demanded. "It is a piece of juggling on the part of this journalist! . . . Take a fresh imprint of my hand, my fingers, my thumb, and you will see whether my hand could possibly leave such an impression as that put on the blotting pad, by some sleight-of-hand trick of this much too smart reporter!" He stretched out his arm in the direction of the blotting pad, as though begging for a fresh trial. . . .

Fandor marched up to Nanteuil.

"Useless," said he, in a curt tone. "I have been watching you! . . . I know the trick!"

Nanteuil stood stock-still, dumb. Fandor lifted the cuff of Nanteuil's coat, and pointed out to Monsieur Havard, and to Juve, a sort of thin film of glove-like form. It was fastened to the wrist by an almost imperceptible piece of elastic.

"This is human skin," said Fandor. "Human skin marvellously preserved by some special process: all its lines and marks are intact. Can you not guess whence it came? Do you need to be told whose dead body has supplied this phantom glove?"

Monsieur Havard was as white as a sheet.

"The body of Jacques Dollon," he murmured. . . . "Yes, that is it! . . ."

There was a moment's intense silence in the room.

"How do you imagine this wretch set to work?" demanded Monsieur Havard.

"Simple enough," replied Fandor. . . . "Fantômas knows the danger criminals run, owing to the exact science of anthropometry: he knows that every imprint denounces the assassin: he knows that it is difficult to do anything without leaving such imprints — and that is why, every time he has committed a crime, he has taken care to glove his hands in the skin of Jacques Dollon's hands."

Nanteuil, at bay, attempted denial.

"You are talking mere newspaper romance," said he.

Fandor looked the banker in the eye.

"Fantômas!" said he. "Do not attempt to deny what is no longer possible to deny! . . . The trick is remarkably clever, and you have reason to be proud of your invention. Perhaps I should never have discovered it, if in this very room, this very night, you had not been imprudent enough to leave those imprints on my collar! . . . No one had left the room, therefore the guilty person was in the room — of necessity he was:*therefore, it followed, that someone had the hands of Dollon!* . . . But how could this someone have the hands of Dollon? . . . Of course, naturally, the idea of these gloves occurred to me! . . ."

Fandor turned to the chief of the detective force.

"Monsieur Havard, Madame de Vibray committed suicide because she lost her fortune through Barbey-Nanteuil mismanagement — she might even have been poisoned by them! But that does not matter! Her death might compromise the Bank: they carried her dead body to Jacques Dollon's studio, and they tried to poison this painter, in order to put the law off their track. You know Dollon was saved! He was a dangerous witness. They killed him in his cell, some warder being accessory to the fact — killed him before his innocence could be established! Then they took his hands, that they might commit murders with them! . . . Dollon is dead, as I have held all along. It is Nanteuil who has committed the crimes ascribed to the most unfortunate Dollon. These crimes have profited the Barbey-Nanteuil Bank — as I pointed out just now!"

Whilst Nanteuil stood speechless, whilst Barbey, whom they had lifted to a sofa, was gasping out his last breath, whilst Juve was giving little nods of approval to what his dear lad was saying, Fandor was treating Monsieur Havard to a further version of the affair.

"When I telephoned to you I was morally certain of the approaching arrest. Not a soul quitted the room after the hands of Dollon had left imprints on my collar and on my neck. Therefore someone had the hands of Dollon. The finger imprints of all the personages present were known to me — therefore someone had a method by which he changed his own finger-prints into those of Dollon. . . . How was it done? It must be a removable method or means . . . why, of course, it could only be by a pair of gloves that the trick was done . . . of course it must be by means of *a pair of gloves made with the skin of Jacques Dollon's hands*! . . . I noticed that Nanteuil kept his hands obstinately behind his back. I guessed that it was he who had played the part of Dollon to-night, so I managed to prevent him removing those Dollon gloves, that I might take their imprint before your eyes — the rest can be guessed, can it not? . . . The imprint taken, profiting by the confusion, Nanteuil slipped off the glove which, as you see, was no thicker than a cigarette when rolled up. . . . To throw it aside was risky: he pushed it up his sleeve while pretending to arrange his cuff, and at the same time to put ink on his ungloved hand and so hide his trick! . . . Only I saw it all. . . . Monsieur Havard, it is not only the false Jacques Dollon I denounce, for Juve and I fully realised that he was also the elusive Fantômas! Here is this cloak with hooded mask, which is an irrefutable proof: besides he himself declared he was Fantômas. . . . Monsieur Havard, all you have to do now is seize this man: Juve and I will hand him over to you!"

It was a thrilling moment! Juve and Fandor, in this hour of decisive victory, mutely embraced. Monsieur Havard advanced with raised hands towards Nanteuil who retreated.

"Fantômas," he commenced, "in the name of the law I arr . . ."

The word was strangled in his throat! . . .

As he advanced another step, Nanteuil suddenly sprang backwards, and his hand rested on the moulding of a wooden panel. . . . At the same moment, Monsieur Havard, as if hampered by some invisible obstacle, stretched his length on the floor!

Juve and Fandor were about to rush to his aid . . . but while Fandor, in his turn, measured his length on the floor also, Juve yelled:

"Good lord! . . . We are caught! . . . He escapes! . . ."

Whilst the detective made a frantic effort to move a step — *he seemed nailed to the floor* — Fantômas, quick as lightning, leaped over the prone body of Monsieur Havard, gained the door, and banged it to behind him! . . . They heard a triumphant burst of laughter. . . . Fantômas was escaping!

"This is sorcery!" shouted the chief of the detective force, in a voice hoarse with rage.

"Take your boots off! . . . Take your boots off!" yelled Juve, who, with bare feet, was rushing through the house, revolver in hand, hoping to come up with the banker bandit! . . .

But, when the detective arrived at the entrance gateway of the house, he found the policemen brought by Monsieur Havard chatting away quietly . . . they had not seen a thing . . . the street was deserted . . . in a second Fantômas had disappeared, vanished into thin air . . . he, the elusive one, had got away: once more he had escaped those who were pursuing him with such keen determination!

"It is very simple," explained Juve to Monsieur Havard and Fandor, who seemed deprived of speech. "Yes, it is simple enough; I guessed it at once when I saw you fall, Monsieur Havard, just after Fantômas had pressed the woodwork."

"He pressed an electric button, did he not?"

"Yes, Fandor, he established a current! . . . The wretch must have placed powerful electric magnets under the floor . . . and the moment he realised that it was impossible to brazen it out any longer — was on the very point of being arrested — he established the current . . . so we three were nailed to the ground by the attraction exercised by these electro-magnets on the nails of our shoes — he, Fantômas, was then free to cut and run for it, whose shoes must certainly have had soles made of some insulating material. . . ."

Monsieur Havard and Fandor made no answer to this.

To have held Fantômas at their mercy, if only for a minute; to have believed that they were going to lay hands on the atrocious criminal, at last; to have seen him slip through their fingers — the thought of this almost brought tears to their eyes: they were in a state of the deepest despondency.

"There's a curse on us!" cried Fandor. "This time, at any rate, we have nothing to reproach ourselves with! We could not foresee that! . . ." Then, to himself in a low tone, he added:

"Poor Elizabeth! . . . How are we to tell her that we have let her brother's murderer escape?"

XXVIII

COURAGE

"Have some more chicken?"

"No, thanks: I am not hungry."

"But you should eat all the same!"

"Are you eating anything yourself?"

"Faith, I am not!"

"Well, then?"

In the private room of the Fat-Pheasant restaurant, where Juve and Fandor were dining, silence again fell. The two men sat motionless, gazing into space. They neither wished to eat food nor do anything at all. They were depressed to the last degree; they felt baffled: they were sick of every mortal thing!

All of a sudden, Fandor burst into tears. Juve, looking at his dear lad in such grief, bit his lip; his face with wrinkled brow wore a dejected, worried look.

An hour or two previous to that, Fandor, on returning to his flat, had found a black-edged envelope: the address in Elizabeth Dollon's handwriting. Fandor had opened it with fast beating heart and trembling hand!

For these past days, an evil Fate seemed relentlessly pursuing them. Now he feared to read of some fresh catastrophe.

He was reassured by the opening lines; but as he read on, and took in the meaning of Elizabeth's words, Fandor felt as though his heart were bursting with grief.

Elizabeth Dollon had written:

"I seem to be going mad . . . yes, I love you! . . . Yesterday, I should have been glad to become your wife; but there came by the same post as your letter, another, which contained terrible revelations, proofs of their truth were given me! . . . I have not the right to curse you — or rather I have not the strength to do it; but never will I marry you, Jérôme Fandor, you, Charles Rambert! . . ."[11]

It seemed to Fandor that everything was turning round about him. . . . He took a few steps, staggering. The weight of this terrible past, a past in which he was the innocent victim, but of which he could not clear himself, overwhelmed him!

Fandor cried, in a voice of despair:

11   See *Fantômas* and *The Exploits of Juve*.

"Fantômas! Fantômas has taken his revenge!"

And before the astounded portress, the unhappy young man turned about and fell in a heap on the ground.

On the other hand, shortly after the extraordinary flight of the banker — Nanteuil to the world in general — but Fantômas to him and Fandor — Juve had received from Monsieur Annion, the supreme head of the police detective department, who only manifested himself on sensational occasions, a note sent by pneumatic post:

"Regret keenly that you revealed your personality in such ridiculous circumstances, and that you failed to arrest a great criminal."

As Juve read these observations, he clinched his fists: he grew livid with rage!

Dinner was a mere farce to the two friends: they did not dine: they had no appetite! Juve and Fandor went over and over in their minds the deplorable events of which, all said and done, they were the victims. They gazed at each other full of self-pity. They felt they were two derelicts afloat on the immense sea of indifferent humanity.

"The worst suffering," said Fandor, with tears of misery in his voice, "is the pain of love."

"The most painful of wounds," said Juve bitterly, "is a wound to self-respect! . . ."

These two, men every inch of them, might have their moments of discouragement, but they were a sporting pair of the finest quality.

"Fandor!"

"Juve?"

"You are courageous?"

"I have courage, Juve!"

"Very well, my lad, let us sponge out the past, and start off afresh in pursuit of Fantômas! . . . I tell you the struggle has only begun. . . . Listen! . . ."

THE END

www.ingramcontent.com/pod-product-compliance
Lightning Source LLC
Chambersburg PA
CBHW050419260626
47156CB00003B/1078